BRENDAN AFLOAT

The Adventures of an Irish Lad in the Merchant Navy 1957 to 1963

David R. McCabe

Brendan Afloat

Copyright © 2014, 2016, 2017, 2019 David Raymond McCabe

All rights reserved.

No part of this publication may be reproduced, stored in a retrieval system, or transmitted, in any form or by any means, without the prior permission of the publisher, nor be otherwise circulated without the publisher's prior consent in any form of binding or cover other than that in which it is published and without a similar condition including this condition being imposed on the subsequent publisher.

The moral right of the author has been asserted.

Editing, formatting and typesetting:
Beaten Track Publishing,
Burscough, Lancashire.
www.beatentrackpublishing.com

Acknowledgements

My many thanks are offered to my late partner Joan for her great support and the welcomed help given by my friends when writing *Brendan Afloat* and especial thanks are offered to Debbie McGowan for her great patience.

Table of Contents

1. The Accident — 1
2. Leaving Ireland — 9
3. Early Days in Hospital — 15
4. Joining Ship — 19
5. Hospital — 29
6. First Date Mary — 31
7. Hospital Visit — 41
8. Set Sail — 45
9. Injuries in Accident — 63
10. Entertainment in Bombay — 65
11. Caring Nurses — 81
12. Night Club in Cape Town — 85
13. Who's Got the Diaries Now? — 105
14. Christmas at Home — 109
15. The Dreadful Diary — 123
16. Ship on Reef: Takoradi — 125
17. Hiccup at the Hospital — 135
18. Polly at the Party — 139
19. Join Ship in Liverpool — 151
20. Trouble at Hospital — 155
21. Visit to the Cavern — 159
22. Twelfth Day in Hospital — 169
23. The Bombing and Enjoyable Visit to Philadelphia — 173
24. Where's the Diary Gone Now? — 191
25. Back to the Beginning — 195
26. Brendan Begins to Recover — 201
27. Last Sea Trip — 211
28. Visit to Outpatients / Next Step: the Future — 223

About the Author — 228

By the Author — 229

What is an Apprentice?

1

The Accident

Well I won't be bothering with her again, thought Brendan Harris to himself as he sped along the brightly lit Merrion Road on his way home to Dunlaoghaire. Riding his elder brother's Vespa motor scooter in the gathering evening dusk, Brendan was on top of the world. He was just returning from a failed date with a girl whom he had recently met at the Crystal Ballroom in Dublin City but, more importantly, he had only that day signed a two-year provisional officer's contract with Calvex Tanker Company. Over the previous four years he had served an apprenticeship as a cadet deck officer with the company. They had offered him a deck officer's contract, subject to him taking and passing his Second Officer's Certificate. Age twenty-one, with the wind in his hair and a clear road ahead, he sped along the wide well-lit Merrion Road looking forward to the future.

Seeing there was very little traffic around, Brendan accelerated to forty. *Wonder how fast this machine will go? Will it do the sixty it has on the clock? No, stick at the forty, no, give it a bit more throttle. Wow! That's fast. Better slow down a bit.* Reducing his speed, with an open road still ahead of him, Brendan thought about the girl, Polly, who was a close friend. He knew her before going to sea and had made a date to go dancing with her the following night. Thinking the world a marvellous place, although he could do with a bit more money, he noticed a car headlights at the entrance to a road on his right. *They'll come out behind me* was his instinctive reaction.

"God. No, it's comin' out fast. I'm going to hit it…" he screamed.

"Motor scooter accident, Meehaul, right leg quadriceps severed, severe bruising right leg, damage frontal part head, cut lips, in a state of unconsciousness. Name: Brendan Harris, male, early twenties."

"Thanks, George," acknowledged Michael the hospital orderly to the two ambulance men. "It's going to be a busy night. Where was this?"

"Oh! Merrion Road on the way to Dunlaoghaire," answered George, as Michael started to wheel the hospital trolley, with the inert body, into the admissions department. "Poor lad had no protective clothing, or even a helmet. Will they ever learn?"

"What was the name again? Oh! You have his licence. Thanks, George. Ah! There we are, born 1940, it's 1961, makes him twenty-one. Hope he lives to see his next birthday. Let's wheel him away, lads, and onto the next one."

Relieved to have the responsibility of the result of another road crash off their hands, the ambulance men went off for a cup of tea, awaiting their next call.

"Hello…Mrs. Harris?"

"Yes," came the sleepy response.

"This is Laurence's Hospital here. We have a Brendan Harris who has been admitted due to a road accident in the last hour…"

"Oh! My God! Brendan. Where did it happen? That bloody scooter. Is he bad? Can I talk to him?"

"Afraid not, Mrs. Harris. He's being treated at the moment."

"Is it bad? Hen-ryeee! Quick, get the car out. It's Brendan. He's in Laurence's Hospital—something about a road accident. That bloody scooter…"

"Come on, Hen, put your foot down, forget the bloody speed limits. Will this old wagon not do more than thirty?"

"All right, Alice…there…we're doing fifty now," came the calming voice from her husband. "That suit you now?" *Laurence's, now that's closer into Dublin, just off the canal,. Poor Brendan,* mused Henry, as the old Ford Consul sped into Dublin in its unaccustomed speed. *He's to do his exams in a month's time. Four years at sea. Hope it's not too bad… Is it only four years ago when he went to sea?*

"Brendan, can you hear me? It's your ma and pop. Can you hear me?"

"I don't think so, Mrs. Harris," advised the nursing sister. "He's gone through an awful lot and is in a deep coma. He's lost a lot of blood, now please step back and let the porters take your son into theatre."

"Did you see, Hen? His head was all cut and his arms were tied down on the bed an' his leg looked awful. Oh God! Will he live?"

"Now, now, Mrs. Harris, no histrionics. He's in good hands and I'd advise you to go have a cup of tea. Nurse Dolan?" called the Nursing Sister. "Will you be after takin' Mr. and Mrs. Harris to the waiting room."

Dismissed by authority, Alice and Henry reluctantly followed the nurse to a small room off the long forbidding corridor. With a smile to her retinue, the nurse stood on her toes, leaned into the big square delph sink and half filled a large copper kettle from a pair of brass taps.

"We've only got de mugs ye kno', Mrs. Harris," she apologised in a deep country accent. "A terrible ting that, yer son wid de accident, but I kno' Mr. Larrigan, who's on tonight, will do a good job. He's a lovely man. I'll make a small pot of tea for yeas. Now der's sugar an' milk, help yerselves please, as I hav' got to go back to the ward. I'll keep me eye on yer boyo."

"Thanks, nurse. That's very kind of you. We'll stay for a bit to find out how things go with Brendan," acknowledged Alice, as she lifted the blue-patterned teapot and started to pour the strong tea into one of the stained white mugs.

"I'm not sure if I'll have the condensed milk," said Henry, as Alice held the half-full tin of the white silky cream, waiting for his acknowledgement. "But give me a drop of it. I'll try it before I have any sugar."

Discarded in their concerned little island in the large echo-filled hospital with its harsh unidentified smells, sudden sounds of rushing feet and the odd raised voice or stifled scream, Alice and Henry, both in their early forties, glanced at each other. Henry—a tall, broad-shouldered, handsome man with a head of black curly hair going grey at the sides—was at a loss at times to know what was expected from him. He was a slow-moving, dependable man who was often taken aback by his wife Alice's forceful attitude. Alice was slightly aggressive in her manner, and attractive in appearance, with a tall slim figure and ash-blonde hair. They were a well-suited pair: Alice made up for the slow thought process of her husband, whilst Henry could sometimes put a curb on Alice's excesses.

"God, Hen! Will Bren live?" she cried, leaning against Henry's large body for reassurance.

"Don't you be worrien then, Alice. He's in good hands now and we can just wait and see. Look, it's gone one o'clock. What do you wanna do?"

"Let's stay, Hen. Bren might need us."

In the early hours, after a restless and worrying time, the surgeon, Mr. Larrigan—a tall, impressive young man, wearing a white skull cap and gown—came to tell Alice and Henry, that Brendan had had a major operation on his head to relieve the concussion and to drain excess fluid. The muscles and tendons on his right knee that had been severed by the impact with the car window had all been sewn up, and the cuts to his face had all been treated.

"Don't you be worrien now, Mr. and Mrs. Harris," consoled the tired surgeon. "Yer son has had a great shock to his system and he's as well as can be expected. He's had a bad blow to his head and only time will tell how well he recovers. I must admit," the surgeon advised with a weary smile, "he has been coming out with some choice words as the anaesthetic has worn off."

"He's spent the last four years at sea ye kno'," interrupted Henry.

"Will he live, Doctor?" cried Alice. "Come on, Doc. He's not going to die on us?"

"He's a strong healthy lad, Mrs. Harris, with a strong will. It's all in the lap of the gods. Now I must leave you. Nurse Dolan will see to your needs. Good morning, try not to worry."

On to the next one, the tired healer of the battered and bruised seemed to say to himself, as he smiled at the worried couple on his way from the room.

***

"Yes, Polly, he's settled down a bit now. God, he must have gone through hell." It was now the following evening. Alice had phoned Brendan's friend Polly, to tell her about the accident, and that they wouldn't be going dancing that night.

"Yes, Polly love. The nurse took us into the side ward to see Brendan. There he was, in a large bed with the sides up, his head covered in a turban of white bandage, his right leg completely covered in plaster. There were plasters on his face, with blood drips an' all those things hanging over him and, Polly," cried Alice with a gasp. "An' his arms were tied to the side of the bed. Oh! God! What will happen to him? We talk to him but he doesn't answer."

"Look, Mrs. Harris," consoled Polly, somewhat surprised with the outpouring of grief from Brendan's mother, who was known only to her as Mrs. Harris and whom she had met only twice before. "Look, you must be exhausted. Do you think you could perhaps…get some sleep? Is there anything I can do? As you know, it's Saturday…"

"No, it's OK, Polly, you've been great. You go on now, but keep in touch an' let's pray he…lives. Henry is arranging to recover the scooter. Ye kno' it was Jono's and the Garda are interested in a statement about the accident. God! I hope he doesn't die!" exclaimed Alice, ever dramatic, bursting into a flood of tears as she put the phone down.

The following day, after a visit to the house from the Garda, it was discovered that Brendan had borrowed his brother's Vespa motor scooter to visit that girl in Dublin. He was returning home when he apparently crashed into the side of the car, smashed his head on the roof and put his right knee into the side window, resulting in the injuries now treated.

"It's going to be a long haul, Hen. The doc says it might be weeks before he recovers, or that he might not awaken at all." Giving an involuntary shudder and nearly breaking down again, Alice continued, "I was looking through Bren's things and came on this book, a sort of diary that he had written while at sea. Do you think Polly might be interested? She certainly feels for him. Do you think I could ask her to read him some of the diary? It might help him recover?"

"Whatever you think best, Alice," said Henry. "Though there might be something in it that she shouldn't see. Ye never know." He grinned.

"Shure, Hen! If she were to read him some of it whilst he's unconscious it might help him. It's worth the risk. Doctor Larrigan suggested we should talk to him to help him recover. I could read some of it to him as well…"

"Hold on. There's the phone ringin," interrupted Henry.

"Hey! Ma," came the youthful voice of Brendan's younger brother Billy from the hallway. "It's Brendan's bit of stuff. The Polly one wants to speak to you."

Surprised to get a return call so quickly from Polly, Alice took the heavy Bakelite receiver from Billy and hesitantly asked, "Yes! Polly…?"

"Oh, Mrs. Harris," came the anxious voice in a rush. "I just remembered Brendan telling me in one of his letters that he kept a diary over the years he was at sea. Maybe…if you've got it there, I could read some of it to him—"

"Polly," interrupted Alice. "How marvellous. Henry and I were just thinking the very same thing. He likes you a lot. I'm sure it would be a great help."

"Look, I could come up on my bike an' collect it now and go into the hospital and read some of it to him tomorrow." *Maybe get to know this guy a bit better*, thought Polly to herself. "Would that be all right?"

Getting Alice's agreement, Polly dutifully cycled the two miles from her parents' home in Dunlaoghaire. After a quick cup of tea, forced upon her by Alice, she wondered if she had done the right thing, but she liked Brendan and as she was getting old now—in her mid twenties—maybe they could get married. Polly was somewhat in awe of Alice; she thought Henry was a lovely guy, but Alice scared her, with her sudden change of moods and dictatorial attitude.

So were the innocent thoughts of Polly, not having seen how bad Brendan was, especially with the head wound, as she cycled home with the treasured diary in her mother's shopping bag slung over her shoulder. She was eager to find out what was held within the multitude of foolscap pages complete with drawings, sketch maps, photographs and compact hand-written prose.

The following day, quite apprehensively, she steeled herself to open the forbidding curtains sheltering her dream of the future. Dressed in a tight-waisted short grey skirt which showed off her long legs, topped by a full white blouse and smart light tan jacket with a suggestion of shoulder pads, she felt she looked quite attractive. With her new high heels and hair cut emphasising her natural blonde curls, she hoped she looked the part. Polly had recently looked to marrying Brendan and settling down with children. Brendan seemed very suitable: a church-going Protestant, with a secure future, albeit one where he would spend most of the time away at sea; Polly had stayed up late the previous evening to read the diary and was somewhat dismayed at some of the antics contained within it.

Whilst Brendan had been at sea, the communication with him, by letter, had been sporadic. He contacted her whenever he came home on leave, but never made any commitment about the future. Here she was, now twenty-two years old. He was the only male who had given any sign of interest in her. She realised she was a bit of an old maid, and a regular church-goer. Brendan had encouraged her to go dancing and had awakened bodily reactions she had not really been aware of. She was unsure on how far she should go in accepting these advances.

What will I see when I pull these curtains? she wondered. *Will he recognise me…? What's that? He sounds in pain.* "Oh? Brendan, what are they doing to you?" she gasped in dismay.

Instead of the smiling Brendan to welcome, there was this writhing body with a light blanket pushed to the bottom of the bed. The restless body had its right leg in plaster, from the top of the leg to toe; its head was swathed in a white turban of bandage. It was unshaven and its hands were lashed to the bedside rails. The body was constantly twitching and complaining in expletive-ridden shouts of horror. There were plastic bottles full of blood and other life-giving liquid swinging above the bed, and connected to the body by tubes. Sometimes the body went into repose and a smile came to the lips, which muttered unintelligible words.

This is not the Brendan Harris I knew—the light-hearted boy who left me some four years ago. We went dancing together. He was tender, thoughtful. When he went to sea I thought…this is the end, but he wrote to me. Somehow, however, I feel a bond with this complaining body in front of me. What's he saying now?

Polly watched as the body in the bed stopped twitching and its eyes opened, staring into space as it started muttering and then, with an unaccustomed smile on its youthful features, clearly announced, "That's all right then," followed by a sudden strenuous bout of endeavour to free its bound hands, while filling the air with expletives.

Startled by the sudden swish of the curtain surrounding the bed and the appearance of a nurse, Polly stood back, recoiling from the sheer horror of this unknown body twisting and shouting its anguish at the world.

"Would you be steppin' outside the curtains, Miss, while I give him the injection," requested the nurse with a fixed smile on her young face as she waited for Polly to move outside the curtained-off area. Stepping back from this foreign world of pain and discomfort, with the body in front of her tied to the protective railings, the smell of urine and the thrashing limbs, Polly thought, *I could get away from this world of anguish and pain. His mind must be going through terrible thoughts. I could get away from all this.* As she backed away from the sounds emanating from behind the curtains she stumbled against an adjoining bed. She turned around to apologise and was confronted by an elderly grey-haired man propped up by a mound of pillows.

"Is he dying then, Miss? Ye kno', he never shuts up with the swearin'. I hear he's a sailor, they're all the same, an' he had wit' him those letter things the heathen English use," complained the pyjama-clad man, sucking his teeth. "Poor lad, but he's a Prod, ye kno'."

He looked as if he had been there forever, as did the rest of the room, filled with male bodies in their beds, and the odd visitor, all looking at her.

"Dat's all right den, Miss," came the call from the bed, as the nurse stepped out between the curtains and deposited a large syringe onto the trolley.

"Thank you, nurse. Look, I'm havin' to hurry. Could you pass these papers to Mrs. Harris when she's next in? Thanks." *Wonder what the old guy meant by the letter things?* thought Polly. She decided she could not continue with the smells and this unwelcome demand on her feelings. The content of the diary was uppermost in her mind and with some of the content being so explicit, she decided she didn't want anything to do with this Brendan Harris. *The things he got up to, nothing like the boy I have waited four years for.* Putting her head inside the curtain, she called out to the unconscious form, "Goodbye, Brendan. I hope you recover," and, crying softly to herself, self-consciously strode down the ward, avoiding the staring eyes from the line of beds on each side.

This looks interesting, thought the nurse to herself, feeling the weight of the parcel passed to her. *I'm just due for a break. I'll have a look at it den.*

"Hey, Mary. See what I've got. Ye kno' the long fella in ward six, always swearin'?"

"Yeah. I remember, Kathleen. He was the fella with the…" Mary, a nurse sitting at a bench in the canteen, drinking a cup of tea, looked around to make sure there was nobody else listening, and whispered, "Ye kno' de fella with the…willy covers. Oh God, what am I sayin? Father Murphy will have me give a million Hail Marys fer thinkin' such evil things." She laughed nervously. She continued, "Nurse Dolan told me he had dozens of them in his wallet when he was admitted. God! I'll have to go to confession for sayin' such a word," she admitted with another nervous laugh and crossed herself.

"Dat's right," agreed Kathleen. "He came in a few days ago, nearly killed hisself on his scooter. Yeh! You're right," she stated airing her greater knowledge. "They call dem French Letters, those willy covers. God only knows why. Do you get them from France in the post? I wonder. Anyway you know he's a Prod as well."

"God! Is he den? A Prod...no wonder der's so few of them here in Ireland iffen der always using these...French letter things. They put them on their—Jeasus...what am I sayin? On their willies to stop havin' babbies, isn't that right, Kathleen?"

"Yeah! That's right. It's a heathen thing to do. No God fearin' Catlick would use such tings," Kathleen announced. "But look, Mary, look at what I've got." Kathleen held out the brown paper parcel with Brendan's diary in it. "Look, Mary. His girlfriend gave me this to give to his mother. Look, it's a diary he's kept, look." She opened the parcel and flipped through the pages. "It's all in longhand, look and der's photos and drawings. Nobody knows I have it. I had a read of a bit earlier an' came across a story in the book when he was in South Africa. You should see the things he got up to. Jeasus, Mary and Joseph. Look!" exclaimed Nurse Kathleen in triumph. "Doan tell anyone I've got it, Mary. We can read it later."

And so the reputation of Brendan Harris began: the tall Prod, the sailor guy with the willy covers and the diary full of explicit adventures. Brendan remained in a coma, oblivious to the effect he was having on the nurses of ward six and others who read this diary. Over the next few weeks, there was delight and disgust with the contents of Brendan's diary, as it moved from hand to hand, whilst Brendan remained in a severe coma.

But let's now go back to the beginning—back four years to when Brendan left his family and country to make his way in the disturbed world of the 1950s, to start his career as an apprentice ship's officer.

2

Leaving Ireland

"What have ye innit, Long John? God! The weight of it."

These were the laughing comments from the young seaman Brendan had asked to help move his sea chest as they stumbled across the deck of the Irish ferry.

Embarrassed, Brendan mumbled some unintelligible words in reply. *God!* he thought. *What am I going to do when I join the ship in England? I'll feel a right fool lugging this behind me.*

It was way back in the mid 1950s when Brendan Harris, a virgin in mind and in body, went to sea at the time when his native Ireland was shedding its youth through the short-sightedness of the politicians. Of course, the politicians were second in line to the all-powerful Catholic Church and, being a Protestant, Brendan had very little chance of securing employment. So it was on the sixteenth of May, 1957, that Brendan packed his bags, having secured a seagoing apprenticeship with the Calvex Shipping Company to become a ship's officer. He had now set sail from Dublin to join his first ship in England.

"Goodbye! Ma, Pop, I'll write and let you know how I get on."

He remembered his mother standing in the light rainfall, hugging his father's arm, dressed in her mock fur coat, with Pop, tall and solid, holding an open umbrella to shield them from the rain, both of them waving in the dim light as the ferry pulled away from the quay. With a last wave to the darkness, Brendan turned back into the light of the companionway to recover his luggage. He was very conscious of the large wooden sea chest his thoughtful parents had presented to him: *all sea dogs use a sea chest, don't dey?* For a self-conscious seventeen-year-old a sea chest standing some three foot long, two foot wide and two foot tall, with an oval top was bad enough. But with the whole dreadful thing covered in green paint, with black bands and brass clasps—all carefully painted by his father—it was dreadfully embarrassing. Along with his pirate's chest, his other luggage comprised a large, cheap suitcase and canvas holdall. These containers were filled with his personal possessions: the new uniform and officer's cap, a civilian suit, overcoat, jerseys, boots, shoes, tropical shirts, shorts and books. *Come prepared for all climates and eventualities* were the instructions in the lengthy list supplied by the company.

At six foot tall and weighing eleven stone, Brendan was very conscious of his height and thin body. His light brown hair refused to take a parting and retained its stubborn styleless shape. His regular features were broken by a few aggravating spots, but with his disarming smile and relaxed air, Brendan found it easy to make friends. So, wearing his one spare pair of corduroy trousers, (had to be lengthened), sports shirt and jersey (knitted by his mother), Brendan relaxed and looked along the rows of wooden seats with their sprawling occupants and squalling children. There were a few young men, all chattering away together. However, there was an empty seat alongside a pleasant-looking girl, wearing a long overcoat and scarf, reading a paperback. With his readymade smile, Brendan walked toward the seat. The girl kept her head down and her eyes on the book and, either unconsciously or deliberately, adjusted her coat over her bare knees, keeping her eyes on the green-and-white Penguin paper back.

"Excuse me. Is this seat taken?"

Without answering or raising her eyes, the girl's head went deeper into her book. Her left hand pulled the green overcoat protectively to her side and her body moved an inch to the right.

Brendan acknowledged her move with a 'thank you' and, leaving the suitcase against the wall, sat down with the canvas holdall on the floor between his legs. The offending sea chest had been stowed in the luggage bay. As they were now an hour into the seven-hour trip to Liverpool, the ship was well out into the Irish Sea and had started to roll and shudder slightly in the disturbed waters. Brendan settled into the uncomfortable wooden seat and thought back over the past year. It had gone so fast. To think, it was only in the last nine months he had considered starting a sea-going career, and here he was on his way to join an oil tanker as an apprentice deck officer—four years before the mast, or maybe behind the mast. *Whatever! What will it mean? Where will I go? Have I got everything I need?*

Dropping into a fitful doze, Brendan recalled the day he received the important Company Indentures, his signature to be witnessed by persons of authority. After the company had approved his application and he had undergone a rigorous medical, a telegram arrived instructing him to report to the captain of the *Calvex Renown*. The *Renown*, as proudly advised, was a brand-new, deep-seagoing tanker ship, docked in Sunderland close to the city of Newcastle-upon-Tyne somewhere in the north-east of England.

BRENDAN AFLOAT

The Indentures, on impressive parchment paper with red seals all over it, made between Brendan Harris and the Calvex Company with his dad as surety and witnessed by Brigadier Baker—that rather pompous, beefy British Army Officer (he won the war for the Allies, by the way)—offered the following terms:

> The said apprentice will receive £575 paid over the four years with a further twelve shillings per annum in lieu of washing and a further sum of £30 payable after satisfactory service and had served at least four fifths of the four years at sea.

Four years...that's a lifetime, wonder what lies ahead, Brendan thought to himself. *How often will I get home to Ireland? Whatever, I'm ready for anything.*

So, Brendan—equipped with his smart uniform, a set of tropical clothes, a 1939 brass sextant, a present from Polly his girlfriend, and an arm pockmarked with injections against all diseases known to man—was all prepared for what the world had to hold for him.

Deep in thought, he found himself sliding off his seat as the ship had begun rolling side-to-side and giving fitful jumps. Through his half-opened eyes he could see stumbling bodies rushing from side-to-side with arms out wide, frantically searching for stability. The weather had worsened. Clambering back onto his seat, Brendan's eyes caught those of the girl alongside him. She was grinning at his discomfort and laughed spontaneously at his un-seamanlike attempts to regain his seat. Settling onto the uncomfortable wooden bench, Brendan acknowledged her amusement with a laugh and looked at the clock on the wall.

"Only one o'clock. There's hours to go yet," he exclaimed in mock distress. "Have you sailed on one of these before?" he asked, hoping the girl would respond and help to break the expected monotony of the hours ahead.

"I'm on my vay home from holiday in Dublin," was the reply. "Thees is my second time to sail. Oh! Oh! Oops! Merde!" was the frantic call, as the ship gave an extra deep roll ending in a sudden jerk. There being no arms on the wooden bench to hold onto, Brendan impulsively grabbed the girl's coat and stopped her from falling forward. With a further lurch, her light body was thrown sideways against Brendan. Quite embarrassed and aroused by the close proximity of the female body as his hand had accidently touched her bare leg, Brendan blushed and sat back in his seat. The girl, somewhat older than Brendan, smiled and settled into her uncomfortable seat, laughing at the sight of Brendan's embarrassment.

Over the course of the next few hours, Brendan discovered that Michelle was French and a student of politics attending Oxford. He was enthralled with her accent and her insight into the politics of the time. His knowledge of the subject was very sparse and when she found that he was going to sea in an oil tanker, she gave him a blow-by-blow account of what was later to become known as the 1956 war.

"After Egypt had nationalised ze Suez Canal last year, England and France invaded the country, and Monsieur Nasser sunk lots of oil sheeps. Ze Americans said dey would not help France or England no more and Monsieur Eden put his hanzs up and deed not tell ze French. Oh! Ette was terrible, so, mon ami, I hope you will be safe on your beeg oil tankers. One leetle thing Bren-dan—are you going to keep a diary of your adventure? Theese are important times. What do you theenk?"

Brendan had always felt he should keep a diary and was very smitten by the lovely accent, flattered that this intelligent and attractive young lady, pretty as that film star Audrey Hepburn, considered him her ami. He agreed with her suggestion and, feeling very grown up, rose to his feet. Swaying in a seaman-like manner, in his best impersonation of Gregory Peck as Captain Ahab in *Moby Dick*, Brendan invited Madame for a cup of tea in the café.

Taking the proffered hand, Audrey Hepburn rose from her seat and the two of them staggered across the deck. However, as it was now four o'clock, everything had shut down, although there were still a few solitary boisterous drinkers stretching their hands out, reaching for friendship like street beggars.

Laughing in unison at the antics of one poor unfortunate drunk, the two new amis returned to their seats and wrapped up in their respective overcoats to try and get some sleep.

"All ashore, all ashore in half an hour, six o'clock."

Wakening to the sound of the calling voice, Brendan stretched out his long legs. Cold and stiff he half opened his eyes. The ship's uncomfortable movements had settled down into a long steady roll with the drumming sound of the engines in the background. His fellow passengers were beginning to rouse themselves; the drunks were oblivious to everything, whilst some surprisingly lively youngsters were peering out of the portholes. A steady procession to the lavatories was forming. Brendan looked at his companion of the early hours, snuggled down in her coat snoring gently, her pretty face grey in the early morning light. She was a stranger again. Rather than waken her, Brendan, needing to answer the calls of nature, left the sleeping body. On his return with two cups of coffee—*the French only drink coffee, don't they?*—she had gone. The seat was empty and there was nothing left behind. The small suitcase, her coat, her smile, her lovely accent…were no longer.

Brendan stood with the two cups of cooling coffee, and for a second, all dreams of the future—visits to her home in France, taking her home to Ireland, showing his brothers how cosmopolitan he had become, learning French, living in Paris—all the fantasies of a seventeen-year-old had disappeared. One of Brendan's neighbours, an elderly man wearing a cloth cap with a peak as long as his weeping nose, nodded at Brendan with a smile, his hand held out for the spare cup,

"Dat's life, Son. Here tiday gon' timorro'. Shure, der's plenty mor' fish in de sea. Ye won't be needin' dat now, will ye?"

With a rueful smile, Brendan passed the spare coffee over and thought, *Yep! He's right but she was very nice. But 'merde'*, he laughed inwardly, *how am I going to get this bloody sea trunk to the station in Liverpool?*

With a lot of hustle and bustle, the ferry boat progressed through the various locks to eventually tie up at Princes Dock, Liverpool, and the many foot passengers made their way ashore. Brendan was in a quandary: how *was* he going to get his luggage to the Lime Street station? The sea chest was too heavy for one person and he did not want to spend too much on a taxi.

"Excuse me!" he called, catching the eye of one of the seamen at the passenger exit. "Do you kno' any way I can get this thing to Lime Street station?"

"Take a taxi, mate, the only way. Oh! Wait a minit Hey, Pete, is yer brudder still runnin' the fruit to the traders on Lime Street?"

Getting an affirmative from Pete, who was helping a woman carry her suitcase down the gangplank, the seaman suggested Brendan had a word with him.

"Young man! Perhaps I can help."

Surprised at the address, Brendan, who had noticed the elderly, well-dressed businessman standing by the gangplank, looked over.

"If you are going to Lime Street Station, son, perhaps you might like to put your wonderful sea chest in my taxi."

Delighted that his problem could be solved so easily, Brendan smiled his agreement and signalled to Pete that he did not need his 'brudder'. With the help of one of the seamen, directed by his new friend, Brendan put the sea chest and suitcase in the back of the large taxi and joined the smiling businessman in the backseat, shoving his canvas holdall between his feet.

In a cloud of cigar smoke, the taxi sped away from the docks and made its way through the crowded streets of Liverpool to deposit its passengers at the busy entrance to the station. Brendan's benefactor waved away his unenthusiastic offer to help with the fare and directed the porter to the London train.

"Where are you going to, son?"

"Newcastle, sir. Joining an oil tanker."

"Good luck, young man. I'm going to stuffy meetings in London. I envy you. All the best."

With that, the elegant businessman, still puffing his cigar, turned away and strode through the streams of anxious people, followed by the porter carrying the man's small suitcase.

What a nice man, thought Brendan, as he grabbed a spare trolley and heaved the overweight and awkward green-and-black monster onto its base with the now much scratched cheap suitcase. He swung the holdall over his shoulder and headed for the station forecourt. *Where is the 9:15 to Newcastle?* Signs pointing to important cities—Leeds, London, Preston—directed the crowds. There were long benches full of disconsolate people with luggage stacked up beside them. The murky light from the high, smoke-stained skylight added to the claustrophobic feeling, along with the noise of shouting voices and the bored unintelligible drone announcing the departure and arrival of trains. *Where's the Newcastle train? Ah! There it is.* Joining one of the many queues, Brendan confirmed with a smartly dressed man reading a newspaper that he was in the right queue for Newcastle.

Leaving the trolley, Brendan ran over to a news stall to buy a paper and a bar of chocolate and rejoined the line of patient people to await this next step of his journey.

Through the countryside of northern England and the many unattractive grimy cities of the north, the steam train, with a final shriek of enveloping, scalding white clouds, came to a halt in Newcastle-upon-Tyne. Brendan's instructions were to make his way to the Calvex agents in Newcastle. Taking a deep breath and feeling quite tired after all his travelling, he deposited his sea trunk in the left luggage office, ignoring the grinning attendant. After asking the way, he found the agent's office.

"Yes, Mr. Harris, you are to join the *Calvex Renown* on Corporation Quay, Sunderland, tomorrow morning. Here's an accommodation voucher to show at the seaman's mission. Good luck."

With his sea chest and battered suitcase, a weary and apprehensive Brendan headed for the seaman's mission in Sunderland. Only twenty-four hours earlier, he had left the security of his home and family for what was a foreign country—new smells, and new voices, a new life ahead of him. He had spent the first seventeen years of his life in the relative comfort and security of his home in Laurel Cottage. His parents and friends were always to hand; now here he was, entering a completely new world, the unknown—exciting but worrying. What would be expected of him?

3

Early Days in Hospital

"Hey! Mary! Just bin in to see Rudolph. God! The things he's saying." Due to Brendan having the 'French Letter' in his wallet, when the porter went through his pockets, he had been nicknamed Rudolph, after Rudolph Valentino, the famous Latin American lover of the 1920s.

"Dey do a lot of swearin' on those English ships, dey do. Have you heard him? Do all Prods swear as much? Father Murphy would be disgusted. Are you enjoyin' his diary book, Kathleen? I do like the pictures an' am lookin' forward to the next chapter. He was a real innocent then, wasn't he? Our Rudi. Wonder what happened to the French girl?"

"His big brother is in visitin'. Isn't he a dish with his curly hair? You know, you wouldn't think dey were brothers."

Mary Sheelin, a second year nurse from County Clare way in the west of Ireland, was a farmer's daughter, the youngest of eight children. Aged nineteen, five foot two in her socks, she had a pleasant, enquiring face, dark, straight hair and a plump body. Endowed with great enthusiasm, she spoke her thoughts.

"I was givin' Rudolph a drink of water this mornin' an' he opened his eyes, looked straight at me—didn't look like he saw me though—smiled and told me to f--- off. God! It was scary. Lucky his hans are tied to the bed. We shuddent have to put up with this blasphemy, should we, Kath?" suggested Mary with a big grin on her face.

"Hav' a word wid Sister Sullivan, Mary, doe it's a bit excitin' to see how Prods get on. I'm learnin' a few things about Prods from his diary. Ye kno' Nurse Dolan? God she's a one. She was on night duty when he came in. Poor guy, I am sorry for him the poor fella, his willy. God, I shouldn't say this," stated Kathleen, looking around and leaning toward Mary. "Ye kno' his willy was standin' up straight an' Joe, the porter, said we'll have none of this and gave it a knock wid' his han' an' Lord Blessus it went over like that…" laughed Kathleen in her Dublin accent, as she described the motion with the side of her hand. Aged eighteen, Kathleen was somewhat taller than Mary with flaming red hair, a thin lively face and slim, in comparison to her compatriot Mary. Both girls went into a conspiratorial giggle.

"I'm goin' in to the ward to have a look at the brud. Keep yer eye out fer Sister Sullivan, will ye, Mary? As I shud be on ward three."

Nurse Kathleen peered around the entrance door to the ward. Seeing Brendan's brother Jono parting the bedside curtains, she walked over and followed him into the slight intimacy of the situation and started adjusting the bed sheet. "He's lookin' well now isn't he, sir," she stated, nodding toward the now relaxed body.

Ever the man to flirt with an attractive female, Jono said, "It's the result of the dedication you good-looking nurses devote to your patients that has kept him alive, no doubt about it."

"Thank you, sir," blushed Kathleen, feeling very small beside the tall Jono. "It's the blood and glucose is what's keepin' him alive. It was a bad accident I hear, air," she stated, hoping to hear more news.

"Yes, Nurse it was my scooter he was riding," laughed Jono resignedly. "It's a write off, smashed up. He rode into the side of a car—a Hillman Minx, I believe. The driver must have had a few too many as he drove straight out into the road in front of Brendan an' bang!" Jono demonstrated, smacking his right hand into his left. "He must hav' hit his head on the roof an' put that leg—" pointing to Brendan's right leg in plaster "—through the car window."

"Isn't he a sailor, sir? An officer in the English Navy?"

"Yes, Nurse. He has spent the last four years on big tanker ships and has just come home to take his officer examinations, next week. Not much hope of that now," admitted Jono, looking for agreement from the nurse.

"Yeah," agreed Kathleen. "You kno', the nurses are all talkin' about him—a girlfriend in every port, they say." She noticed Mary peering anxiously from the side doorway and waving her arm. "Gotta go now, sir. I hope he…lives," was her hopeful comment as she hurriedly walked out of the ward.

Jono had only in the previous six months returned from a period of time in the British army and was now employed as a salesman for a souvenir firm in Dublin. The firm offered to pay travelling expenses if he could provide his own transport. Fortunately he was now in a position to buy a second-hand Austin 8, with a reasonable mileage on the clock, and the loss of the motor scooter, which had been only insured third-party, now consigned to the scrap yard, wasn't such a bind as earlier thought.

He was a good-looking man, was Jono, some six foot tall, with tight curly hair, strong features, prone to needing a shave five minutes after applying the razor, of wiry build and very conscious of his appearance. Very popular with the girls, Jono was now doing a strong line with a Roman Catholic girl. Alice was not in favour of her eldest son consorting with a Roman Catholic but there weren't a great many Protestants in Jono's social group. When he got back to Laurel Cottage later that evening, he brought up the subject of Brendan over the evening meal.

"Hey! Ma! I've just been to the hospital to see Bren, poor guy. All the apparatus around the bed…" Jono stroked the black stubble on his chin reflectively. "You know, they're all calling him Rudolph in the hospital. Not the red-nosed reindeer, but after Rudolph Valentino. Wasn't he a film star in the twenties?"

"Well is that so?" mused Alice with the hint of a smile. "Brendan is no Rudolph Valentino." She smiled again. "Rudolph Valentino," she repeated laughing. "Even before my time, Jono. He was known as the great Latin lover in the silent movies around the time I was born. I remember when he died." She stopped talking for a moment whilst she thought. "Yes! I think he was only thirty when he died. Bren being linked with Rudolph Valentino—I wonder why? Bren the great Irish lover…well what do you know? Ha! Ha! He will shure laugh about that when he recovers. God! Hope he does."

"Don't you be worrien, Ma. He's going to get better. But Bren the great Irish lover, that's a good one." laughed Jono, as he tapped out a filter tip cigarette from the carton of twenty. "I wonder what's prompted them to call him that? By the way, where's that diary thing of his?"

"I left it with Polly yesterday," replied Ma. "I'll give her a ring after tea. She said she'd read him a bit of it. I just wonder now if she did. She hasn't been in touch…"

"They reckon," continued Jono, "it could take a few weeks for Bren to come out of the coma an' that his memory could be affected."

"God, I hope not. He has done so well. There's a letter for him from the shipping company. Here it is." Ma proudly showed the embossed Calvex letterhead to the group. "It's askin' him to agree a two-year contract as a third officer when he finishes his exams."

"They must think well of him to offer that," interjected Henry. "But it doesn't look like he'll be going back to the Nautical School in Dunlaoghaire for some time. We'd better let dem know Alice…"

Laurel Cottage

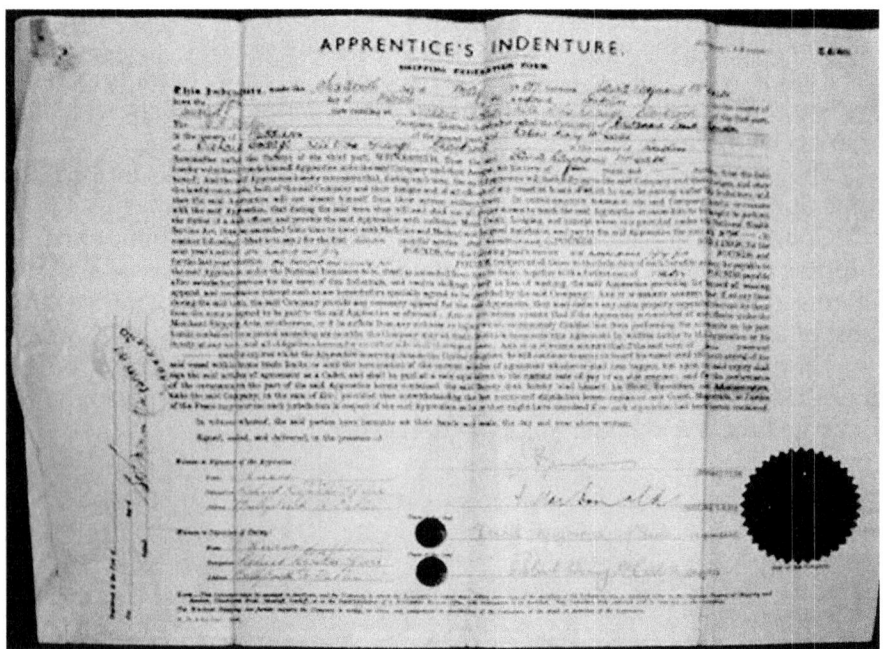

Apprentice's Indentures

4

Joining Ship

That evening, after Brendan had settled into a shared room in the seaman's mission, he met the three other apprentices he would be spending the next undetermined number of months with. Two of them were old sea dogs: the elder, Kenneth Johnston, was a tall young man with pleasant welcoming features, age nineteen, very positive in his attitude but very guarded in his initial approach to any new venture. He was coming to the end of his third year of apprenticeship, and Brendan was wary of him. The other experienced apprentice was Donald Marshall; the *Renown* would be his second ship. Brendan took to Don's friendly welcoming, laughing attitude immediately. Don's stockier muscular build, with curly brown hair and striking blue piercing eyes were in direct contrast to Brendan's lightweight, tall, slim body. They took an immediate liking to each other.

Then there was Barry Jones, a first timer like Brendan. However, Barry showed no attractive qualities whatsoever. He looked like a confused bulldog, with his pudgy body and florid features. His eyes sunken within his prominent cheeks were all balanced upon a rounded body; Brendan's immediate comparison was to Billy Bunter of Greyfriars School from the *Knockout* comic.

Whilst Ken and Don discussed their seagoing experiences, as all old sea dogs do, Brendan and Barry briefly talked about their recent past. Barry, in his strong melodious Welsh accent, rambled on about how fortunate the Calvex company were to have his services, as he came from a family with a long seagoing tradition. Raised in Swansea, Barry had gone to private school and won silver cups for achievements in the Welsh language. His father, now retired, had been a commander in the Royal Navy and it was ordained that he, Barry Jones, was destined to become a ship's master in record time. Barry was not Brendan's idea of a shipmate.

Endeavouring to assert themselves with their new associates, Brendan felt he had lost some credibility on the appearance of his black and green 'Long John Silver' sea trunk. Johnston made a reference to Irish pirates, while Don Marshall, grinning mightily, helped Brendan carry it to his room, expressing his sympathy when Brendan explained that his parents had proudly presented it to him and he couldn't hurt their feelings.

After an unsettled night's sleep (Brendan had been paired off with Barry, who snored pretty badly), Brendan was feeling quite apprehensive—a new life ahead of him and new people he would be associating with for goodness how long. Where was he going, what was expected of him? His three associates were each apprehensive and wary of the others and there was some forced laughter on their way down to Corporation Quay to report on board the *Renown*. All four, resplendent in their uniforms and naval caps, arrived at the *Calvex Renown* tied up alongside the dusty unkempt quayside.

The *Renown*, just built at a local yard, towered above the quay, all magnificent in its white superstructure and dark blue hull. A 16,000-ton tanker built to transport oil to and from most ports in the world, she had just finished her seagoing trials and was now loading stores and equipment for her first voyage.

Brendan decided he would follow the confident and experienced Kenneth, as Kenneth had done it all before. However, the dumpy Barry, who had already become quite overbearing with his constant critical comments, pushed his way to the front and bounded up the accommodation ladder tied alongside the towering hull. The two seniors looked at each other and smiled. Brendan kept quiet and followed the three others up the long steps to the ship's deck.

With a feeling of destiny, Brendan stepped off the gangway leading to the ship's main red painted deck. All he could see was a profusion of black pipes leading to black tank covers, with upright white topped narrow valves alongside each tank lid. Down the centre of the deck, front to rear, ran a raised walkway with white rails. *One day soon I'll know how it all works* were Brendan's immediate thoughts as he walked onto the red deck.

"Well welcome you four beauties!" was the shouted greeting from the white superstructure to the right, as a tall, young man dressed in a blue jersey and dark blue trousers with officer epaulets came towards them across the deck. "We'll soon get you out of that gear and get you working, lads. My name is Michael Read, third mate. Where's your gear?" the smiling officer asked in a very English accent.

"Still at the mission, third," answered Johnston.

"OK! Come with me and I'll introduce you to the Chief Officer and figure out what to do with you. Come on then," he instructed, as he rapidly strode back towards the white structures. Dutifully, the four splendidly dressed officers-to-be followed the quickly retreating figure, ignoring the grins from a small group of men gathered around a pile of boxes containing ship supplies.

Brendan, again following the other three with Barry bouncing ahead, looked around at the myriad pipes and masts and vents, steps and rails, with three dominant colours: white, black and red. The air was filled with the smell of new paint and bare metal, and the atmosphere of preparation. *Gosh!* thought Brendan to himself. *There is so much of everything. The third mate seems a nice guy. Wonder what the Chief Officer is like?*

"Come on, Paddy," called Don Marshall. "Put your cap straight. We're going to meet the Chief Officer."

Must put these guys straight about my name before they get used to calling me Paddy, thought Brendan as they entered the officer deck, the hushed atmosphere of oak panelled walls and subdued lighting contrasting with the bright sunlight they had just left.

"Those two cabins," pointed the third mate, "are for you apprentices. That door on the right is my cabin, next to it is the second mate's and this," he stopped outside an open door, "is the mate's cabin."

"The Chief Officer's cabin, Third," admonished the shirt-sleeved male figure sitting at a desk with his back to the door. Swivelling around in his chair, the Chief Officer faced the group standing in the doorway.

"What have we got here then, Third? A delegation from the Pirates of Penzance?" he asked in a deep Irish accent.

God! He's a Dublin man, Brendan recognised immediately.

"No, sir," answered the third mate with a strained laugh. "They are the new apprentices."

Raising to his stockinged feet, the first mate, with a commanding body surmounted by a completely bald head—*the man responsible for the running of the ship*—called out, "Come in, lads. Let's see the colour of yer eyes, den. Be quick. I've got a lot to do. Me name is Tom Cassidy."

"I'm Johnson, sir. Kenneth Johnson."

"I'm Donald Marshall, sir."

"Brendan Harris. Sir."

"Barry Jones reporting for duty. Shir." Stepping forward and standing to attention, Barry made a start to salute but thought better of it and kept his hands down to his side.

"Right, Third. What are you goin' to do with them?"

"We've got no bedding on board for them as yet, sir, an' it appears they have no working clothes with them."

"Well, we can't get them to work in all their finery. Book them in for another night in the Mission and—" turning to look at the four and raising his voice "—now the four of ye git yer backsides out of here and report back tomorrow morning with yer gear at ten. And be ready to work yer bollocks off. Now dismiss an' let me git on wit me work. Third, go see the Chief Steward about the bedding."

With that, Chief Officer Tom Cassidy swung back to his desk, sheltering a grin on his face.

"Third, any idea when we should sail?" questioned Don Marshall, as the four of them were being shown their quarters for the forthcoming months.

"As you know—it's Don, isn't it? You are two to a cabin, see there, the luxury. I remember my first trip on the *Venture*. God, the squalor. When do we sail? It's Wednesday today, I reckon we should be away by Saturday."

"Any idea where to, Third?" asked Ken Johnson.

"No idea… You're the senior, aren't you?"

"Yes, Third. Just come off the *Rover*. How long have your been with Calvex?"

Half listening to the conversation, Brendan examined the cabin he would be sharing over the coming months. *Please, God not with the little Welshman*. A small room some ten foot square, with two curtained sleeping bunks, one over the other, was visible through the open door. A fitted desk lay alongside the wall to the right with two chairs and knee room under the desk and two respective desk lights. At right angles to the desk, facing the doorway, was the outside wall of the ship, or, bulkhead, with two portholes: round windows with brass fittings, stretching the width of the cabin. On the left of the room at right angles to the outside wall were two small wardrobes with a wash basin to the left of the open door. With the furniture finished in oak veneer and the wall a light cream and everything smelling very new and fresh, it all appeared very satisfying.

"Look, Johnson," called the third, "I've got work to do. You take the new lads around; show them what they have let themselves in for. OK by you, Harris?" he nodded towards Brendan, "an' you, Jones?"

Receiving nods of affirmation from all, the third mate hurried away and the senior apprentice started to outline the layout of the ship to the first trippers, excusing the experienced Don.

"I'll be brief, guys. Excuse me if you know this already. We are now in the midships section, officer accommodation. Aft—that's the rear end—" with his hand pointing to the right "—that's where the crew lives. The engine is down there, as is the galley, where the food is cooked, and up the front end—the bows—we have the foc'sle or forecastle, with the anchors. Got that?" Receiving affirmatives from the two first trippers, he continued, "Now, I'm going back into town. Got some things to do. See you back at the mission."

"Well, what do you think of that, now?" growled Barry. "Who does he think he is, now? Tellin' us the obvious."

"Well, whatever." answered Don who had returned. "Look, it's mid afternoon. The mate said to turn in tomorrow, so let's make the most of what's left of the day."

"That's fine by me, Don. Let's get back to the mission and get out of this gear," suggested Brendan. "What about you, Barry?"

"Oh! I'll stay on and have a look around."

Somewhat relieved to get away from Barry, Don and Brendan made their way back to the seaman's mission to change. Don, not as tall as Brendan but of heavier build, looked well in his uniform but was glad to change into his slacks and sweatshirt.

"Paddy—" he started to say when Brendan stopped him with a smile.

"Don, before you go any further, my name is Brendan. Call me Brendan or even Bren. My name is not Paddy, OK?" he said, looking Don in the eye.

Slightly taken aback, Don replied with a grin, "Bren..." He hesitated slightly. "I was just going to say, what you think about us sharing the cabin? Barry would share with Ken."

"That's a relief, Don, that's fine by me. Have you any plans for the evening?"

"There's a dance on here in the mission—thought I'd look in at that after phoning home. Money's pretty short."

"Great. I must phone my mother as well."

After his dutiful call to his ma, Brendan got the spare pair of slacks and the rather creased brown sports jacket out of the sea chest, kept the white shirt and tie on, gave the pair of brown leather shoes a polish with the bathroom towel, ran the broken plastic comb through his hair, took a deep breath and gave Don a call on his way to the main hall, where the dance was to be held.

Feeling a bit guilty that he hadn't been in touch with his girlfriend, Polly, back in Dublin (telephone calls were very expensive), Brendan promised himself to write her a letter when he knew where the ship would be going.

"Right, Don, let's see what the talent is like here in England," grinned Brendan.

Later that afternoon, after returning to the mission and changing into their shore clothes, the two young men made their way to the reception room in the old building.

"Gosh! There's only a few people here, Don."

"It's still early, Bren," declared Don. "Look. There's a tea bar over the other side of the room."

The two matelots walked self-consciously across the wooden floor of the well used room, trying not to appear too interested in the small groups of girls sitting on chairs placed against the white distempered wall. Approaching the white-cloth-covered table with the steaming tea urn on it, Brendan unconsciously turned on his *I would like to be your friend* smile and commenced to charm the plump elderly tea lady with his warm Irish accent.

Armed with their stewed tea in delicate porcelain cups and a couple of plain unappetising biscuits, the two sat down on unsteady spindly chairs at the side of the hall.

"Bloody hell, Bren!" complained Don in slight disgust. "What are we doing here? Look! Let's ditch this and go somewhere else. Maybe have a drink in that pub down the road." Rising, to leave the two hesitated.

"No hold on a mo, Don," cautioned Brendan "Look what's just come in. I'll take the tall one, OK by you?"

Somewhat surprised by his newfound bravado, Brendan looked to Don for his agreement. Don—surprised himself, as he had thought Brendan was a bit slow and reticent—nodded his agreement. "Yeah, Bren. The smaller one looks fine."

The two girls were both in their late teens. The tall one, some five foot eight, wore a white blouse and swinging skirt over a pair of elegant, brown legs extending down to smart brown shoes with small heels. With her blonde hair in a pony tail, she sent Brendan's heart aflutter as she looked in his direction and smiled. *Gosh!* thought Brendan. *Did she smile at me?*

"Yer on there, Bren lad," said Don in a mock envious voice. "I'll have to do with second best."

The second girl, wearing a one-piece red dress, with her dumpy legs, high heels and her brown hair piled high to attain some of the height of her friend, kept her head down as the two of them made their way towards the table.

"Finish your tea, Don, quick, and let's get another cup. This is our chance."

So, gulping the lukewarm tasteless tea and putting the biscuit in his pocket, Brendan, followed by Don, sauntered over to the tea table.

"When does the dance music start?" asked Brendan as they reached the table. He glanced at the tall blonde, who looked at her friend, who glanced at her wrist.

"It should start in about ten minutes. Look! There's Tommy the disc jockey. Must introduce you to him, Joan. He's my brother." The second girl had replied in a strong Geordie accent and, before Brendan could intervene, had taken hold of her friend's arm and steered her over to introduce her to Tommy.

Left standing, the two took their second cups of tea, looked at each other and followed the two girls over towards the record player and a smug looking Tommy.

"Look, Bren, would you believe it? He's wearing a wig," exclaimed Don. The slick black hair precariously balanced on the thin head of the middle-aged disc jockey was definitely a different tone of black to the busy sideboards.

With a professional shrug of his shoulders, Tommy acknowledged the introduction and, leaving a nonplussed Joan and his sister, sauntered in his squeaky soft-soled shoes over to the record player. With a smile to his larger audience of four giggling girls and three sulky looking young men, Tommy brought the volume up to the sound of Eddie Fisher singing "Oh Mein Papa".

"Have you any Victor Sylvester records, Tommy?" enquired Brendan, hoping to impress the lovely Joan, knowing he could get around the floor to a foxtrot beat.

"Yeh, I have one here somewhere, a seventy-eight. Ah! Here it is, the 'St. Bernard's Waltz'—a bit scratched, but maybe a strict tempo for this crowd." Tommy grinned. "I've got Joe Loss with 'Jeepers Creepers' and the 'Woodchopper's Ball' on a forty-five, and plenty of dance music on seventy-eights—even got rock 'n' roll."

"What do you think, Joan? What music do you like?"

Somewhat startled at being addressed by Brendan, Joan, who had been shuffling through the stack of records on the table, looked up. In a soft, educated voice, in contrast to the harsh Geordie accents around her, replied, "I like Nat King Cole and any by Johnny Mathis. Have you seen any, Mary?" she asked Tommy's sister, giving Brendan a half smile.

"Look, girls, don't mess my records around," exclaimed Tommy, pushing his sister aside. "Now go an' look after yer boyfriends while I get on with my job. Now…"

Leaving Tommy to get on with his work, Brendan winked at Don. "Come on, Don. Let's leave Tommy to get on with playing the records… are you…?"

Don neatly stepped in. "Mary, I see you have finished your tea. Come on. Let's be mad and have another. Maybe they might have some coffee, my name's Don, by the way."

Mary, by now slightly overcome by the sudden attention, allowed herself to be guided towards the tea table. Brendan gestured to Joan with a smile, *let's follow them* and after some nervous laughter, the four new friends sat around a small table at the side of the empty floor. Both girls were as eager as the two boys to cultivate a friendship and, after a few embarrassed starts, Brendan's dancing improved under Joan's guidance. After initial nervous attempts to create conversation—*is the new rock 'n' roll style of dancing going to catch on? Did you see any of the latest films*—Joan, who appeared to be an avid film goer, wanted to discuss the merits or otherwise of the new style of film on the market: James Dean, *East of Eden*, or *Blackboard Jungle* with Glenn Ford. To lighten the conversation, Brendan asked if anyone had seen *The Lady and the Tramp*.

"Yes! Wasn't it cute?" agreed Mary. And so, as the evening continued, the conversation relaxed into general topics, the room filled up with animated talk and Brendan got to hear some of Joan's story. She was born in London, was a nurse, and was nineteen years old. She was staying with Mary's parents before sailing to America to take up a nursing job in Philadelphia. Brendan, quite amazed at his good fortune to meet such a polished woman, was now dancing on air, delighting in the touch and smell of this mature nineteen-year-old. What could this lead to? What a pity he only had a day or two before sailing to *goodness-knows-where* and she is away to the US of A at the end of the week.

"Joan. I have had a lovely evening. Oh! That it could continue."

"Yes I have enjoyed myself, Bren. Let's keep in touch. Look, here's my address when I go to America. Oh! Tommy has just announced the last dance."

Rising from his rickety chair to the sound of Rosemary Clooney singing "Goodnight Sweetheart", Brendan Harris took his newfound love in his arms and swept around the ballroom, nodding his acceptance to the applause from the crowd of ordinary people wishing they could be as successful as Brendan Harris. *Brendan Harris, ship's officer, captain of the world, successful in love, the accomplished dancer…*

"Yes! Mary, what is it?"

…Back to the unpolished floor of the seaman's mission, the smell of dust and stale cooking odours, the distempered walls, back to reality.

Joan walked off the dance floor, unconsciously holding an enraptured Brendan's hand.

"Oh! Your Dad is here to take us home. Mary. OK! I'll be with you in a minute…" Turning to Brendan, Joan took his other hand and smiled her enchanting smile. "Bren! Thanks for a wonderful evening. You've got my new address and Mary's telephone number. Try to get some time before you sail. I am leaving next week. Do write… Bye! Bye!" Reaching up on her toes, the vision of perfection and dreams kissed Brendan and, with a wave, disappeared through the doorway.

"Wow! Don, what a night!" exclaimed Brendan as his senses returned to reality. "I'm in love, Don. I've got to meet her again. By the way, how did you get on with…Mary?"

"Nothing much, Bren. Look I'm away to bed. It's getting near midnight and we've got a hard day ahead of us tomorrow. Look, there's Ken just come in. Hi, Ken, how was your evening?"

"Rubbish. Let's get out of this dump and onto the open sea. Where's Barry Jones?"

"No idea," chorused the two tired sailors.

"Probably gone back to Wales," muttered Don under his breath.

Returning to the empty two-bed, characterless room, Brendan hugged himself with delight. Glad to be on his own, particularly to be without the irritating Welshman, he prepared himself for bed, letting his mind conjure up thoughts of the future. *Must get that diary going. Wonder how Michelle is doing?*

"It's pissing down outside, lads." So announced a less than cheerful senior apprentice, as he sat down at the heavy oil cloth covered wooden table to his breakfast. "Typical northern weather. Look, this egg is congealed and the fried bread is soaked in grease."

Brendan looked up from his plateful of fried eggs, fried bread, bacon and sausages, wondering what the guy should be complaining for. *What a feast. What's this pissing down business?* he thought to himself, not having heard the expression before. Quickly realising the miserable Englishman probably meant it was raining—*piss, water*—he concentrated on his eating.

"Where's Barry Jones? Has anybody seen him?"

"No, not a sign of him, Ken," answered Don Marshall, pushing his grease-covered plate away from his body and picking up a mug of tea.

"Paddy here says he hasn't seen him since last night. What's the little bugger up to? Wonder if he got his end away?" laughed Johnson.

Keeping his head down, Brendan hoped the guy wasn't in trouble. *What's he mean by 'end away'? God, it's like a new language. Anyway, what of it, wonder if I can see Joan today? Gosh! She was lovely.* Starting to daydream, he settled down to finishing his tasty, if not very healthy, breakfast.

"Right, lads, all ready for a day's work. Come on, off your backsides. It's eight thirty now, want you on board by ten. In yer workin' clothes. I'll leave it to you, Johnson. Don't see Jones. Everythin' all right there, Johnson?"

Jerked out of his dream, Brendan looked up to see the third mate Michael Read at the end of the table directing his comments to Ken.

"Everything's fine, Third. Don't worry. We'll all be on board by ten, providing we're not delayed too much at the shipping office when we sign on."

"God, you haven't signed on yet? You've all got your discharge books, haven't you? Well, get finished here as quickly as possible and sign out. The company is paying the bill, so take a taxi, with your gear, to the shipping office. Then get back to the *Renown* as quick as you can. Right I'll see you all on board later in the day. Now get a move on." A slightly harassed third mate pulled his raincoat on and, with a worried frown, turned and strode out of the room.

"There's a worried man," laughed Johnson to the table. "Well, would you believe it? The Welshman returns. Where the hell have you been, Jones?" questioned Johnson to the diminutive figure of Barry Jones as he entered the breakfast room, resplendent in his full uniform with peaked cap.

"Just stayed in a hotel overnight. My parents came up to see me off. That all right by you, Kenneth, boyo?"

A seething Johnson, whilst annoyed that Jones hadn't told him he would be staying elsewhere for the night, was further irritated to be addressed as 'boyo'.

"Look here, *boyo*," answered a tight-lipped Johnson. "Get your fat little Welsh carcass down here with your gear within the next ten minutes with your discharge book. Go on, no argument. And don't you ever call me boyo again."

A slightly crestfallen Jones turned on his heel and, muttering under his breath, left the room.

Poor little guy, thought Brendan to himself. *He's doing it all wrong. Thank God I'm sharing with Don.*

By eleven o'clock that morning, the four of them had taxied to the shipping office presented their discharge books—their passports to a seagoing career—and were registered as crew on the *Calvex Renown* for the duration. Brendan arranged to have four pounds a month—half of his monthly wage—sent to his parents, as he knew they needed the money and had spent a lot on equipping him. *Yes! I wonder how Ma and Pop are getting on and Jono and Billy. And Polly. Polly? What do I do? She surely can't expect me to stay in and not enjoy myself. I wonder if she is still working for Lotimers the accountants. Hope she doesn't find someone else but that's not fair on her. Anyway I'm going to get the best out of life and it's looking pretty good at the moment. A pound a week to spend, though, I'm not going to do much on that. Must write to her when I get back to the mission and write some notes for the diary.*

Small North Sea Coaster

5

Hospital

"Hello, Polly, it's Alice Har—"

"Oh, hello Mrs. Harris," interrupted Polly. "I've been meaning to ring you about Brendan. I feel very guilty now. I left the hospital earlier today and gave the diary thing to one of the nurses to give to you."

"Oh! Why did you do that, Polly? What's wrong? Anything we've said or done? You know we are depending a lot on you to help him recover."

"Yes! I know, Mrs. Harris, but that body in the bed is a stranger to me." Polly hesitated and started to cry. "It's not the Brendan I know and there are some things in the diary thing that upset me. So I don't want to read any more of it."

Oh! What the hell have I done, thought Alice taking a deep breath. *Hen was right. I shouldn't have given it to her. Must give it a read myself. Wonder what she read?*

"Polly I'm so sorry. Could I plead with you to perhaps talk to him, den? The doctor says it's important he has familiar sounds and voices and he knows your voice." *I'll bloody well get her to go in if it kills me,* thought Alice fiercely. "Please, Polly. It means a lot. Just remember the times you were with him," Alice appealed in her sincerest voice.

"I'll think about it, Mrs. Harris—"

"Look," interrupted Alice, "Henry and I are going in to visit tomorrow. Please come in with us," pleaded Alice, nodding to Henry who had been listening to the conversation. "… At six o'clock … that's wonderful, Polly. … Yes! Yes! We'll pick you up at your house. Thank you, Polly. Goodbye." Alice put the phone down. "That's great, Henry. She's coming—anything to help Bren. Come on now, Hen. I could do with a drink. I'm gasping—" she laughed "—and I must get down to reading some of this diary of Bren's. It sounds interesting."

"Hello! Anybody interested in me?" was the sudden question from young Billy, who had been standing at the sitting room door.

"Oh, Billy, we're a bit pushed for time. Could it wait until tomorrow?" Alice replied, reaching up to pat Billy on the shoulder, before turning around to follow Henry. Billy was the youngest of the three sons, close to six feet tall, and, like his elder brother, endowed with a head of close-cut black curls, but with an immature childish face. he was feeling somewhat forgotten with all the attention being given to Brendan.

"Go on to the pub then, Ma. Anyway, how is Bren? I haven't been in to see him yet. How is he, Pop?"

"That's all right, son. He's as well as we can expect," replied Henry, turning back from the front door. "We'll be back in an hour or two. Bren is not much better, still fighting for life…"

"Come on, Henry" called Alice impatiently. "We'll be back shortly, Billy. You must have some homework to do." Alice stepped out into the dark, followed closely by a hesitant Henry, who realised Billy wanted some attention.

Billy resignedly watched his parents walk down the garden pathway, his father's tall figure short-stepping behind the fast-moving smaller figure of his mother as they exited through the garden gate and disappeared in the darkening evening light. Billy shut the hall door and with a deep sigh made to return to his room to prepare for that evening's visit to the technical college. Billy, some five years younger than Brendan, was now sixteen years of age, had left school and was going to take a course in accountancy. He was working as a junior in a large surveyor's office and going to the college in the evenings. Wishing to discuss his career choice with his parents, he had found—and could understand to some degree—that they were more interested in the welfare of his elder brother.

Sketch of the Creole in the Mediterranean

6

First Date Mary

On their way back in the taxi to the ship, Brendan couldn't get his mind off the delights of the previous evening and wondered if he could get to see Joan again before the *Renown* sailed.

"What do you think the chances are, Don, to get to see her before we sail?"

"This is only Thursday. I heard we could sail either Friday or Saturday. What do you think Ken? This Irish bugger hit lucky last night."

"Yeh, I heard. We'll see what the mate wants us to do. I, like the rest of you, I'm sure, would like some more time before we sail. Are your parents still in town, Barry?"

Having recovered his confidence in his own abilities following the earlier rebuff by Johnson, Barry replied in his attractive sing song accent, "Yes, they are going home on Friday, Kenneth, and they would like to see me again before sailing."

Ken was pleased to notice the absence of the word 'boyo' but slightly irritated by Jones emphasis on his full name. "Look, Barry, it's a long shot, but on my last trip the mate invited my parents on board for a tour of the ship before we sailed. If you like I'll see if this mate would allow it."

"Thanks, Kenneth. That would be great now. My father would be pleased, as he was in the Royal Navy in the war."

With peace restored with Barry and with a fair rapport with the other two, Ken was quite pleased with his leadership. He had joined Calvex three years previously as a deck apprentice and had been on three different vessels. This was his first trip as a senior and he was beginning to enjoy his new status.

"Right, lads, let's get this lot on board," Ken ordered as the taxi drew up alongside the high accommodation ladder—portable wooden steps leading up to the main deck of the tanker. "Barry, as we're sharing, could you see to my luggage whilst I see who is going to pay the taxi."

"Don't worry, mate. I have an account with Calvex," interrupted the driver. "A tip wouldn't go amiss though."

Ken chose to ignore the hint, as did the other three as they dismounted and recovered their luggage.

"God, Brendan. It must weigh a ton," exclaimed Don, as he and Brendan self-consciously took the green and black eighteenth century wooden monstrosity from the rear of the taxi. "Look, Bren put your coat over it. Maybe no one will notice," Don suggested.

An embarrassed Brendan acknowledged Don's help—*I owe you one, Don*—and they made their way up the unsteady steps of the accommodation ladder. Reaching the top, a few seamen looked enquiringly at the two of them as they struggled on to the large deck.

"What have ye got there, lads?" One grinning seaman called. "A dead body, or is it filled with whiskey den?"

Brendan kept his head down, blushing furiously. "Oh! God let's get to the cabin, quick."

Don, stumbling backwards and looking over his shoulder, called out, "Right, Bren, this could be difficult." They had reached the midship's accommodation and the steep metal steps up to the next deck level presented an obstacle.

"Having trouble then, lads? We could have got the derrick rigged up and lifted it on board for you," called a mocking third mate from the next deck.

By now the cover had fallen from the trunk and Brendan was balancing it on his shoulders, whilst Don pulled it up the steep steps. Reaching the top of the ladder, there was a cheer from the group of seamen on deck.

"Only one more deck to go, lads," was the encouraging call.

"God! Sorry, Don," apologised Brendan as they stumbled to the next steep steps. Ken and Barry by now had recovered the rest of the luggage from the taxi and were standing, watching the humiliating spectacle. Brendan, who would normally have capitalised on the attention, was very concerned; after all, he was a prospective officer and this debacle wouldn't help his career.

"Thank God that's over," was the sigh of relief from the two of them as they eventually reached the cabin deck and stumbled over the step into the officer accommodation.

"It'll take a bit to live this down, Bren," Don said. "Come on. Empty the bloody thing and get it hidden away in the store room."

"That was a right shambles, Harris," roared the third mate from the deck outside. "Johnson, get that long streak of an Irishman sorted out and come back to me for orders."

"This third mate is turning out to be a bit of a bastard," muttered Don. "Don't worry, Bren. It will all blow over. What are you laughing at, Barry?"

"Oh! Sorry, Don, but it was funny seeing the pair of you struggling with the treasure chest, and when the cover came off and the crew when they saw the colours…they had a good laugh."

"Come on, Bren. Let's get this bloody thing emptied and hidden away," called an exasperated Don again.

With some relief they dropped the offending trunk on the cabin floor and recovered their remaining luggage from the deck. Brendan, feeling somewhat subdued, allowed Don to make claim to the desk nearest the porthole.

"Are you there? Don? Bren?" called Johnson from the next cabin. "Get your working clothes on. pronto! There's some more stores coming on board and the third wants us on deck in ten minutes."

"I wonder if I'll be able to get to a phone to give Joan a call? You remember the girls we met last night?" asked Brendan.

"Yeah! You lucky bugger. She seemed keen. I don't know why, looking at you." Don smiled enviously, looking Brendan up and down.

"It's the Irish magnetism, Donald, boyo. You English have a lot to learn."

"I shure would like to meet her again. What about her friend, Mary? She seemed nice and friendly." Brendan laughed.

Don grinned, replying, "Brendan…boyo…you owe me one. Come on. Let's see what Ken wants us to do."

Dressed in their working clothes—an assortment of dungarees and boiler suits—the four officers-to-be were delegated to carry the last delivery of stores from the deck to the storage rooms, under the officers' quarters, in the centre of the ship.

Brendan was paired off with Barry to carry the heavier parcels, whilst Ken and Don, to emphasise their seniority, took their time carrying the lesser parcels. Barry began to grumble at this, saying it was beneath him; he hadn't joined to do the work of a labourer. Brendan, a realist, put his head down and did more than his share, glad to be doing something positive.

"Get stuck in, Barry," he advised. "This is what we are expected to do. You'll be captain soon enough." With the stores all safely under lock and key, Brendan turned to Barry. "Right, Barry, I'm nipping ashore to make a phone call. There's a phone box at the dock gates. Will you cover for me? I'll be back in time for lunch."

***

"Speak to Joan Turbitt, please … Brendan Harris … Yes! She is expecting me to call."

God! Will she remember me, thought Brendan to himself. *What if she says yes? Where will we go? I've only got five bob on me. Maybe she'll pretend not to know me.* Silence…the phone was lifted…

"Hello? Brendan? How lovely to get your call, are you going to take me out? I'm flying to Philadelphia on Saturday…"

Gosh! She sounds very nervous. Wow! She wants me to take her out.

"Love to see you, Joan. I'm sailing tomorrow or Saturday. This could be my last night in the UK. What could we do? I'm pretty short of cash."

"Don't worry, Bren. I'm spending the last of my English money. I've even arranged to borrow a friend's car, so come on. Where can I meet you?"

"Well, as you've got yourself a car, could you meet me at the dock gates at half five? I'm sure I can get away then."

"Any chance of seeing your lovely ship? I've never been on a tanker."

Gosh! That would be something, show her off to the other lads. Golly she's keen. "OK, Joan. If I ring you back in, say, twenty minutes or so… I'll have a word with the chief officer. I'm sure it will be OK."

Replacing the phone with a flourish, Brendan took a deep breath and raced back to the ship.

"Hey, Ken! What do you think the chances are the mate would allow a friend of mine on board to have a look around. Remember? She's the girl I met last night? Is it OK if I go and ask him, Ken? You know the procedures better than I do."

"No harm in trying, Bren. Wish you luck. I think he's in his cabin. By the way, we're sailing at eight in the morning, to the Isle of Grain for cargo."

"Right thanks, Ken. That's great news. Where's the Isle of Grain? Later…tell me later. I'll go see the mate."

Full of anticipation, Brendan raced to the chief officer's cabin, stopped at the cabin door, composed himself as best he could, smoothed down his work trousers, ran his fingers through his thick hair, and knocked.

"Excuse me, sir. Harris, apprentice."

"Yes, Harris. I know who you are. What do you want?" answered the mate swivelling around in his desk chair.

"Sir! Ahem! Sir!"

"Out with it, laddie."

"Well, sir! A very good friend of mine is coming to collect me, sir, to go out this evening, sir, and wonder if she could have a look around the ship, sir."

"You know we're sailing in the morning, laddie, an' there's a lot of work to be done. Now we can't have new apprentices gallivanting all over the place with their floosies. No! Son! Get what work you've been given done and be back here on board by ten tonight. Right, Git."

With a wave of dismissal he swung back to continue with his work from before Brendan's interruption. Slightly nonplussed, Brendan turned on his heel, wondering whether he should salute or say thank you, pulling the cabin door closed behind him.

"Any joy, then, Bren?"

"No! Well sort of, Ken. He said I could stay out until ten tonight. Can he do that?"

"Brendan, he can do anything he wants. He's only responsible to the captain. He's the boss. Anyway, has Barry not told you his dad has invited the four of us for a meal in Newcastle?"

"No! He hasn't, Ken. I don't mind, anyway," Brendan replied with a grin. "I bet you would rather be seeing who I'm seeing, rather than Barry's dad."

"Yeh. Don told me she's a peach. Thought you had a girlfriend, anyway."

"God! Polly—I never called her or wrote a letter. Ken! Where's the Isle of Grain? I could ring her from there."

"On the Thames, Bren. We should be there by tomorrow night."

"Thanks, Ken. I'll call her then. Any idea where we go from there?"

"I believe we're going to Swansea for more cargo and then to Bombay."

"Gosh, Bombay. That'll be through the Mediterranean, won't it? Is the Suez Canal open yet?"

"Don't know the detail yet, Bren. But it could be."

"Wow! Wait until I tell Joan. You know, Ken, she's going to Philadelphia in the USA. Do tankers go there? What a great life. Right, what work do you want me to do?"

"Go see Don. He's in your cabin. The time's your own now, until we sail tomorrow."

Must get ashore and call Joan, Brendan thought to himself. *Yeh! I remember, that French girl on the Irish boat mentioned it, that a guy called Nasser sank a few dozen ships in the canal. Something about him nationalising the canal and Eden got his nose bruised. Gosh! That would be great. What a life.*

"See you, lads. Sorry, Barry, can't meet your dad," Brendan called out with a big grin on his face as he left the cabin. "I'll be back about ten."

Humming to himself, he stepped out onto the wooden deck, feeling very confident in his rather cheap grey suit an inch too short in the leg—it was difficult to get a suit off the peg for an inside leg of thirty-two inches. His jacket, strained slightly across his broad shoulders, hung loosely around his tapering narrow waisted body. His black, size eleven shoes shone after some severe polishing; his dad had always impressed him that well polished shoes showed a polished person. However, he was quite conscious of the acne spots on his face and his awful brown straight hair that would not fall into a quiff.

Later, a very pleased Brendan Harris met Joan at the dock's entrance, where they decided to pool their money and go to the pictures.

Here am I, he thought to himself, *sitting in the Odeon Cinema in Newcastle-upon-Tyne, my left arm around a smashin' girl, a bag of popcorn balanced between us, her head on my shoulder and Audrey Hepburn singing "S'wonderful". What more could a sailor want?*

After the initial shyness when they met, they had decided to go to the early showing of *Funny Face*: a film with Audrey Hepburn and Fred Astaire. Brendan surprised himself with his newfound boldness and, after they took their seats in the smoke-filled auditorium, was delighted with Joan's willingness to allow him to put his arm around her and to be kissed. His senses were at a peak; his body ached with the closeness of her, her fresh, sweet smell, her newly washed hair and the taste of her lips. Too soon the film ended and they stepped out into the cold early evening air.

"Wish I looked like Audrey Hepburn," she mused.

"Don't be talking like that, Joan. You're lovely. Bet you can dance better than her and you've got more 'up there' than her too." Just realising what he had said, Brendan was thankful she couldn't see him blushing.

There I go again putting my foot in it…got my mind on a girl's diddies. Oh! God I ache.

"Look there's a pub. Let's go have a drink, Bren. It's only half eight. I hear Newcastle Brown is the drink to have here. Let's try some."

Brendan pushed open the heavy pub door and held it open for Joan, as the warm smell and the low hum of conversation overcame the cold outside air.

"Look. There's seats through that door," Joan pointed out as they entered the smoke-filled bar room, with its strong smell of beer, unwashed bodies and cigarette smoke.

"Grab them, Joan, will you? I'll go get some Newcastle Brown," Brendan offered, as they entered a further room with a large bar full of cloth-capped men, along with the occasional shawled female.

"What'll you have then, pet?" the smiling, big busted, barmaid called out from behind the polished bar top.

"Two Newcastle Brown ales, please?"

"Yer new here, kidda. Is it a bottle of the dog ye wan or a glass? Fer yerself an' the lass?"

Recognising the word 'glass', Brendan smiled and agreed to two glasses of the 'dog', which he assumed must be Newcastle Brown. Handing over half a crown, he was surprised, and pleased, to get two pence change.

"Here you are, Joan," Brendan said, placing the two half glasses of watery brown beer on the stained wooden table before her.

"A glass of the dog, or brown ale. It looks awful doesn't it?"

"Knock it back, Bren lad. You've paid for it. Here, do you want a cigarette?" Joan asked, offering Brendan a cigarette from a ten-pack of John Player.

"Shure, thanks, Joan," answered Brendan, taking the offered cigarette and casually knocking it gently on the table top, as they did in the films. Not having smoked a cigarette before, he tentatively placed the firm, round tube between his lips and watched Joan put a lighted match to the end of her cigarette. When it was glowing, she drew in a lungful of smoke and exhaled the waste smoke in a cloud of grey, giving a smile and gasp of satisfaction.

Right, thought Brendan, *nothing to it*...a deep draw...lapsing into a sudden dreadful fit of coughing, he frantically threw the cigarette towards the large ashtray on the table and held his head in his hands until the fit of coughing subsided. "Golly! Joan, what was that? God! That was awful. I've never smoked before."

"Gathered that, Bren. Come on. Let's have another Nu-castle Brun. We can afford it. Finish that one off, sailor," laughed Joan, having already emptied her glass.

Hoping a further drink might ease his throat, Brendan gulped down the remaining brown liquid and bought another two glasses.

"That's better, lass. Let's have another of your fags. I'll be more careful this time."

Lighting up another John Player Special from Joan, he commenced to puff it gently and sip the glass of beer. *This is the life*, he thought, *a beer in one hand, a fag in the other and a good-looking girl beside me.* Sitting close to Joan, he put his hand on her knee and leaned over toward her and gently blew some beer-flavoured John Player smoke into her face. Unfortunately, the romantic moment was destroyed by a loud burp from Joan, who commenced to giggle, knocking her half-empty glass, spilling some beer onto the small table. Brendan, feeling a bit unsteady, went to grab the glass by the hand with the lighted cigarette in it, fell over onto Joan's lap, dropping the cigarette and sending the glass smashing to the floor.

God, what have I done? thought Brendan as he recovered himself, looking up to see a silenced room and staring faces.

"It's all right, everyone," he called out. "'Tis a trick I do, you kno'." Don' worry, Miss. I'll pay fer de glass," he addressed the smiling barmaid who had materialised from behind the bar.

"Now, Paddy, jus' sit back ther an' keep quiet. It's all reet, everyone. Git back to yer drinkin'," she called out to the now disinterested spectators and patted Brendan on the head.

"Look after him, Miss," she said to Joan "He's a cutie, isn't he?"

Joan smiled at the barmaid and looked Brendan in the eye.

"I just overbalanced, Joan. I'm not drunk/ I'm only feeling a bit comfortable." Brendan straightened his jacket and patted down his hair as he returned the gaze, relieved to see a smile forming on her lovely face.

"Ye kno', Bren I'm feeling a bit uncomfortable meself. I thing, doe, I could do with going to the lav."

"What's the time?" exclaimed Brendan. "Must be gettin' late. I don't have a watch, you kno'."

"Plenty of time, Bren. Time fer another Brown and a fag."

Brendan was beginning to feel a bit dizzy from the beer and the smoke. *OK! One more small glass and then back to the ship, maybe 'get to know her better' in the car. Wow, I'd like to get my arms around her and…stop it, ye eejit. There's no way.*

"Come on, Paddy. Get dat down ye, ye big lump and less go for a drive in the car. I'm feelin' a bit wonky mesel'…myself." Joan giggled, putting on an Irish accent. "Come on, you poor eejit. Let's get you back to your ship before you drop dead." Joan smiled in a motherly manner and caught Brendan's arm.

"You've got a reet one there, lass," commiserated one of the cloth caps blowing a plume of nicotine-loaded smoke into the air. "Wha's the world comin' to whin they can't take their beer or draw a tab." And nodding his wise old head, the resigned sage looked towards his wise old friends, who all nodded their wise old heads in unison.

Feeling rather foolish, Brendan smiled weakly at his audience, drank the remaining dregs of the 'dog' and stumbled his way toward the door.

"Hod on, Bren. I wanna go pay a visit."

"Yeh, I'm with you there Joan—I mean—God, there I go again. I'll go on my own—not wit you—ye kno' what I mean. Excuse me, sirs, where's the toilet?" he asked in general to another group of caps.

"Ye mean the netty?" questioned one. "'Tis over there." He pointed toward a doorway alongside the bar.

"See you back here, Bren. Less go," declared Joan, pushing through the door marked 'ladies'.

What do I do now, thought Brendan, *this is going great—maybe we can have a bit of a snog in the back of the car*, as he washed his hands in the stained ceramic sink in the toilet.

Outside the toilet door in the dark corridor, with the sound of laughter in the background and the smell of beer in the air, Brendan waited in great anticipation. The door opened and Joan came out. Looking anxiously around and seeing Brendan, she gave a relieved smile and linked her arm through his. "Cum on, Bren," she grinned. "I'm feeling quite tipsy. What's the time? Quarter past nine, still early. Let's go for a little drive."

"Come on then, let's go," a delighted Brendan called, unlinking his arm and putting it around her slim waist.

"Where's the car?" asked Joan laughing.

"Back of the pub," answered Brendan, leading Joan down the dark side road. Stopping to steady themselves as they stumbled on the pavement edge, Brendan faced Joan and put both arms around her body. They looked at each other and on impulse Brendan kissed Joan on the mouth, overjoyed with the immediate reaction. She tightened her arms around his waist, pressed her body against his and kissed him hard.

Taking Brendan's hand, Joan ran down the road to the car with him following behind. Laughing and gasping with anticipation, they squeezed into the back seat of the A40 car and wrapped themselves around each other, kissing madly. Brendan pushed his hand under Joan's light blouse; the feel of her warm skin made him gasp. He moved his hand to the front and pressed it against her right breast.

"No, Bren, no. Please don't."

Not knowing how far to go or really what was expected, Brendan removed his hand and after the first minutes of this frantic kissing, they sat back in the tiny seat of the A40 car, their legs touching, their bodies boiling with expectation.

"We'd better stop, Bren, my love," breathed Joan in Brendan's ear. "It's too risky, but come on. Kiss me again."

They continued petting and testing each other, until Brendan, realising the time, gasped in frustration, "I've to be back on board for ten."

Reluctantly they dragged themselves out from the backseat and returned to the dock gates, where they started kissing again.

"Write to me, Bren. Do keep in touch. We are…will be…worlds apart," Joan cried.

"You have my address at Calvex. You never know. I may go to Philadelphia someday. Goodbye. I must go. It's nearly half past ten."

With a last big hug and long kiss, Brendan waved goodbye and made his way back to the *Renown*, wishing he had a few more days to get to know this lovely girl.

Sketch of Cargo Boat

The Dover Tunnel as considered in 1957

7

Hospital Visit

"Are you ready, Henry?" called Alice loudly, muttering in exasperation. "Come on, Hen, and stop farting about. We're picking up Polly at a quarter to two, hospital visiting is at two to four. Get your skates on. It's half one now."

"Just got to tie my shoelaces, dear," was the patient reply from the resigned Henry. "Is Billy comin', Alice?"

"Billy, are you comin' to see Brendan? We're going right now," called Alice in a loud voice implying *if you don't come immediately you can go fly a kite*.

"OK! Coming, Ma," was the reply from the side bedroom. "Won't be a minute."

Ma Harris, dressed in a short, hip-hugging skirt with a roll-necked sweater and her long blonde hair tied back in a bow—ever the exhibitionist—looked as if she were going on a film set as she shrugged on her mock fur coat and waited impatiently for her two men.

Both suddenly appeared in the hallway. Pop, in his grey trousers and green cardigan, wearing highly polished brown shoes, grinned at Billy, who was wearing brown corduroys with a white sweater and black shoes.

"All right," acknowledged Ma, putting her hands up and smiling. "Wear whatever you like. I'll pretend I'm not with you. But come on, times passing."

"Still got the curtains around the bed. What's it now? Three days since…?" stated Alice, grasping Henry's hand for comfort as they approached the curtained-off bed in the large ward. There were beds each side of the long, wide room, all occupied by male patients, some with their legs dangling from the ceiling on pulleys, others with their arm in a plaster cast jutting from their bodies at odd angles. Some were propped up with pillows, looking at old magazines, or just sitting staring into space. Overall, in the startling white clinical room, there was a feeling of permanence; the bored and sleeping occupants appeared like plasticine models propped up in the beds for effect. There were a few visitors sitting at the bedsides, glad to look at something new to relieve them of the effort to make conversation.

Alice curled up her nose in distaste at the overall smell of disinfectant and human bodies, and peered hesitantly around the bedside curtain.

"How are you, Bren, love?" she asked in great anticipation that there would be a response. Silence. Brendan was in a drugged sleep, unconscious to the world. "Hen, call the nurse—go on quick—he's not breathing."

"Just wait a minute," suggested Henry, motioning Polly and Billy to wait outside the curtains. "Now, it's all right, Alice. He's breathing," he consoled, patting Alice on the shoulder. "I wonder if he is just asleep or unconscious? Billy, Polly, it's OK," he called, putting his head outside the curtains.

Alice leaned over the protective bed railings to give a Brendan a kiss, with her short skirt riding up her backside revealing bare leg and suspenders.

"Careful, Alice," cautioned Henry.

Giving up the futile attempt, Alice struggled back to her feet, quite red in the face, and stepped aside to allow Polly and Billy a clear sight of the recumbent patient.

Brendan's head was still enveloped in a turban of bandages, with red strips of stitching on his chin and right cheek. The light sheet covering his body had slipped, showing his right leg was still encased in plaster. The white gown he was wearing had ridden up, revealing the drainage tube from his penis to the receiving bottle and what, with the various bottles hanging from pulleys over the bed, Brendan Harris looked as if he was hanging onto life by a thread. His wrists were still loosely tied to the protective railing around the bed and he had not had a shave, which did not help the viewers, especially Billy.

This was the first time Billy had seen Brendan since the accident and he was quite shocked to see his big brother—the one he admired and envied—so helpless and vulnerable.

"Gosh! Ma! exclaimed Billy in a hushed voice. "Will he live? God, He looks awful."

"Come on, Billy, don't cry," commiserated Henry, putting his arm around the young lad's shoulder and leading the hesitant body outside the curtains.

"Are you all right, Alice?" asked Polly, startled again by the sight of Brendan, so helpless, the fellow she had had such dreams for. "Do you want a moment on your own? I'll step outside if you like."

"No, Polly, it's all right," sniffled Alice.

Polly put her arm around Alice. "Look, Alice. Look at that guy on the bed. He's alive. He could have so easily died. Now there are qualified people looking after him, and I will help you all I can to get him back on his feet again. Is that all right?" Polly was somewhat startled in what she had said; she stood back from Alice, a determined look on her pretty face.

"Thanks, Polly," sniffed Alice with a smile. "Thanks a lot. I am very grateful." Turning to lean over as close as she could to Brendan, she caught his wrist and in her most motherly voice said, "Hi, Bren. Can you hear me? Come on, Bren. Give us a smile. Look! I've got Polly here. She's looking as pretty as ever. Billy is outside with Pop. We're all thinking of you." No reaction. "Polly, come on you give a try."

Somewhat self-consciously, Polly in her pleasant, clear south Dublin accent called out, "Come on, Brendan. Polly here. Hurry up and get well so we can go dancing. Come on, give me a smile…" Unable to continue through the tears, Polly squeezed Brendan's wrist and stepped outside the curtains with her head bowed. The moment that Polly stepped away, Brendan's eyes opened and in a very weak but commanding voice, he said, "Port ten, sir," smiled and shut his eyes again.

Billy and Henry looked at each other. Henry gripped Billy's arm and called out, "Did you hear that, Alice? Brendan spoke! He opened his eyes!"

"Bren, Bren, are you there? Please answer me. It's your Ma here," pleaded Alice, pushing past the two large males leaning on the rail attached to the bed. "Come on, Bren…come on…"

"No, Alice. He seems to have drifted off again. Maybe one of the nurses or the matron might have some news. I'll go and have a look for one," suggested Henry, glad to get away from the tears. He was feeling a mite upset himself and didn't want to show it.

"Ah! Nurse!" Noticing a nurse with her large white cap tending to a patient further up the ward, Henry walked towards her, signalling for some attention.

"Be wid you in a mo, sir," was the waved reply, as the nurse spooned some medicine into the recumbent body in the bed.

"Yes, sir. Can I help? Of course, you are Mr. Harris. Rude—" quickly correcting herself "—I mean Brendan's father."

"Can you tell me something about Brendan? How he is and what can be expected."

"I wish I cud, sir. Perhaps I cud see if Sister is free to have a word wid you," Nurse Mary Sheelin replied, thinking to herself, *I hope they don't ask for that book of Rudolph's. Kathleen's got it an' she's off today.*

"Thank you, nurse. Would you please? We'll wait," agreed Henry, returning to the party grouped around the hospital bed.

Within minutes, with a swish of the curtains, the imposing figure of Sister Sullivan in blue skirt, dark blue jacket and glorious white starched head piece announced herself. "Yes, I'm Sister Sullivan. Now how may I help you?" was the no-nonsense question—*don't please waste my time.*

"Sister," returned Alice with her *don't you question me, lady or you're in for trouble.* "An update, please, on Brendan Harris. Thank you."

"Yes." Sister Sullivan was somewhat taken aback with the retort from Alice. To regain command of the conversation, she requested they all step outside the curtained bed.

"Mrs. Harris, Mr. Harris," declared the starch bedecked sister, nodding to Alice and Henry. "Your son is doing very well; everything is being done to ensure his comfort. His leg will be healing under the cast. However, we are being very cautious regarding his head injury, and—I must be adamant about this—" she nodded commandingly at the four visitors. "There should be no more than two visitors at any one time." In a final statement announced in her broad Dublin accent, she said, "The comfort of your son is paramount. He is in excellent health, but dear me, his language at times is quite dreadful."

Somewhat shocked, Henry and Alice meekly held their heads down. Billy had to restrain himself from laughing outright and Polly retorted, "Where does it state only two visitors, Sister? I did not see any notice."

"That is a ruling on this ward, young lady. Please abide by it in any future visits. Thank you. Will that be all?"

Receiving a half smile from Alice, Sister Sullivan turned on her heel, her skirts swinging around her and the imposing starched monument on her head bobbing up and down as she strode away, victorious.

"I agree with the sister, Hen," exclaimed Alice, turning to face Henry. "Bren never cursed like he does now. God!" she exclaimed. "He does come out with some choice sayings. I've never heard him cursing before."

"It must be what they do at sea," ventured Polly. "Curse a lot..."

Polly was now in a difficult position: she had committed herself to help in Brendan's recovery, but was in doubt about Brendan's feelings to her. She had found out he had been to see another woman on the night of the accident, and the entries in the diary he had written gave the impression he was a woman chaser—nothing like the innocent Brendan she had known before he had gone to sea. There were, however, some nice references to her in his journal, voicing his thoughts about her and he had written her a number of letters.

However, this body in the bed was a stranger and she now wondered if she had the strength of mind to continue giving her time to what could be a lost cause. *When Brendan recovered will he remember me? Or, again what if he didn't recover? I've told his mum—what a woman—that I'll stand by him to help however I can. Poor Bren. I wonder where that diary is?*

8

Set Sail

"Right, you lot of lazy sods. Up you get. We're sailing at eight."

Brendan, from a deep sleep, sat up with a start, knocking his head on the bunk above him. *Who is it? Where am I? Gosh! I'm on the ship. Oh! My head. I smell of drink and cigarette smoke. Oh! Lord.*

His mind whirling, Brendan stretched out in the wooden sided bunk bed, his feet pressed against the bunk's end. He could hear raised voices and the sound of a ship's hooter.

Suddenly a pair of legs in striped pyjamas swung into view and a body dropped from the bunk above.

"Are you awake, Bren? We don't have much time. I'm going for a quick shower. See you," called Don as he grabbed a towel hanging under the small sink in the corner of the cabin and rushed out the doorway.

Brendan slowly came to; he immediately recalled the previous night. *What a night, what a girl, what do I do? I feel like jumping ship.*

"Come on, Bren. Get off your backside and dress for breakfast."

"You mean put on the dress uniform, Don?"

"Yeh! Got to look our best when we use the saloon—the old man or the mate may be there. Anyway, the chief steward would report us if we weren't dressed properly."

Suitably attired and presentable, the four apprentices entered the 'saloon' on the deck below the accommodation deck, to be greeted by a steward dressed in white uniform, who directed the four prospective officers to their table. The main table, alongside the forward bulkhead with a line of glass filled portholes, was already occupied by the senior officers. The third mate acknowledged their entry with a nod. The chief officer smiled toward them and the captain, a portly, grey-haired, sullen looking sea dog, raised his head from his plate of egg and bacon in response to the third mate's comment and nodded. There were three other officers seated at adjoining tables.

"They will be the engineers and the lecky—electrician," Ken advised in a muted voice. "You can have grapefruit or cereal, lads. Help yourself from the table over there. The steward will take your order for breakfast."

Brendan was very impressed with this grandeur for breakfast. White tablecloths, large white serviettes, an array of cutlery, even a menu and service from a steward, who followed Ken and Don to collect their starter.

"Rice Krispies, Wow! Crackle and Pop. Luxury," exclaimed Brendan grinning at Don.

Don ignored the comment and Ken's shoulders stiffened as he spooned the grapefruit into a small bowl. Brendan filled his bowl with Rice Krispies and milk and returned to the table.

"Not having any starter, Barry, then?" asked Brendan as he sat.

"Yes, Brendan, I'm having some porridge. The steward is coming with it."

"Let's see what's on the main course," exclaimed Brendan picking up the embossed menu. "Egg, sausage, beans, tomatoes, mushrooms and fried bread. I'll have the lot. Toast as well, and coffee. What about you, Barry? Never had this lot at home. Gosh! Isn't the menu impressive? It's got the Calvex flag on it."

Don and Ken returned to the table, talking in muted tones and gave their respective main course orders to the simpering steward. After that, the breakfast meal continued in scattered silence.

"After we've sailed we had better—would you agree Don—tell these two—" smiling in Barry and Brendan's direction, Ken continued. "Tell these two what's expected from them. When we've finished here, you three change into your working clothes. We sail in half an hour. You, Barry, go aft with Don, and you, Bren, can go on the foc'sle. I'll be on the bridge with the third mate. Finished? OK, let's go."

In unison, the four eager souls deposited their serviettes on the table and hurried back to their cabins.

In the pouring rain, with a stiff cold wind blowing off shore, Brendan made his way to the front of the ship or for'rard , as the seamen say—*for'rard to the foc'sle, that scans nicely*. He was dressed in his wet weather gear: a rather thin unsatisfactory windcheater, a pair of heavy trousers tucked in a pair of black wellington boots and a black sou'wester that he had used when fishing for mackerel back in Dunlaoghaire. He felt very self-conscious as he walked along the flying bridge: the raised walkway some six feet above the wide deck toward the front of the ship.

There were six seamen preparing to unwind ropes from the bitts, large heavy low posts on the deck, all very busy; other important figures dressed in a variety of oilskins bustled around in the pouring rain. Brendan, feeling quiet redundant, approached one shrouded figure he recognised as the chief officer.

"Sir, Harris here…"

"Oh, yes! Harris the first tripper. Stay around but keep out of the way."

Feeling more than ever in the way, Brendan pulled his windcheater tighter around his body and wiped his cold wet face with his now sodden handkerchief.

"Tug attached, sir," was the call from another rain drenched sou'wester-garbed seaman.

"OK, Bos'n," acknowledged the chief officer, raising his hand to the small, stout, one-funnel tugboat dwarfed by the high bows of the tanker, to signify the tow rope was now attached to one of the bitts on the forecastle.

"Oh! Answer that phone, will you, Harris, and tell 'em tug attached."

More than happy to be doing something, Brendan lifted the receiver to hear a loud voice instructing, "Single up for'rard. Yes! We see the tug."

"Single up, sir?

"Right, Bos'n," called the mate. "Single up an' let's get out of this miserable place."

With a lot of shouts and muscular effort, the seamen pulled the heavy sodden rope hawsers from the shore leaving a wire rope, termed the spring, stretching from the foc'sle back along the ship side connected with the shore.

With a sudden blast of whistle and a plume of steam ejecting from the funnel, the mate shouted, "Let go spring." The shore gang lifted the 'spring' from the shore bitts and the tugboat started to pull the tanker's bows out from the shore. The ship's screws started to turn and push the ship forward.

Feeling quite excited, Brendan forgot the rain and cold, as the tanker—his home for the undetermined future—left the bare dock and cranes and started its way out of the harbour. He looked back to the midships section with its lines of portholes surmounted by the control bridge with its larger windows and the dim shape of moving figures. He could feel the vibration of the engines as the whole vessel quivered under the power of the turbine driven twin screws, or propellers. *Here I go. This is the start of my new life. I should get this all down in my diary, as you never know—it could be a bestseller some day. Ha, ha.*

"Right, Barry, Brendan. Before we start work, let me tell you what the position is." Ken in his smart slacks and roll neck jersey swung his desk seat around to face the two new apprentices awaiting the reason for their senior's call. "I'm senior apprentice only because I have more sea time in than Don, and my duties are to show you the ropes and tell you what is expected of you. Firstly, an apprentice's life—yes, Barry, some companies call us cadets but in Calvex we are navigating deck apprentices.

"Navigating, because we learn how to navigate the ship, take it safely from A to B. Deck, because we work on the deck as opposed to the engine room, and apprentices as we are at the call of the officers for anything they wish us to do. Ha, Ha, Yes, Bren, we are the bottom of the officer pile. Over the next few months, you will be expected to study hard, work hard and put up with some miserable conditions. The crew will pull your leg, but they are mostly pretty good-natured. Now, it's coming up to nine o'clock. You have an hour to look at the study books supplied and some paperwork to complete. You sit for two exams a year. Don and I will be sitting our half-year tests next month. You both will probably, over the four years, spend time on different ships. The fleet has smaller coastal ships and larger deep-sea vessels. There are still larger ships being built, and Calvex go anywhere in the world there is a need for oil. Don will be on hand to help you out, Bren."

With a conspiratorial grin, Ken dismissed Bren as Barry turned his chair to face his desk. As Brendan rose from the side of the bunk bed he had been sitting on, the ship gave a sudden lurch rather than the steady repetitive roll from side to side.

"The wind must be picking up," remarked Ken as some papers on his desk slid off onto the floor. Brendan, steadying himself by clutching at the door jamb, tried to balance against the unaccustomed unsteady footing. Staggering out into the corridor he bumped into the first mate on his way to his cabin.

"Settling in OK, Harris? You'll get your sea legs soon," remarked the officer as he smoothly balanced his body against the roll of the ship.

The *Calvex Renown* was now out into the North Sea, having left Sunderland, and was forcing its way through the increasingly unsettled heavy seas in the teeming rain, on its way to the oil refinery in the Isle of Grain. *Must ring Polly from Grain. She will be wondering why I haven't been in touch. I'll write a couple of letters tonight. The Doc has asked I keep in touch as well.* The Doc, or Doctor James Courcy—Brendan's favourite school teacher—had a close affinity with the sea. He was a doctor of philosophy, spoke some dozen languages and had helped Brendan in his later years in school. He was an eccentric but very likeable man.

Sitting at his desk with the ship rolling in the disturbed sea, Brendan tried to assemble his textbooks and papers into order and, with some amusement, found them sliding across the desk.

Don, studying for his half yearly exam, due in a month's time, was becoming slightly exasperated with Brendan's attempts at order, and resigned himself to helping Brendan.

"Now, look. There's a list of subjects for your first exam."

Brendan looked at the studying required for the months to come. Navigation, ship handling, cargoes, learn the Morse code, learn semaphore. A multitude of new subjects. *I'll look at all that tomorrow. Got to first find my way around my new home. Ah! Here's a plan of the ship.*

> The ship is a long cylinder divided into separate tanks with the anchors at the front, the foc'sle - and the engine with the

propellers at the stern. On top of this, over the engine there's the crew's quarters and in the middle, midships, there's the centre castle in four levels: the saloon for eating, with the engineer officer's accommodation, over this the deck officers and then we have the captain with the bridge control and the flat roof on top of this, called the monkey island.

"Right, lads, get your working clothes. Don, could you get some brooms and waste bins and with Bren clean up around the wheelhouse and other decks," called Ken, as he and Barry, resplendent in his new blue corduroy trousers, brown expensive windcheater and heavy working boots, made their way to some other exciting pastime.

"Morning, Third," called Don to the third mate on the bridge. "Bren and I are here to clean out all your rubbish."

The third mate, in his dark blue uniform trousers and jacket with the gold strip on the cuffs, poked his head out from a door at the back of the bridge "OK, Marshall, there's a fair bit of waste here in the chartroom. Hi, Harris. Settling in alright?"

"Yes! Thanks. Sir, Third!"

Grinning at Brendan's confusion, the third mate disappeared back into the chartroom.

"Bren, here a mo," Don called. "I'll put you straight. Come out onto the bridge wing. It's quit raining." He pointed to the side extensions to the wheelhouse.

"Didn't want the helmsman to hear, Bren," cautioned Don, as he nodded towards the able seaman in control of the ship's wheel at the back of the wheelhouse. "You call the third mate, Third, the second, Second and the mate, Sir, as with the captain."

"Thanks, Don. The protocol! Is it the same with the engineers?"

"Yes, but you don't call the chief engineer Sir, you call him Chief," he answered with a further grin. "Now, let's start sweeping. It'll soon be smoko."

Brendan, feeling somewhat overcome by all the changes in his life, the new people, new attitudes, whom to report to and finding his position in the hierarchy, picked up the long-handled broom and looked around the wheelhouse, or bridge, which stretched the width of the ship. An impressive long wide room with sliding doors at each side offering entrance to an open platform, this was the centre of operations; the small wheel beside the giro compass was used to steer the ship. There were a range of other ship control aids in strategic positions on the wooden floor. To aid the officer of the watch, toughened windows giving a one-eighty-degree of the aspect ahead were installed in the front wall.

The apprentice's task was to keep this room clean and ensure the many brass items were polished.

Brendan's first day on board ended with a very tired young man collapsing into his bunk with confused thoughts. Had he done the right thing? One minute he was dressed in his uniform, being served his meal by stewards; the next he was in dungarees sweeping the deck. What a contrast. What was the balance between himself and Don and the third mate? Who do you call 'Sir'? *Well whatever*, Brendan thought to himself, *I'm told we get into the Isle of Grain early next morning and even though the ship is rolling quite badly I haven't been seasick. Don's good to work with, haven't quite sussed out Ken, whilst Barry seems a bit of a pain. I'll phone home tomorrow. Wonder how Polly is keeping…?*

"Right! Up you get…Sirs! Mate says yer to get yer backsides on deck 'mediately."

Awakening to a loud knock on the cabin door and the ceiling light switching on, a startled Brendan pulled his bunk curtains aside to see Don's legs appearing from the bunk above as he answered the call from the seaman sent to awaken them.

"OK, Bren!" called Don as he began dressing. "Looks like we're on our way into Grain. God! It's only six in the morning," he complained with a grin. "It'll probably be quite cold down aft and we'll be there for some time."

Taking the advice, Brendan put on his heavy trousers and roll-necked sweater knitted by his mother and, suitably attired, the two sleepy sailors made their way out on deck.

"Gosh! Look at all the tankers at anchor," Brendan exclaimed as they made their way aft by the raised open passageway over the red metal deck, all very peaceful now, as the ship was making its way through the calm sea—nothing like the rolling and shuddering and howling wind and turbulent seas they would encounter over the months to come.

"There's the Grain Tower ahead of us, Bren. As a youngster, I remember walking out to it with my dad. During the war it was used as a boom control point. You know they had a chain with a net fitted on it to stop the U-boats getting in. I live in Chatham just down the road from here."

"Don, are you going to go home?"

"Probably not. My parents may come over to the ship though. They are very busy. My dad's an MP, you know, and my mom is an actress. She's playing in a musical called 'Damn Yankees' in London."

"An MP, Don? Is he a doctor?"

"No! A member of parliament, a politician. Hold on, here's the second mate."

"Right, which one are you?" asked the short and burly figure of the second mate, dressed in a stained brown duffel coat and officer's cap, still with its tropical white cover very soiled with use. He strode over to the two apprentices.

"I'm Harris, second," answered Brendan, remembering Don's advice that this officer was not to be addressed as 'Sir'.

"OK, Harris, yer the first tripper, huh! An' you're Marshall?" he asked, nodding to Don. "OK! Let's get this f---ing boat tied up."

To Brendan, this officer was very out of place; his appearance, his attitude and the use of the F word. His assumption that all officers were 'gentlemen' was shaken.

"Right you," called the second in his broad London accent to one of the seamen, a tall angular bald-headed man garbed in a white roll-necked sweater that hadn't seen soap for some months. "Get your arse in gear and prepare the mooring ropes for tying up."

The three seamen, including the one addressed, who were already preparing the mooring ropes, stopped momentarily, looked at each other with an unspoken message and continued their preparation.

"Here, Harris, you look like you played cricket. Get a hold of the heaving line an' throw it to those miserable looking dockers on the quay. Come on, quick!" was the sudden order by the second.

Brendan, quite startled, looked at Don, who grinned and pointed to a coiled rope on the deck alongside one of the mooring ropes. One end had a large knot in it, no doubt to take the line to the waiting dockers. Brendan got hold of the rope and started to swing it to get some momentum but just before letting the weighted end free, there was a roar from the second.

"Harris, you stupid f---er! Tie the end to the mooring rope before you let go. Jeasus, what have we got here?" exclaimed the second, looking to the seamen for agreement.

The three averted their heads and Don stepped in to tell the second he had already tied the heaving line to the mooring rope. Once the first rope had been looped over the shore connection, the two tugs which had been pushing the tanker towards the oil jetty backed away and, with a lot of shouting and grunting, the *Calvex Renown* was tied up alongside the oil jetty.

Brendan's first port of call: the Isle of Grain. First of many over the following years, it was a platform festooned with cranes and pipe connections, with a walkway linking to a group of unattractive buildings with further pipes interlinking with each other, all no doubt with important destinations. *How far to civilization? The romance of the sea, where are the dusky maidens, the guitar music? Come on, be patient. We are still in England. We still have the excitements of Swansea to look forward to and then though the Mediterranean and the Suez Canal to Bombay. Wait, wasn't there some trouble with a guy called Nasser nationalising the canal? That lovely French girl on the ferry told me about him.*

"Right, Bren, we are on watch from eight tonight to eight tomorrow. Twelve hours. The tanks are being cleaned today and we're going to start loading clean oil for Bombay overnight. We're on with the second mate. Do you want to come with me into Chatham today? My stepmum said she can't get out to the ship but could meet me in town. What do you think?"

"Shure, Don, I suppose clean oil is petrol and such. Yeh! I'd like to go with you," replied Brendan. "Looking forward to meeting your mother. Never met a real actress." *I mustn't forget to ring home and Polly.*

"Wait until you see her, Bren. You're in for a treat. She's my stepmother an' not much older than me—a real dish. My mother died some years ago and my dad married Catherine. Catherine Le Fevre—can't believe she's supposed to be my mother. She's an American; her dad is a radio personality or such."

With a shrug of his shoulders, Don started getting dressed for the run ashore, leaving Brendan thinking of his normal, settled childhood, but looking forward to meeting this actress.

"There we are, Bren, The Prince of Wales. Let's go in. I wonder if she's there?" Don grinned apprehensively at Brendan as they pushed open the well used door on Railway Street and entered the dimly lit interior to the smell of stale cigarette smoke and beer fumes.

His eyes becoming used to the darkened room, Brendan's attention was caught by the striking of a match as a customer in the customary cloth cap lit up his Senior Service. Then, looking further into the room towards the bar with its gleaming pumps, he saw a pair of long, nylon encased, crossed legs stretching up to a short, tight, red dress around the narrow waist of a female body. Brendan's eyes took in the white blouse shaped around a pair of prominent 'diddies' and the manicured hands—one holding a small glass and the other hand in an elegant poise with a lit cigarette. The head of this breathtaking figure was surmounted by a sleek helmet of black hair around an attractive face with dark eyes and sensuous red lips.

Gosh! What a stunner! thought Brendan, as Don self-consciously introduced him.

"Hi! Honey!" she greeted Don. "And hi to you, big boy" were the softly spoken, teasing, American accented words from the tall busty hour glass figure offering a limp slim hand to Brendan.

"Hello, Mrs. Marshall," answered Brendan in a hoarse voice as all his senses came to attention.

"Yes, Cath. Brendan is from Ireland, straight from the bogs," chuckled Don, as Brendan glared at him then turned back to the vision in front of him, grinning inanely. Slightly taller than Don and not much older than him, Cath recovered her hand and in her soft American twang instructed the admiring 'landlord' behind the bar to provide her 'friends' with a drink.

"I'll have an Irish with a small drop of water, thank you, landlord," were the words in a pronounced Dublin accent from Brendan. *An Irish whiskey. God, what am I saying?* he thought…

"We have, for the discerning Irishman, a choice. Which would Sir like?" enquired the landlord, pointing to the row of different sized labelled bottles on the glass shelf behind him. Dragging his eyes from the stunning figure in front of him, his right hand in his trouser pocket endeavouring to adjust himself, Brendan recognised the name on one of the bottles.

"Shure, Mr. Landlord, I'll have the Power," he replied, hoping that was the correct way to ask for a whiskey. Blushing furiously and feeling most uncomfortable, Brendan leaned against the bar and accepted the small glass with a disappointing amount of brown liquid in it.

"I'll have a glass of Brown, thanks," Don ordered. "What about you, Cath?"

"Oh! I'm all right with my gin and orange, thank you, son." She answered, pronouncing 'son' in a playful manner. Cath was enjoying herself, having two young men ogling her.

"What play are you acting in at the moment, Cath?" Brendan asked, remembering Don had mentioned she was an actress.

"Play? Brendan, not me. I'm a singer in a night club—the Raymond Revue Bar. I worked in the Windmill Theatre before that."

"That must be great, Cath. Must come along to hear you someday." Don, overhearing the reference to the Raymond Revue, thought *that's that new strip club in Soho*. Looking at his stepmother in a new light, as his dad had not told him this, he asked, "Are you a stripper then, Cath? You're not an actress?"

Cath was smiling broadly and enjoying the moment. "I am a very good actress Donald and," with a pout of her lipsticked mouth, "I have been known to take my clothes off on the stage."

Brendan looking at this glorious female; the news that she was a stripper, that she took her clothes off on the stage, had his imagination working overtime. No clothes on, no bra, no skirt. Not having ever seen a woman without clothes on, only aware of their shape and allure, Brendan was now, what, with the whiskey and this vision, beginning to get very hot. This woman had suddenly changed from his friend's mother to an attractive however unattainable prospect.

Cath, looked at Don, who was in somewhat a state of mild shock. "Donald, your dad has asked me to keep my job a secret but I thought you should know what a popular girl I am. I am so glad to meet you again and your lovely friend, Brendan," Cath exclaimed in a sexy voice, turning to Brendan and placing her hand on his knee.

What's she up to? was Brendan's immediate reaction to the knee trembler. *God, what do I do? What's happening to me? Don, go away, disappear. Does she fancy me? Oh! Mother, what do I do? All I want to do is touch her, wrap my arms around her. God, if I don't do something I'll explode.*

Don didn't know whether to be annoyed or amused with this revelation. *What has my father done? Why has he married such a slut?*

"I'm going back to the ship, Bren. I've had enough of this slag," Don suddenly announced with disgust and disappointment in his voice. "Are you coming back with me?"

Before Brendan could make his mind up whether to stay with this attractive dangerous feline or shrug his shoulders to all the hinted excitements of remaining, Cath rose from her bar stool and rummaged in her shoulder bag. "There you are, Donald. Your dad asked me to give you this." She proffered a sealed brown envelope to Don. "Sorry you don't like me but I'll go. Goodbye, sonny, enjoy yourself. Sorry I can't help you down there." She smiled, looking at Brendan's lower body. "But I'm sure a good-looking guy like you will find a willing girl someday."

With a shrug of her shoulders, a glare at Don, and a further smile at Brendan, the slim body—Brendan's dreams—strutted away with a swing of its hips and a clatter of high heels on the wooden floor.

Silence reigned, the barman coughed, Don shuffled his feet in embarrassment and Brendan smiled in sympathy and regret.

"Come on, Don," Brendan said. "Let's get back to the ship. Thanks, barman." With a cursory wave, the two sailors walked out into the sunlight, both immersed in their thoughts, Don annoyed and upset, and Brendan excited with the thoughts of what might have happened but feeling some sympathy for his friend.

"Right, Marshall," announced the third mate. "You know the drill. You and Harris here will be on twelve-hour watch daily until we sail. At the moment we are discharging water ballast, and then the tanks will have to be cleaned and mopped by the crew as we will be loading a part cargo of lubrication oil for Bombay. So it will take the best part of the next day to finish the ballast. Johnson and Jones will relieve you at eight in the morning. If you need me I will be in my cabin." With a smile, the third mate—who had only recently been an apprentice himself, taking orders from the office of the watch—turned on his heel and ascended the ladder to the officer's deck.

After the abortive visit to Chatham, the two sailors had returned to the ship, taken a meal and had tried to gain some sleep before standing watch that night. Don was quite morose and in a bit of a sulk over the episode in the afternoon, unlike Brendan, who was excited with the feelings in his body and also keen to learn the intricacies of a tanker's workings.

That evening, when they started their watch duties, Don had gone into the watch room and taken the only seat in the small space and started to read a book. Brendan resigned himself to a long night. Always eager to know exactly what was required to succeed with a given task, Bren wanted the answers to questions. He was very conscious of being judged on results, even when someone else was ultimately responsible. Knowing that water ballast was necessary on an empty ship to balance the ship in the water, which was now being pumped out of the ship's tanks to make way for the oil cargo, he wondered why three men were needed to supervise the procedure. *Ah, well*, he thought to himself. *Who am I to question my superiors?*

During the night, finding he was responsible for nothing more than to make tea for the third mate and Don, and to close and open the large valves on the deck—shutting down one tank when empty and opening up a full one—he found it very hard to stay awake and was exhausted when eight in the morning arrived. Ken and Barry took over, and he and Don, who had become more communicative over the night, changed into their dress uniforms and had a large breakfast before crashing out—as the nautical term was—for the next few hours.

Over the next couple of days at the Isle of Grain, Brendan surprised himself that with just a few hours' sleep after the twelve hours on watch, he was quite alert and found out a lot about the ship, ship's procedures and loading oil. He tried a couple of times to telephone home but found a delay on the line of an hour or so each time made it difficult and anyway it would cost a small fortune to ring—something like eight shillings—so he settled down and wrote a note to his ma and Polly, saying all was well.

***

"Right, Harris, you go for'rard, with the mate. And Marshall, you make your way to the bridge. Call the other two and have them go aft." So instructed a weary third mate to two tired apprentices at three o'clock on the Thursday morning. The *Calvex Renown* had now loaded its part cargo of lubricating oil and was on its way to its next port of call: the sea port of Wales, Swansea.

When the ship cleared the Isle of Grain, Brendan had gone to bed. An hour later at eight o'clock, when the ship cleared the dock, he was roused for breakfast, an hour's study and a day's work.

On their way through the English Channel, leaving the majestic cliffs of Dover to starboard, around Lands End and into the Bristol Channel, Brendan found it hard to credit that it was only a week since he had joined the Merchant Navy. This was his new life now, at the beck and call, as a junior apprentice, to all officers on board, certainly a far call from the relaxed days in Ireland. *Let's make the best of this experience. My whole life ahead of me—I'm being paid to travel the world. Next stop: Bombay…the mystic east, rebellion, over-population, poverty—is it still under British Rule?*

Whatever, a seventeen-year-old Irish lad was out to see the world and paid not very much with which to do it.

Back to reality: one o'clock on a windswept morning, in driving rain, the *Calvex Renown* prepared to weigh anchor prior to entering the lock gates on the entrance to Swansea harbour. All apprentices were roused to report to their various posts for docking.

God, thought Brendan, as he stood on the high foc'sle of the ship in his sou'wester hat and light windcheater, back to the wind and his nose dripping from the rain and a head cold, *I could be in bed. I'm not needed here. All the others know what they are doing.*

"Harris," shouted the mate, resplendent in his long black oilskins and a red sou'wester, leaning against the rain washed black windlass barrel. "Get me a cup of tea. We're going to be here some time yet, an' bring the bosun a cup as well."

"Don't forget us, Paddy. I'll have two sugars in mine," laughed one of the crew members all shrouded in their assorted wet weather gear. Brendan, realising his leg was being pulled and that he'd better rise above the miserable picture he must portray, raised his head and, pretending to take a note pad from his pocket and licking the end of a supposed pencil, called "Now that will be tea all round then? Anyone like a piece of cake or a chocolate biscuit?"

The mate laughed. "That will be all right, Harris. Just myself and the bosun. One lump and little milk. Get one for yourself."

Brendan, feeling better in himself, made his way carefully along the raised walkway over the tanker deck to the midships structure and put the electric kettle on to boil. The only mugs in the top drawer of the desk in the watch room were both tea-stained and unwashed. The tin of condensed milk with its lid pierced by a penknife was a week old and the Tate and Lyle sugar bag was one big lump of solidified caster sugar. The teapot still had used tea leaves in it, so Brendan emptied this over the side of the ship and with the stained tea spoon scooped out two large spoonfuls of tea leaves from the bag in the drawer. While waiting for the kettle to boil, he took stock of his surroundings. He was looking to the rear of the ship on a level with the stilted walkway linking the rear structure to the midships accommodation. The high streamlined funnel with wisps of steam emitting from its cowl stood out against a background of the city's lights intermittently winking on the hills behind through the windlashed rain. Out of the dark announced by their navigation lights and searchlight, approached two tugboats from the land.

They must be the tugs to guide us into the dock. Great there's the kettle boiling. This officer—tea boy more like it—must do his duty: two mugs of tea coming up. With a mug in each hand, Brendan made his way up the rain-washed stilted walkway to the front of the ship and passed the now cooling mugs to their recipients.

"Thanks, Harris. Now go over there and help those guys pull the towing hawser up from the tug," instructed the mate, pulling a face as he drank from the mug.

By half past four they had passed through the lock, down a short canal and entered the Queens Dock to tie up alongside one of protruding oil jetties.

Don and Brendan were put on duty until midday, when they helped the crew prepare the remaining oil tanks for the expected cargo of white spirit and other high volatile oils. That afternoon, they went for a short visit into the town and bought a few items. Brendan had got a few pounds' advance on his wages to buy a heavy rain jacket. They both had haircuts and were back to the ship for some sleep before going on loading watch from eight o'clock that night. The next two days were spent either sleeping or on watch for when, at one o'clock on a cold and rainy morning, the *Calvex Renown* and her first tripper Brendan Harris sailed on their maiden voyage overseas.

***

"God, its cold," complained Brendan Harris to the short statured helmsman beside him. The *Calvex Renown* had developed a steering malfunction and could not be controlled from the bridge. This meant the officer on watch, situated on the bridge of the ship, needed a link between him and the helmsman steering the ship from the emergency wheel at the stern.

It was now two o'clock on a cold and wet morning with a strong wind on the starboard side of the ship, and Brendan had been called by the officer of the watch—the foul-mouthed second mate—to get his miserable body down to the aft deck and relay steering instructions to the helmsman. Feeling quite important at being chosen to attend to such an essential task, Brendan had dressed in his wet weather gear and, after instruction from the second mate, made his way as quickly as possible, in the tossing ship and driving spray along the flying bridge towards the stern and the emergency wheel. The tanker now fully loaded with its different cargoes of oil was very low in the water with only some six feet of freeboard. The high waves were washing over the tanker's deck in spume-filled sheets of water, smothering the raised walkway over the tanker deck, colloquially called the flying bridge. To get to the stern of the ship, Brendan had to run along the flying bridge, hanging onto the guard rails whenever a larger than usual heavy wave crashed over him.

The *Calvex Renown* was now driving south through the Bay of Biscay, heading for the more protected waters of the Mediterranean on its way to deliver much needed petrol and other oils to the port of Bombay in India.

Brendan, fairly bouncing in his exhilaration with the wet spray in his face and his newfound confidence, aided the helmsman to get the steering wheel connected to the emergency steering system and settled down to a few hours of a cold but exciting experience. Balancing his body to the lurching and swaying of the large tanker, he watched the stormy seas rushing past, the dark clouds scudding across the moon, and he felt for the first time a part of this newborn ship on its first voyage, just as he was himself. *Gosh! This is the life. Oh! God where am I going,* as a sudden extra lurch of the deck destroyed his carefully adapted balance and he had to grab a stanchion to save himself from toppling over the side into the racing water.

A snort of derision emitted from the shrouded figure at the wheel. "First tripper. Huh!" With that, there was a shrill ring from the telephone. "Second Mate here, Harris. The engineers reckon they should have the steering repaired in an hour. Enjoying yourself, are you? Keep the helmsman on his toes on a course of one-eighty degrees. Now keep awake an' I'll have a relief to you at oh-four-hundred."

Feeling now quite a part of the organisation, Brendan replied with a positive, "Aye, aye, Second," replaced the phone and unfairly admonished the helmsman for being a couple of degrees off course.

The next hour passed with the wind abating somewhat. Brendan was relieved at 0400 by Barry, who came to take over until 0800. Feeling very satisfied with himself, Brendan made a most seaman-like walk back to his cabin and fell into a very welcome bunk.

Three hours later…

"Come on, Bren. It's seven o'clock. Time for breakfast. Saturday morning, your turn to scrub the wheelhouse decking. I'm doing the brass."

This was the custom every Saturday morning; the apprentices took it in turns to scrub the wheelhouse deck and polish the various brasses.

"But, Don," complained the sleepy Brendan. "I've only had a few hours' sleep. I spent half the night saving the ship."

"I know, Bren," grinned Don "We are all very grateful, but orders are orders. Now you'd better get moving."

On his bare knees with a scrubbing brush in his right hand, a galvanised bucket full of soapy water beside him, attired in a pair of once-white short shorts, the officer-to-be scrubbed the surface dirt off the wooden decking. His muscles aching from the unaccustomed exercise and lack of sleep, he muttered to himself at how unfair the world was. The steering gear had been repaired at five o'clock and Barry had been given the morning off. Don was polishing the brass fittings. Ken, the senior apprentice, was nowhere to be seen.

"Come on, Paddy!" chortled the third mate as he paced by. "You've got the bridge wings to do as well. They need a good scrub."

"My name's not Paddy," muttered Brendan to himself. *And I didn't join the navy to do this, my knees are all soft from the wet deck. My arms ache, but if they want it done, it gotta be done. Nobody is going to say I'm a whinger.*

By ten o'clock, after an hour's scrubbing, Brendan stretched his long frame, dried his knees and proclaimed with some satisfaction, "There. That's done."

"Looks lovely," agreed Don. "I've done the brass and I'll sweep out the chartroom. You had better get down to the cabin and change the bed linen. The steward will open the linen room at ten thirty. It's the junior apprentice's privilege. Ha, ha, you do it each Saturday morning."

Feeling quite hard done by after his night on duty, a tired Brendan trudged his way down to his cabin only to meet an ebullient Barry full of his endeavours of the night: the stormy seas, his adept handling of the helmsman, how he had singlehandedly saved the ship from collision.

With his pillow case bulging with the sheets from both bunks slung over his shoulder, Brendan felt like bringing it down in full force on the chattering little fat Welshman, droning on in his sing-song accent as they made their way to the linen room.

"I'm only doing this as a favour to Ken," explained Barry. "We have reached an agreement where we share the work."

"Where's Ken now?" enquired Brendan.

"Oh! He's with the mate, no doubt discussing how well I controlled the ship this morning," replied Barry in a smug voice.

Brendan, quite nonplussed on how to retort to these outlandish statements, shrugged his shoulders and passed his pillow case to the simpering steward.

Allowing the overacting Welshman to pass out of his sight, Brendan walked to the side of the ship and leaned on the salt encrusted wooden bulwark, the protective rail running alongside the tanker, and took a deep breath of the warm Mediterranean air. The tanker had entered the Mediterranean at six o'clock. The sea had calmed a lot from the early morning and a warm breeze was now wafting in from the African coast, the clear blue sky mirrored in the colour of the waves running alongside the tanker. Sometimes a larger sea would wash over the side and race over the red-coloured deck, crashing against the coaming of one of the black tank lids. The sounds and the smells of the sea, and the gentle roll of the deck beneath him gave Brendan a satisfying feeling of achievement. Only seven months since his fruitless endeavours to find a career in Ireland, and he was now an apprentice deck officer in a large tanker company with a career mapped out ahead of him. Lots of hard study lay ahead: the secrets of navigation, ship handling, and ship's cargo—the trans-shipment of anything from bananas to locomotives and, of course, oil.

With a sigh of satisfaction, Brendan climbed the bulwark ladder back onto the accommodation deck, looking forward to the future.

***

"Yes, Paddy, another day or so and we will be at Port Said, five to port. That tanker to starboard is a bit close."

"Third," enquired Brendan. "Third, I heard there was a war just in the last few months over the Suez Canal. Is it all over now? Has the fighting stopped?"

"Five to port, Paddy," repeated the third mate with a short sigh of exasperation.

"Oh! Sorry, Third, five to port it is," replied Brendan, turning the wheel a few spokes to the left to bring the ticking giro compass on the display in front of him to show a changed direction to eighty-five degrees, thinking he must tell the third not to call him Paddy.

"You know about Nasser and the nationalisation of the canal?" With a half nod from Brendan, the third continued, pleased to air his knowledge. "Well a few months ago, peace was declared and they have cleared many of the ships sunk in the canal. It opened a couple of months back so it will be interesting to see the results."

Seeing his reflection in the wheelhouse window, Brendan was pleased with how he looked in his tropical uniform. It was a uniform comprising a short-sleeved white shirt with navy epaulettes on the shoulders, white shorts reaching above the knee with white knee-length socks in polished brown shoes. *Pity Polly can't see me now*, he thought as he adjusted the wheel to settle the sixteen-thousand-ton tanker on a steady course eastwards through the Mediterranean Sea towards Port Said: the port at the entrance to the Suez Canal.

This is the life. Here am I, steering this big ship through the Mediterranean Sea, on this lovely Sunday morning, Italy somewhere to the left, and Africa to the right—

"What's that, Third?"

"You're drifting a bit. Get her back on course, Paddy. Anyway, another ten and we'll put her on automatic. Not bad for a first try. When the second mate comes on at noon we'll take a sight. Have you got your sextant with you?"

"Third," said Brendan in a hesitant voice. "Third, I would rather you called me by my name: Brendan."

Before Brendan or the third mate could speak, the short portly figure of Captain Fergus Mitchell rolled in from the sunlit wing of the bridge, dressed in very casual tropical wear: white shorts that came below his knees and open-toed brown sandals. A pair of very white stocky hairy legs balanced the heavy-set upper body covered in a short-sleeved white shirt with navy epaulets sporting the four golden bars of his rank.

"Who's steering this boat, mister?" the portly figure demanded in a strong Scot accent, of the third mate. "Look we're going all over the f---ing place."

"It's Harris here, Sir. First time on the wheel. Hasn't done too badly at all, I thought," answered the third mate, unconsciously standing to attention in his smart tropical uniform.

With a loud clearing of his throat, the captain glanced over at Brendan and back to the third. "Third, if I say we're all over the place we-are-all-over-the-f---ing-place," admonished the rotund figure. "I'm your captain—Captain Mitchell—an' what I say—" Stopping mid sentence, he wagged his finger at Brendan and the third mate and swung back to stand on the prepared stool to see out the bridge window, exuding sweat and petulance.

The captain, being short in stature, was unable to see through the wide bridge windows and required a stool to stand on. This problem was to lead to many instances of petulance from the 'leader' as whenever the 'leader' moved, the stand had to move with him. The senior officers had had many meetings to resolve the problem. Should there be an apprentice available to move the stand, or should the mate on watch do it? Could a set of wheels for the stand be considered with a rope stretching from each wing to aid in a speedy movement? Of course, in stormy weather, wheels would be dangerous. Many was the laugh at the thought of the 'leader' in rough weather, balanced on his stand, rapidly moving across the deck, eventually tipping over the side of the ship never to be seen again. It appeared a compromise had been agreed. The stand should stand alone, 'like Custer with the Sioux Indians', whilst at sea but when docking the ship, it would be the responsibility of the apprentice to anticipate the captain's movements.

Brendan's feeling of peace within himself evaporated. This wasn't what he expected the captain to be like—the most important person on the ship, the leader of men, and the pinnacle of his own ambitions—not this disappointing sweaty grunting little porker of a man using swear words instead of adjectives.

This was the first time he had been close to the captain since joining the ship. They had left Swansea in the early morning a week ago in rain and mist, and Brendan had entered the routine of dressing for breakfast, spending an hour of studies, changing into work clothes to do the menial jobs that a first-year apprentice was expected to do. Change again for lunch at twelve, back into working gear for the afternoon and change again for dinner at six. He had met the other officers in an official capacity and the third mate socially, but the captain had had his meals in his cabin.

"OK! Harris, go get your sextant," ordered the third mate, conscious of the captain's presence as he changed the steering control to automatic. "And back here in five."

Brendan took a deep breath of the clean fresh air as he moved out from the enclosed bridge structure onto the open bridge wing, adjusting his body balance to counteract the steady roll of the ship as it thrust its way through the moving white-flecked sea.

"Hi, Don. Great, I see you've got my sextant. Gosh, I've met the captain—what a miserable old sod," exclaimed Brendan under his breath, as a hurrying Don passed the wooden box containing the instrument on his way towards the bridge.

"Have you used a sextant before, Don?" asked Brendan in a hesitant voice.

"Yeh. Nothing to it," shrugged Don. "The sextant gives you the angle between the sun and the horizon. That gives you your latitude and, with a bit of spherical trigonometry and a chronometer, you can work out the longitude. You'll get the hang of it, don't worry." He grinned. "I'm still trying to figure it out."

"Right, you two, on the bridge wing now," ordered the third as he acknowledged the presence of the second mate, who had come on watch to take over from him.

With the captain, Brendan, Don and the third mate all pointing their sextants at the sun, Brendan watching Don to see what he did, and the third mate very conscious of the captain grunting and farting, it became very crowded on the bridge wing. Brendan, somewhat taller than any of the others, stood at the back and made an attempt at working the sextant.

"Right, you've got the angle and the time, go get your lunch and back to the bridge here, where you can work out our position in the chartroom. OK, Second?" enquired the third mate with a nod towards the second.

"Don, I'd love to come up with an answer, but haven't a clue what to do." admitted a contrite Brendan in an aside to Don.

"Don't worry, Bren. You're not expected to. Now let's get some food into us."

With the sun high in the sky and the ship steering a steady course through the blue Mediterranean Sea, Brendan Harris with his newfound friends and his future mapped out ahead of him, let out a whoop of joy and punched the air in satisfaction. "This is the life."

View from Tanker: Port Said

9

Injuries in Accident

"No more than two students, Doctor. Mr Harris has had a very disturbed twenty-four hours and is in need of sleep." These were the cautionary words from the sister to Doctor Larrigan as he prepared to sweep aside the curtains surrounding Brendan's bed.

"Very well, Sister. Thank you! I will be as quiet as possible. Nurse?" he called. "Could you arrange for two of these intelligent persons—" smiling at the student group "—to accompany me when I examine Mr. Harris?"

Pulling aside the curtain in the darkened area, a somnolent body could be seen under a light sheet, its hands still tied by the wrists to the raised side of the large bed. The sounds coming from the body were the troubled noises of someone having a bad dream. The body twitched in spasms, with frequent pulling of the wrists, which were wrapped in bandage to protect them from the cords tied to the metal bedside.

"It's three days since I operated. The minor cuts on his face seem to be healing all right." Standing back from the bed, Larrigan addressed, in a lowered voice, the two students gathered around him. "What is the main worry here, the patient has had a severe blow to the right side of his head to the frontal lobe. What damage, would you say—" directing his voice toward the younger of the two students "—could this cause to his brain function?"

In a hesitant voice, the young man, small and thin, with a face rampant with acne and startled to be asked the question, took a deep breath and stuttered in a broad Dublin accent, "De-de…frontal lobe, Doctor. It controls the mo-mo-motor function of the brain." Receiving a nod of affirmation from Larrigan, he continued with added confidence, "an' de temporal lobes here—" pointing to the part covered by the ear "—are involved with memory and hearing—"

"Yes!" interrupted Larrigan. "Very good, young man. That is the more worrying point. The patient, on recovery, may have some memory loss due to damage of the temporal lobe. When Mr. Harris was admitted, there was liquid emitting from both ears and I suspected immediately there to be… What would be your diagnosis, young lady?" questioned Larrigan to the other student: a very nervous young female who blushed furiously and stuttered an unintelligible reply. "I immediately suspected epidural haematoma, bleeding between the skull and the brain, young lady. I opened both sides of the skull and removed clotting blood. Clotting blood, as you well know—" smiling at the embarrassed student, he continued "—will swell and most probably result in death.

"Our patient here is very active, I am pleased to say, but a further concern is possible damage to the occipital lobes. Again, I would ask your opinion as to the possible result of damage to these lobes. Have you an opinion, young man?" Larrigan directed his question to the now smiling young male doctor, who obviously knew the answer.

"Sometimes, sir, in cases like this, the patient on recovery will have diplopia."

"Yes, very good young man. Diplopia, or double vision. We can but wait and see. Now…" Larrigan moved to the lower part of the bed. "The right leg, the upper muscles are called?" He pointed to the top part of the encased leg.

"The quadriceps fermoris muscle. This was severed in the collision, where the right knee smashed the glass in the rear window of the car and the muscle was cleanly cut above the patella."

"Yes! Young man you are fortunate to be alive," consoled Dr Larrigan patting Brendan's encased right knee.

Disturbed by the voices and proximity of the group, Brendan, still unconscious, began cursing under his breath and pulling against the wrist ties.

Gentleman of Port Said

10

Entertainment in Bombay

Port Said harbour: the entry to the East, an immaculate morning, a cloudless sky, the temperature in the low eighties Fahrenheit, a light breeze coming off the land. Brendan Harris, feeling very smart in his clean, hot weather gear, creased white shorts, an immaculate white shirt with black epaulettes, white stockings and black shoes, stood beside the well polished ship's telegraph awaiting instruction from the important officers: the captain, the second mate and the pilot.

The pilot, a very foreign-looking gentleman wearing scruffy khaki shorts even more ridiculous than the captain's, and a white soiled shirt straining over a well-fed body stood aloof from the ship's officers. Before the war, the majority of pilots recruited to traverse the canal had been British, but now Mr. Nasser had sacked them all and given the job to his Russian allies. The pilot had boarded the ship, which was now entering Port Said harbour. Brendan was very apprehensive of his duties: to affect the telegraph orders, to enter the movement instructed in the log and to anticipate when to move the captain's 'stand'. The nuances of the war and foreign pilots were the furthest things from Brendan's mind.

"Slow ahead," instructed the second mate.

Gosh, that's me, realised Brendan, more concerned with watching the captain step off his stand.

"Slow ahead, sir," acknowledged Brendan, sweeping the telegraph arm to rest on the required slow ahead instruction to the engine room.

"Harris," called the second, nodding to the captain's waddling movement to the bridge wing. Brendan raced toward the captain's stand, only to see the little man had stepped back on his stool. He returned to the telegraph position to scribble the time and telegraph order he had taken.

With the hot and humid atmosphere on the bridge, Brendan began to sweat profusely as the tanker progressed closer to the shore, the square dusty brown buildings shimmering in the heat. The atmosphere on the bridge was very tense, the captain visibly showing his distain of the pilot who had deliberately snubbed him when he boarded. For many years, the canal had been run and serviced by the British, and Captain Mitchell of the *Calvex Renown* did not take too kindly to a foreigner controlling his ship. However, this was as now ordered and he had to abide by the rules. He refused to speak directly with the intruder and would only converse through the second mate to an interpreter, who would pass on whatever message he wished to convey to the pilot.

So the passage to anchorage in the harbour was conducted in stony silence, apart from grunted instruction from the pilot to the interpreter, who would repeat it to the second mate, who would then pass the message to Brendan. Brendan would record all engine movements in the log. They proceeded at a very slow pace into the overcrowded harbour, ignoring the many bumboats—small boats manned by traders selling ornaments and trinkets, all shouting and calling for attention, milling around the ship, racing out to sell their wares to these hopefully unsuspecting limeys.

Reaching their anchorage position, on the signal from the second mate, Brendan rang the *finished with engine* instruction to the engine room and entered the exercise in the log book. The pilot grunted something unintelligible, the captain snorted his derision and waddled off the bridge. Not forgetting to place the captain's stool in the backroom, Brendan went to find Ken to discover what the orders were for the rest of the day.

"OK, Bren, we're taking on some fresh water. See that small water tanker alongside? When that's finished loading, you and I shall be going on watch through the canal. Don and Barry will be on deck duty. It's oh-eight-hundred now, Friday nineteenth." Looking at his watch, Ken smiled at Bren. "We'll have our breakfast now and should enter the canal about ten-hundred. I'll take the first few hours, you go on at midday and I'll take over from sixteen-hundred. I'll come back on at twenty-hundred to midnight and as you brought us into Port Said you go on at midnight and take us out at Suez. Don't worry there will be very little to do," said Ken, as Brendan stepped back with a frown at all this unexpected responsibility.

What about that little Welshman? He's getting off lightly.

"Don't worry about Don an' Barry. They will be on ship-cleaning duties, a bit of scrubbing here, a bit of paint scraping there," interjected Ken with a smile. "When we return to the canal, roles will be reversed."

Happy with the outcome, Brendan had a quick wash and a satisfying breakfast. Feeling somewhat weary after his early morning duties, he thought he would have a doze for an hour or so.

"Come on, Bren. Quick. We're goin' into the canal. You're to be on the bridge in five minutes. It's five to twelve. Come on, git yer arse up there quick," called Don anxiously.

"Shure, shure. Is it, Don? God, I only lay down for a minute," stuttered Brendan as he threw his legs over the side of the bunk. "Where's me good shoes? OK, thanks, Don. Must have a slash, plenny of time. Lucky I'm still in me best."

"I got you a cup of tea, Bren. It's on your desk. Now shut up and get moving," urged Don as he left him alone in the cabin.

With ten seconds to spare, a rather crumpled looking first-trip apprentice arrived on the bridge and a relieved Ken passed over the log book.

"Note, Bren, engine room on standby—we're weighing anchor an' the cap'n's stool is on the port wing. Good luck. I'm away now, Third," Ken called to the third mate, who was speaking with the second.

"Oh! I've got the Irishman, have I? Make us a cup of tea then, Paddy," the second mate instructed with the emphasis on the *Paddy* in his sentence. "Pilot, would you like a cup?" he enquired, with a glance toward the bulky, foreign-looking body dressed in short, tight, off-white shorts and red shirt, long white stockings and heavy white boots.

Without turning his body, the answer, "Nein," came in a guttural burst, followed by a string of what seemed like oaths to the English ear. This pilot for the trip through the canal seemed no different to the first unpleasant uncommunicative man.

"OK, be like that you miserable bastard. You're just like the last one," the second mate muttered under his breath. "What about you, sir? Would you like a cup?" he called in a loud voice to the figure standing on his stool on the port wing.

Receiving no reply, the second turned back to Brendan. "Just me then, Paddy, You kno'—milk and two sugars. Right. Jump to it—hold it. You're looking a mite scruffy, lad. Pull you stockings up and get the tail of your shirt tucked before the old man sees you."

Annoyed with himself, Brendan did as instructed and, recognising the signal from the forecastle advising the anchor was aweigh, entered it in the note book, at the same time acknowledging the instruction from the pilot to put the engines on *slow ahead*.

"Second, I'm leaving the bridge now. Call me if you need me," the captain called out in a loud voice as he walked past the pilot. Passing into the chartroom at the back of the wheelhouse, Brendan heard him mutter to the second, "Keep yur eye on that Russian bastard out there. I doan trust him."

Having made the tea for the second, Brendan walked out onto the bridge wing to look at the monotonous stretches of red and yellow sand stretching to the horizon on either side of the sixty-foot-wide canal. Joined by the second mate on the bridge wing, Brendan was quite startled when he started to speak in a conversational tone.

"What do you think of the goings on, Paddy?"

"What do you mean, Second? Do you mean the sunken ships we've seen in Port Said and the Russian pilot? I've heard about a guy called Nasser—"

"Yeah, there we were, mindin' our own business running the canal—the canal we helped to build—making a nice profit and Nasser last year decides to nationalise it. Our f---ing prime minister Anthony Eden, along with the French and the Israelites, decided to teach Nasser a lesson. The Yanks wouldn't help, the bastards. So we, along with the French, started to bomb the Gippos. The United Nations put an end to that and Nasser said 'up yours' and sunk a few dozen ships in the canal. The Russians backed Nasser, so that's why we have a Russian pilot, not an English one."

"So that's why there were those wrecks at Port Said?"

"Yep, Paddy, they started clearing out the canal late last year. Only opened it a month ago—that's sometin' for your diary. When all the stupid fighting ceased and as they were losing a lot of money with the canal closed, they cleared a lot of the wrecks out to get it opened again. They towed some of the boats to the Bitter Lakes; we should see a few when we arrive there later in the day. Now get on with your bloody work," dismissed the second, realising he had dropped the hard-man guise.

Grinning to himself, Brendan looked down to the fore deck to see Don and Barry busy with paintbrushes, both stripped down to shorts. Don's brown well muscled upper body stood out in contrast to Barry's white sweaty blubber shape. Brendan, feeling pretty privileged in his important position on the bridge, returned the wave from Don.

Later that afternoon, the *Renown* anchored in the Great Bitter Lake to let the northbound convoy pass through.

"See there, that's one of the Ben line ships. It's been here since Nasser blocked the canal exits. They have had a skeleton crew on board for the past few months. See, there's an Elder Dempster ship." Ken pointed out the various dilapidated looking cargo ships anchored in the lake.

"Look, there's a few of the crew going for a swim," exclaimed Barry.

"Go ahead, lads," suggested the mate who happened to be close by. "Get the pilot ladder over the side first, though, as I don't want to be fishing you out of the water."

With close on a full cargo, the ship's freeboard—the distance between the main deck and the water surface—being only six feet or so, Brendan quickly divested himself of his sun hat and plimsolls. He had finished his watch on the bridge, and, climbing over the ship's rail, made a less than spectacular dive into the salty water. Ken was a close second, followed by Don. Barry leaned on the side rail and signalled his dislike of such nonsense. From Brendan's perspective of the ship at sea level, it appeared huge, immense, towering over him. Treading the thick salty water he thought, *this is the life*, and letting out a whoop of joy, he went into his

Johnny Weissmuller Tarzan crawl—more a splashy overarm giving the appearance of a drowning man.

Too soon there was the call to come back on board and amid loud chatter and laughter, they dried themselves off and prepared for dinner.

That evening, they sailed out into the Red Sea, heading south for their next stop the magical sounding Bombay.

Just under a month out from the UK and Brendan was beginning to find his feet in his new environment. His home was now this moveable unit moving at the whim of the market demand for oil. The UK needed oil to refine into its more useable products, and here was the *Renown* with its complement of twenty-eight males—this long tube of steel now taking refined products to its customer and preparing to take part in its sole purpose: the transport of oil in its crude state to a refinery. As the ship's tanks had not been soiled, corrupted by a cargo of crude, the shippers had taken advantage of the clean tanks and used the *Renown* to transport the petrol and white spirit from the refineries in Swansea and the Isle of Grain. After leaving Bombay, the *Renown* would then head north to the Persian Gulf and the oil fields of Kuwait to load a full cargo of crude oil for a refinery in Europe.

Brendan's responsibility as a navigating apprentice was to learn the workings of seagoing vessels. Not only would he have to learn the requirements for the trans-shipment of oil, but also how to load and ship anything from grain to cars, and learn how ordinary cargo ships worked.

As a beginner, Brendan, along with Barry, was expected to do the housekeeping for him and his senior cabin mate. To fill his day, as ordered: to chip rust, to paint, to scrub decks, to polish brass, to make tea for officers, to learn seamanship, how to sail anything from a row boat to a super tanker, to navigate anywhere in the world from the Arctic to the Antarctic and to prepare for six-monthly exams set by the head office. He was a healthy seventeen-year-old, six feet tall, slim build with presentable features and the normal sex drive of a young male, having to adjust to male-only company for weeks on end, with the frustrations of only a few hours ashore and limited time to seek out female company.

Brendan was now also introduced to the painting style referred to as wadding. With the constant battle with the elements to prevent the multitude of oil pipes crisscrossing the decks becoming too rusty, a fast, whilst very messy method, called wadding was used. The applier of the paint—usually an apprentice—would strip down to the barest essential in clothing, in the warm weather of course, cover all naked skin with a cream called Rosalex, grab a lump of cotton waste, dip it into the pot of paint and apply it liberally to the rusted metal. This was an uncomfortable exercise, as clambering over the large pipes would incur scratches and tears in the skin. Not a very popular pastime.

Eight days after Suez, the *Renown* entered Bombay harbour and tied up at the oil jetty at Jawahar Deep.

"We'll be here a couple of days at the most," advised Ken. "Whilst here, we've to get cholera jabs and there is an invite from the seaman's mission. They are laying on a bus to take officers to visit a posh club outside Bombay called Breach Candy. Anyone for it?" Ken paused for a response. "OK, from the grins on the three of you, I'll be the martyr and do the first eight hours watch. The bus leaves at midday. You, Don, and Brendan, back ready to go on watch from twenty-hundred and then Barry and I will take the next eight from four in the morning. Who's this guy?" questioned Ken, taken aback, as a rather large, overdressed male with double chins and a bulky, well-used large suitcase, apologised for his presence by bowing deeply whilst balancing and opening his large suitcase on the taffrail.

"I come speak with you officers, please. The captain he say OK I show you suits of clothes. OK with you, sirs?"

Recoiling somewhat from the strong odour of the perspiring body and unhealthy appearance and amused at the Welsh intonation in the overdressed salesman's voice, Brendan was interested in the contents of the case.

"They look pretty good, Buster," exclaimed Ken taking out a pair of well-made khaki shorts and placing them against his work shorts. "Look, the shirts are pretty good too. How much you ask, Buster?"

"For you, sir I only ask…" replied the perspiring body, assessing Ken's size. "Turty rupee for suit, include spare short. Same for all." The anxious salesman smiled.

"That's just over two quid," expressed Ken in a pleased voice. "Maybe I'll have a set."

Brendan, thinking of his shortage of clothes, smiled at the salesman and agreed to buy a set. With a flourish, the pleased, overdressed, perspiring introduction to this outpost of the British Empire produced a cloth measuring tape and proceeded, in an apologetic manner, to measure Ken and Brendan, affirming the finished product would be ready the next morning.

Receiving a negative response to his smiling question from the other two, he bowed deeply and backed away, repeating he would be back in twenty-four hours. Brendan was very pleased with the chance of getting some clothes so cheaply and was only sorry he couldn't afford two pairs. With great anticipation, he changed into his best tropical gear: white shirt with black shoulder epaulettes embossed with a gold circle denoting his lowly position in the officer ranking; white shorts, long white stockings and black shoes, and joined Don and Barry to await the news of transport to Breach Candy. Barry, looking very tubby in his white shirt and extra long white shorts, announced that he had seen a large van or bus pull up at the end of the long jetty.

"Let's go, boys. That must be our transport," called Don, as he made his way out of the cabin. Followed by Brendan and Barry, Don led the resplendent duo out on deck towards the gangway leading down to the jetty.

"Don' forget to be back for twenty-hundred lads. I hear there's some great talent at the club," called out Ken over the rhythmic beat of the oil being pumped through the throbbing pipes connected to the shore.

With a wave and grin, the three acknowledged Ken's wave and started their way along the jetty to the waiting green painted bus.

"Well, would you believe it, lads? It's a 1940 Volvo B12 twelve-seater. Look, it's rusted to hell. My dad had one years ago," exclaimed Don.

With a welcome greeting, the driver directed the three of them on board, and after a number of false starts, the bus pulled away from the jetty. With very little suspension the short trip out of the docks over cobbles and railway tracks was quite uncomfortable. The hard tyres bounced their way onto the dirt and concrete road toward Breach Candy.

In the dusty heat, they passed faded mansions, unloved palm trees, streets crowded with ancient cars, rickshaws, beggars and children sitting at the side of the pitted road covered in dust.

Entering the grounds of the club, the driver parked his bus close to the entrance and directed the three to the club reception.

"I come for you at the four o'clock, all OK?" enquired the driver, leaving a large plume of exhaust behind him as he roared away.

"God. It's hot, what a fantastic place," exclaimed Brendan. "Look, there's a coolie coming towards us."

In this very British club, a leftover from the days of British rule, they were led into the reception hall of this once-grand building to be approached by a young Indian man in white slacks, white jacket, very commanding appearance and educated voice.

"Gentlemen," he announced himself, "my name is Keith Fordyce. I am on the management and you are most welcome to the club. Please accept our offer of hospitality. Do take advantage of the amenities we have. There is a swimming pool. If you need, we have swim trunks. Luncheon is available from midday. Shall I arrange coffee?" Receiving three rapid nods of agreement he continued, "Please do make your way to a table beside the pool and I shall arrange it. Thank you."

As quickly as he had appeared, the member of management faded into the lightly populated reception hall and the three lads looked at each other in their surprise at such a welcome.

"God, Bren, look at the talent," exclaimed Don, nodding his head toward a group of European girls dressed in shorts and shirts. The girls were glancing toward the three sailors, who stood out amongst the few persons in Indian dress saris and the occasional turban. "Come on out to the swimming pool. I'm looking forward to this. What do you think, Barry?"

"I'm looking forward to a cup of coffee, laddo. The talent can wait," was the reply from the Welshman.

"Don't they look cute?" replied Brendan. "Hope they're going out to the pool."

As the three walked out of the building, they could see the blue sea shimmering under the cloudless sky and heard the sound of female laughter from a swimming pool ahead of them. Self-consciously, they walked toward an empty round, white-topped table surmounted by a large blue parasol. Most of the other tables surrounding the pool, were occupied in the main by families. The table alongside them was occupied by an English couple with a teenage daughter and a male child. Brendan had noticed the girl, about his own age, was wearing a blue summer dress with white top and a ponytail. She had lowered her head when he happened to look her way.

The father, dressed in white shirt, red parasol hat and very long white shorts called over, in a very refined English accent, "Would you gentlemen be from the ship just docked?"

Before anyone had time to answer, a waiter came forward with a tray containing a large coffee jug, three cups and a plate of crustless sandwiches. Whilst Barry attended to the waiter, Don replied to the question and Brendan tried to catch the daughter's eye. The father introduced himself and warned them to cover the plate of sandwiches as the crows were apt to swoop in and steal them. The black crows were certainly evident, hopping around the tables ready to break up any spare crumbs, there was a laugh from the table on the other side, which had just been occupied by three young women; a crow had swooped down from a nearby tree and snatched a sandwich from an unguarded plate. The girls were all wearing bathing costumes, with one in a very revealing bikini.

"Are you from the new ship in?" called the girl in the bikini.

"Yes," replied the three lads in unison and laughed.

"We have just come from London through the canal," said Brendan. "The weather was nothing like this back in England." He pointed to the sun.

"London—haven't been there for some years. I come from Chiswick," informed one of the less scantily clad younger women.

"I know it well," said Don. "Come from Chatham."

Brendan was mesmerised by the bikini, with all the alluring flesh pushing against the pink bikini top and the long, shapely, sun-tanned legs stretched alongside the table, and didn't know where to look.

"Are you from England as well?" he asked, unconsciously speaking in his deep musical Irish brogue.

Leaning forward, emphasising her breasts, the bikini replied, "Yes, I'm from Worcestershire. I gather from your accent you are from Ireland. My name's Helen."

Brendan, now with all sexual senses in full power, blushed, crossed his legs and tried to stop looking at the girl's bikini top.

"I'm Brendan," he stuttered. "From Dublin's fair city, where the girls are so—Oh! God! What am I saying? Yes! We are off the *Calvex Renown*, just came in this morning. Do you live here?"

By now, Barry and Don were in conversation with the other girls.

"Pull your table closer to ours. We would like to hear more about your days at sea," called the older of the girls, all of twenty-five.

With much heaving and laughter, the boys tried to move the heavy table closer to this delightful group of females, but they gave up when the Indian servants came rushing over to carry their wicker chairs around, tut-tutting and shaking their heads. Brendan made sure he was beside the bikini. Whilst moving his chair he nodded an apologetic smile to the English family and acknowledged the father's envious wink with a grin.

With the six of them endeavouring to sit at a table for four, there was every reason to push up closer and whilst doing so, Brendan accidently brushed against the bikini and apologised. Helen smiled and caught his arm, pulling him down onto the adjoining chair. Brendan, looking up caught Don's eye, who grinned and nodded his head toward Barry, who was in deep conversation with a small, brown-haired girl in a severe one-piece bathing suit. Don was sitting close to the other friendly looking plump, well-endowed young lady who had her hand on his knee.

With the cool air blowing in from the sea and the muffled sound of the surf beating gently against the shore, the light hearted conversation around them and their newfound companions, the three boys could not believe their luck. After a meal of fish and chips, they all went for a swim in the large seawater pool and shortly after said their goodbyes, as the bus had called to take them back to reality, to the smell of oil, the all-male environment and their moveable home.

Back to the ship, the three weary but very contented young men were full of their conquests. Don and Brendan tried to get some sleep before going on watch at eight o'clock that night, as the watch would not end until four o'clock the next morning, with Barry and Ken relieving them until midday.

Disturbed from a deep sleep, Brendan could hear the voice in the distance.

"Rise and shine, lads. It's time to go on watch."

Is that me he wants?

"Come on, Bren. We have ten minutes to take over from Ken. Come on, get your arse out of the bed. What a day that was, did you get your lady's address?"

Rolling his six foot frame out from the tiered bunks, Brendan stretched and grinned hugely. "God, Don I can't stop grinning. What time is it?"

"Ten to eight. Have your cup of tea. Ken left it there on the desk. But get a move on. By the way, there's a couple of letters for you."

Letters! Great! thought Brendan. *Three—that's Ma's writing, one from the Doc, this other must be from Polly. Never wrote to her as I promised.*

"Come on, Bren."

"Right, Don. Roll on four o'clock when I can get back to bed. Don't we have to have cholera jabs tomorrow?"

"Of course!" he exclaimed, kicking the side of the desk in frustration. "I'd forgotten all about that. Third said to be at the agent's at ten in the morning. I'm supposed to be studying for exams as well. Bloody hell, what a life."

***

"Right we're on eight across at the moment, just about empty. Should be clear by twenty-thirty. We switch to five centre and that's the last of the white spirit. The second mate is on watch until ten, haven't seen him for a few hours. Now I'm going to get my head down, on again at four in the morning." So a weary Ken passed over responsibility for the watch to Don and Brendan and trudged off to his cabin.

"Right, you pair of wankers, get down on deck and take ulllages of eight across," instructed the second mate suddenly appearing in the deck office. "Right, Irishman, after that, get me a cup of tea. I hear you guys had a fruitful time ashore."

"That's right, Second," replied Don, swinging the brass lead weight at the end of the ullage tape. "Come on, Bren. You get the log to record the measurement.

Hi! Pumps," Don called to the pump man, a bald, oil-stained Corsican who was now standing in the doorway of the small office, wiping his hands on a rag.

"The pump, eet is playing de silly buggers, Mr. Second. I stop eet for a short while. Not bad, I hope? OK!"

"If you must, Pumps. It sounds all right to me."

"Mr. Second, if you wish to leave it on it OK by me. But it will go bumph soon." The pump man demonstrated by throwing his arms in the air. "Eet go bang!"

"OK, stop the pump. Go tell them on the shore what we're doing and tell me when the pump is in service again. Now I'm going up to my cabin. Don't forget the tea, Paddy," so instructed the unpleasant second mate as he exited the office.

After obeying the second's instruction, Brendan settled down in the office to read his letters. His mother just wished him all the best, thanked him for the money sent each month, £4 from his £8 monthly earnings.

The orchard was beginning to blossom. Pop was well, Jono had joined the British Army and Ma was now enjoying herself in the British Legion with two of her sons serving in the British forces.

There was another from Doctor de Courcy, offering congratulations on joining the Merchant Navy and his concern that De Valera, at the age of seventy-five, was still in control after the Irish election in March. The Doc was worried at the resurgence in the support for Sinn Fein. He was involved in the recent growth in Irish shipping and was away to Algeria to discuss some political question; he looked forward to hearing from Brendan soon.

Polly's letter was held over to last.

Opening the letter from Polly and feeling very guilty that he had not written to her, Brendan was pleased to hear she was well and wishing he were at home. She recalled the dances they had gone to and the fun they had had together, and hinted strongly they might have a future together and that she longed to see him again. Enclosed was a small black and white photograph of her in the one-piece swimsuit he had admired.

Putting the letter in his pocket, Brendan went out on the deck in the evening gloom and leaned on the ship's rail, looking at the lights coming on over Bombay city amid the haze of smoke. *Do I want to consider marriage, children? I've got so much to see and to do, the world, people, experiences, other women. I do like her a lot, flattered that she feels like she does—*

"Come on, Bren. Quit the daydreaming. The pump's working, get down on deck—"

Time passed slowly with the monotonous *thump, thump* of the pump, the closing and opening of tank valves, taking ullages—measuring the distance from the level of the oil to the top of the tank. Don and Brendan took it in turn to doze and read. Don got on top of some studying. Brendan did some reading and the second mate popped his head in every so often to ensure all was going well. He went off watch at midnight, to be relieved by the third mate. Around one o'clock, some of the crew returned very drunk and with a lot of singing and tomfoolery they traversed the gangplank and stumbled their way aft. Silence reigned apart from the odd toot from a tugboat announcing its presence. At a quarter to four, Brendan woke Ken and Barry, and by four fifteen was fast asleep.

"Come on, Don, Bren. Up you get. Time for breakfast."

"What do you want, Barry? Go away," growled Don, suddenly wakening. "Oh, yes, of course. Our bloody jabs. Thanks, Barry."

"Yep, Bren, the Indian is here with your shorts. Must get back on deck," said Barry as he left the cabin, leaving the sharp smell of oil behind him.

"Just one moment," answered Brendan to the knock on the door frame. "I'll be with you in a minit. Don, it's the tailor. OK! Come on in."

The beaming Indian pushed aside the door curtain to present himself and suitcase, and produced two sets of well-ironed shorts and shirts, brand, sparkling new.

The clothes fitted perfectly, and a very pleased tailor took his thirty rupees from each before bowing his way out of the cabin.

"Better be quick, Bren, with the breakfast. Let's get a taxi to the agent's office. It's a couple of miles away. It's eight thirty now, we could walk back and be ready for watch at twelve," Don suggested, as they rushed down to the dining saloon.

"Shipping Agencies—Signal Hill Avenue, pronto, if you please," ordered Brendan to the swarthy taxi driver behind the wheel of a rusty Ford Prefect car. "Look, Don. It must be a forties model still going strong. Janey Mac, he's going fast."

The driver, with flowing black hair and a big grin, was weaving his way through the crowded road, with his hand pressed on the car horn, swerving around pedestrians, racing past beggars sitting on the pavement with their feet on the road, and narrowly missing slow moving rickshaws.

"What a dump, Don. Look," Brendan said loudly. "There's an old red English bus. It's advertising Bovril; Bovril is Best. Look at all the rubbish."

The dirty streets in Dublin were sparkling clean by comparison to the filth he could see. Brendan mopped his brow, sweating heavily in the extreme heat. Wrinkling his nose to the unaccustomed smells he called out over the sound of the racing engine, "Don, I don't fancy walking back through this lot. Let's take the taxi back again."

"Nor do I, Bren, can't afford it though. I'm keeping my eye on the way we are going so that we'll know our way back. It's gone nine. We're back on watch at noon—hope there's no delay at the doc's."

With a dramatic sweep of the wheel, the taxi swerved to a halt in the forecourt of the 'doctor's', covering a small queue of ill-dressed natives in a cloud of red dust. Don and Brendan stepped out of the creaking vehicle, avoiding the malevolent stares of the dust-covered patients, and turned to the driver. Grinning mightily and with obvious disdain for his fellow countrymen, the driver directed Don and Brendan to the closed wooden door in the scruffy whitewashed building, stating he would wait for the Sahibs.

Wondering whether he should knock on the unwelcoming door, Brendan glanced at Don and, noticing the natives stepping back, pushed it open to see a room crowded with white-robed men, all standing facing turbaned men sitting behind a long metal grill. There was sudden silence; all heads turned and a hushed sigh sounded from all around—*who were these infidels in their shorts and bare legs, with their pink faces and short hair?* Brendan bowed his head to everybody, smiled, and greeted all present with the little Hindi he had learned from his phrase book, "*Shuha prabhas, shamma kare*"—good morning, excuse me. There was a startled silence, as turbaned heads looked at each other, *white men excusing themselves*. The atmosphere eased and to save the day, an Indian in European dress materialised and greeted Meesters Marshall and Mcabeee and ushered them apologetically into a side room.

"You are coming for the injections, sirs? My name is Hassan. Please be sit." He pointed to two rattan chairs at the side of the grimy whitewashed room and clapped his hands as a signal for two white-robed men to appear from behind a paper screen, one carrying a cloth covered tray and the other rubbing his hands down the side of his off-white gown. Mr. Hassan bowed to Brendan, pointed to his left arm and signalled Brendan to stretch his out. The robe carrying the tray produced a cloth, scrubbed a spot over the vein on the inside of Brendan's arm. The other robed man took a loaded syringe from the tray, shot some liquid from it into the air and then plunged the needle into Brendan's arm with some relish. Brendan stepped back with a startled, painful grunt. Mr. Hassan offered an apologetic smile and directed the syringe bearer to do the same with Don. A further cloth-covered phial of liquid was produced. With the needle wiped and transferred from Brendan's syringe, the robed assistant, smiling behind two gleaming dark eyes, jabbed Don's left arm with a flourish, producing a yelp of shock from the recipient. Mr. Hassan offered a further apologetic smile and produced a small piece of cotton, as if from the air, to each to mop up the blood. He then directed the two of them from the room, smiling and bowing.

Holding the cotton to stem the small spot of blood on the crook of their left arms, they re-entered the crowded adjoining room, eager to get away, expecting to be viewed again by the white-robed patients. It appeared they had found something more interesting to them than two pot-boiled Europeans.

"Can you see anything, Bren?" asked Don, wrinkling his nose at the smell of so many sweaty bodies. "You're a bit taller than me."

Stretching up on his toes, Brendan balanced against a white robe and looked out into the dusty hot yard.

"God, Don, it's our taxi driver. There are guys pulling him from the car. Look, they're beating him up."

Horrified, Brendan watched as the taxi driver was bundled into the back of the large Citroën car, which sped away, followed by an ancient Ford Popular car, driven by a policeman. "What's going on, Mr. Hassan?"

"We do not know, sirs. Now come quickly. I take you back to your ship."

Climbing into the large Mercedes car which had arrived alongside, Mr. Hassan directed Don and Brendan into the back seat and, with a wave of his arms and some rapid instructions in Indian, the car screeched away, covering the remaining queue of assorted patients in a cloud of red dust.

"My! He's in a hurry," exclaimed Brendan. "Hey! Mr. Hassan, what's the rush?"

"You have no need to know, sirs. I will return you safely back to ship. As agent of Calvex it is my duty," came the worried voice of Mr. Hussan as he looked anxiously to his left and right.

With a grunt of exasperation, the driver muttered, "*Soower ke bachche*"—son of a pig—and pulled to a stop behind a large wooden cart slewed across the road with its real wheel broken. The cart driver, with his robe caught in the edge of the cart, was shouting at the skinny horse rearing up in fright. Rickshaws had stopped with their riders shouting instructions. Mr. Hassan, looking over his shoulder, struck the car driver on the arm pointing to a space on the earthen pavement where he could squeeze the Mercedes. Blowing his horn furiously, the driver mounted the pavement, such as it was, scattering beggars and traders, a few being brushed by the cars fenders. With the way clear, the car sped up, leaving a scene of devastation behind.

"Wow, that was exciting," exclaimed Don. "Wonder what the hell is going on? Hey we should have turned right there. I remember the bank was on our left coming out. We're on the wrong road. Hey! Mr. Hassan! What the hell is going on?"

"Do not worry, sirs. We take short side to ship. We are losing them, Abdul, down there."

With a sudden turn of the wheel, the car banked heavily to the left, knocking over a few traders' stalls and, with a solid muffled bump, settled back on its four wheels, passing the waving angry stallholders.

"Thank God. There's the ship."

The *Calvex Renown* could be seen on the other side of the dock gates and as the Mercedes raced toward the gate, the keeper, recognising the agent who was waving furiously, unaccustomedly against his orders raised the barrier. Screeching to a stop at the end of the gangplank, Mr. Hassan instructed the two apprentices to get back on board and he would go speak with the captain.

Don and Brendan, slightly flustered, apprehensive and indeed very curious as to the reason for the race were instructed to go get their lunch and be ready to take watch at 1200. However, both were called to the captain's cabin, instructed to say nothing to anyone of their escapade and to continue with their duties. The captain also emphasised they were not to go ashore again and the police may call to interview them.

"Our lips are sealed," stated the two of them as they relieved Barry and Ken.

"We have been told to say nothing, all very secret," said Brendan.

"Wish we knew what was going on ourselves," whispered Don in an aside, "but let's get the most out of this. What's the cargo situation, Ken?"

"We finished discharging an hour ago now, and taking ballast," replied Ken in his official voice. "Should be finished in a few hours. The third mate is on. Look what's that car coming?" he said, pointing to the dock entrance. "Looks like police. What have you two been up to? This is getting interesting."

"Johnston, Jones, don't go anywhere. Our two smugglers have been called to the captain's cabin," called the third mate. "Pumps wants you down on deck. The wing tanks are near full."

Entering the large captain's cabin with its sofa and easy chairs all occupied by the police, the first mate, the agent, Brendan and Don were beckoned to stand in front of the captain's grand desk.

"Right, you two. What have you been up to? The police are here to interview you," glowered the captain.

"Have no idea, sir. We were just having our jabs" Don answered, pointing to the swelling on his left arm, as did Brendan. "The taxi driver was beaten up and then Mr. Hassan rushed us back here."

Standing up to his full height of five foot nothing, the captain leaned forward as far as his belly would allow and in a severe voice, looking to the police, asked in measured tones, "Did you take anything from the taxi driver?"

Both Brendan and Don answered emphatically in the negative.

"There you are, gentlemen," said the captain. "No. They took nothing. Now, may we proceed with the running of the ship and put an end to this nonsense?"

"One moment," interjected the taller and more impressive of the two uniformed men. "One moment. We wish to search the bodies." He instructed the other officer to approach the two young men.

"OK! Go ahead," Don replied. "We have nothing to hide."

After a fruitless search, the two policemen took Don's and Brendan's names and backed out from the cabin.

"Now, Mr. Hassan, explain yourself," ordered the captain and, in his best pidgin English, the agent explained that realising the two boys had been in the cab with the driver and there was some illegal contraband being exchanged, he considered it wise to race the two boys back to the ship to avoid any trouble.

"Well done, Mr. Hassan. Say thank you to Mr, Hassan, Boys, and get back to your duties," instructed the captain, dismissing Don and Brendan.

On their way down to relieve Ken and Barry, both boys breathed a sigh of relief and agreed they owed Mr. Hassan for his prompt action.

"How's your arm, Bren?"

"Bloody sore," replied Brendan. "Yours looks pretty painful too. What a day!"

Canal in Venice

Cape Town Harbour

11

Caring Nurses

"An' how's Rudolph, our favourite patient keeping today?" greeted Nurse Kathleen as she stepped between the curtains shrouding the bed from enquiring eyes. "I hear you've been a naughty lad again, cursin' Sister Sullivan. Tut! Tut!" admonished the nurse quietly as she tucked in a stray sheet corner. "I've bin readin' your diary, Rudie. You are the one for the girls. That nurse you met in England—" *how I envy her, sailing away to the US of A* "—she sounded very nice, Rudie. Did you ever meet with her again?" she asked, not expecting an answer, looking at the unconscious body lying on its back with wrists still tied to the bedside. "It must have been uncomfortable in the heat in the…where was it…Oh! Yes! De Persian Gulf. Reading your diary is shure helpin' me with me geography." She laughed to herself. "You're de talk of the nurses' quarters. We're all hoping you live. So come on, Rudi, giv us a smile," encouraged the nurse, as she stroked Brendan's brow and he slept in a deep drugged sleep. "What is it, Mary?"

The bedside curtains suddenly parted and Nurse Mary's head appeared, with her hat askew and her forefinger pressed against her pursed lips. "Sister's on the prowl. I could hear yu talkin' to Rudi—yes, I heard you. You quite fancy him, don't yu, Kathleen? You an' he would make a fine pair. I saw ye stroking his brow."

"Arr, go on wid ye, Mary Sheelin. I don't know what ye mean. Me fancy him? A long streak of a Prod." Nurse Kathleen recoiled and stood back from the bed, looking at Mary in feigned astonishment.

"Still an' all he does look a bit cute…"

"What are you about, Nurse Sheelin? Now get on wid your work," were the sudden orders made by Sister Sullivan as she brushed aside the curtains. "An' what are you doin' here, Nurse Fitzgerald? Now both of youse get on wid your duties an' leave this young man to recover. He does not need two worthless girls gossipin' over him."

As the two nurses scurried away, the curtains fell together and Sullivan stood with her hands on her hips, looking at the long thin body covered by a light sheet. *Yes! Mr. Harris. You have disturbed our existence here with your aura of mystery. What am I going to do with you? You've got a few of my nurses here in a tiswas.* She laughed silently to herself. *You've even got me wondering what you're like, an' who ye are. I haven't come across many prods in my life an' you're an interestin' one. There's talk that you brought a book in with you that you've written. Wonder where it is?*

In deep thought, Sister Sullivan absentmindedly tucked in a bedside corner before stepping out into the ward.

"Is everythin' all right der wid de young fella, Sister?"

The sudden question jolted Sullivan back into the present.

"I wish I could get half the 'tension that fella gets in an hour. It's like the market in Mullingar, wid all the nurses comin' to look at him," complained the farmer from County Westmeath, who had just lost a foot in an accident with a threshing machine and wasn't too sure whether the false teeth returned to his mouth were the right pair. *God Almighty what am I goin' to do widdout me foot?* he wondered. Not expecting an answer from this strict senior nurse, he was startled to get a reply.

"Mr. Fagan," admonished the sister in her well-practised withering tone. "Mr. Fagan, consider yerself lucky you only lost yer foot. That young man in there could lose his mind an' even die." With that retort ringing in the air, Sister Sullivan stormed down the ward, her large headdress swaying like a ship's sails.

"God, Paddy," exclaimed the farmer to the next bed. "I only arsked."

"Thank you both for coming in to see me regarding your son Brendan," offered Dr. Larrigan to Alice and Henry, both sitting on the edge of their seats after their call from Larrigan's secretary. "It is now a full week since he was admitted and this is just an update on your son's position. Don't look so worried, Mrs. Harris. All is going as well as can be expected. The trauma of the initial blow to the head has been overcome and your son is settling down to treatment. Looking at him in the bed with all the tubes and bottles around him I must agree is quite daunting," smiled Larrigan in sympathy. "They are all necessary and are used to regulate the flow of life. We are now spoon-feeding him with soups and he is responding well. We feel within the week he should regain consciousness. I must warn you, however, the full extent of his head injury will not be fully known until he awakens. I must say, young Brendan—" smiled Larrigan "—is quite a favourite with the nurses and everyone here wishes him well. Have you any questions? Oh! Of course, I forgot. Brendan's right leg appears to be knitting well and should offer no problem after a course of physiotherapy." Larrigan now looked enquiringly at both parents.

"Thanks, Doctor, we are very grateful," answered Alice. "Aren't we, Henry?"

"Of course…yes…we are both very grateful for all the attention given to our son, Doctor," answered Henry, shifting uncomfortably in the small wooden chair.

"Thank you, both. Things are looking very promising," offered Larrigan, rising from behind his desk to show the grateful parents to the door.

"That wasn't too bad, Hen. Bren seems to be recovering. I know it's not visiting time, but maybe they will let us into the ward to see him," suggested Alice, catching Henry's arm by the elbow and propelling him down the long corridor to the ward.

"Oh! Hello Mrs., Mr. Harris," greeted the nurse. "You'd like to see Rudolph? *Oh God, I've done it again!* "So sorry. Brendan, I mean. I'll go an' ask Sister."

Given permission to see Brendan for ten minutes, Alice and Henry stepped inside the bedside curtains to see Brendan propped up by pillows behind him. The turban had been removed, replaced by a light bandage around the head. His wrists were still tied to the bedside, whilst a nurse fed him with a white liquid from a spoon. Brendan's eyes were closed and he was eagerly drinking the liquid.

"Oh! What a relief, Hen, to see him like that!" cried Alice, squeezing Henry's arm. "Maybe we'll be able to talk with him in a week or so. Must tell Polly. She will be pleased.

***

"Hello, Brendan. It's Polly here. Can you hear me?" Not expecting any response, Polly tucked her dress under her thighs as she sat on the uncomfortable hospital chair alongside the bed. "Your ma says the doctor is very pleased with your recovery and has every expectation you'll be up and sailing before the month end." *Am I wasting my time here? When I touch him…there again, I just touched his face, and he turned his head away. If only I had that diary of his I could read some of it to him.* "Oh! Hello, Mrs. Harris. There's no change. Poor Bren is still in another world."

"Hello, Polly. Thanks for coming in. How did you get here? We could have brought you in."

"Gordon, my brother, drove me in. He's out in the car park, waiting for me."

"Henry and I could take you back home after visiting hour. Do you want to go down and tell him?"

"No! No! Thanks, Mrs. Harris," answered Polly, "we're going on into the city, but thanks. Oh! I see Billy is with you. Hello, Billy. How're you keeping? Bren seems to be improving."

"Yes. From what I hear, he should be up and chasing the girls in a week or two," answered Billy in a light sarcastic tone.

"Look, Mrs. Harris, I'll leave now. There are too many of us an' the matron might get annoyed again. By the way, have you seen the diary? I left it with the nurses a few days ago," Polly asked as she stepped out between the curtains.

Catching Polly's arm, Billy called out, "There's a nurse I recognise—she was here a few days ago. Hey, Nurse?" he called out to the hurrying Nurse Mary Sheelin, carrying a rather full bed pan.

"Yes, sir, I'll be back in a jiffy," Nurse Mary replied, nodding her head to the cloth-covered bed pan, wrinkling her nose in distaste. "Kathleen, Kathleen," Mary called out anxiously, "the good-lookin' lad with the Harris tribe—ye kno the one—wants to talk wid me. What do I tell him?"

"Ye mean about the diary thing? Oh! Jeasus, Mary and Joseph, what do we do it's still in the flat." After a moment of deep thought, Kathleen stood to attention, stuck her chest out and announced, "I kno'. I'll be honest and tell 'im the truth. I'll flutter me eyelashes an' say I took it home an' will have it for him tomorra. Leave 'im to me, Mary."

With that, Kathleen strode out into the ward toward Billy and Polly standing outside the curtained bed. Her footsteps faltered, she slowed… *What if they tell Sister? What if Matron hears of it? God, I'll have to do some charmin'.*

"Hello, Mr. Harris, I'm Nurse Fitzgerald. How can I help you? An' you, Miss?" Kathleen asked, directing her gaze at Billy and nodding a welcome to Polly.

"Yes, Nurse," replied Billy, somewhat startled by the appearance of this attractive female in blue uniform with starched hat. *Wow, she is a looker.* "Hello, Nurse. You sound as if you're from Wicklow."

"Yes. I'm from Enniskerry. You're a Dublin man, I can hear. About your brother's diary…will it be all right if I give it to you tomorrow. I must admit I took it back to my flat," she smiled at Billy, "and I hope you don't mind I read some of it. Found it very interesting."

"One moment, Nurse," interjected Polly in indignation. "You had no right taking this private property. I've a good mind to report this matter to the sister."

"Don't do that, Polly," interrupted Billy, not wishing this striking nurse to get into trouble. "Everything will be all right. We will have it tomorrow, won't we?" questioned Billy with a conspiratorial glance at Nurse Kathleen.

"Yes, Miss, I will have it to you tomorrow. I shall put it in Rudy's—I mean Mr. Harris's locker," offered Nurse Kathleen.

Getting a disgruntled nod from Polly, Nurse Kathleen caught Billy's eye, gave him a dazzling smile and turned away in triumph.

12

Night Club in Cape Town

"Well that was a bit of an adventure, Don. Wonder how our Taxi driver is? He looked in a bad state when those guys were beating him up."

"Could have been us, Bren," replied Don. "We were lucky to get away as we did. Damn, I've got a splinter in my knee." Don sat back on his haunches, throwing the metal scraper to the deck as he examined his bare knee. Both apprentices were scraping paint spots off the wooden decks at the accommodation structure. Brendan was getting used to doing the menial jobs allocated to apprentices; scraping paint off wooden decks was not what he had expected but if that's the way it goes, so be it.

"Have you been to the Persian Gulf before, Don?"

"Came here before Nasser sunk the ships in the canal on one of the crude oil boats. Went to Abadan right up to the north of the Gulf. This time, as you know, we're heading for Mena Al Amadhi in Kuwait."

"God, must be time for 'smoke'. I'm fed up with this wind blowing up my shorts," laughed Brendan.

"Better wait until Ken calls us. Seems like a bit of a sandstorm blowing up. Yep! There's Ken. OK, Ken?" acknowledged Don with a wave as Ken made the motions of lighting a cigarette from the bridge wing.

The four gathered in Ken's and Barry's cabin, having first got their tea at the saloon kitchen and settled down for twenty minutes or so with their fags. Tipped cigarettes were the choice of the day. The tip filtered the smoke, supposedly reduced the nicotine content, and made them healthier. Brendan, who had only started because everybody else did and they seemed to enjoy inhaling the smoke, smoked his twenty Kensitas a day.

"There's a bit of a storm blowing up," advised Ken. "Better give up the scraping for the moment. The centre castle needs a sweeping out. Bren and Barry, you could do that. You and I, Don, are needed up in the chartroom—the third mate needs a hand. God! The wind is sure increasing."

The *Renown*, now riding very high in the water after discharging its cargo in Bombay, was beginning to roll and lurch quite dramatically.

"Right 'smokoes' over. Let's go."

Brendan, finding it difficult, as they all did, to keep his footing with the erratic rolling of the ship, struggled to reach the cabin door. One moment he was lurching toward the door the next he was falling away from it. "Grab hold of what you can, lads," called Ken, laughing.

When Brendan stepped outside, facing the stern, he was hit by a strong hot wind filled with rain and sand coming over the starboard side. The ballasted ship was riding a deep swell with the hull high in the water, rising and falling, with the engine noise roaring as the propellers left the water when the ship plunged its bows under the large waves. The air was hot, with menacing grey bulky clouds on the horizon, the startling sight of lightning forking through the layers; a knocking sound could be heard coming from the centre castle.

"Wonder what that is, Barry? Wonder if the doors are shut?"

The centre castle was the large space under the officers' accommodation on the main deck, with storage space for all things necessary for running the ship—ropes, paint, lifeboat parts, laundry, oil drums and whatever other spare parts could be needed in the future.

"Look, there's the bosun!"

The bosun, along with three of the crew dressed in their assorted warm weather clothes—shorts, dungarees, paint-stained shirts—came racing down the flying bridge, their arms out, leaning against the strong wind.

"C'mon you two. Giv' us a hand to shut these doors." called the bosun, as he and the others split up in pairs, two to starboard two to port. Brendan joined the boson's group, slid down the ship's ladder to the main deck and proceeded to help pull the heavy storm door from its grip on the bulkhead wall.

"Hey, Bosun, before we shut this, hadn't we better see there's no one in there an' check what's knockin'?"

"Gud thinking, lad. Hold on, boys. Go on, Paddy, have a look inside, Jeasus this wind is strong," shouted the bosun as a sheet of sand-laden water swept over the deck.

"Anybody there?" roared Brendan stepping, over the coaming and into the dark, large, echoing chamber. Calling again, Brendan was ready to step back into the wind, when he thought he heard a call over the noise of the wind and the creaking of the ship. "Wait Bos'n. I think I hear someone. Who's there?"

"Here! Over here!" was the reply from deep in the dark room. "Over here at the paint locker. I'm caught. Ooh! That hurt."

"It's the cabin boy, lads," called the bosun. "Mick, Joe, com' on. Paddy, will you hang on here?"

"OK, Bos'n," Brendan replied.

"He's just bruised, Paddy. Silly little shit. What was he doin' here?" an exasperated bosun shouted over the wind as he and a shivering youngster, supported by the two grinning seamen, stepped out onto the open deck. "We'll get the chief steward to have a look at him."

The cabin boy, about Brendan's age and dressed in a pair of torn dungarees and T-shirt, broke away from the seamen, favouring his right leg and crying out he was all right and he didn't want help from 'you bastards'.

"Hang on to him, Mick, while we shut this door," ordered the bosun, struggling with the heavy metal storm door. With a resounding thump, the storm door shut and a wet but exhilarated Brendan went to the cabin boy to see if he could help.

"I doan wanna your help, sir," cried the bedraggled cabin boy. "I'm all rite. Now f--- off. No! Sorry, sir." The confused lad tried to struggle way from the seaman's grip, only to fall against a ship's railing as the ship again rolled suddenly, bringing the seaman with him.

"God, they were nearly over the side," yelled the bosun. "Jeasus, let's get this little bastard locked away. We've got better things to do."

"You go ahead, Bosun." shouted Brendan over the screaming wind. "I'll take the lad up to the steward. Do you know his name?"

"Why the f--- should I know the little shit's name? Right, lads, we've got to look at that lifeboat. Cum' on."

"What's your name?" asked Brendan, as he staggered toward the wet and shivering cabin boy hanging onto the ship's railing in terror. "Come on. Let's get out of this shit, fella." Brendan stretched out his hand.

"What are you up to, Bren?" It was Barry, leaning on the rail of the deck above. "Throw the bugger overboard."

The now submissive cabin boy caught Brendan's hand and the two of them staggered to and climbed the ship's ladder to the deck above.

"This lad is hurt. Will you help me get him to the chief steward?" Brendan asked.

A grinning Barry complied and between the two of them they got the exhausted and weeping cabin boy into the small hospital room. Barry went to get the steward: the nearest member of the crew with any first aid knowledge.

"Just bruises and a few pains and I think he has been interfered with," grumbled the chief steward. "I'll have to report this to the captain and you, young Irishman, will have to make a statement, along with the bosun."

Poor lad, thought Brendan. *What does he mean, interfered with?* Brendan knew the cabin boy was labelled as the lowest in the steward's pecking order. The youngest member of the crew seemed like he was very frightened. *Wonder what happened? Why was he in the centre castle on his own? What was he up to? God, he's the same age as myself and he called me sir. Called me sir and I a lowly apprentice. Suppose to him I must appear like an officer with authority. Gosh! Wonder what happened? Better write down some notes.*

Musing these thoughts over in his mind, Brendan staggered his way up to his cabin to get a shower and dry off.

As quickly as the storm started it ceased. The seas began to settle, the wind reduced, the masts whipping some thirty degrees from the vertical, all settled down.

After the severe storm the sky had turned a wonderful blue, with a very hot sun beginning to scorch the decks and any unwary humans. The decks were, however, covered in sand brought in by the wind from the deserts in Saudi Arabia, and the bosun with a few of the seamen had begun to hose them down. The stewards began sweeping out the accommodation; the sand seemed to get everywhere. Brendan and Barry, being the lowest in the officer pecking order, were delegated to sweep out the wheelhouse and chartroom. Brendan, whilst working in the chartroom, noticed Michael Read the third mate, making an entry on the chart attached to the table top.

"We're just going through the Straits of Hormuz into the Persian Gulf, Brendan. Look, that's our dead reckoning position. We are in the traffic separation lane—keeps northbound tankers separate from the southbound ones."

"How wide is the strait? I see that's Iran to the starboard. Is that Oman to port?" asked Brendan, examining the large paper chart with the pencil lines marking the course taken by the *Renown* through the strait.

"The narrowest part is about thirty-four miles wide and the only sea passage to the open ocean for the Persian Gulf. Over the year, many thousands of tankers go through here. We're heading for Mena, the oil port of Kuwait. It's a very interesting part of the world this…"

The third hesitated here and looked at Brendan with the question in his eyes—*Do you want me to go on or just shut up?* Brendan, eager to hear what the third had to say, acknowledged the look and the third continued.

"Over there to starboard we have Iran with the Shah, there's going to be trouble there in the near future. At the moment, Britain and the US are supporting the Shah in his wish to suppress communism. Over there—" he pointed to port "—is Oman. The Sultan is repelling forces supported by Nasser of Egypt, and Iraq to the north has restless natives.

Kuwait, where we're heading for, way back in 1899 entered into a treaty with the US that gave us control over their foreign policy in exchange for protection and money. This was before oil was discovered in 1930. Kuwait is now independent under the protection of the British Empire."

"I am impressed, Third, very interesting. Why was Britain bothered about Kuwait in—when did you say?"

"That was in 1899, Bren. Britain feared that a railway between Berlin and Baghdad would lead to an expansion of German influence in the Gulf and as there was a suspicion of oil, the UK wanted some control. The dispute between Britain and Germany over the railway was settled somewhere around 1914. Now that's enough history lessons for the day. Must get on with looking after the ship." With that, the third with an embarrassed smile strode back out into the wheelhouse.

What a guy. I'm very impressed. Must get to know some more about him. Maybe he can give me some help about the cabin boy. What did the steward mean by interfered with? I don't want to ask the other guys about it, as they will all just jeer me.

"OK, lads!" called Ken as they all met in the saloon after dinner that evening. "We're due into Mena tomorrow. Now. this will be a quick turnaround. I'll take first watch with you, Bren and you, Don and Barry, take the next eight hours. If all goes as expected, we will take about ten hours to load fifteen thousand tons of crude and we will be heading out of this hothouse within twenty-four hours. The latest news is Lands End for orders. So we could end up at any refinery between here and the UK. Have you got a minute, Bren? Like a word with you. Piss off, Barry. I don't want any comment from you."

Brendan followed Ken out onto the deck.

"It's about the cabin boy, Bren," Ken said.

"Yeah! Thought as much, Ken," Brendan confirmed, as he and Ken leaned on the rail at the ship's side.

"Just look at those stars—thousands of them. What a lovely night. Quite a life, isn't it, Bren?"

"Yeah, I agree with you there, Ken. The cabin boy, the poor lad. What's going on? He was terrified, scared out of his wits."

"The mate has asked me to talk to you about that. I'm not too sure of the exact detail but apparently…you know the cabin boy is there to wash dishes, make beds and do whatever he's told? He's grouped with the stewards and there's often one or two of them who's a bit queer. Well, there is one of them got the lad in the centre castle and did his thing with him."

Still not quite understanding the subtleties of Ken's words, Brendan realised, "You mean he interfered with him."

"Yeah, Bren," answered Ken, relieved Brendan had understood so quickly.

"God, I feel so stupid Ken. Does that mean the guy who attacked the cabin boy is a queer?"

"Quite probably, Bren. Now don't say anything to anyone about this. OK? The mate has it all in hand."

"Shure," agreed Brendan, "Ken, I won't say a word, but I hope that cabin boy is OK."

However what's a queer? Must find out somehow. I have the idea it's when a man fancies a man. But for a man to beat up a young boy, it must be something else…

These were Brendan's troubled thoughts as he went to bed that night. Why was he so fortunate to be in however lowly the ranking position he was in whilst the cabin boy was at the bottom of the abyss?

"There we are, Bren, there's where the money is," mused Don, pointing to the low-lying coastline ahead of the ship. "Mina Al-a-bloody Madi. We will have a hectic few hours ahead of us. Look! There's another Calvex boat anchored. Wonder if any of the guys I know are here. God, it's getting hot."

It was only ten o'clock in the morning and the sun, high in the sky, was remorseless in its scorching rays. All exposed metal was red hot and the temperature on the main deck, by midday, reached one hundred and twenty degrees.

Brendan in his working shorts and old torn shirt was feeling on top of the world. He'd had a good night's sleep, was up-to-date with his studies, had settled in with some new friends and found his place in the running of the ship. He was well fed, beginning to get a sun tan, still being plagued with acne but otherwise in good health, age seventeen and with the world ahead of him. He and Don were washing down the bulkheads around the accommodation decks. Not a very uplifting task but part of being a navigating apprentice.

"Enough of the chatter, you two. Get on with your work," grinned Mike Read, the third mate, as he walked past in his immaculate white officer's uniform.

"Sorry, sir," apologised Don, bowing his head in mocking submission. "We know our place."

Mike acknowledged their submission with a wave as he mounted the steel steps to the bridge.

"A nice guy that, Bren," said Don. "He was an apprentice only six months ago. Won't be long before we're doing the same. You've missed a patch there, you Irish nit," laughed Don as he threw a soaked sponge at Bren.

***

"The oil is coming in at a hell of a lick. It's estimated to finish in ten hours. Ken keep your eye on tank five and you, Paddy, on seven. Number five should be about max in ten minutes."

The *Renown* was now alongside the oil jetty with two land pipes connected. These were straining and leaping with the pressure of the oil racing through.

"OK, Second, I'll go stand by five. We want ullage of three feet, isn't it?" confirmed Ken as he made his way down to the red-hot deck with the brass-headed metal tape to determine the remaining ullage: the space between the oil surface and the top of the ullage plug standing eighteen inches above the deck level. The metal deck was now becoming so hot they needed to wear leather-soled shoes, and the sickly, overpowering smell of the oil fumes forcing through the only outlet—the six-inch top of the ullage pipe—was making them quite nauseous.

"Ullage six feet," called Ken. "Eighteen inches to go."

Brendan dropped the brass plug into the ullage pipe and, holding his breath, placed his head into the stream of noxious rushing gas to measure how high the swirling oil had reached.

And so, for the next six hours, they took ullages, closed valves, opened valves, had their hats blown off by the force of the expelled gas from the tanks and wiped the smelly crude oil from their faces and their eyes. Protective glasses were worthless, as they were immediately covered by the fine oil spray. They sweated profusely in the searing heat and by the end of their watch felt pretty sick from the heat, the exertion, the smell and, of course, the accidental breathful of gas.

Five hours later, the *Renown* pulled out from the jetty, fully loaded, to head to Lands End for Orders (LEFO) and allowed the next in the queue to go alongside.

After an uneventful ten days, the *Renown* joined the convoy of ships in the canal, still on her way to LEFO. When she reached the Bitter Lakes to let the southbound convoy through, the eagerly awaited orders arrived: discharge at Venice. *Venice: 'white swan of cities'*. Immediately on hearing the word Venice, Brendan thought of his favourite poem by Longfellow. The only full poem he ever remembered from school days.

After that, it would be the boring trip back to Mena. But Venice, thought Brendan, this was something to look forward to—St. Mark's Square, The Bridge of Sighs, The Doge's Palace and the beach, The Lido where the film stars disport themselves. Summertime, though—unfortunately there would be lots of visitors.

The *Renown* arrived at Venice in the early hours of Friday the twelfth and anchored until midday, when they steamed into Port Maghera and tied up alongside the San Leonardo landing stage. The crude oil was pumped ashore by pipeline, eleven kilometres long, under the lagoon to the storage tanks on the Isola dei Petroli: a small island at the side of the lagoon.

    Duties done, Brendan decided that evening to go and see some of the highlights of this wonderful city. After obtaining directions from the shore men and with a few thousand liras in his pocket, dressed to kill in his light brown slacks, fawn shirt, brown jacket and open-toed sandals, he made his way to the nearest bus stop. In his hesitant Italian, he paid the fare to the Piazzala Roma on the island and then found a ferry that would take him to San Marco Square.

    Amongst the chattering people on the ferry, Brendan felt great anticipation as he stepped off at the Piazza San Marco. He had done some reading about the city, as he wanted to savour the atmosphere and history of such a famous place and had purchased a guide to the island. As he walked slowly into the square, on his left could be heard the string orchestra laying a Strauss Waltz in the Cafe Quadri. There was the stunning Basilica San Marco and the famous slender Campanile di San Marco with its bell tower. Alongside this were the Doge's Palace, the old headquarters of the Doges. *God look at the girls! Wow! There are some beauties look at the dresses.* With some envy, he passed the café with its patrons all chattering away in the warm twilight evening. Couples with linked arms walked by, talking animatedly in a multitude of languages. *Oh! To be part of this, to speak the language, to have the money, enough money to even buy a coffee.*

    "Excuse me, *senorita*," smiled Brendan as he bumped into a couple of attractive sun-tanned, well-dressed ladies.

    "That's a'right, son," came the acknowledgement in a rolling American accent. "That's a'right. Tell me—which is the Doggies Palace? We canna make it out," the taller of the two ladies questioned him with a quizzical smile.

    Brendan, always the one to take advantage of any opportunity to impress the ladies, answered in Irish Italian, "*Buena sera, senoritas*. The Doge's Palace across the square over there, ladies. Beside Saint Mark's Basilica is the Doge's Palace or, as we call it here in *Venitio*, the *Palazzo Ducale*."

    With a further quick glance in the growing darkness at the travel brochure, as the two interested ladies looked to where he was pointing, he continued in a mix of Irish American and Italian, "The paved area, you may see if you look closely, that stretches around the Doge's Palace, is known as the *Piazzetta* and as we know, the word *piazza* means a square in Italia and, of course, a *piazzetta* is a little square." In his most seductive voice, enjoying the reaction to his play-acting, Brendan indicated with a nod of his head the café behind him. "And, of course, we have behind us the famous Gran Caffe Quadri and Caffe Lavena here for many years with the wonderful orchestra playing—is that now a Strauss waltz?"

Catching the younger of the two ladies by the waist, Brendan, who was quite practised at dancing the waltz back in Ireland, began to swing the surprised woman around in waltz time, both laughing an apology on bumping into the passersby, who stepped back grinning. Some called out *bravo* and joined in with the impromptu dance. Suddenly, out of the onlookers, came a jeering English voice.

"Well, look who it is! If it isn't our Irishman." It was the second mate from the *Renown*, with one of the engineer officers. Putting on an Irish accent, he continued in a mocking tone, "Hello der, Paddy, an' who's yer little lady?" He pushed aside anyone close to him and grasped Brendan's partner on the buttocks. "Oops! Sorry, lady!" The second laughed drunkenly, breathing stale beer fumes into the woman's face as she turned in surprise. The atmosphere immediately changed as the smiling onlookers all melted away and Brendan's two ladies linked arms and pushed their way back into the passing holidaymakers, looking back in disgust. Brendan was horrified.

"You bastard!" he confronted the grinning second mate and walked away seething.

His evening ruined, he made his way back to the ship.

***

Brendan was now into his first year at sea. He had travelled many miles, had seen the aftermath of war, the effects of poverty, the attitude to life in lands with hot climates, as opposed to his upbringing in a temperate country. He had visited cities steeped in history and just touched in Kuwait a way of life completely foreign to his norms.

On a personal note, he had adjusted to living in close proximity to others. He was learning to take orders to attend to the most menial of jobs. He was learning about his attraction to the opposite sex—he had heard so many stories of his peers' conquests. He was eager to reach his own. He was aware of his good fortune to be in the position he was in: being paid to travel the world.

There was, of course, the requirement to study and live within the paltry salary as an apprentice, but with confidence and ambition he knew he would make his way through his chosen profession as a ship's officer. Sometimes he had his doubts, though. He wished to impress. The latest episode with the second mate disturbed him. He didn't know whether to make a complaint to the chief officer, but thought he'd probably be laughed at.

He was quite pleased with the way he had adjusted to ship's life; it felt very far away from home. The studying was quite hard. There was a lot to learn—both the theory and the practical side. His first exams were due in three months. *But that's a long time away. Right, I've a good pal with Don. Barry is a pain and Ken is a bit aloof. Wonder if I'll ever meet that French girl I met on the boat coming over? Gosh! Was that only three months ago? What about Joan at the Seaman's Club in Newcastle. She was going to Philadelphia as a nurse—really fancied her. That girl in the bikini at Bombay—she was a bit of a smasher. What's this about prostitutes? The seamen are full of talk about what they do to them and some of them get the clap. What's the clap? Was that VD for Venereal Disease? They were weird pictures that seaman showed me the other day—he thought donkeys and women. God! How awful. He got them in Port Said. What do I do about Polly? Hope she's enjoying herself and gets that letter I sent from Venice.*

What about smoking? Twenty fags a day seems to be the usual. The mate was boasting about the forty a day he smokes. His voice sounds all husky. These Senior Service ones I'm smoking...maybe I should go on to those tipped ones, Kensitas. All the same price. These Passing Cloud cigarettes—the guys all laugh and say they're for the poofters or queers. Tried one the other day, oval in shape and smell of perfume. What exactly is a poofter or a queer? Wonder how the cabin boy is faring. Haven't seen much of him over the last weeks. Of course, his part in the running of the ship is miles away from mine.

...So Brendan mused to himself, leaning on the taffrail one moonlit evening, as the empty tanker made its return journey south through the Red Sea, heading for Mena Al Ahmadi to load cargo with LEFO the next destination.

"Heard the new orders, Bren?" Receiving the negative, Don explained, "After loading at Mena, we're heading south around Cape Hope, bunkering at Cape Town and then across the South Atlantic to La Plata, in Argentina. Probably load a cargo of crude somewhere in America and back to the UK. Let's see, it's now the middle of July, we go back through the canal up to Mena, load—that should be about the end of July. Then it's head south another three weeks over the line to Cape Town, then across the south Atlantic to La Plata, another few weeks that's the end of September."

"Yeh, Don. Do you think there's any chance we could dock at Philadelphia? Is there a refinery there? Fancy surprising that nurse Joan I met in the UK. She was going to Philly. That would be a surprise for her."

"You bet, Bren. I'm sure she's just waiting for a randy Irishman to turn up," laughed Don. "I do think there is a refinery there. Yes, a lad I was with on the *Calvex Cruise* was saying he went there a few years ago."

***

Sailing through the Indian Ocean leaving the coast of Africa to the right the *Calvex Renown* passed by the island of Mozambique, rounded the Cape of Good Hope and picked up the pilot outside Cape Town harbour.

"Gentlemen," came the announcement from the tall rangy South African pilot as he directed the tanker toward the harbour entrance. "Gentlemen, the flat top of the mountain is often covered in orographic clouds. Clouds formed when a south-easterly wind is directed up the mountain's slopes into colder air, where the moisture condenses to form the so-called 'table cloth' of cloud. Legend attributes this phenomenon to a smoking contest between the devil and a local pirate called Van Hunks. When the table cloth is seen, it symbolises the contest. That is your introduction to this wonderful part of the world Cape Town Table Mountain… Slow ahead."

"Slow ahead," repeated Brendan, as he brought the shiny brass handle on the telegraph anti-clockwise to signal to the engine room an engine instruction was to follow, with a sharp forward move to rest at the labelled instruction. The engine room answered and the engine beat reduced.

The bows of the *Calvex Renown* entered the harbour, guided by the tugboats, between the pier heads. The Table Mountain stood out as a cragged backdrop, with the devil and Van Hunks having a little tiff on the summit, fronted by the many town buildings, cargo ships and passenger liners along the waterfront.

What have I got to look forward to here? Wonder if we'll get ashore? thought Brendan as he completed the log book, the *Renown* now being alongside the bunker terminal.

"Hey, Bren," came the call from the deck below the wheelhouse. "Come on, quick! The third wants us in the saloon."

"Comin', Don." *Wonder what this is? Maybe some post. Hope Polly got my letter — hope there's one from her.*

"Come on, Bren! The third has some news."

Following Don into the saloon, Brendan nodded to the other three apprentices, the radio officer and the third mate, all with expectant faces and smiles.

"Right, we're all together, then," announced the third. "I have some news you might be interested in. Has anyone heard of the Blue Moon Hotel?" Looking around the expectant faces with no response, the third continued, "The captain has been offered by the British Consul six tickets for a dance tonight at the Blue Moon Hotel in Lakeside. Anyone interested?"

"You bet, Third," was the immediate spontaneous response.

"I take it you all want to go then," laughed the third. "The Consul has been very generous and laid on a taxi for us, so get a meal into you, get your gladrags on and be ready for twenty-hundred hours tonight.

The chief steward will fund you some local money. We sail tomorrow at oh-eight-hundred. It's the six of us so let's have a good night of it and all come back sober."

With enough South African rand to buy a few moderately priced drinks, and in great anticipation, Brendan joined the other five as the taxi, a Chevrolet De Luxe 1950 monster coloured a dark blue with dashing silver edging and sweeping winged bumpers, pulled up alongside the ship. The third mate, dressed in a double-breasted grey suit with brown shoes, wearing a plain tie and his hair close-cut, led the way down the gangplank ,followed by the radio officer in brown slacks and grey sports jacket with a brown bow tie. Don looked very smart in a brown suit with brown tie and his hair in his well coiffured wave. Ken wore grey slacks with a grey sports jacket with red tie and hair well greased. Brendan followed up with well polished brown leather shoes, grey slacks with the twenty-two-inch bottoms, a white shirt with blue tie and a grey sports jacket with light grey flecks…and his brown hair in that cursed fringe. Barry surpassed all, with his double-breasted, brown-flecked, worsted suit, with shiny brown shoes and his hair well greased to his head.

The driver in a smart uniform bowed them all into the Chevy: the third mate and radio officer on the front bench seat and the four apprentices squeezed into the back.

"Sit back, genteelmen," announced the driver in a marked Cape Town accent. "My name is Kurt. Ve are on our way to Blue Moon, as they say 'Bop and Spoon in the old Blue Moon'."

With a loud roar, the heavy Chevy pulled away from the ship and with dextrous movements, the driver had the large car and its expectant passengers smoothly on their way to adventures new.

"The Blue Moon, gentlemen, opened its doors in 1939, on the eve of the war, and has been very popular ever since. It has a lovely spring floor—when you stand on it, you can feel yourself moving—it glides under your feet. I met my wife there ten years ago an' have glided through life ever since. You've just come from England I hear?"

"Yes!" replied the third. "On our way to Argentina. What time does the dance hall close, Kurt?"

"Any time after one a.m., sir. I'll be there waiting in the car park for you. Now, there can be some rough gadms, so beware. Oh! Gadms are baddies, gangsters. You're all looking very neat and English, so keep together as you never kno'. Should be there in twenty min or so. Di ye mind if I put the radio on?"

With an OK from the third, Kurt turned a few dials and the radio blasted out the rock 'n' roll tune "Rock around the Clock" by Bill Haley, followed by "Check your time with the LM chime—it's eight o'clock".

"Here we are, lads—the Blue Moon Hotel. As they say, 'Bop and spoon at the old Blue Moon'. Enjoy yerselves. I'll be here from midnight. Keep your eye out for the gadms. Ye know, the baddies."

Pulling to a halt in the car park outside the custard-coloured building with its many lights and square Art Deco style front, the six young men stepped out into the cool night air all in great anticipation. Mike Read—the third—enjoined them all to stay together until they had discovered the 'lay of the land'.

"Here are your entrance tickets. I see the Consul has catered for one drink each. Remember what Kurt said—beware of the gadams. Now let's get in there, fellas, and let's Bop and Spoon!"

To the sound of the recent hit song "Long Tall Sally" beating out in the main room, the six lads presented their pass tickets, feeling somewhat conspicuous in their rather formal clothes compared to the surrounding dance goers in their varied relaxed gear.

"Good evening, gentlemen," greeted the large, dinner-jacketed, bow-tied doorman in a put-on English accent and with a big grin on his red face. "Good evening. Are you all from England? 'Tis not often we get Poms here, but welcome."

"I'm not a Pom, buster," bristled Barry. "I'm a Welshman and this guy here's an Irishman."

"Blimey. Sorry, Taffy," grinned the doorman. "And you, Paddy. You're all welcome here, even the Poms. That all right by you, sport?" He nodded toward Mike Read.

"That's OK… sport," replied the third. "Now let's get in before there's any trouble, especially from you, Taffy."

Barry reacted to the slight admonishment by stepping back, ready to defend his race, only to be hustled in by Ken.

"Come on, Barry. Don't be so touchy. Come on…"

"An' now, ladies and gentlemen," interrupted the band leader from the stage at the far end of the hall "We are going to play a medley of quickstep songs starting with 'So Rare', made popular by the Mills Brothers, followed by the 'Isle of Capri' by the Gaylords, finishing with that Guy Mitchell favourite 'Singing in the Rain'. So get your partners and let's dance."

Swinging into a quickstep, the ten-piece band filled the air with rhythm and a few couples started to dance on the large sprung floor. Brendan, who fancied his ability, had the rhythm but hadn't perfected the steps, started to swing to the beat.

"Where's the bar?" called Don, his voice raised over the sound of the band. A few heads turned at the sound of this very English voice. There were groups of youngsters, males with their tight trousers, and bopper shoes and varied hairstyles, and girls with their short, tight-waisted dresses and ponytail hairstyle. Some in flat shoes; all contrasted with the old-fashioned clothing of the visitors.

"Hiya, girls," waved the radio officer: the only one of the group dressed to suit the occasion, wearing tight trousers, check shirt and an unfortunate yellow cardigan. His white plimsolls matched the boppers worn by the youngsters.

"There's the bar, boys. Look, they have glasses already filled. Hello, miss," Don called to the woman behind the bar—a smart, slim woman in a short black pleated dress with low neckline. "What's in the glasses?"

Obviously surprised by Don's London accent, the woman turned to face him with a large smile on her face.

"Well, cobber, it's a treat to hear an accent from home. I'm a London girl. It's Brandy and coke—the favourite drink here. I see you have chitties. Let's have 'em, boys. You'll like 'em." She handed out the glasses half full of the brown concoction. "Hey! Mary, a bunch of lads from the UK," the smiling girl called over to another smartly dressed girl serving behind the bar. "My name's Alice. Mary's from Dublin."

"Well would you believe it? You might know it—we have our own Dublin man here," said Don.

"Hiya, Mary," interrupted Brendan. "We're off the tanker in Cape Town just for the night. You're not very busy here now. My name's Brendan Harris, from Dunlaoghaire."

"God bless us, a man from Dunlaoghaire. I'm from Finglas meself. Hold on. What is it? Two of the brandies? OK! Sorry about dat, Brendan. Are you here for the dancing? I'll be busy all night but a few of my friends are here. Would you like to meet them? Hey, Nuala," called Mary, waving through the cigarette smoke at a small group of girls sitting around one of the tables at the side of the dance floor. "Hey, Nuala, come over and meet Brendan and his friends. Der looking for some company for the evening. Off one of the ships in de town."

A small slim girl, dressed in the swinging pleated skirt which seemed to be the fashion, with tanned legs and a low cut blouse showing a deal of cleavage, beckoned Brendan and the others.

"Come on, lads," encouraged Don, waving back. "Let's join the party."

"Pull one of those empty tables over," suggested Ken.

"That's a good idea," said Nuala. "There are four of us and six of you lot. Hold on, Francis, Margi, do you want to join us? There's some lads here looking for a bit of company," she called over to two girls at a table on their own.

Barry, surprised all by striding over on his short legs and bowing to the two hesitant girls, and in his Welsh accent suggested, "Francis, Margi, we would be delighted for you to join us."

The girls, giving the impression that they didn't understand what he said, giggling, joined the group.

"What is it girls, fellas?" Mike Read asked from the bar. "Brandies all round? I'll need some money from you fellas. Come on, dig deep."

As with the others, Brendan passed the rand dollars he had to Mike, not terribly interested in the drink and anxious to get on the dance floor, as the band were now playing a jazzy quickstep. Having caught the eye of one of the taller girls, he inclined his head to the floor and grinned, delighted to find she reciprocated and rose to accompany him to the dance floor. Catching her hand and putting his arm around her slim waist, he found himself intoxicated with her perfume, her body against his, and swung naturally into a very passable quickstep.

"Yeh, you can dance pretty well. Are you the Irishman?" questioned the girl in a Cape Town accent, leaning back in Brendan's arms, pushing her body against his groin.

"Yes," gasped Brendan. "From Dublin. What's your name?

"Elizabeth. Oops! Watch my toes."

Grasping her body closer, enjoying the feel of her against him, Brendan surpassed himself in the dance and ended in a dramatic finishing backstop swing.

"Can you jitterbug, Bren?" Liz asked. "I love the rhythm. Listen. They're playing my favourite, Little Richard and 'Tutti Frutti'."

Caught up in the euphoria of the moment, Brendan went into overdrive and jitterbugged himself into near exhaustion. Entranced by the dexterity of his partner, he was mesmerised with the sight of her short skirt swinging parallel to the floor, revealing brief white shorts over long tanned legs. *Concentrate on your dancing, Brendan,* he told himself. *The lads are all looking. Let's give them something to talk about.* "Come on, Liz, let's show 'em. Let's swing, girl."

"Yep, Bren, they're playing 'Rock around the Clock'. Let's rock, daddio." Catching her partner's hand, Liz and Brendan went into rock 'n' roll mode, Brendan swung her under his arm, pushing her into a spin, twisting around on his heels, moving his feet in double time to the captivating beat.

With the music ending and Liz going into a final swing, their bodies collided and, laughing breathlessly, they supported each other and stumbled to the table.

"Well done, Bren. God! Didn't think you had it in you," exclaimed Don. "By the way, this is Clare, Bren." Don proudly showed off a girl about his own age, dressed in a short cotton dress and tight white top with her arm linked to Don's.

"Hi, Clare. This is Liz, Don. Isn't she the gear?" exclaimed Brendan with his arm around Liz's narrow waist. "What's the time? Half ten?

Great—plenty of time. I see the other lads are enjoying themselves. Look, there's Ken. Who's she, Liz?" Brendan asked, as Ken went sweeping by in a waltz with a buxom girl in a long dress.

"That's Elaine Butterworth. She's great fun—was my school teacher. I see the Welshman has palled up with Pauline. She likes little important men. Listen, Bren, come on, let's dance. I like a smoochie number."

Thankful that he had concentrated on dancing at the local hops and dance halls before he started his seagoing career, Brendan caught Liz's hand and swung her onto the floor with a flourish. Holding her close, he ventured to press his cheek against the side of her head, breathing in her intoxicating perfume. He pressed his body hard against her yielding slim form, not believing how bold he was becoming, and felt her hand pulling him closer.

"Bren, would you like to get a bit of fresh air? That door at the side leads out to the garden. Come on, let's go."

Not waiting to be asked twice, Brendan walked briskly behind Liz as she trotted to the side door and pushed it open to reveal a passage running alongside the dance hall. Brendan, finding it hard to believe this was happening, caught the willing girl in his arms and kissed her fiercely on the lips. Another startling discovery, she started pushing her tongue against his closed lips. Parting his lips, her tongue shot into his mouth whilst she started fumbling at his trouser belt. Drawing her head back, she whispered in his ear, "Put yur hand under my skirt, go on..."

God! Does she mean play with her...? Janey Mac! God, she's got my trousers down!

Over the next few minutes, with the expert guidance of Liz, Brendan now really knew what girls were for—not only for dancing and chatting up... *But this, God. Why didn't my mother tell me about it?* he laughed to himself.

Helping Brendan to hitch his trousers back around his waist, they held each other in their arms, leaned back, looked at each other and grinned.

"Janey Mac, woman," exclaimed Brendan. "Come and sail around the world with me and we could do that fifteen times a day."

"Come on. Let's go back in. They'll be wondering where we are." Linking arms, they re-entered the dance hall to the sound of a slow waltz and drifted their way slowly around the dance floor, to the table where the others were all in different stages of friendship, Barry still talking furiously, Don holding his partner's hand, staring dreamily into her eyes. The R/O was nowhere to be seen.

Ken came up behind them with a dazzling blonde on his arm. "Where have you two been? No, don't answer that. All I have to do is look at you. Look at them, Agnes, both knackered. Come on, let's dance."

"What's this knackered, Bren?" asked Liz as the others waltzed away.

"We must both look a bit tired, Liz. That's what knackered means." Brendan was a bit overcome with the events of the past few minutes. "Let's go get another one of those Blue Moon brandies and a cigarette. Do you smoke, Liz? Here, have one of mine," Brendan suggested, as he produced a pack of Kensitas tipped and dextrously ejected one skywards, it landing on the floor. "Here, have another one instead. I'll have that one," he laughed as he ejected another and bent over to pick up the errant cigarette, stumbling against Liz.

"God, we haven't got much time, Bren. Give us another kiss. Come on, let's forget about the drink and go outside again."

Not terribly eager, but willing to have another go, Brendan began to follow Liz to the entrance to heaven, when Mike Read suddenly materialised with his school teacher.

"Hey! Bren, we're going now. The driver is waiting for us. Sorry, miss, but I've got to take lover boy from you." He laughed.

"No you're not going, Bren," replied Liz, grabbing Brendan's arm. "You're mine. I'm not letting you go," she cried in mock anguish. "Go away, you *dom kop*," she shouted at Mike.

"Come on, Mike. Let's all have one of those brandies. We could buy the driver one," pleaded Bren.

"Good idea, Bren," interrupted Ken, still wrapped around his blonde. "Let's all get together and have a last drink."

"OK," replied Mike. "I'll have a word with the driver. You get the other guys together. There's Don. Where's Barry?"

"There he is. Ha! Ha!" laughed Ken. "Look—he's still talking to that girl. Probably all about Wales. Come on here, Barry," he called. "Anyone know where the R/O is? Hope he turns up."

"There's the third—there's Mike. He's got Kurt with him. Come on, Charlotte. Let's get another dance. They're playing 'Swinging the Blues', or is it 'Singing the Blues'? Anyway, let's swing."

"Come on, Liz," called Bren, downing his brandy. "Let's swing too."

Full of euphoria and the brandy, Brendan swung Liz onto the dance floor, closely followed by Don and his girl. Barry stood looking quite aloof to this frivolity; Ken was already on the floor; Mike bought Kurt a drink and he started swinging with the school teacher. The radio officer came staggering in to join Kurt. On this high note, when the dance ended with hugs and kisses and frantic fumblings, the couples made their partings whilst Kurt tumbled the drunken R/O into the Chevy. Brendan scribbled Liz's address on a Blue Moon leaflet and, both nearly in tears, they said goodbye.

With a roar of exhaust, the Chevy pulled away from the parking lot, with arms waving from the open windows and shouts of 'goodbyee' as the lights of the Blue Moon faded in darkness. Don shouted out above the roar of the engine, "Bop and Spoon at the old f---ing Blue Moon. What a night!"

In unison, the others with a roar all agreed, "Dance and SPOON at the old Blue Moon." What a hell of a night.

"All rise and shine. We're sailing at ten. Come on, Bren, Don, it's oh-seven-thirty hours. Get your arses on deck, you randy buggers."

Wakening with a start, Brendan grinned from ear to ear and with a loud whoop exclaimed, "What a night, Ken, what a night!"

"Yeh, Bren," laughed Ken. "What a night—even Barry scored. We're sailing at ten. It's half seven. How did you do, Don?"

"I'm in love, leave me alone. Boy! What a night. Let's hope we come back here again. Bop and bloody Spoon in the old Blue Moon. What a night. Oh! Clare, are you thinking of me?" called Don as he hugged his pillow.

"Right, it's back to reality, lads. We're sailing at ten. Bren, will you go up for'rard with the mate? I'll be on the bridge and that leaves you, Don, and Barry—oh, there you are, Barry. Did you get your end away last night?" Ken enquired with a smile and before receiving an answer, continued with his orders. "And you, Don, go aft with the second."

Slightly annoyed by the tone of Ken's voice, Barry replied in a reserved tone, "I had a very pleasant evening. Freda's a very intelligent girl. We're getting married next year."

"You're not?" Was the astonished exclamation from the other three.

"Yes!" Barry replied in a smug voice and burst out laughing. "Got you there, guys."

It was a cold and blustery morning with some heavy rain and wind, as the large tanker slowly edged its way from the wharf assisted by tugs fore and aft. With the engines going at slow speed, control was difficult as the ship, with a full cargo, was very deep in the water. A sudden extra strong gust of wind coming from the right started pushing the tanker's bows to the left as they approached the harbour exit. The for'rard tug went into full power, as seen by the sudden surge of water at its stern, but it wasn't enough. The ship's head kept swinging to the left and collided with the jetty point. However, with the pull from the tug, the tanker sluggishly bounced off the stone jetty and slipped clear of the harbour. As soon as they were off the shipping lane, the anchor was dropped and a surveyor called to assess the damage. Fortunately this was quite minor. Both the chain locker, where the anchor chain was kept, and number one tank, which fortunately was empty, had some plating buckled, but the ship was deemed safe enough to proceed.

Next stop: La Plata in the Argentine, four thousand plus miles across the South Atlantic, taking a full cargo of sixteen thousand tons of crude oil from the Persian Gulf in the northern hemisphere to Argentina in the south; two weeks' sailing without sight of land, across the southern Atlantic directly west, on Latitude thirty-four degrees, with the frozen wastes of Antarctica to the south.

Here am I, thought Brendan to himself, *ploughing through the immense waves of the south Atlantic in a huge oil can, rolling from side to side. I've seen new countries, had new experiences. Gee! Haven't I had new experiences! Cape Town—what an evening. Wonder if Liz thinks of me? If we had been there any longer, I wonder if I would have got her into bed…the ultimate. Get her into bed. Didn't Sub Lieutenant Lockhart on the Compass Rose get—was it Virginia McKenna?—into bed on his shore leave? Must get a copy of the book Cruel Sea by Nicholas Montserrat. Must answer that letter from Polly—she sounded a bit doubtful about our relationship. Gee! What do I do? I can't not follow my instincts. Hopefully she's enjoying herself. Wonder what's happening in Ireland?*

So Brendan's thoughts crisscrossed themselves, as he tried to balance his body against the erratic rolling of the ship whilst on his knees, scraping paint from the wooden deck.

Scraping paint, what a waste of my time. I know a first-trip apprentice must learn everything about ship construction, ship handling, cargoes, navigation, and seamanship. Surely I could be doing something better than scraping paint off the deck? Probably put it there myself when we painted those deck railings in the Mediterranean. Wonder if it's near smoke time? Could do with break. Could do with a fag. That was a big sea.

Standing up and grabbing a metal stanchion, Brendan looked aft from his position on the side of the ship as it rolled again to the left, with waves surging over the main deck. *Yeh! The deck is only seven feet above sea level. The waves must be ten feet and more. Wow! There's another crashing wave washing straight across the main deck. Is that Chippy coming along the flying bridge? Hang on, Chippy here's another big one.*

With that, a further large wave swept across the deck, as the body of the ship rolled to port and the top of the wave engulfed the flying bridge. Chippy had seen it coming and had hung on to the railing. When the ship righted itself, Chippy shook himself like a dog just getting out of a river and staggered the remaining yards to safety before another wave followed. *Ah! There's Ken Yep! Smokoe.* "OK, Ken. I'm coming."

Gathered in Ken's and Barry's cabin, the four lit up their various styles of cigarettes: Ken on Senior Service untipped, Don on Woodbines, Bren with his tipped Kensitas and, of course, Barry, who had to be different; he rolled his own. Always crooked and flat, sometimes they went up in flames. He rarely got a good drag out of one.

All very relaxed, with Springboks Radio and Eric Egan the announcer coming out with his corny greeting 'I looovee Yoouuu' followed by some rock 'n' roll music.

"Have you heard the news this morning?" asked Ken, always the one with the news and knowledge. Gaining the others attention he continued, "Remember the news about the biggest tanker ever built, last Feb—*The World Splendour*, built in Sweden? Well, she went on fire just a couple of days ago, on her way to The Persian Gulf—sank just off Gibraltar."

"Makes you think," commented Don. "That could be us at any time. When we're in ballast. The tanks full of gas. Anyone killed, Ken?"

"Apparently everyone got off safely. Sixty-nine crew. Right, back to work. We should be picking up the pilot off Montevideo in a couple of days' time. Wonder what the talent's like in La Plata?" he grinned.

That's a couple of days away, thought Brendan, as he stubbed out his cigarette. *Must get a letter written to Polly before then and one for me ma. Must write to Joan in Philadelphia—there's a rumour we may be taking a cargo to Philly in the near future. It would be great to meet her again. That seems a long time ago when I met her in England…*

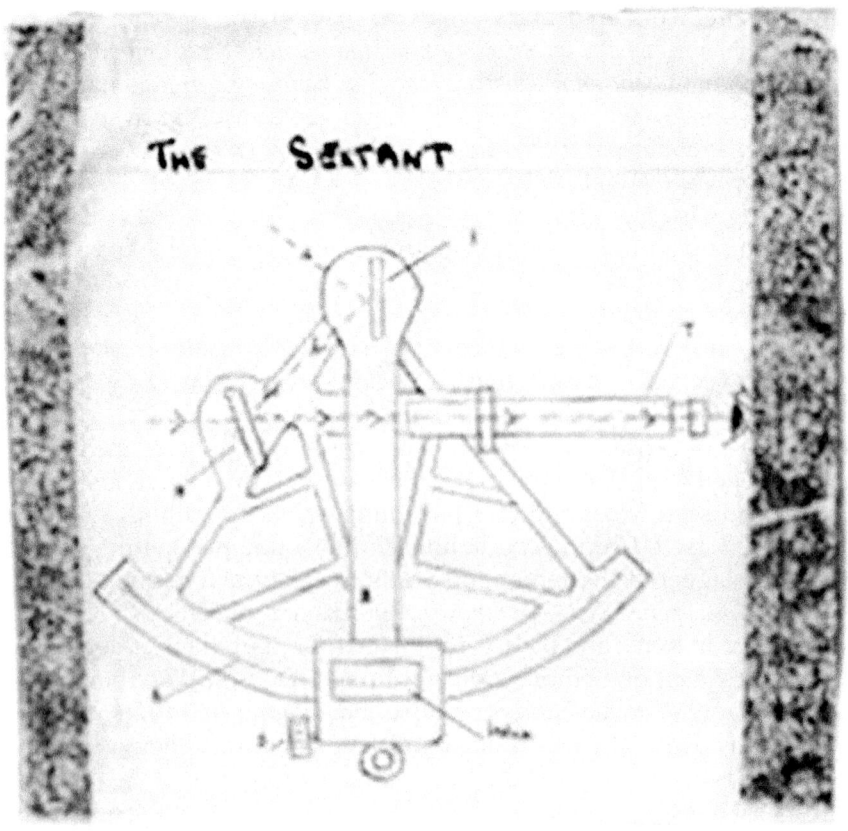

A Sextant

13

Who's Got the Diaries Now?

"What'll I do, Mary? What'll I do? I've got into a real interesting bit. He's in America an' going to see that nurse. You know..." Nurse Fitzgerald, whenever in a panic, adjusted her skirts by pulling them down at the sides. "I'd better bring in the diary thing tomorrra... Oh! Jeasus, I'm off tomorra, Mary. Cud you bring it in?"

"What time is the young lad comin' in, Kathleen?"

"I dunno, it was afternoon visitin' today when he was there," replied Kathleen.

"All right," said Mary in a positive voice. "I'll bring it in. In the mornin' I'm workin' earlies, I'll leave it by his bed. Den when the young lad comes in, there it is for him," Mary announced in jubilation at resolving the problem so easily.

"Doan let anyone see you," cautioned Nurse Fitzgerald.

"But tanks, Mary, you're a pal. He's a right woman chaser is our Rudolph," declared Kathleen. "I wonder if he ever does it, Mary? Ye know what I mean," grinned Kathleen.

"Oh away with ye now," laughed Mary, slightly embarrassed by her more broad-minded friend. "Ye shouldn't be saying such tings. Now we'd be better getting on wid our duties, Kathleen." Mary put down her half-finished cup of tea.

"God, not another soiled sheet, Rudi, you've gotta control yerself," complained Staff Nurse Carrigan, just finishing off the night shift. Sheila Carrigan, in her early twenties, cringed a little as she cleaned up the thin white body of Brendan Harris and deposited the soiled sheets in the bin alongside the hospital bed. Transferred from another ward two days before, Carrigan was a broad-minded Dublin girl, tall, with a plain angular face, large brown eyes and a smiling mouth.

"Come on, Rudi lad, give us a smile," she pleaded gently to the relaxed unconscious body now more comfortable in clean sheets, as she rubbed some cream on the bed sores appearing on his buttocks. "How long are you going to stay in this far away world you're in? When did you come in?" she asked. "It's all of seven days now!" she exclaimed, looking at the hospital record clip at the end of the bed. "Oh! Hi! Mary, you must think I'm mad talking away to myself? Anyway," she exclaimed, stepping back from the bed in slight surprise, "you're a bit early. It's not eight yet, an' what have ye got there?"

"Aw it's just some papers," answered Mary, as she stepped inside the curtains. "I've bin told to leave them for Rudi's brother when he comes in later today—wanna make shure der here for him," Mary retorted in a dismissal tone, as she placed the parcel of papers on the bedside cabinet.

"Der not Rudie's diaries, be any chance?" laughed Carrigan scornfully. "The famous diaries. Let's have a look." She leaned forward to grab the papers.

"The nurses are all talkin' about dem. Oh! Shit! I've dropped dem," Carrigan called out in disgust. "Look, Nurse, you go on an' sign in, I'll tidy dem up an' leave dem on the cabinet," she called out as she leaned forward to recover the papers which had fallen from the paper bag. *I'll have a quick look at some of them before I go home,* she hastily said to herself, pushing a wad of papers inside her apron.

"What's this, Nurse? What are you doing?" was the sudden voice of authority from the large figure of Sister Sullivan standing between the sharply pulled curtains. "Nurse Carrigan, what is that I see in your apron?"

Taken aback by this sudden confrontation, Carrigan, who had been on duty for eight hours, replied in a weary resigned voice, "They're just some papers I found on de floor, Sister, an' was going to put them on the cabinet." *Honest, you big pudding,* she muttered under her breath.

"What's that, Carrigan? What's that you muttered?

"Sorry, Sister. It's all about nuttin'."

"Listen to me, young lady. I will decide whether it's nuttin' or not. Now go an' get some sleep an' we'll say no more of it."

Suitably admonished, a relieved and somewhat overtired nurse replaced the papers and sidled out into the ward.

"Dat's you told off, Nurse," called Farmer Murphy from the adjoining bed. "Is somebody going to look after me? Me foot is hurtin' awful."

"Mr. Murphy, how many times have we told you it's all in yer imaginin'? The foot is no longer der. Do ye understand, Mr. Murphy, yer foot is away wid the fairies. Will that be all now, as I'm going te bed? Goodnight." With that, Nurse Carrigan stormed off down the ward.

"Jeasus, der we go agin', I only arsked. I don't arsk fer much."

Whilst this little scene was being enacted, Sister Sullivan, alone beside the bed, was curious to discover what was contained in this diary that the restless body had produced. In Sullivan's eyes, being a country girl who had travelled no further than a hundred miles from her home in Limerick town to Dublin, Brendan Harris whilst only twenty-one years of age, was a much-travelled man. He had been to places she had only seen in the dog-eared school atlas. Her education had been solely in the Irish language, which was very restricted in its understanding of the modern world. Brendan Harris was a foreign body to her narrow entrenched views and was also a Protestant, a member of the old feared and despised ruling class. *What's in this diary thing?* she wondered, hesitating beside the bed. *Nobody will notice if I take it overnight,* she thought to herself, glancing over her shoulder. *I could say I confiscated it.* Rapidly collecting the many loose sheets and placing them in the large paper bag, she concealed them in a towel and strode purposefully from the ward with her dangerous cargo.

Brendan at the Helm

14

Christmas at Home

Orders came through on their way north: bunker at Punta Cardon and load a full cargo of Venezuelan crude at Maracaibo and then head back to the UK. And so life went on for Brendan, docking at exotic sounding places: Cabimas, Punta Cardon and, of course, Swansea. Another trip to the Persian Gulf followed, with a return to Swansea, in the early weeks of December 1957, with a full cargo of crude to satisfy the thirst of the UK for oil. As the *Calvex Renown* needed some repairs to the fore peak, after the damage done in Cape Town, it was decided to affect the required repairs, pay off the crew and send the apprentices home for some leave.

A sun-tanned and much matured teenager bid farewell to his many friends on the *Calvex Renown* on a bitterly cold Welsh morning mid December and made his way to Swansea railway station to start his marathon train journey to Dunlaoghaire. After many weary hours travelling to London then traversing the country to North Wales and the port of Holyhead, he boarded the passenger ship *Princess Maud*, crossing the Irish Sea, and arrived in Dunlaoghaire port. Back to Ireland, his parents delighted to see him, appeared to have aged in the months he had been away. His brother Jono was still in the British Army and was serving in Cyprus. Billy was at school and Polly was nowhere to be seen.

Glad to return to such familiar ground, Brendan took some time to adjust to the cold. The weather had turned very bitter, with north winds and flurries of snow. He met up with some of his friends and spent many hours reminiscing about his travels. There was very little change in his parents' circumstances; Pop was still making the daily journey into Dublin. He was now an area manager, collecting the pennies from the gas meters but in charge of a large area and a number of other collectors. Ma was still chasing the dream of a higher social status and was a regular with Pop at the local British Legion branch.

"Bren," called Ma from the fireside in the sitting room, "can you put some more coal on the fire? God! It's cold. Is the bundle against the door? Stop the bloody draughts. Has there been any contact from that girl, Polly? You were going quite strong with her before you sailed away," questioned Ma through the clicks of her knitting.

"Yeh, I wonder what's going on there, Ma! I rang her yesterday and her brother answered the phone. Don't like him. Her ma is nice. I'll try again later. Jim, you know he's with the Alfred Holt as deck apprentice?"

Ma wasn't terribly interested in what Jim was doing. He really wasn't the sort that her Brendan should be associating with. A bit of a chancer and a smooth talker. She pulled the hem of her dress further down her legs to protect them from the heat of the coal fire.

"You like Polly, don't you, Bren?" she suggested. "Haven't seen her since you went away. She is nice and she is a…Protestant." This statement was made with some emphasis and a faint smile.

"Yep, I do like her, but there are many more fish in the sea, Ma. I wrote to her from Cape Town. Hope she got the letter. Ah! Cape Town—Bop and Spoon at the Old Blue Moon. Ah! Memories." He chuckled to himself.

"What's that, Bren, the Blue Moon?"

"A night club in Cape Town, Ma. What a night. I learnt a lot that night. Wow!"

"I wouldn't like to guess what you got up to," snorted Ma, "you sailors. There's the phone. Would you get it, Bren? You never know, it might be Polly." Ma picked up her knitting and altered her position before the fire.

"Hello," came Pop's rich sounding voice from the hallway. "Hello! Who is it? You're very faint. Hello! Oh! You want Brendan. Who is it? Polly? Oh! Hello, Polly, how nice to hear from you. I'll get him."

"Hey, Brendan!" called Pop in a loud voice. "Brendan, it's Polly." He winked as he handed the heavy black Bakelite phone receiver to Brendan.

"Hello, Polly."

"Hello, Brendan," was the hesitant reply. "Brendan, I was not aware you were home, I have been away for the past week and got your lovely letter. Gordon only told me you had rung. How long are you home for? Do you want to meet me?"

"Of course I want to meet you," Brendan replied with some emphasis. "Where are you now? I'm sure to be home for the Christmas and then will be on standby to join my next ship. Probably early January. What are the roads like where you are? I could come down on my bike to see you."

"Yes! I'm at home at the moment. Just came back from Limerick in the last hour. I'm bushed. There was quite a bit of snow. Would it be all right if we met tomorrow? The journey was terrible."

"That would be fine, Polly. Like to go to the dance at the Top Hat tomorrow night?"

"Look, Bren, I'm very tired. I'll give you a ring in the morning. You don't mind? Do you?"

Realising Polly was anxious to get some sleep, Brendan agreed and replaced the phone. *Well she didn't agree to go dancing. What do I do? Time is short I want to make the most of what I've got. I'll give Jim a ring and see what he's doing.*

"Hey! Jim lad, Brendan here."

"Brendan bloody Harris, is it then. God! I thought you must have gone down with your ship. You have just got me in time. I'm away in the week, joining my next ship in London. Shall be in Africa for Christmas. Sunshine and girls. Are you still doing a line with that Polly one? Still fancy yourself as a dancer?"

One of the things about Jim was he never shut up, forever chasing the girls, however great company.

"How's Sonja, Jim?" The last time they had met, Jim and Brendan had had an adventuresome trip in Jim's father's yacht and the girl of Jim's dreams was a comely wench called Sonja.

"History, Bren. Come on let's have a night out, it's a Friday, go into town and pick up a couple of country girls or maybe a nurse or two. The Arcadia in Dublin is a hot spot. We can lay it on, two sailors far away from home looking for love. On the way you can tell me all about the boring life you lead on tankers. I've got the Da's car for the night."

Brendan sometimes wished he had joined a general shipping company carrying different cargoes to exotic ports rather than oil to refineries usually situated miles outside the centre of activities. Jim's ships seemed to spend weeks in port giving the crew time to get to know some of the natives and see some of the country.

That evening, with two green Irish pound notes in his pocket, dressed in his rather old-fashioned double-breasted grey flannel suit, trousers rather too large for his twenty-two-inch waist, also with twenty-two-inch turn-ups some inches above his black leather polished shoes, the dashing six footer joined his pal Jim. Jim in contrast was rather small, just over the five feet eight tall with smartly cut light tweed trousers and light blue blazer. Jim prided himself on his quiff, his over-long blond hair swept back in a wave any respectable ocean would be proud of, made a contrasting couple of teenagers.

Who would succeed with the ladies? Jim generally shuffled around the dance floor, tossing his hair back and charming the girls with his wit. Brendan prided himself on his dancing and with his height and natural smile succeeded where Jim floundered. However by mid evening, Jim had dazzled a striking blonde nurse from Carlow, and Brendan had paired off with her friend, a tall willowy secretary from Dublin.

Brendan was delighted to practise his dancing, as he found Marcella was taking dancing lessons, but unfortunately kept giggling to herself whilst they were dancing. When they sat in a group, drinking their orange juice, Jim entertained them with some of his heroic deeds whilst at sea, all the time putting his hand on Mary's knee and making suggestive comments. Brendan, sitting close to Marcella, put his arm around her and was delighted to find he wasn't repulsed and complimented her on her perfume choice.

As time went by, the two boys, very pleased with themselves, discussed their separate 'conquests' whilst visiting the toilet. As eleven o'clock approached, the girls became somewhat fidgety. Jim had suggested driving them home to Finglas. Brendan, excited at the thought of a possible snog in the back of the car, was somewhat concerned, as he knew Jim's knowledge of North Dublin was as sparse as his own. He was somewhat relieved when the two girls nodded to each other and rose like a couple of sparrows, hovering in the air, and declared they were going to catch the bus home and flew away, giggling together.

Rather dismayed, Brendan looked at Jim. "What did we do wrong there, Jim lad? I thought we were away. You scared them when you asked your one where she was sleeping tonight. Saw her bridle. My one stiffened like a horse ready to jump Beecher's. Anyway," Brendan laughed dismissively. "Didn't fancy going to Finglas."

"Well," admitted Jim, "you get nowhere if you don't ask. She did fancy me though. Come on, let's go home and I'll tell you all about Mademoiselle Fifi when we called into Tangiers. Now there was a bonny lass."

The following morning, Brendan woke up to a cold and miserable day, the sky overladen with heavy grey clouds, wondering whether to throw down freezing rain, a few million hailstones or maybe some fluffy snowflakes. The windows in this the spare room at the side of the cottage were rimed with ice; the air in the room was freezing cold. His immediate thought was the time.

Wow! Ten o'clock. Must get up. What time will Polly ring? What a waste of a night. Gosh! It's cold.

"Phone for you, Bren," came his ma's voice from the faraway hallway. Grabbing his father's large overcoat from the bed to keep warm, he rushed out into the hallway. "It's Polly, Bren!" Ma giggled at the sight of Brendan in his bare feet and his father's large overcoat trailing behind him.

"Thanks, Ma." Taking a deep breath to calm himself, he took the phone. "Hello, Polly."

"How's my sailor boy?"

"Cold and miserable, Polly. Everything OK for tonight? Look forward to going dancing."

"Me too, Bren. Look, I'm doing nothing this morning, what about a coffee in the Roman Café? You know the café in Dunlaoghaire?"

'Is that still goin', Polly? What do you say, at eleven, that OK?"

BRENDAN AFLOAT

"Hey, Ma," called Brendan as he put the telephone receiver down. "You'll be glad to hear I'm meeting Polly in Dunlaoghaire later this morning an' were goin' dancin' tonight. Do I smell some rashers fryin'?"

"Yeah, your pop is frying a few eggs and rashers. Do you want some? Or need I ask?"

"Yeh, I'd love some of Pop's fried bread as well," answered Brendan as he raced down the hallway and rounded the doorway into the spare room, throwing the coat onto the bed. He dressed hurriedly, singing away to himself as he made his way down from the bathroom along the stone-tiled corridor to the kitchen and went directly to the red-hot stove to warm his hands.

"Mornin', Jono," he called out to Jono, sitting in his pyjamas at the kitchen table with a plate full of his father's special fry up in front of him. "Haven't seen you since I got home. Still in the army? How are you keeping?"

"Yeh, I'm fine," replied Jono. "As ye say, still in the army. I'm a corporal now. I've been down the country for the past few days. You're looking well, Bren. Hear you're doing OK. Have you been around the world yet?" he asked through a mouthful of breakfast.

'Only halfway, Jono," Bren replied, sitting down beside his brother. "Look, Jono, are you doing anything special tonight?" he continued. "There's a dance in the Top Hat and I am going with Polly. The only trouble is transport."

"Here's your brekki, Bren," interrupted Henry. "Two fried eggs, a couple of rashers and fried bread. There's tea in the pot. Will you give Billy a call, Jono? He'll sleep the day out. Do you pair want to use the car tonight? It could do with a few shillings' worth of petrol, though."

Bren looked at Jono in the hope that he would take up the offer of the car.

"Well, Una and I had made no definite plans for tonight," Jono mused. "Could have a word with her. Thanks, Pop, for the offer. I'll think about it, Bren. You know we were going to stay in and read a book tonight."

"Come on, Jono. Stop fooling about," called Brendan as he threw a piece of fried bread at his grinning brother. "I'm meeting Polly in the Roman Café later this morning…what do you say?"

"OK, Bren, just teasing. I'm sure Una will agree. She's looking forward to meeting my sailor brother."

"You agree then—great. Thanks, Pop. I could put five bob to the petrol."

"Same here, Pop," agreed Jono as he rose from the table "I'll go give Billy a call."

"Mornin' boys," came their mother's voice as she exited the 'pantry', leaving the sound of a flushing toilet behind her. Known as the pantry this, the smallest room in the house, was used as a lavatory, an airing

113

room and a storage for tinned foods. It was also the warmest room, as there was always an oil stove lit. Making her way over to the large stone sink with its brass taps, she ran some hot water from the noisy gas cistern and continued.

"Now that you're all home, we will all be here for Christmas day. Pop is collecting a turkey in Moore Street later today. Oh, and by the way, Bren, the Rev Draper has asked if you wouldn't mind reading the lesson tomorrow morning at church. I told him you would do it. The readings are on the hall table. You don't mind, do you?" she asked, looking straight at Brendan without blinking in the old Ma style of *you will do what I tell you.*

Slightly taken aback, Brendan, who had read the lessons many times before going to sea, and knowing his ma wanted to show him off to the congregation, agreed with a shrug of his shoulders. Pleased to be asked, he thought he'd better get the bible out and see what the lesson was all about.

"And I'm going with you, Pop. Like a visit to Moore Street," called Billy as he entered the kitchen ahead of Jono. "I'll have the eggs and a rasher, Pop. Are there any mushrooms?"

Billy, just age thirteen, was becoming quite demanding and feeling left out of things, as he was still going to school whilst his two brothers were earning money, going dancing, and being grown up.

"Say please, Billy," commanded Alice.

"Please, Billy," replied Billy with a half smile. "Hello, Bren, or is it Captain Harris I'm talking to?" Turning to Brendan, he covered his envy and admiration with sarcasm. Brendan, knowing his younger brother, didn't rise to the bait.

"I hear you're doing well at school. Ma tells me you have been picked for the senior hockey team for the school championship?"

Getting a suppressed grin from Billy, Brendan continued, "That's something, Billy, I was fourteen before I even got on the junior team." *What a lad,* Brendan thought. *He must be good. But why so unpleasant?*

"Where's the bike, Billy? I'll be using it later this morning." The bike, a Raleigh roadster, was Brendan's pride and joy. Before going to sea, he had kept it in pristine condition and knew it was being used by Billy when going to school.

'It's in the shed at the back, Bren. Haven't used it for a couple of weeks. Think one of the tyres is flat," was Billy's dismissive gesture as he started on his breakfast.

Catching his pop's cautioning eye, Brendan held back the sharp retort he was ready to come out with and rose from the table. "Hope the air pump is still working, Billy. I'll go have a look and thanks…little brother."

Leaving the warm kitchen, he hurried out into the back yard and made his way cautiously over the frozen stone flags to the open shed. Amongst the broken prams—*are they still there,* he thought, *and the gardening tools and that broken wheelbarrow*—was his Raleigh bike. The bicycle he had bought for half a crown three years ago and spruced up, even spending a small fortune of three shillings on straight handlebars. Here it was, lying on the floor of the shed, discarded like so much junk.

Lifting the bike from the floor he stood it up against the shed wall and saw both tyres were deflated but the frame and wheels looked in good order, and the air pump was still clipped onto the crossbar.

God! I hope they're not punctured or I'll have to walk the two miles to Dunlaoghaire, he thought to himself. Fortunately the tyres inflated as he pumped them up, without the dreaded hiss of escaping air.

After a fairly hairy ride to Dunlaoghaire, slipping and sliding on the frozen roads, Brendan arrived at the Roman Café full of anticipation. *What will she think of me, haven't seen her since the beginning of the year. Hope she's there, maybe I should have gone to her house.*

Parking his bike against the street wall he took a deep breath and, taking off the stupid hat he was wearing, pushed open the door of the café. The window looking out to the street was covered in condensation and the café was full of the babble of voices, the juke box roaring full blast with Elvis and his "Hound Dog". All the tables were full of youngsters laughing and shouting their comments over the juke box noise. The cigarette smoke was already beginning to form a grey blanket covering the low ceiling. There was a healthy smell of human mixed with the sweet tang of coffee beans.

"Hey! Bren, come and join us," came a shout from the far side of the narrow room. Looking over, Brendan saw Trevor Brown who he had been to school with, along with a few others he recognised. *Monica, now what's her surname? Daphne Taylor, and look there was Winston Blackwell: wonder if he is still the same creep he was in school?* He acknowledged their greeting with a wave, looking anxiously around. *Can't see her.* With that, a blast of cold air hit his back and he felt the presence of a figure behind him.

"Hello Brendan, looking for me?" came the voice he recognised—that lovely dusky tone, that wonderful welcoming voice.

"Is that Pollyanna Blackwell I hear behind me?" He smiled, turning around with his arms wide. With a big grin on her pretty face, reddened by the outside cold air, she spontaneously stepped into his arms and they kissed a long awaited kiss which sent the occupants of the room cheering.

Trevor Brown rose to his feet and called over, "Come on, you two, is it coffees you want? Di, will you squeeze over and give this pair room. Can yu giv' us a couple more of your lovely cups, Mike?" he called over to the elderly man behind the coffee counter. "Now, Bren, get your coat off and introduce us to yer lovely girl," coaxed Trevor. Brendan took off his overcoat and after helping Polly with hers looked around for somewhere to hang them.

"Put 'em on the floor, Bren. Here, there's room beside us. Squeeze up, Di, go on."

Brendan recognised Di, an old flame, sitting beside Pauline, who moved closer on the bench against the wall and patted the bare wood beside her. To the sound of Johnny Ray now "Crying" buckets of tears from the throbbing juke box across the crowded room, he squeezed in beside a smiling Diana and made room on the bench seat for Polly. Producing a pack of Senior Service cigarettes, he offered them around to be welcomed with many shaking heads as some either did not smoke or were smoking the tipped brands.

Lighting up his own (Polly didn't smoke), whilst he was pleased to be the centre of attention he would have much rather had a meeting of closer intimacy with Polly. However, he recounted his experiences of the past few months as much for Polly as for the others. The conversation then turned to the recent news of the Russians putting the first artificial satellite into Earth orbit and the further news that they had now put a larger satellite with a dog into space. Winston, who had been very quiet, announced the dog's name was Laika and that man would be on the moon within the next ten years. Laughed to silence by the others, Winston nodded his head wisely and bet them all a tanner that there would be a man on the moon within the next ten or twelve years.

Wanting to make the most of his time with Polly, Brendan suggested they go for a walk and, wishing their noisy friends goodbye, left the warm atmosphere of the café and made their way out into the cold air.

Still slightly uneasy with each other, to Polly this Brendan was not the same slightly bemused innocent young man she had said goodbye to a year ago. He was now more confident and assertive but still had a quirky sense of humour. She was still undecided to his intentions. She was now nineteen, certainly more mature than Brendan, in a settled job in the city of Dublin with prospects of advancement. She had been approached by a few male colleagues over the past year, had had a liaison with one or two, but the thought of this enigma called Brendan who kept in touch and said the words she wanted to hear.

To Brendan, age seventeen, still a virgin in many ways, Polly was the girl back home. Very attractive, very personable, someone to boast about to his peers, but for him at the age of seventeen, there could be no long-term commitment. There was a world to see and he was viewing it. He did not think too deeply about their relationship, looking, like all selfish young men, to realise the physical attractions of a good-looking intelligent female without the long term commitment of marriage. Although Brendan, through his upbringing and his parents' stable marriage as an example, considered this as the eventual outcome, whether it be with Polly or some other attractive member of the opposite sex so be it, but let's see and sample the delights of the world, however restricted by the lack of cash.

That evening, he joined Jono in his father's large Ford Consul car. They waved goodbye to the envious Billy and drove to Dalkey, a small seaside town south of Dunlaoghaire, to collect Una from her flat. Una turned out to be a talkative horsey-looking blonde, taller than average. Jono and Brendan were both over six foot tall, so when they collected Polly in Dunlaoghaire, and after parking the Consul, made a striking foursome as they entered the ballroom. Jono, the debonair, tall, striking man of nineteen, experienced soldier with erect stance, offered to buy drinks all round. The squaddie in the British Army certainly appeared to get a deal more in finance than a poor apprentice in the British Merchant Navy. Brendan declined the expensive Irish whiskey and settled with Polly on a glass of orange juice as, lighting up their cigarettes, they all sauntered over to a table alongside the empty polished dance floor.

Una, who appeared to be somewhat older than Jono, in a very Dublin accent, began to dominate the conversation, expounding her knowledge of the newly formed Irish dance bands. "Ye see," she continued, "ye see these lads call themselves the Royal Show band. The singer there—" pointing to the stage "—is called Brendan Bowyer. He plays the trombone and comes from Waterford, as they all do, and they all came from other bands. The fella on de gee-tar is Jim Conlon. The music dey play is great, there's a bit of jazz, ye know the trad jazz, played by—who is it now?" She thought as she leaned on her right hand, the end of her fag sizzling her hair. "Got it. An Englishman called Kenny Ball. He plays the trumpet. Marvellous music. Do ye rock 'n' roll, Bren?

"Not that I know of, Una, but I'm willing to try. Do you?"

"Jono and I are the champions of Dalkey. They talk about us in all the pubs in the area. Don't they, Jono?" Una laughingly directed the question to a startled Jono.

"Well not being one to boast. Ha! Hum!" he replied, making an apologetic gesture of his hand. "We have been known to rock the night away after a few drinks, we are pretty good at rockin' and rollin'. We are known but not in all the pubs, Una. Come on, be fair."

Brendan was beginning to like this odd lady and asked if she knew anything of the Chris Barber jazz band. She then went into great detail about a clarinet player called Monty Sunshine, and Lonnie Donegan on the banjo and Barber on the trombone.

"Hey, Bren." Polly nudged him, annoyed with all the attention Brendan was giving to Una. "We're here to dance, they're playing a quickstep. Do you want to have a go?"

Brendan, his foot tapping to the music from the stage, excused himself from this very interesting woman and with great confidence started his version of the quickstep, with Polly following as best she could. After the first tour of the dance floor, bumping into other couples, Polly whispered into Brendan's ear, "You haven't done much dancing since we last met, Brendan? Have you? You've got the rhythm, now just follow me. Now listen to the beat—slow, quick, quick, slow. That's it, you have certainly got the music in your feet. Oh! Darn! The music has stopped."

Before they had time to return to their table, the band started playing an Elvis number, and Jono and Una started jiving, or rock or rolling, to the lively beat. Swinging to the beat, Una called over to Brendan and Polly.

"Give it a go, you two. Let it rip, Jono," and the two of them went into a fast arm swinging, foot stepping dance, matching the rapid beat of the drum, with Una singing along in a pretty amazing voice.

> *The warden threw a party in the county jail*
> *The prison band was there and they began to wail*
> *The band was jumpin' and the joint began to swing*
> *you should've heard them knocked out jailbirds sing.*

Matching the rhythm, Brendan and Polly tried to keep up with the gyrations of the other two, making a creditable try of it, and when the dance ended were both exhausted with the effort and sheer enjoyment of the rapid movement. "Jailhouse Rock" was followed by "All Shook Up", and another pair of lively Elvis songs. Polly and Brendan sat this out to watch Jono and the mad Una sweep the floor with their exhausting movements to the beat.

"So ye all can get yer breath back, let's swing gently to 'Blue Moon'," was the gratefully received suggestion from the stage.

Adapting the steps learned from the quickstep, Polly and Brendan joined in, enjoying the slow beat and the closeness of their bodies. Polly's hair, naturally wavy, was just high enough to tickle Brendan's nose, but he didn't complain.

Treating themselves to another glass of orange juice, the evening continued, with Brendan and Polly getting to know some more about each other and found they could dance quite easily together. Una came out with some surprising statements during the evening. Brendan when dancing the foxtrot—or the Brendan derivation of a foxtrot—with her got the full force of her personality as she pressed her groin up hard against his and asked if he had got into Polly's knickers yet. Startled by the intimacy of this forbidden female—*isn't she with my brother? What's she up to?*—Brendan, who had already been slightly overpowered by her perfume and the closeness of this alluring female, shocked himself with his reply that he would be happy getting into hers. He blushed mightily and was glad when the dance ended.

Winking at Brendan whilst seating herself beside Jono, who had been dancing with Polly, this dangerous female wrapped her arms around

Jono. Polly must have sensed something had happened on the floor as she was slightly shocked by Una's direct approach; even Jono was getting a bit disturbed. They had both had a couple of whiskeys.

The rest of the evening passed by with both couples keeping to themselves. After they had stood for the soldier's song at midnight, Brendan and Polly snuggled together in the backseat of the Consul and Una sat close to Jono in the front on the bench seat. Driving carefully on the frozen road, Jono dropped Polly off first. She was still living with her mother in Dunlaoghaire and they waited whilst Brendan said goodnight. He then dropped Brendan off at the cottage and with a wave headed back to Dalkey. Brendan, feeling envious of his big brother, thought perhaps he had the better of the deal with Polly, but there again… *Wow—What should a man do?* So he went to bed in the large cold room with ice on the window and went into a restless sleep under some threadbare blankets and his father's large overcoat.

"Rise and shine. Time to get up. Come on, Bren lad. You have an important day ahead of you."

"All right, Pop," was the sleepy reply from Brendan as he grudgingly slid out from under the warm covers and stood on the cracked lino, pulling the coat off the bed. "God, It's cold. What time is it? Didn't wind my watch."

"Nine o'clock. I'll get some brekki going for you. What time did you get in last night. Where's Jono and the car?"

Jono's not back yet. He must have stayed with Una, thought Brendan enviously.

"Don't know, Pop, he dropped me off this morning, about one, and then took the Una one home."

"That one," snorted Pop in disgust. "She's a load of trouble. Hope Jono knows what he's getting into."

"I think he does, Pop, lucky sod," answered Brendan as he made his way out along the stone passageway to the pantry, with the bible, to look over the lessons he was going to read in church later in the morning.

"And now to God the father—that's me, away I go," whispered Brendan to Billy, standing beside him in the pew of the local church.

"Good luck, Captain," encouraged Billy.

Stepping out onto the worn carpet, Brendan made his self-conscious walk to the front of the church, bowed his head to the vicar, who smiled and nodded toward the tall lectern.

Now standing behind the tall lectern, with the well-used heavy St. James Bible resting on the back of a golden eagle with its wings spread before him, Brendan faced the seated congregation.

Raising his head he began to read, or was it James Mason the famous film star who now, in a deep commanding voice, held the thousands of believers in thrall as he read from Exodus 14—the parting of the Red Sea.

"And the children of Israel went into the midst of the sea upon the dry ground and the waters were a wall unto them on their right hand and on their left. And the Egyptians followed them and it came to pass that the Lord said onto Moses stretch out thine hand that the waters may come again upon the Egyptians—and the waters returned and covered the chariots…"

The lesson went on for some further five verses, and at the end, James Mason turned the bible to the second lesson and stepped down to face the vicar as the congregation then proceeded to recite the *Te Deum Laudamus*. Brendan, still very nervous after the recitation, read the second lesson and was quite relieved to return to the family pew at the rear of the church. The Reverend KDB Draper then came to the front of the church and, after reading the church notices, cleared his throat and announced: "Before we proceed with the service, I would wish to thank Brendan Harris for reading the lesson. Why it is so relevant today is that Brendan is an officer in the British Merchant Navy and has recently sailed through the Red Sea and was involved in the recent problems with the Suez Canal."

Heads turned to look at this interesting new attraction to the congregation: an officer in the British Merchant Navy. *Was this Alice and Henry's little boy, Brendan? Was he involved in that distant fighting at the Suez Canal?*

Brendan blushed and kept his head down. *Ma must have been talking to the Rev. They are a year out. Still, it's nice to be famous for a while.*

"Oil Tankers, that must have been scary? You have been through the Suez Canal. Did you see any fighting? What rank are you? Was the weather hot? How long are you home for? These questions came from all ages and sexes as Brendan with a very proud mother and sceptical brother waited outside in the church grounds for Henry to finish counting the collection monies in his role as church warden. There were a couple of invitations to Christmas parties from parents, especially those with daughters. Brendan said he would be delighted to go but would have to look at his diary. *What would they say if I asked to bring Polly?* he wondered to himself.

Enjoying his newfound fame, Brendan walked back to the cottage with the others, Pop worried about the absence of the car, Ma wallowing in the success of her favourite son, and Billy full of admiration but very envious and wishing he were older. Arriving at the cottage to find the Consul parked in the driveway, Pop went to check there was no damage, whilst Ma gave out in no uncertain terms, taking no excuses from Jono for the worry he had caused.

Over the following couple of weeks, Brendan saw Polly again, turned down the invitations to parties, met up with Jim for a few drinks and had a few evenings out to the local pub. His parents held a party over the Christmas for friends. Polly came but there was no sight of Una. Jono brought another girl this time: a lively brunette twice his age. Brendan kept well clear of her. The New Year's Eve passed over very quietly. Ma and Pop went to a pub to celebrate, Jono disappeared with the brunette and Brendan spent the evening at Polly's house. As the roads were still too dangerous to cycle, he was happy to walk the two miles back to the cottage, meditating on his good fortune. Looking at the dark star-filled sky, he wondered how the poor dog Laika was getting on in Sputnik Two. The Americans had apparently tried to match the Russian success and launched a rocket with a test satellite, which exploded shortly after launch.

Due to worsening of the weather and the need to prepare for the company six-monthly examinations prior to the final second officer's exam at the end of his four-year apprenticeship, Brendan got down to some serious studying using the text books he had purchased on navigation, mathematics, spherical trigonometry, ship handling and the multitude of cargoes carried by ships to every part of the world. Money was very short and he was eager to find which of the ships of the fleet he would be posted to next.

A letter arrived in the first week of January, in the New Year, with a travel pass for Navigating Apprentice Brendan Harris to join the *Calvex Commander*, which was due to dock on the fourteenth of January at the Isle of Grain Refinery. From the company literature, he found the *Commander* was one of the older tankers, built to take refined oils, white spirit, petrol lubricating oils *et cetera* to anywhere in the world. With this exciting prospect ahead of him, Brendan bid goodbye to all and sailed to Holyhead on the mail boat from Dunlaoghaire and took the London train.

Isle of Grain

Our stay in Grain this time lasted for the best part of five days. We left our anchorage on Sunday morning and tied up at number one jetty. By Wednesday we were fully loaded and sailed with the morning tide. As usual the majority of jetties were occupied by British Tankers the more interesting being the 'Lantern', which is on her maiden voyage from Italy, the 'Flag', 'Ambassador', 'Premier' and 'Chancellor'.

On our way out from Grain, we took the passage through the Thames Estuary which brought us to the Tongue light vessel and dropped the pilot at the E Spit buoy. We have a powerful motor tug of twits passed, leaving a large

Sketch of a Deep Sea Tug

15

The Dreadful Diary

"Sister, I think we may consider freeing Mr. Harris from the wrist restraints. He appears to have settled down quite remarkably. Would you think so, Sister?"

Dr. Larrigan stood back from the bed where Brendan still lay on his back. It was ten days since he was admitted and upon review, Larrigan was becoming concerned. Brendan was now eating liquid foods and drinking copious amounts. All his senses were quite acute, tests on his eyes and hearing all produced suitable reactions. His speech was still clear whenever there was a burst of spontaneous reaction to intimate touch. However, his cognitive function could not be assessed as he was unable to communicate verbally.

"Whatever you suggest, Doctor. However, I would remind you Mr. Harris can be quite violent in his speech and physical action. Could we consider a lighter restraint, perhaps giving greater movement of the arms?"

"Certainly, Sister, the protection of your nurses is paramount," agreed Larrigan, pulling Brendan's eyelids back and shining a torch into the eyes. "I am pleased with the young man's resilience and would suggest within the week he may regain consciousness. Your nurses would be pleased, I gather. He has become somewhat of a favourite. Oh! Yes, Sister," Larrigan turned to face the sister, "there is something about a diary that Mr. Harris has with him. Apparently it is very…interesting." He smiled knowingly. "Have you seen anything of it?"

He asked in passing, not even expecting an answer and was rather surprised to hear Sister Sullivan retort with, "Yes! News of this dreadful literature that that man," she glanced at Brendan in the bed, "has written has come to my attention. You know, Doctor, he has spent the past four years as a sailor—a sailor I will have you know, in an English ship—an' he a Protestant as well." Full of mock indignation, Sister Sullivan became quite red in the face and began to wish she had not taken the now probably very interesting document. If she were to be caught with it she would certainly be in trouble.

Somewhat taken aback by the sister's vehement attack, Larrigan stood back from the bed, retrieved his instrument case from the floor, stopped to look at the figure in the bed, and commented on his way out. "Yes, Mr. Harris, you have certainly made your presence known in this hospital. We all look forward to your recovery, don't we, Sister?" Larrigan smiled to himself, acknowledging Sister Sullivan's grunted reply.

Shipping Water

16

Ship on Reef: Takoradi

Feeling very self-conscious, Brendan Harris experienced matelot, stood at the bottom of the gangway reaching from the jetty to the deck of the *Calvex Commander*, a weary looking ship. Brown rust stains streaked the once white accommodation structure. The ship's sides needed a good cleaning, exhaust fumes from the old-fashioned tall oval black painted chimney stack with the blue band surmounted with a large white C, wandered lazily into the clear cold air.

Paying off the taxi, Brendan bent to lift his two suitcases when he heard a shout from the main deck.

"Hi! Hold on a moment. Is it Brendan Harris?" questioned a tall figure, with a very English accent, dressed in windcheater and woollen cap, leaning over the rust stained ship rail.

Receiving a confirmatory wave from Brendan, the tall male came striding down the gangway calling out, "I'll give you a hand, old chap. Hello, Brendan, I'm Leonard Bennett. Welcome on board the *Calvex Commander*. Here, let me take that suitcase. You'll be sharing with me, old chap. We're sailing in three hours, that'll be fifteen-hundred hours. We were getting a bit worried that you might not make it."

A rather weary Brendan—he had been travelling since eight o'clock the previous evening—was slightly overcome by this effusive welcome and followed the well-spoken Englishman onto the main deck and to the apprentices' cabins in the officers' accommodation.

"Allow me to introduce David Mitchell, he's from Enfield. David, this is Brendan Harris," offered Len.

"How r'ya, Bren? Hear you come from Paddy country. I'm from Southport, ye know; north of Liverpool. Call me Dave."

"Len, the third wants you on deck. We're switching tanks in ten minits." A flustered looking youngster dressed in a large windcheater, woollen gloves and a peaked cap shading his boyish face had appeared in the cabin doorway.

"Thanks, Tommy. This is Brendan Harris. He's a Dublin man, as you know."

"Hello, Brendan," acknowledged Tommy, raising his right hand as if to make a salute but dropping his arm in embarrassment, muttering, "must go. See you again."

He's just a kid, sounded like he comes from Wexford, or somewhere south of Dublin, thought Brendan to himself.

"Tommy's a first tripper, Bren. A bit of a mother's boy. Been with us three months," advised Dave in a resigned tone of voice. "We bunk down next door, I'll show you. There, you're in the top bunk. The left side of the dresser for your clothes, and the bottom two drawers in the chest under the porthole are yours. I use the desk under the ports. See you, old chap. Tom Doyle, the third, is on watch. You had better check in with him."

"What a nice guy. Dave, how long have you been on the *Commander*?" asked Brendan, as he started emptying his suitcase. He would need his working clothes when they sailed.

"I've been here six months. I hear you were on the new *Renown*. What's she like?"

"More plastic, and a streamlined funnel and goalposts instead of masts. It looks like the owners of Calvex are increasing the fleet. I see there's a thirty-two thousand tonner just been launched."

"Yeh, the *Calvex Faith*. OK for us guys, for the future. When you think the *Commander* is twelve thousand tons, a thirty-two thousand tonner is a hell of a size. I hear they are even thinking of tankers as large as one hundred thousand ton. Dave's a nice guy, a bit posh but OK. Young Tommy needs to grow up a lot. He joined last month. We've just loaded a full cargo of gas oil and white spirit for Stockholm. The rumour goes we're heading for Galveston in Texas after that."

With his newfound associates, Brendan settled into the working of what one could call a tramp ship. After their visit to Stockholm, where they went to three different delivery points for their 'clean' cargo—refined oils rather than the crude oil transported by his last ship—they headed out into the Atlantic for Galveston, Texas. With the ship in ballast—some of the tanks filled with water to keep the ship deep enough in the water to aid steering—they took four weeks to reach Texas, where they loaded a full cargo for Rotterdam.

And so on it went; the *Calvex Commander* loaded and discharged cargoes in ports around Europe and Scandinavia, but special interest was aroused when it was directed to take a cargo of varied products to the Canary Islands and from there to deliver parcels of oil to two ports in Africa: Takoradi in the new independent country called Ghana, and Lagos in Nigeria.

Having successfully completed its visit to the Canaries, the *Calvex Commander* continued its journey south across the equator. It was early one warm June day in 1957, with white clouds high in the sky and low-lying land covered in trees and mist lay to the left, that the *Commander* approached Takoradi. It was expected this would be a fast turnaround, as there was only a small parcel of cargo to unload.

Brendan, in his tropical uniform—company cap with badge, white shorts, white shirt, polished shoes and epaulettes on his shoulders—made his way to the bridge, as it was his turn for bridge duties. The other three apprentices went to mooring stations ready to dock at the oil terminal in Takoradi harbour.

Captain Rogers was on the bridge, a commanding figure in his tropical shorts and perfectly ironed white shirt. *Seemed to consider himself a story book seaman,* Brendan had thought. He demanded that all officers wore their full uniform when on duty, their uniform cap with its white tropical cover and flashy company badge, white shirt with epaulettes, white shorts and long white stockings with polished black shoes. The third mate, Tom Doyle, was officer of the watch and looked quite nondescript with his unattractive white shorts and stubby legs. The captain was a stern disciplinarian and when on the bridge could override any order made by the junior officer.

Directly ahead, in the misty early morning air, the harbour wall of Takoradi could be seen, and to the left there were some distracting flashing lights on the distant shore. There seemed to be some activity amongst the flashing lights, with people waving frantically and launching small boats.

"Wonder what that's about?" the third mate mentioned to Brendan in his nervous pacing due to the proximity of the captain.

"Third," roared the captain from the port bridge wing, the part nearest the shore, "what are they on about, and what's that ahead to starboard? Here, giv' me your binoculars, man…quickly, and put the engines on slow ahead."

Brendan, noticing the worried tone of the captain's voice, shouted out "Slow ahead, Third," and swung the telegraph handle to the new instruction to the engine room.

"Looks like a ship at anchor, sir," answered the third hesitantly, as he passed his binoculars to the captain; looking at the object closer, although the black spherical object hanging from an erect derrick post looked like an anchor ball, he was beginning to have his doubts.

"Have you checked the chart, Third? Jesus, it's a wreck, must be on a reef of some sort. What are the depth soundings? God! I'll have to do it myself," grumbled the irate captain as he strode into the enclosed part of the bridge structure.

"Captain, Captain, it's a wreck, the Monte Negro," called the third from the chartroom in a worried voice.

"Stop engines," roared the captain. "Full astern."

Brendan, repeating the order, rotated the brass telegraph handle to full astern twice to alert the engine room, leaving it to rest at the full astern position. Within seconds, the bell on the telegraph rang as the engine room responded by bringing the engine room pointer to full astern. Brendan recorded the instruction to the engine room in the log book, conscious that the captain was now anxiously looking ahead as the ship got closer to the wreck.

The small boats from the shore were closing on the tanker whilst due to the sudden change in engine beat the ship was shuddering badly, with objects falling off the walls, and the captain's cup of tea crashed to the deck.

The third, very, very worried, came out to the wheelhouse and looked anxiously at the nearing wreck. Brendan could see he had his fingers crossed behind his back. The first mate, on the foc'sle, was waving frantically as he went to pick up the phone.

The engine, by now, had stopped and was beginning to go full astern, but before the propellers had time to gather the weight of the ship and go into reverse, with an immense final jolt the *Calvex Commander* suddenly stopped moving forward. Brendan prevented himself from falling forward as he was holding onto the telegraph handle, but he could see the captain on his knees, holding onto his head, shouting confusedly, "Stop engines! Stop engines!"

The third mate, frantically trying to remain on his feet, fell against the wheelhouse wall, hitting his head on a projecting wall mount and collapsed on the floor. Brendan clung onto the telegraph as the bows of the ship rose with the momentum, pushing the front of the ship higher on the underwater obstruction. With the engines stopped, the *Calvex Commander* settled on the reef alongside the Monte Negro.

There was dead silence. Everything stood still for a moment. The helmsman stood looking at his redundant wheel, the third mate lay on the wheelhouse floor, either unconscious or unwilling to accept reality. Captain Rogers, no doubt realising the enormity of what had happened, stood leaning against the radar stand with his head bowed and his smart badged cap lying on the deck beside him.

Reality returned with the entrance, onto the bridge, of a breathless first mate, Brian Goodwin, who went directly to the captain, on whose head a noticeable swelling was arising. Instructing Brendan to take the dazed captain into the chartroom, the first mate took over, checking that Brendan had entered all movements in the log, instructed the second mate to look after the bridge whilst he, with senior apprentice, Leonard Bennett, went forward to assess what damage they could see.

By now everybody was out on deck questioning what had happened. There was talk about abandoning ship or maybe even launching the life boats, but with the tanker embedded firmly on the reef she certainly was not going to sink for the moment. The signals from the shore had stopped and the canoes and boats were now milling around the stricken tanker. The fear of fire was imminent, as high octane petrol was seeping out from the holed tanker. The mate was now in a difficult position. With the captain in a daze he had to take over, but the captain was still responsible for the ship. What to do now, try to go astern and try to free from the reef? That could increase the damage to the hull.

"What's the tide at the moment, Harris? The tide tables are there beside the charts. Second, will you get a loud hailer or something and tell those interfering sightseers to get away from the ship," the mate shouted out as he went to see to the captain, who had collapsed on the wheelhouse floor.

"Two hours to high tide, sir," called out Brendan from the chartroom door.

"Thank God for that," a relieved mate called out. "Hopefully the rise in water level will be enough to refloat. Call the shore and see if they have a tugboat to help pull us off…no…the second will do that. Good man, Harris, take the megaphone and get rid of those bastards trying to get aboard. Go get the bosun to help."

Taking the megaphone from the second, Brendan ran over to the ship's side to see four canoes with waving shouting natives backing away from the ship as a light film of oil was seeping out from the hull.

Fortunately there was little wind, so come full tide, aided by an ancient tugboat belching black smoke, and after transferring oil from the forward tanks to the few empty tanks further back in the ship, the ship's head was raised out of the water. With some gentle coaxing from the engines, and tugboat, the *Commander* scraped off the offending reef and anchored away from the harbour. The important task was now to stem the flow of escaping oil before entering the harbour.

Over the next two weeks, the ship was patched up and the *Calvex Rover*, one of the other tankers in the fleet, arrived empty to take the cargo of oil from the *Commander*. This was a fraught operation as the *Rover* had to come within fifteen feet of the *Commander*, because the flexible pipeline was not long enough to stretch any further. Six heavy coir fenders were brought in from the town and placed between the two large metal hulls, and hawsers joined the ships fore and aft to prevent them moving any further apart.

With the sea quite calm and the ships some fifteen feet apart, the lifeboat was used to take the pipelines across the short gap. The empty *Calvex Rover* seemed huge alongside, as it towered over the *Commander*, being low in the water, still with cargo. All was going well, with the pumps working hard, transferring the oil, when a small general cargo ship swept past. Orders had been given to all visiting ships to stay well clear of the tankers, but unfortunately this ship had apparently not heard the instruction and as the offending ship swept past, the surge of water displaced by it started the two tankers rolling heavily and moving together at an alarming speed.

The pump man fortunately was close at hand and raced down to the deck to stop the pumps as the flexible pipeline began to rise in the air as the hulls closed together. The coir fenders were able to cushion the impact of the two hulls, but unfortunately the life boat—some twenty-four foot long, six foot wide, and made of light aluminium—ended up crushed between the two hulls, and when they parted sank with a sigh of bubbles. The pipeline between the ships buckled and split, throwing oil over the *Commander's* deck. It was fortunate that the cargo pumps had been stopped.

It took some time for the ships to settle, and it was decided to halt the movement of the oil until something more secure was devised to keep the ships apart.

Having worked twelve-hour shifts for the past week, helping to shore up the damaged front of the ship, the four apprentices were relieved to know there would now be some time to relax. However, as they were gathered in Len and Brendan's cabin, wondering whether they could get ashore to see something of Takoradi, the second mate popped his head in and advised the mate wanted to see the four of them.

"Gentlemen," announced the first officer, as he stood up from behind his desk. "You are probably aware of the present circumstances where cargo shipment has been temporarily stopped and Captain Rogers has been relieved of his duties. I am now in charge and look forward to your support in the coming weeks. There is one small problem: the principal of the local school, here in Takoradi, has requested an officer from the *Commander* to visit and give the children a short talk about the ship and our circumstances. I see you are interested, Harris." Brendan had involuntary raised his head. "With your Irish approach and gift of the gab, I think you would be quite suitable. Mitchell, you could hold his hand. A car will be at the jetty tomorrow morning at ten to take you to the school. So you could spend some time preparing your talk, Harris, and make sure both of you look smart. OK! Dismissed. Bennett, could you stay, please?"

With a wave of his hand he motioned the others to leave.

BRENDAN AFLOAT

"Wonder what he wants Len for?" questioned David Mitchell. "That's a bit of a chore, Bren. What are you going to talk about?"

"Well," answered Brendan. "I dunno. Maybe—haven't they—Ghana just got their independence from England? I remember my stamp collection had some stamps from the Gold Cost. That was what the country was called, up to last few months."

"How'd you know that, Bren?" exclaimed Dave in mock astonishment.

"Education, Dave, a good Irish grammar school education, and some pretty Gold Coast stamps. Tommy, where did you go to school?" Bren asked, to bring Tommy into the conversation.

"Blackrock College, you know—it's near Dunlaoghaire, Brendan," was the hesitant reply.

"Blackrock College, I am impressed," exclaimed Brendan. "Your parents must be pretty well off to have sent you there."

"Well, my father's a solicitor in the city," was the proud reply. "He's got his own practice in Dame Street and—"

"Well, Bren," interrupted Dave, "what are you going to do about tomorrow? I don't know why the mate didn't ask me."

"Shure, Dave, don't worry I won't let you down, we can do it together. Probably will be a class of youngsters. We'll impress them with our tropical uniform and flash a bit of braid. That always impresses."

So the following morning, prompt at ten o'clock, an old motor boat came chugging out from the harbour for the two resplendent youngsters in their white shorts and shirts and smart white-topped peaked caps. The only braid on an apprentice's uniform were single strips of gold on their shoulder epaulets. They were met by a smartly dressed native in a rather old white Ford Escort. The many obvious rust spots were liberally covered in off white streaks which gave the well-used car the appearance of an albino zebra on wheels.

Full of chat, the smiling driver introduced himself with a somewhat unpronounceable name, and when both passengers had settled on the hard leather seats, he revved up the engine and sped away from the wharf, leaving a whirling cloud of dust behind him.

Racing down the wide dusty main street with the engine screaming, the driver turned to Brendan and, through his grinning white teeth, shouted "You like? I go faster like Fangio, I go." With the battered Escort hurtling down the street and people leaping out of the way, Brendan and Dave hung on to anything they could. As they left the main street and bounced over a rough track for a mile or two, they came to what looked like an abandoned military post, deserted turrets and dilapidated timber houses, and came to a slewing, dust raising, halt outside a high freshly painted wooden shed.

Waiting until the cloud of dust had settled, Brendan stepped out of the car door, opened by the very active driver, to be greeted by a smiling elderly black gentleman, dressed in a stained black dinner suit.

In a cultured London accent with musical undertones, he proudly introduced himself as Mr. Eyeore, the principle of this, the first secondary school in Takoradi since independence from Britain. Brendan, immediately recalling the stories of Winnie the Pooh and Eeyore, Pooh's, donkey friend, and catch phrase 'Thanks for noticing', nearly addressed him as Mr. Donkey, and introduced his co-passenger.

Mr. Eyeore was very effusive in his welcome and led the two very dusty young men into the large shed, which had been changed into a temporary school. There were a number of doors to both sides of the distempered room, with two windows opposite the entrance door. The hot sun peered through the small windows, shining on rows of desks all with a smiling black child rising to their feet, and in one attractive sound welcoming Mr. Harris.

Slightly overcome by this welcome, Brendan was then also introduced to an extremely attractive young female teacher, dressed in store bought summer clothing, who curtsied when she shook hands with the 'tall weather-beaten sailor' from across the sea—a representative from the mother country.

"Mr. Harris, Mr. Mitchell, I am sure you would like some refreshment after your dusty journey," offered Mr. Eyeore, bowing slightly and directing the two sailors to the nearest closed door. "I do hope Nero, our driver, kept within the speed limits." He smiled knowingly. "Miss McKinley, would you please continue with your lessons. Our guests will return shortly."

After a short break and pleasant conversation with Mr. Eyeore. Brendan and Dave were introduced to the very attentive class, and Brendan explained who he was, where the *Calvex Commander* had come from, and the many countries they had been to.

Miss McKinley caught Brendan's eye and requested permission to refer to a well-used book on geography and arranged for the children to gather in groups to follow, in the three books available, their guests' journeys around the world. Finding it necessary to stand closer to the young teacher to point out on the map where the ship had been, he became very conscious of her attractive body and perfume. How fresh she looked, how warm and appealing with her shiny black face and flashing smiling white teeth. Brendan was smitten. *Control yourself, Harris.* With a nod to Dave, he passed the talk over. Dave surprisingly started to emphasise how beneficial it must have been to the population to have had the benefit of British expertise and backing prior to independence in March the previous year. There was spontaneous applause, started by

Miss McKenzie and followed by the children, all nodding their heads in agreement. Somewhat surprised to see this, Brendan, who had read so much about the dreadful treatment by the English over the native Irish population before independence, thought he would bring this to the attention of the children and asked did anyone know where Ireland was. Looking somewhat bemused, the children looked at each other and shook their heads. Miss McKenzie then stood in and, smiling at Brendan, explained that Ireland was a small island alongside England and was part of the British Isles, and before Brendan could make any further comment, Mr. Eyeore, who had been sitting at the side of the room, rose and thanked these two gentlemen from England for their wonderful talk and helpful information about the big ship in the bay, and did anyone have any questions. There was an immediate forest of hands, and Miss McKenzie pointed to one alert looking anxious youngster.

"Yes, Rufus, you have a question."

Rufus, dropping his hand to his side stood up behind the desk and, in a positive but nervous voice, asked the question on all the other's faces.

"Why, Sir, did the big ship hit the wall under the sea, and why didn't it sink?"

Brendan looked at Dave, and Dave nodded. "Up to you, Bren."

Gotta be careful here, thought Brendan to himself. *Can't say the captain was an idiot and the officer of the watch should have looked ahead. A bit of diplomacy needed here, maybe a bit of waffle.*

With the very nervous youngster still awaiting a reply, Brendan smiled at him and went into reasons why the tanker hadn't sunk. Buoyant tanks, oil lighter than water, skill of the officer on watch. Why did the ship hit the reef? A board of enquiry will decide that. Maybe an error on the chart, the steering might have been faulty. Any number of reasons. Any other questions?

"But, Sir!" interrupted Rufus.

"Now, let Mr. Harris take another question, Rufus," ordered Miss McKenzie, realising the difficulty Brendan was in. Between them, Brendan and Dave answered the many questions, and after Mr. Eyeore had thanked the two of them the youngsters all stood up and clapped politely.

Brendan said his goodbyes to Mr. Eyeore and lingered a bit in his goodbye to Miss McKenzie, but could not catch her eye, and boarded the waiting Ford Escort with Fangio impatiently revving the engine. With a roar, leaving a trail of smoke and fumes, they left the two school teachers in a cloud of dust.

The following days were spent discharging the cargo into the adjoining ship and when this was completed they limped back into the port and unloaded the remaining parcel of oil ordered by Takoradi.

Len proudly announced that he had been promoted to what was termed as an uncertified third mate as he had served his time as apprentice. This made Dave into senior apprentice, and he was quite annoyed that Brendan had been given responsibility for the talk at the school and made it plain that he thought Bren was stepping out of line.

Now that the ship was patched up and cargo had all been discharged into the *Calvex Rover*, the *Commander* was readied for its trip back north for repairs to be effected. During this leisurely trip back to the UK, Brendan sat a further six-monthly exam in preparation for the next step at the end of the four years, when he would sit for his officer's examination to become a third officer.

The Calvex Rover on left, receiving oil cargo from the Calvex Commander

17

Hiccup at the Hospital

"How's he keepin' den, Nurse? How's that brother of mine? I see he's still got a lot of gadgets attached to him." The ever ebullient Billy had paid an unexpected visit to Brendan. He covered up his concern with his usual mock cheerful approach, and Nurse Mary Sheelin was taken aback as to how to respond to this rather grown up schoolboy.

"Yes, sir. Your brother is in great form. You will see we have loosened the wrist straps as he has settled down a great deal. We're hoping he comes out of the coma soon."

"God, but he looks so thin. Are you feedin' him at all, Nurse?" Billy enquired in his straightforward manner. "There's not a scrap on him."

Mary, deciding not to answer, turned to smile at the good-looking Billy. He was dressed in a white roll-necked sweater and grey slacks, and with his black curly hair and fresh complexion, along with his height, made an attractive figure to a lonely country girl living in a flat in the big city.

Billy, thinking Mary looked cute in her blue and white nurse's uniform with white cape, smiled back. Billy now seventeen was growing up fast and looked a couple of years older than his age.

"What part of the country are you from then, Nurse?" was the only thing he could think of to say.

Smiling to herself as she leaned over to punch the pillow under the somnolent Brendan, Mary answered, "'Tis from Carlow, I am from, den, sir. 'Tis from Dublin ye will be from yerself, is it now?" Mary questioned, giving Brendan an accidental mild blow to the side of his head as she punched the pillow…*sorry, Rudi, hope I didn't hurt ye, did I? Yer little brudder is makin' a play for me, I'm thinkin'…*

"Nurse Sheelin, Nurse Sheelin," was the call from the ward, quickly followed by the curtain being drawn back. "Oh! Der you are, Sheelin."

135

*Could have thought as much. The nurses all seem to flock to this corner…*thought Sister Sullivan. Noticing Billy, she recoiled slightly. *Another Harris—they'll be the death of me.* "Oh! Hello, Mr. Harris, sorry to disturb you, but Nurse is wanted on the ward," she addressed Billy whilst indicating to the nurse to leave the bed.

"Hello, Sister," greeted Billy, smiling at the disgruntled woman. "Everything all right? Oh! By the way, I hoped to collect Brendan's diary. I don't see it by the bed. You haven't hidden it, Bren?" He looked at the sleeping body, waiting for the sister's response.

Oh! God! The diary thing… "Yes! I seem to have heard of this diary, Mr. Harris. Have you not got it den?"

"No, Sister," replied Billy, slightly exasperated by the silly question.

"Perhaps somebody else has taken it. Your elder brother was in a short while ago…" suggested Sullivan, "or maybe your mother. There are a lot of visitors for your brother, der. He's lookin' much better now. Would you agree?"

Billy, unsure of himself, agreed that anything she said could be possible, said his goodbyes, and passing through the ward on his way out, waved goodbye to Nurse Sheelin.

Later that day, Billy sat down to the evening meal in Laurel Cottage with Alice and Henry and Jono, who had dropped in for a short visit. Billy brought up his visit to the hospital.

"Ye kno', Ma, Bren is not lookin' so well at all, now. He's been unconscious for nearly two weeks…"

"I know, Billy," answered Alice, resting her knife and fork alongside the potatoes and meat on her plate. "Yes, I agree with you, Billy, he does not look at all well." Pointing her finger and looking towards the other diners, she continued, "He's so thin. They mustn't be feeding him properly. But what can we do? What do you think, Hen?"

"Well, Alice," answered Henry, balancing a forkful of mashed potato on his knife, "I am sure the hospital know what they're doin'. The poor lad has brightened up a bit. And I think…now don't take this wrong," Henry looked around the table and raised his voice, "I think there should be somebody from the family beside that bed, talking to him all the time. We know he can hear. Larrigan did say that could help Bren survive…"

"Yes, Pop," interrupted Jono, "the fear is when he comes out of the coma he could be in a vegetative state. We've gotta do something more positive."

"What do you mean, a vegetative state, Jono?" interrupted Billy.

"I've been reading up a bit about results of comas, an' Bren, from what I read, is in a deep one. If the brain is damaged he could lose, say, the power of reasoning, or even the ability to speak or even hear. That's what they call a vegetative state, Billy." Jono took a drink of tea, saw the shocked faces of the others, and continued pointing his fork at Alice. "Ma, as I was going to say, I'll take time off work and we could arrange to be with Bren…"

"Yes, Jono. Hen, can you take any time off work? You're right, Jono." A reinvigorated Alice began to take command. "Maybe you could get in after school, Billy," Alice suggested, looking directly at Billy, who looked quite startled at the thought.

"I'll give Polly a ring. She has been in to see him the most, believe it or not. She probably thinks badly of us."

"But Ma, wait a minute," continued Billy, "if Bren is in this vegetative state, as Jono says, would our talking to him all day long be any use?" He put a forkful of meat and mash into his mouth with a flourish, as if to say that's the end of the discussion.

"I kno' what you mean, Billy," replied Henry, being more forceful and positive than he had ever been in his life before. "But we've gotta do something. I'll take the day off tomorrow and you and I, Alice, can go in an' see Larrigan an' get things moving."

There was silence; Alice looked at Henry, seeing a husband she had never seen before, so positive. *Where has this forceful man come from?* Billy, who had never heard his father raise his voice or hold an argument, looked on in astonishment, whilst Jono applauded his father with a cheer and pat on the back. The most startled of them all was Henry himself. *What have I done? I've never taken a day off work before, what about all those calls I have to do…no, this is more important.*

"Right, you, lot," he said, looking at the startled faces, "get that food into you an' let's get into that hospital an' show them."

The atmosphere in the room changed. There was purpose in the air. They weren't going to leave their Brendan to the mercy of others. "Hold on, everyone," were the sudden cautionary words from Jono, who had lit up one of his smelly cigarettes. "We just can't go storming in and take over." Looking at the surprised faces around him, Jono took a pull on his cigarette. "You know what I mean. We can't just storm into the hospital." He laughed scornfully. "They would probably throw us out. Sorry to interrupt, Pop…"

"That's OK, Jono, I know what you mean," answered Henry, enjoying his newfound confidence. "If you and Billy, or maybe your Una, were to go in…there's another hour for visiting. You could check if Larrigan is around, and your ma and I could go in tomorrow to see him."

"OK, Pop. What about it, Billy?"

"I've got a college class to look after tonight. Could knock off early from work tomorrow and call in. Sorry, everyone." Looking very guilty and sheepish, Billy hung his head.

"That's OK, Billy," offered Jono. "I'll go on my own, maybe get Una, or what about Polly? A female voice may be good for Bren. He likes the girls."

Henry and Alice, very relieved that Jono was now taking some responsibility for Brendan's recovery, decided to relax and pay a short visit to Moron's Pub that evening.

we hauled off from the jetty. Turning in the dark and gloomy basin aptly named Chaudron d'Enfer, where the current attains its maximum force of ten to eleven knots and the many eddies and whirlpools make steering difficult, we proceeded down river at the tremendous speed of fifteen knots and were soon out into the open sea.

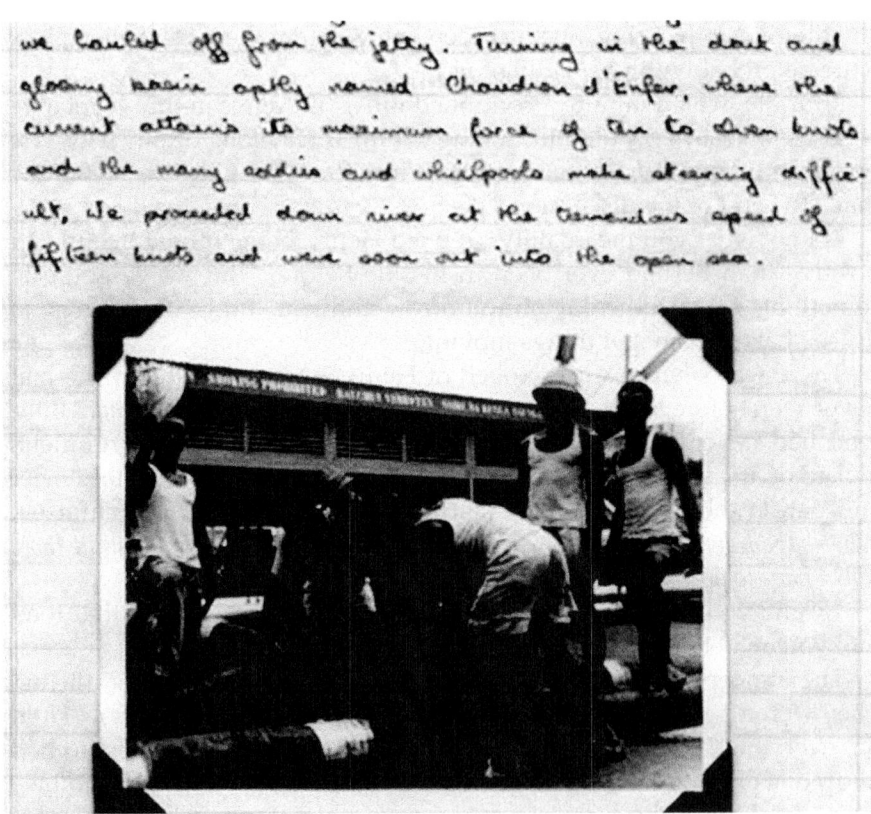

Jetty Workmen, West Africa

18

Polly at the Party

Upon reaching Sunderland on the east coast of the UK, Brendan, along with the rest of the officers, was given shore leave and provided with a travel pass for a return trip to Ireland, and was told to report back to the *Commander* in fourteen days' time. On his way back, during the train journey across England and the overnight B&I ferry to Dublin, Brendan looked back over the months he had spent at sea.

He had put on a bit of weight, gained himself a sun tan and a lot more confidence. He felt he had grown up a great deal. The world was a lot smaller from the time, some two years previously, he had left his sheltered life in Ireland. He had seen the world in its different guises: the wealth of some countries contested with the poverty in others. He was shocked with the class divide in India and the sheer poverty of some compared to the riches of others. He wondered at the grandeur of Venice and the loudness of Cape Town. Ghana was a surprise; would their new country succeed in its newfound independence? What a complex lot the human race were, with such a mix of black people, brown people and all shades of white people. The world was full of gorgeous girls, coming in all sizes and colours. Even the smell of oil and paint had its charms The breathlessness of the severe heat in the Persian Gulf compared with the freezing extremes inside the Arctic circle tested the mettle of all. One overriding feature, over all in these years, was the exhilaration of stormy seas, the immense power of the oceans when in turmoil, and the sleeping dangers of a flat calm.

Brendan was now learning how to relate to his peers, to give and take, to study new subjects, spherical trigonometry, ship construction, ship handling, how to load a banana boat from a book, how to handle people. Learn how to dance, find out, with as much practice as possible, what girls want. Not to worry too much about the lack of money. In fact, take a deep breath and look forward to the next two years. The exam results from the company, to date, had all been positive. *I've got a lovely girlfriend at home and a few others around the world, so,* Brendan thought to himself as he arrived on leave in Dublin, *I've got a pretty good life.*

"Hi, Ma, Pop, thanks for collecting me. You must have got up early, it's only seven o'clock. What about work, Pop?"

"Hello, Son," greeted Henry, smiling at Brendan, whist Alice did her best to squeeze the air from his body in a welcoming hug.

"Have a good trip?" continued Henry, picking up one of the two suitcases Brendan had deposited at the side of the ship's gangway. "How long did you say you'd be home for? I'll drop you both home to the cottage and should get back into the city by nine."

"You're looking well, Brendan. Oh! It's so nice to see you again," enthused Alice. "We've arranged a small party for you over the weekend. Polly is sorry she couldn't get off work today to meet you. But she sends her love."

Is Ma cooking up something here? What's this new closeness with Polly? I'll give her a ring tonight. She should have had my letter posted in Takoradi.

"Thanks, Ma, I'll look forward to that. Got a few souvenirs for you both. They're in that suitcase, Pop. I see you've still got the old Wolseley 8. God, it must have a fair mileage on it now. How old is it, must be somethin' like twenty years old?"

"Yes, Bren, well on its way to a hundred thousand. Over ten years old now," a proud Pop replied, patting the shiny bonnet in affection. "Right, in you get and we'll make our way home."

Climbing into the rear seat, the smell of the gleaming leather upholstery and the sight of the dark wooden dashboard brought back memories of weekend drives into the Wicklow Mountains for a picnic, or a trip down to Killiney beach for a dip in the Irish Sea.

Brendan settled down as best he could in the cramped seating space and listened to the local news from his ma—how the neighbours were and how his brothers were managing. The council had just tarred the road outside the cottage and when it got hot, the tar melted. Back to humdrum attractive normality.

"You know we've just got rid of Dev. This new guy, Sean Lamass, might do some good, even though he's still Fianna Fail," announced Pop suddenly from the driver's seat, as they wandered along at a strict thirty miles an hour. The Wolsey's maximum speed in any case was a slow sixty miles an hour.

"Dev—that's Dev Valera, the prime minister, isn't it, Pop? Wasn't he one of the rebels in the twenties?"

"Now, boys," interrupted Alice, "now don't get started on politics. Time is too short. Do you know, is that pal of yours, Brendan, Jim Curtis, at home now? Didn't he go to sea? Do you think he would like to come to the party on Saturday?"

"Questions, questions, Ma," Brendan suppressed a yawn. "Look, Ma, I'm half asleep. I'll dig out his number when we get home."

"OK, Bren, I'll shut up now, but you're not getting away that easy," called out Ma as the atmosphere in the car settled down to a relaxed silence.

Arriving at the cottage, memories were brought to the fore; the long roughly built wall surmounted by the laurel hedge leaning over it, the small green door in the wall with the unpolished brass notice stating *Laurel Cottage*. Humming the tune "The Green Door" by Jim Lowe, a recent hit song, Brendan remembered when he was four years old and the great excitement when the family moved into Laurel Cottage. Now eighteen years old, worldly wise and grown up, to Brendan the once high wall looked smaller, and the door minute. The white plaster, once clean and unbroken, was crumbling in parts showing the red brick. When he stepped inside the door everything looked so much smaller; the long lawns which seemed to stretch for hundreds of yards up to the imposing double-fronted cottage now looked so much shorter. The grass needed cutting and the hedges trimming. *That's something I can do over the next few days*, thought Brendan, *but doesn't the cottage look imposing, with its large chimney breasts and the walls covered in Virginia creeper? Ah, yes, this is home.*

The orchard stretching down the left side of the cottage was, as ever, full of apple trees with young fruit beginning to ripen. The loganberry, gooseberry, blackberry and currant bushes peered out from the long grasses and colourful yellow dandelions, all displaying their ripening fruits. Looking to the right, the pine trees edging what was called the paddock were as tall as ever in their green glory. *Remember climbing a few of them when a youngster. Oh! Memories.* "Hey, Ma, where's Billy?"

"Probably still in bed," snorted Ma in a resigned tone. "Loves his bed, does Billy. God he'd better get moving or he'll be late for school. What's the time, Hen? My watch has stopped."

"It's only eight, Alice, plenty of time. I'll put the car up the avenue at the side and have a quick cup of tea," announced Henry, striding back to the green door.

Over the next few days, Brendan relaxed into the comfortable feeling of home and security, although Pop seemed somewhat subdued. Never one to display emotion, not like Ma, he was quieter than usual. *Perhaps I'll have a word with him, see if he will talk*, thought Brendan in his newfound adulthood. Billy, ever the independent youngster in his early teens, still going to school, whilst proud of his seagoing big brother did not want to show too much admiration and was a bit distant.

Jono was now a Lance Corporal in the army. Ma and Pop were both very proud of him and had become members of the local branch of the British Legion in Dunlaoghaire. Ma was reaching the social level she had always aspired to.

"Maybe you and Polly could come down some evening next week, after the party," Ma suggested. "You're ringing her tonight, aren't you?"

"Come down where, Ma?" Brendan asked, slightly confused.

"Sorry, Bren, I was wandering a bit, was thinking of the Legion. Be lovely if Jono were here, we could all go down together. Wonder what Billy will do when he leaves school? He'll be leaving soon, thank goodness, as the fees are getting a bit steep."

Wonder if that's what's bothering Pop, thought Brendan. "Yes, Ma, I'll come down after the weekend. Will give Polly a ring after tea. Have you asked her about the party?"

"Yep, Bren, she's coming. She's been looking forward to it. Is that the phone I hear? Just a minute, Bren. Be back in a sec," said Ma, as she left Brendan sitting in the front room whilst she went into the hallway.

"Hey! Bren, it's Polly, she's ringing from work, come quick."

"Hello, Polly, just got in this morning. I was going to call you tonight."

"Hello, Bren, lovely to hear you again. Got your last letter. Dying to meet you."

"Me too, Polly, not me, I mean you…you know what I mean," he laughed. "It's a lovely day, what would you like to do?"

"Could you come down to my house? I should be home about five thirty, have my tea and be ready at half six. We could go to the pictures, or maybe a walk down the pier and have a cup of coffee in the Roman."

"Not too keen on the pictures, it should be a nice evening, a walk down the pier—"

"Sorry, Bren, got to go, see you at the house at seven, OK? Bye."

"Hey, Ma. When's tea? I'm going down to Polly's for seven. Must get the bike out. Hope Billy has been looking after it. Are you there, Billy?"

"I'm using it tonight, Brendan, going to the club, sorry you can't have it," came the voice from the back room.

"But Billy, it's my bike."

"Don't care, I'm going to use it. You come home thinking you can take over. Well I'm having it and that's final," came the loud deliberate statement from the back room.

I suppose he's got a point, thought Brendan, *he must feel out of it. Must get around to having a chat with him.*

"OK, Billy," called Bren. "You win. Any idea how I can get down to Dunlaoghaire?"

"Get the bus," was the scornful reply.

Better give up, Bren, or I'll go in and hit him. Suppose I could leave early and walk. It's only a couple of miles. Wish I had a car. Maybe Pop, when he comes home, could drop me down. Or maybe not, he'll be tired after work. OK, Shanks's pony it is. Boy I'm looking forward to this. She seems keen. Mustn't forget the present I got in Cape Town. Where is it?

Humming the tune of "The Green Door", Brendan danced down the hall and into the side room where his bed was—the same room he had slept in as a youngster. The water pipes running along the top of the wall were still unpainted, but the walls were now white-washed. The same dirty curtains were hanging limply by the windows.

"Ah, there we are," he exclaimed as he produced the small oblong box, with the words 'The Lion's Head Gold Mine' embossed on it, from his suitcase. Lifting the thin lid, he checked the silver chain enclosed; the piece of gold clipped onto it was still there, with the small fancy written certificate stating it to be a nugget of real gold from The Lions Head Gold Mine, Cape Town, South Africa. It had cost £4 in English money—half a month's wages—so it must be real. *Probably not, but Polly won't know how much it cost. Cape Town, the Blue Moon. Wow!*

With his newfound knowledge of the world, and especially of girls, Brendan, after a meal of egg and chips, set off on his walk to Polly's. Up past the Vee cottage, memories of the old dead woman and the lost penny came back. Next, Moran's Pub, again memories of his first pint and Timothy Spangles, the tramp with the wonderful voice. Then down the hill past the reformatory school, memories again, picking potatoes for a shilling an hour and cleaning out the pig sties. *Wonder why they hired me when the school was full of able-bodied young men?* He walked along past the houses in Mountown, down York Road and past the grammar school. The school hadn't changed; imposing iron gates leading into lawns on both sides of the drive, up to the wide, tall building, with large windows framed by Virginia creeper. Memories again, some good some bad.

However, I'm grown up now, going to meet my girl. Feeling quite exhilarated, he ran the last half mile, remembering when he had first met Polly at the parochial dance a few years ago. He jumped up and punched the air in exuberance and sheer delight, realising how fortunate he was. Reaching his destination, he raced up the steps to the large door framed by marble pillars, stubbed his toe on the top step and crashed into the doorway. Fortunately he had brought his arms up in time to cushion himself and ended up in a heap on the concrete. Feeling quite the fool, with painful arms and a throbbing right big toe, he began to rise from the hard concrete when his eye caught the bottom of the heavy door swinging open. *Oh! God! What do I say?* were his first thoughts, then, *Boy my arm hurts.*

It was Polly, all anxious. "Are you all right, Brendan? Why are you down there, trying to get in the letter box, were you?" she asked, stifling a laugh. "Why didn't you use the bell?" she asked in a mock serious voice. "That's what most people do." With no movement from Brendan, she crouched down, becoming a mite anxious. "Are you all right, Bren? Speak to me."

On his knees, Brendan bowed his head. Beginning to laugh he caught Polly by the shoulders and looked her in the eyes. "I'll feel a lot better if you give me a kiss."

"Oh! You silly eejit," snorted Polly. "Just the one…" Without any more prompting Brendan rose to his feet, took her in his arms and kissed her hard on the lovely lips, holding her tight. The pain in his arms and foot forgotten.

Leaning back, still with his arms holding her, Brendan smiled at Polly, her face flushed and her eyes bright.

"Hello, Polly, I stubbed my foot, it hurts awful. Have you any iodine or something to put on it?" He laughed.

"Iodine?" she asked leaning back. "What would that do for you?" She snorted. "Come on in and meet Mum, she's dying to meet you again." After reintroductions to Mrs. Hughes, and a laugh about Brendan's entrance, Polly took Brendan into the kitchen to administer to his bruises and to catch up on all the news.

"You're a lucky guy then, Brendan. She adores you. Look she's smiling at you now."

The time for the party had arrived and Brendan was enjoying himself. A lot of people had arrived, along with Jim, his seagoing pal. They were both standing at the entrance to the kitchen with drinks in their hands, discussing, as always where Jim was concerned, the girls in his life.

"Aw, shut up, Jim. Isn't she nice, though?" replied Brendan. "Look at those lovely legs, and she's got a real trim waist and her top half looks great. I think she's got marriage designs, though. I'm only eighteen and she's twenty. What about yourself, Jim? How many whiskeys have you had? You're still chasing that Sonja lass? I'd better go on the orange juice. I'm feeling a bit wonky an' I don't even like the stuff. Dat's the whiskey, you know. God, I'm rambling."

"I've had a couple of brandies, Bren, an' I'm quite sober. I can hod my drink, old chap. Shee's a luvy girl," slurred Jim. "Ah! Sonja, the love of my life wh' a girl. What am I sayin', Bren, haven't seen her for a year or more. She married that German geezer, old enough to be her father," explained Jim with a mock resigned smile. He took his comb from his corduroy jacket and combed his quiff back with a flourish. Proud of his quiff was Jim.

Brendan forced himself to stand upright. He'd had two whiskeys with a drop of ginger in each and nothing to eat, as it was still early in the evening, and was feeling a bit frustrated. Polly seemed to have become very involved with Ma Harris and wasn't giving him the attention he had expected. His thoughts turned to Jono's Una, and memories of her teasing at the dance in the ballroom not so long ago. Brendan liked Polly as a friend, but like all young men of eighteen he was looking for something more. What that was he was not too sure, but the lower part of his body was sending out the standard signal.

"Bren," was the call from the kitchen. "Bren, can you come down? We need you."

"That's Ma calling, Jim. Go an' entertain Ada Duffy there. She's been admirin' you all evenin'."

"Just for you, old buddy, I'll give her some of my time," accepted Jim, "but I'm used to more classy talent, ye know, havin' had my way with royalty. Tell you later, old chap," Jim remonstrated with Bren as he walked slowly toward Ada. Ada, who had noticed Bren smiling at her as he pointed her out to the unsteady Jim, dropped her eyes and looked as if she wished to escape.

Over the past minutes the house had begun to fill with guests, mainly the neighbours but with a fair number of Brendan's acquaintances. Jono arrived with Una. She looked quite startling in tight white jeans and a snug white blouse, showing the outline of her bra.

"Comin', Ma," answered Bren to the further call from the kitchen, as he acknowledged Jono and Una's entrance. "See you in a minute. Ma's callin'. Must go." He grinned as he tried to pass a large, corpulent man with a red face and thinning hair, dressed in a sloppy tweed suit.

"You're lookin' well, son," was the greeting in a marked country accent. "I hear you're a sailor now then," and began to recite, "A life on de ocean wave…" which petered out as Brendan's look of astonishment that this tall man in sloppy clothes was the representative of the Garda—the elite police force. He was the sergeant, and Brendan had not seen him out of his smart uniform and peaked cap.

"Oh! Sergeant," exclaimed Brendan. "Didn't recognise you for the moment, out of your uniform. I see you gotta drink. Got to go, the Ma is callin'," apologised Brendan as he made his way across the room. "Hello, Sean; hello there, Mrs Duffy, see you in a minute. Get yourself a drink. Gotta go, Ma is callin'."

"Hey, Brendan! Give us a hand," was the call from the porch as Brendan exited into the hall. It was Pop, with a large crate full of Guinness bottles, followed by one of his many friends from work, 'Moonjoe' Murphy, so called because he entertained parties with his rendering of "Moon River" on his mouth organ and his name was Joe.

Moonjoe was carrying two bags of white buns, one in each hand. "Der's another bag in the car, can you go an' get it, Bren?"

"Sorry, Pop, can't do. The Ma calls. I'll take the crate from you, Pop. Hello, Mr. Murphy, got your organ with you?" enquired Brendan as he took over the heavy crate of drinks.

"Rarin' to go, Sonny, after a few pints. You the sailor?" queried Moonjoe.

"Yep, Mr. Murphy, gotta go. See you later," replied Brendan, turning on his heel to start down the hallway.

"Oops, Sailor, where you going?"

"Oh, sorry. Oh, it's Una. How are you, Una? Sorry, I'm in a hurry." Brendan, taken by surprise, pleased the crate was a barrier between them but also sorry, moved on swiftly down the hallway toward the kitchen.

"Yes, Ma! I'm here. You wanted me?" he called out to Alice, who was busy making sandwiches at the wooden table near the window, with Polly working away beside her.

"Brendan, will you do me a favour and tell this lass of yours she's done enough and to go and enjoy herself. She's made a couple million sandwiches."

"Come on, Polly, I haven't seen anything of you over the past couple of days," invited Brendan, delighted to see the somewhat relieved smile on Polly's face.

"Are you shure now, Alice, the sausages haven't gone on yet an'—"

"Go on, girl. Pop will help out and there's always Jono. I wonder if the Una one knows how to make a sandwich? Come on, Jono, and get workin'."

"Aw, Ma, I've bin workin' all day long," sighed Jono in mock complaint, as he took a bite out of one of the sandwiches from the piled plate on the table. "What do you need doing?"

"Great, get those sausages in the pan…"

Catching Polly's hand, Brendan helped her divest herself of the grubby apron and invited her out in the fresh air to be together.

"Bren, your Ma is lovely, but can't she talk. She told me all about your da's family and the people down the road. Who's Stormy Doyle? And does Ada Duffy really fancy you? Look, Bren, you go entertain your fans for a few moments while I get washed up and put my party clothes on. I bet you will like them. Nobody's looking, giv' us a kiss."

Wrapping his long arms around this delicious warm slender body, Brendan kissed her long and until they were gasping for air.

"See you in a few minutes, Brendan, love," called Polly as she ran back into the house to get ready for the party.

Taking a deep breath of the fresh air in the orchard alongside the cottage, full of the aroma of fruit and grass and the sound of the many birds, the hum of insects and sound of laughter emanating from the cottage, Brendan again thought himself blessed with good fortune. With a jaunt in his step he made his way back to the party.

Every party at this time had to have music, with the record player now taking over from the piano, but Mrs. Duffy was the Winifred Atwell of Killoughlin town. A singsong was very popular, and with Moonjoe adding his accompaniment to the piano with the mouth organ, a strange combination, everyone was having a great time. The cigarette smoke was getting thicker in the room and everybody had a drink. The sandwiches and sausages had all been consumed. Ma insisted on making her usual embarrassing attempt—embarrassing for her family but the guests loved it—at singing "The Woman with the Wooden Leg". Having had a few drinks, she would call for silence and, standing before the piano in her red flouncy dress with the startling low cut white top, and her lips very red from the vermillion lipstick, she would commence singing in a voice full of apprehension until she got her confidence in the second verse, where she kicked up her legs and danced around, pretending to play a fiddle.

> *In the town of Ballybray there was a lassie dwelling*
> *I knew her very well and her story's well worth telling*
> *He father kept a still and he was a good distiller*
> *But when she took to the drink, well the devil wouldn't fill her*
> *She had a wooden leg that was hollow down the middle*
> *She used to tie a string on it and play it like a fiddle*
> *She fiddled in the hall and she fiddled in the alleyway*
> *She didn't give a damn for she had to fiddle anyway.*

The audience all roared and clapped, somewhat disappointed when Alice admitted she didn't know any more of the song.

"I know one," called the sergeant, and in a surprisingly gentle tenor voice started to sing the sad song "Danny Boy", and when he came to the second verse everyone joined in:

> *But come ye back when summer's in the meadow*
> *Or when the valley's hushed and white with snow*
> *'Tis I'll be here in sunshine or in shadow*
> *Oh, Danny boy, oh, Danny boy, I love you so.*

And so the evening continued. Mrs. Duffy banged away on the piano, the singing got louder, the cigarette smoke got thicker, and the Irish accents got broader. Brendan had a go at singing "Don't fence me in", in his Bing Crosby voice, and Polly recited a verse from "Golden Daffodils". Jono told a few jokes about Englishmen, Scotsmen and Irishmen. Una did a mock strip tease, which the older members of the party were somewhat shocked to see. Pop kept the drinks going and Billy, who had been very quiet, made a great attempt at an Irish jig. A great night was had by all and grudgingly everyone started to make exit movements at three in the morning. Ma had agreed that Polly could stay over in the spare bed in the back room, which led Brendan to consider certain fantasies. Jono disappeared with Una in the Ford Consul; Billy fell asleep on the dining room sofa. He'd had a couple of whiskeys, and had to be carried to bed. When everyone had gone, Brendan stood with his arm around Polly in the sitting room, with the cigarette smoke still hovering close to the ceiling and half-empty beer glasses and empty tea cups strewn around.

"What a night, Polly, everyone seemed to enjoy themselves."

"Yes, Brendan, what a night! They all love you, as I've always done," replied Polly, snuggling against Brendan's body.

God, how do I reply to this? Am I feeling the same? What does she mean? An admission of love means commitment, marriage, children, and responsibility. Do I respond with a similar admission? Is that what she wants?

"What a lovely thing to say, Polly. I don't know what love really means, but at the moment you are everything to me," replied Brendan, holding Polly closer to him and kissing the top of her head. "We had better get to bed, it's getting late, Polly…I mean, not we together…but we—"

"I know, Bren, but we had better not. Love the thought, but…"

Brendan was not surprised at Polly's decision, and whilst disappointed he was to a certain extent relieved. They spent the next while on the sofa and he then showed her to her room. With the hall clock chiming three sympathetic rings, Brendan got under the blankets of his lonely bed.

"Bren, Brendan, Brendan, quick, there's a phone call for you, it sounds like an Englishwoman."

It was nine o'clock on a lovely summer morning, shortly after the party. Brendan was just preparing to cycle down to Polly's; she had got the day off to go to the beach with him.

What could it be? thought Brendan as he acknowledged his mother's call and raced in from the orchard where he had been weeding some of the flower beds. *Must be Calvex, I'm due for a recall. It's been a month since I left the* Commander.

"Hello? Brendan Harris."

"Glad I caught you, Mr. Harris, this is Calvex head office here. I'm requested to inform you that you are expected to join the *Calvex Faith* in Birkenhead Dock on Thursday seventeenth July. We are sending travel warrants to your home. That is all right, I take it?"

"Yes! Of course!" replied Brendan.

"Good. Yes, there will be a letter with the warrants outlining everything. Goodbye, and bon voyage."

That gives me another couple of days, thought Brendan. *It's Monday now, sail on Wednesday night from Dublin…*

"Ma, did you hear that? I'll be leaving on Wednesday night. Joining the ship on Thursday, in Liverpool. The *Calvex Faith*."

"Hope you won't be going to any dangerous countries," said Ma as she flicked a duster at the hall table.

"Must get going, Ma. Polly will be waiting. Billy's at school, did he take the bike?"

"You must have a talk with him before you go, Brendan. He feels very much out of things, with his big brothers keeping the world going. I'm sure he took the bike."

"I'll take the bus. What's the time? Must get a new watch. I got one in Italy, a Glorisa, it just gave up. Suppose I'm lucky it kept going for a year."

"Will you be home for tea? I could get Pop to do a fry up."

"That'd be great, Ma. I'll be back about six. Thanks, Ma! Thanks for all you're doin', I'm very grateful," enthused Brendan, giving her an unaccustomed peck on the cheek and a brief hug as he left to catch the bus.

The next couple of days went by in a flash. Brendan waved goodbye to his parents at the Dublin Quay whilst he boarded the B&I boat to Liverpool. Polly did not come to see him off, as she had said a tearful goodbye the previous evening and given him a wristwatch as a farewell present. *Farewell forever*, wondered Brendan, *or just a farewell until we meet again?*

I get the feeling it's up to me, but what can I do? I'm only earning buttons and have a lot of living to do, but she is nice. Hope I don't lose her but…

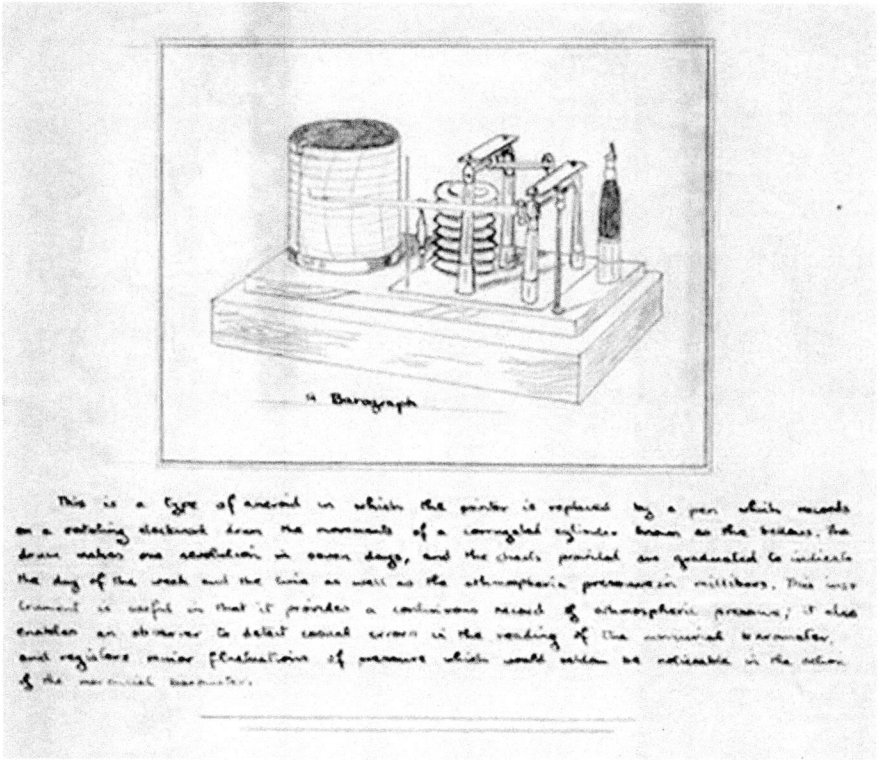

Sketch of Barograph

19

Join Ship in Liverpool

"Seaman's home, Mister. You could walk to it. Ah! I see you have two cases. There's a taxi rank just over there, by the Liver Buildings. Yes! Mam…"

Nodding his thanks, Brendan, in the light rain, dragged his two suitcases under the remaining parts of the now disused overhead railway. He had received, before leaving home the previous evening, a large envelope with a travel warrant and instructions to check into the seaman's home when he arrived in Liverpool and await further information.

"Sailors' Home, Mister, have you der in a jiff," answered the taxi driver in his marked Scouse accent, directing Brendan to put his luggage on the taxi floor. Brendan, enquiring how much it would cost, was relieved to find it wouldn't be any more than a shilling. Lighting up a cigarette and thanking the smiling taxi driver, he looked up to see the famous liver birds on the Liver Buildings welcoming him to Liverpool. Entering the wide thoroughfare, they passed the ancient church of St. Nick's to the left, and within minutes he was left standing in the rain outside the imposing Sailors' Home in Canning Place. The taxi driver, full of information, had explained in his strong accent that as far as Brendan could comprehend, the home was there to provide a refuge from the grog shops—"Drunk for a penny and blind for tuppence"—and the attentions of Judies such as Harriet Lane, Jumping Jenny and 'The Battleship'.

Looking up at all the imposing, but dirty brickwork of the entrance, at the large letters proclaiming he was entering the Sailors' Home, he passed through what must have been the Pooley Gates, or as the taxi driver had laughingly stated the 'Pearly Gates', a pun on Pooley, the manufacturer's name. "It's a bit like a prison, young fella, rather than the gateway to heaven," was the added warning.

The severe lady behind the iron grilles and artwork passed Brendan a key, an envelope from Calvex, and a notice stating drinking and entertaining members of the opposite sex were forbidden and the doors were locked at midnight. Brendan, realising his smiles and laughing witticisms were falling on rather deaf ears, nodded his head in defeat and made his way into the yawning mouth of the ancient building.

Three tiers of cast iron ornamental galleries, all utilising nautical themes of twisted ropes, dolphins and mermaids, stretched ahead of him with a smell of dust and rusting iron work. Finding his cabin on the lower tier, Brendan sat on the bare mattress, placing the blankets and sheets he had been given by the severe lady on the soiled bare pillow. Brendan, sniffing the kippered room, opened the letter from Calvex.

Without any preamble he was instructed to report on board the *Calvex Faith* in Birkenhead Dock, to Captain Alan Holder, by Thursday morning, 17th July. *Great. That gives me the evening to myself, maybe get to see some of Liverpool's night life. Get a bite to eat here at the home then have a wander around the town, back by midnight, only have a couple of shillings to spend anyway.*

In the light rain on a warm sullen night, Brendan, dressed in a light macintosh and black sou'wester—*might as well keep my hair dry*—strolled away from the Liverpool docks towards the imposing buildings harbouring the offices of the many shipping companies based in the city, past the many insurance companies, and across to Mathew Street, a narrow street off one of the main thoroughfares. Brendan had been told about a club there called the Cavern. This club, which had only been open for a year or so, was full of talent and plenty of music. Feeling a slight buzz of anticipation, he made his way down the narrow wet street, along with quickly moving groups of youngsters, overhearing comments and exclamations in a strange guttural accent full of words like 'ye kno', 'Jesus', 'yokes', and 'tarrah'. The girls were all protective of their large hairdos, with some wearing wide flouncy dresses, whilst the boys in the main seemed to slouch along with their hands deep in the pockets of their plastic raincoats.

Following the others, Brendan pushed his way forward, smiling at the noisy girls, past the crudely painted CND symbols and graffiti, and then down a flight of steep wooden steps into a hot, thick atmosphere of dim lights, unwashed bodies, cigarette smoke and amplified sound. Stuffing his sou'wester into his coat pocket, he joined the others as they passed their coats to a young red-headed girl behind a table. She acknowledged Brendan's presence with a comment in a strong Scouse accent as she handed him his cloakroom ticket. Brendan grinned at her but she was busily tending to the coats being handed in. Lighting up a Kensitas tipped, he pushed his way into a long, barrel-shaped room with a low ceiling made of bare bricks, with rivers of condensation running down the walls. There were dozens of teenagers—the boys dressed in suits and jackets with thin lapels and matching thin ties, whilst the girls were in the main dressed in short skirts with tight exciting sweaters, or in wide flouncy dresses with beehive hairdos. The narrow stage was occupied by a small group with guitars and a drummer.

"Who are the band?" Brendan shouted the question to a taller than average tight sweater as she and her friend jigged to the sound of the rhythm music.

"Dat's Paul McCartney, isn't he a dream? They're the Quarrymen. Where have you been, fella?" was the dismissive comment as Brendan realised his blazer, with its wide shoulders and Calvex tie, were somewhat out of context with the Cavern ambience.

"I'm new to the scene here, girls," answered Brendan with his disarming smile, running his fingers through his hair. "Just in from the far east, on the tanker, first time in Liverpool."

"Me brud's on a tanker, he's a steward," replied the taller of the two bouncy sweaters. "What do you do, fella?"

Surprised with the result of this, his first encounter of the evening, and enthralled by the movement of the two girls, he stepped in to join in the gyrating dance. "What's the name of the tune?"

"'That'll be the Day', fella. I asked yeh what you do on the tanker," was the short reply from the moving body.

"I'm a navigating officer," shouted Brendan over a sudden rattle of the drums.

"Is dat so den? Look, Pat, der's Mike an' Jim. Nice talkin' to you, fella...Hi, Mike!"

"Bye, girls, nice meeting you," answered Brendan under his breath as the sweaters and nylon-encased legs went to join the fortunate Mike and Jim.

Lighting a cigarette, Brendan, feeling very conspicuous in his out of context clothes and short haircut, decided as it had been a long day. He might as well cut his losses and get an early night. He had to find his way back to the seaman's home. He collected his raincoat from the talkative redhead and, after a miserable walk back in the rain to the equally miserable seaman's home, he was relieved to find a note at reception, advising there would be a taxi calling at eight fifteen the following morning to take him to the *Calvex Faith*, across the river in Birkenhead.

AARHUS   TO   MALBORG   AND   I.Q.G.R.Q.

Sunday 20th Sept. to Saturday 26th.

Quite an eventful week this week with two ports and the orders. On anchoring off Aarhus on Saturday evening we were informed that we should have to wait until the next day before the clean oil berth was free. So on Sunday afternoon when the "Belgulf Glory"

Fishing trawler
harbouring from threatening storm.

of Gulf Oil (Belgium), came out we weighed anchor and steamed alongside. Much to our surprise and pleasure the shore authorities informed us that they would not be

Fishing Trawler

20

Trouble at Hospital

"Hi, Polly, it's Jono, Brendan's brother here, glad to get you. I know you're concerned about Bren—"

"Oh! Hello, Jono," interrupted Polly. "Yes, I've been thinking about poor Bren. I'm sure the hospital knows what they're doing, but Bren doesn't seem to be getting much better."

"That's exactly what we're thinking here, Polly, and we wondered," Jono paused for a second, "if you would agree to working a rota where, whenever possible, there is someone that Brendan knows beside the bed. A familiar voice talking to him. He knows your voice, and we know he likes you a lot…" Jono paused again, waiting for a reply.

"I'm all for it, Jono," was the relieved voice. "I was in yesterday, and poor Bren looked so lost and helpless…"

"OK, Polly, no time better than the present, there's—" he looked at his watch "—an hour left for visiting. I'm going in right now. Do ye' want to come?" Giving Polly no time to answer, he continued, "I could pick you up in ten minutes an' be in there within the half hour."

"Right, Jono, I'm getting my coat on right now."

"You heard that, Ma?" called Jono. "I'm picking up Polly right now. I'll try an' get someone in authority to get things sorted. See you in a couple of hours." With a wave Jono shouted his goodbyes.

***

"Sorry, sir, nobody allowed on ward," was the 'negative' from the serious and daunting looking nurse put on sentry duty for Ward Six. Jono and Polly had rushed in, giving themselves twenty minutes to see Brendan, and hopefully have a word with Sister Sullivan or possibly the matron, or somebody in authority.

"Oh, what a surprise, Sister. Why, what's wrong? I do hope it is not too serious. We have come a long way to see Mr. Harris," Jono smiled his daunting *I'm your best friend* smile. "You know Brendan is my brother. He's been in a coma for the past ten days and—"

"Mr. Harris," interrupted Nurse, "I am not a sister, and I have told you the ward is out of bounds. This is due to a very serious infection. Now, will you please stand back."

"You heard me say, sir," repeated the nurse to another disappointed visitor, "the ward is closed due to a suspect infection."

"We came to see the sister in charge, didn't we, Polly?" stated Jono, looking to Polly to support his request.

"Yes, Nurse," stated Polly in her *don't question me* voice. "We have some very important news regarding the welfare of Brendan Harris. It is imperative we speak with her."

"I shall take a note of your message, miss, and pass it to Sister…when she is free," was the reply from the over-tired sentry.

"Nurse," announced Polly, stepping forward purposefully between Jono and the desk sentry box. "Nurse, it is essential…we speak…in person…with Sister. About Mr. Harris."

The nurse bristled slightly and sat back in her desk chair, folding her arms. "If you tell me something of your news, I will inform sister. One moment…" She stopped to stare at a small fat man, who had pushed his way to the desk.

"Yes, sir! As you can see, the ward is closed," the nurse advised triumphantly, pointing at a small, handwritten note stuck to the front of a notice advising something about coughs and sneezes.

"Mr. Harris," admonished the staff nurse as Jono began to speak, "if you and this young lady do not step back, I will call a porter and have you expelled from the building."

"We're getting nowhere here, Polly," admitted Jono. "Maybe it's best we leave it to tomorrow. All right, Nurse, you win." He smiled in defeat. "Just hope Bren is OK. Come on, let's get back to the cottage."

The following day, Alice rang the hospital to see if she could make an appointment to see Doctor Larrigan, *or was it Mr. Larrigan—was he a Doctor or a Consultant?* Alice could not get any further than the receptionist in the hospital and was told to write for an appointment. Visiting had been stopped for Ward Six: something about suspected measles.

"Wonder when Larrigan makes his rounds?" Alice asked Henry as she sorted the dirty breakfast dishes in the kitchen sink. "I'm sure he wouldn't mind us talkin' about Brendan and our worries. Oh. by the way, you know Polly rang to say she's going to try to get in to see Bren after work."

Henry, engrossed in repairing the spare gas cooker, was still somewhat shocked that he had phoned in to the gas company office in Dublin that he wouldn't be making his calls—the first time in his working life that he had taken a day off, apart from agreed holidays. "That's nice of her," he said absentmindedly. "Now, Alice," he addressed Alice, standing up holding his back. "I've taken the day off, we've got to do something positive with it."

"I agree," said Alice, drying a large breakfast plate, "but what do we do? It doesn't look like we can make an appointment with Larrigan. I say," she placed the plate on the draining board alongside the kitchen sink and walked over to the malfunctioning gas oven, standing over Henry. "I say we try again an' maybe get a hold of that Sister Sullivan, or even one of the nurses, an' tell dem what we want to do, an' say we're not leaving until we get what we want."

"But Alice, you can't do that," remonstrated Henry. "First of all, they won't let us into the ward. Come on, Alice, it would be a waste of time. Let's try another phone call. Jono said he will have another try this morning."

"OK, Hen," a resigned Alice submitted temporarily, but was ready, if the phone call failed, to storm the ramparts, thinking to herself that *if enough of us bother them, they might weaken and we could get some positive news about Brendan.*

Wheelhouse of the Calvex Commander

21

Visit to the Cavern

After a breakfast of congealed fried egg and greasy fried bread, Brendan bade farewell to the uncomfortable bed and spartan accommodation of the seaman's mission. The taxi driver was full of talk about the test match with New Zealand. England, even without Graveney apparently, had bowled out the New Zealanders for 161 in four hours. Brendan wasn't greatly interested in cricket, and also found it difficult to understand the rapid-fire Scouse as they merged with the heavy traffic through the Mersey Tunnel, out into Birkenhead and then south for a short distance to the Cammell Laird ship yard.

"Well hello, if it isn't Brendan Harris again. Hiya, Bren," were the welcoming words from Don Marshall, at the top of the gangplank. "I had heard we were to expect an Irishman, thought maybe it could be you. What have you been doing since we were on the *Renown*?" enquired Don as he helped Brendan with his luggage.

Looking around as he made his way across the red-plated deck, assailed with the smell of fresh paint, he followed Don up to the officers' quarters.

"Why has the ship been in dock, Don?" Brendan asked. "I've been on the *Commander*—"

"It wasn't you who ran her aground, was it?" interrupted Don with a laugh. "You've gotta tell me all about that. Have you seen anything of Barry Jones? Oh! Yes, do you know who the first mate is, Bren?"

"Haven't a clue, Don. Go on, who?"

"Your old friend. Ha! Ha! You're going to like this, Bren, Brian Turdy! The second mate from the *Renown*. He has had promotion."

"God, Brian Turdy. I remember—nobody seemed to like him. I remember I met him when ashore in Venice—he was drunk, the bastard. He's now a first mate. Well, there's hope for us all."

"Thought you'd like that. The third, a John Brady, seems a nice guy, a bit old for a third mate. Haven't met anyone else, only joined yesterday. There's two more apprentices expected over the next few hours. It would be a laugh if Barry Jones turned up," said Don as he helped Brendan place his suitcase on the cabin bunk. "We might as well share. I've grabbed the bottom bunk. Oh yes! The *Calvex Faith*, she's been in dock for the last weeks—was in a collision with a tramp steamer in the Indian Ocean. Was built here in 1956."

Taking in all this information, and very pleased to meet up with Don again, Brendan remembered Barry Jones, the pompous little Welshman.

"Barry Jones, the little Taff, a bit of a pain, was Barry. Yep! Glad to share with you, Don. I'd better go and report to the mate. Well, what do you know…Brian Turdy?"

"Hi! I'm Ron McManus," was the unexpected greeting as Brendan stepped out into the passageway, "and this is Tim Sound." The other two apprentices had arrived. With introductions all around, the two newcomers moved into the adjoining cabin and Brendan went looking for the first mate.

"Well hello, Paddy! So we meet again. What have I done to deserve this? Marshall and yourself." Brendan had knocked on the chief officer's door and was greeted in this most unexpected manner by the chief officer.

"Congratulations, Sir, with your promotion," smiled Brendan and offered his hand as he stepped towards the seated mate. The chief officer, dressed in a brilliant white shirt and company tie, rose and took the proffered hand. This wasn't the Brian Turdy Brendan knew; the scruffy, foul-mouthed, unkempt second officer. The transformation was startling.

"Thank you, Harris, I hope you had a relaxing few days' leave. Have the others turned up yet? "

"Just arrived as I came in, Sir," answered Brendan, still somewhat taken aback by this new officer.

"Good! Well don't let them bother me for the moment. Have them report to the third mate. Have you done so yet? John Brady—sounds like he could be a countryman of yours, Harris." With that he dismissed Brendan with a wave of his hand as he sat at the desk.

Closing the cabin door, Brendan laughed to himself; the promotion seemed to have changed Mr. Turdy into a human being.

"All right, gentlemen," called John Brady, the elderly third mate. All of thirty-five years of age, John was happy with his position. He had entered the profession in his late twenties and was very competent in his work, and slightly old-fashioned in his attitude.

"My name's John Brady, third mate. Donald, I see from time served you would appear to be senior, with two years under your belt. Brendan you're next, with sixteen months. Ronald, I see you spent six months on the *Rover*, and welcome to you, Timothy, your first trip, I see.

"We sail at ten tomorrow morning, so get all your gear stored away and into your working clothes, as there are a lot of stores that need shifting and the wheelhouse is in a filthy state. An' the bosun will be looking for a hand. Leave that for you to arrange, Donald."

""Right, thanks, Third," replied Don. "Let's get settled in, lads. Oh, Third, do we dress up for dinner tonight?" Don asked, beginning to fall into the role of senior.

"Why, yes, of course," replied the third. "We must keep the standard up. Welcome on board, gentlemen," smiled the third mate as he walked across the alleyway to his own cabin.

"Right, lads, coffee all round, first. You any good at making coffee, Tim?"

Brendan wondered how the new lad was going to settle in, remembering how strange everything was to him on his first ship. He was pleased to hear the young lad answer, "Coming up, gentlemen." He grinned. "Is it milk and sugar all round?"

After a quick coffee and a cigarette, on Don's suggestion, Don and Ron went to give the chief steward a hand to store the food for the next few months. Bren and Tim went to the wheelhouse to tidy it up. On their way to the enclosed part of the main deck, under the midships housing called the centre castle, to gather the cleaning gear, a bearded, bald and paunchy man, dressed in dirty dungarees and a windcheater called out, "Ah! Der ye' are, lads, the thurd mate said you'd be there to gi' me a hand. You're the new apprentices den, aren't you?" questioned the scruffy looking individual as he placed a coil of rope on the deck.

Ron retorted abruptly, in his south of England accent with the question, "Who are you, my good man?"

"I is the bosun, young fella me lad, an' doan' you ferget it."

This bristling untidy apparition was the bosun, the most important of the seamen; he was the foreman of the working crew and snotty-nosed deck apprentices should know their place.

Brendan immediately placated the irritated Liverpudlian by suggesting Ron went ahead to seek out the chief steward whilst he would help the bosun.

"Now, what can I do for you, Bosun, is there much to carry?" Brendan asked, lapsing into his native Dublin accent.

"Doan' worry, there's no need. I jus' doan' like that f---ing poncey southerner's attitude."

That evening, on their way to the saloon for their dinner at six o'clock, all dressed in their respective uniforms, Ron McManus, a tall, self-assured young man, now beautifully dressed in his officer's uniform with its shiny buttons and knife edge creases, taller than Brendan who stood over six feet tall and carrying his peaked cap under his arm pronounced in a laidback, public school voice, "I hear, chaps, there's a great nightlife here in this Liverpool. What do you know?"

Brendan had thrown on his uniform. He had worn it twice before and the jacket was beginning to get a bit tight. He had thought of ironing the trousers but hadn't got around to it, and hadn't even considered wearing the peaked officer cap. Young Timmy, who looked as if he should still be in short trousers, had followed his cabin mate's standard and arrived in a spotless virgin uniform, highly polished black shoes, a sparkling white shirt with Calvex tie, and of course a uniform cap. Don had thought like Brendan—wear at least part of the uniform, just in case, but there surely was no need to wear the cap. A tie was probably necessary, but the cap was overdoing it.

"What do you think, Bren? You being an Irishman, you should know a bit about Liverpool," Don asked as they entered the saloon.

The saloon was quite empty, as most of the engineer officers were either down fiddling with the engines or hadn't yet returned from leave. The captain was apparently having his meal in his cabin and the second mate was ashore, which just left the first mate, Brian Turdy, the third mate, John Daley, and the chief engineer, Alexander MacRory, sitting at the captain's table. The carpeted room was filled with four, four-seater tables, in lines of two, with the captain's table under the row of portholes looking down onto the for'rard deck. A door to the right was the entrance to the kitchen, with a sliding window alongside where the steward, dressed in black trousers and white jacket, passed meal orders.

The officers looked up at the entrance of the apprentices and Daley appeared to look twice and comment to Turdy, as only Ron and Timmy placed peaked caps alongside the one cap already there.

Turdy shrugged his shoulders, but Daly appeared to remonstrate and made to stand up, but was seemingly ordered by Turdy to sit down.

"Looks like Daly thinks we should have carried our caps. God! What a twit," Don muttered to Brendan under his breath. "I don't see the mate's cap."

"Sorry, Ron," continued Don, "you suggested an evening out in Liverpool. I think Brendan here knows a bit about the nightspots. Don't you, Bren, old chap?" Don suggested, smiling apologetically at Ron.

"Come on, Don, I've only spent one evening in Liverpool, I'm no expert. But if you want a lot of noise and plenty of talent, the place I went to last night, The Cavern, could be the place for four randy sailors. There's another, a café called the Jacaranda that's just opened, it's got a steel band, could be OK."

"Let's go there, lads—the Jacaranda. Sounds like the name of a snake. But maybe The Cavern? Any suggestions?" queried Don as he picked up the evening meal menu. "Look, the steward is waiting for our orders. I'll have the soup and the lamb, thanks, Steward."

As the others placed their orders, Timmy, in a semi-apologetic manner, corrected Don on his definition of a Jacaranda; it was an exotic South American flower.

"If sirs doan mine me interruptin'," the steward from Liverpool interjected, "The Jacaranda is a real hot spot. It's in Slater Street, full of talent and the steel band is great. On a Monday night they have the Steel Beetles. If Sirs doan mine me interruptin," the steward grinned as he took the meal orders.

"Thank you, Steward," smiled Don. "The Jacaranda it is. Thanks, Timmy. Anyway how do you know what a Jacaranda is?"

"I liked botany at school and learned a lot about tropical plants. I know the word means fragrant and it's a flowering plant found in the Bahamas and Americas," answered a slightly embarrassed Tim.

Brendan caused a laugh when he interjected, "I fancied Botany at school, as well, but I'm afraid she didn't like me."

The conversation continued over the meal, with Don relaxing in his position as experienced leader. Ron, in his know-it-all voice, made final pronouncements, which sometimes stopped the flow of conversation. Brendan got the conversation flowing again each time with his odd 'Irishisms' and laughter, whilst Tim, feeling very young and inexperienced in this his first trip, kept very quiet.

"We've been ordered to get back to the ship by two o'clock tomorrow morning. We sail at ten," was the gleeful announcement from Don, as the four of them piled into the taxi ready for an evening out. They had all got advancement on their wages, so were feeling quite wealthy and ready to hit the highlights of Liverpool.

"If yer luckin' for dollies, lads, yer best bet is The Cabin," stated the male taxi driver. "Met me wife there, two years ago. Gotta kid now. Livin' in a council flat in Bootle."

Don, sitting in the front seat of the creaking taxi, turned his head to acknowledge Brendan's offer of a cigarette and asked whether they should take the driver's advice.

"Three things stand out here, lads," replied Brendan in his Irish drawl. "I don' want a wife, or a kid, or to live in a council flat in Bootle. Wherever that is. It's The Cavern, for me. That OK with you, lads? No offence, I hope, driver."

With a chorus of ayes, the taxi continued its journey through the Mersey Tunnel and threaded its way into Mathew Street, to deposit the four eager young men outside The Cavern Club.

"Hope ye hav' a gud evenin', lads," wished the driver as he prepared to leave "Oh, by the way, will ye giv' me luv to Cilla. She's on the coats. Name's Cyril."

Brendan nodded his acknowledgement, remembering the talkative redhead he had seen the previous evening.

"Let's go, guys. I'll lead the way," offered Brendan as he pushed open the heavy door to the club and was hit by an oven-blast of air and the loud noise of rock 'n' roll music. "Follow me, guys," Brendan called out as they stepped through the doorway to make their way down the steep slippery staircase to the stifling depths of the catacombs below.

"Where are you takin' us, Bren? God, the smell," shouted Don over the loud beat as they were hit by the smell of cigarette smoke, disinfectant, urine, rotting fruit. And then, of course, there was the solid beat of drums and guitar music.

"Follow me, guys, I think I know where I'm goin'. They used to store fruit here in the old days, so I'm told," shouted Brendan. "Sorry, miss," he apologised, as he bumped into a female in a dark coat who had stopped suddenly at the foot of the steps.

"Dat's all rite, fella. De ye kno' where de cloakroom is den?" she asked in the Scouse accent that Brendan was beginning to become accustomed to.

"There's three tunnels der, you see. The first one has the cloakroom at the far end. Are you here for the dancing?" asked Brendan.

"Hey, Mable," the blonde shrieked over the noise, to a couple of other girls looking lost. "Down there, past that dancin' place to de bottom, Paddy here says." The blonde grinned as she turned to Brendan and gave him a light punch on the shoulder.

Delighted with the friendly response, Brendan turned to his compatriots and gave the thumbs-up sign. However, Blondie was not the most attractive looking girl, standing just over five foot in her shaky high heels, with a long runny nose and prominent teeth.

Passing what appeared to be the admissions desk, with a hulking giant assessing the eager youngsters, Brendan stopped to consider what to do next. "Look, lads, there's three tunnels. That bigger one in the middle seems to be where the noise is comin' from. God! The talent. It's exciting stuff. What do you think, Ron?" he asked his tall companion.

Ron seemed to be aloof to it all, with his posh accent, his height, a head of hair taller than Brendan, who was six two in his stocking feet. "Do you have any idea where we can leave our coats, Bren, old chap? It does pong a bit, Don. All very frantic, isn't it? The music's a bit loud," Ron shouted in reply in his posh London accent. "But it certainly makes you want to swing to the beat."

"Down that tunnel on the right, follow my blonde with the teeth," grinned Brendan as the four of them pushed their way through the crowd of youngsters to the rear of the crowded, black painted tunnel.

"Is Cilla around?" questioned Brendan of the perky little blonde as she took their coats.

"Naw," was the nasal return. "Cilluh is off t'night. Nex'," called the little blonde as she offered to take the coats from a group of girls pushing their way into the enclosed space.

"Let's go listen to the music and see who's playing," encouraged Don. "There seems to be seating in the next tunnel, where the sound is coming from."

Followed by Tim and Brendan, they stepped into the white-painted low tunnel, where the walls were beginning to perspire with the lack of ventilation and the press of bodies. In the lull of the changeover of the band they found two seats, which Don and Bren grabbed, leaving Tim, who seemed somewhat lost, standing at the side.

"Go on den, girls, squeeze up and let Junior have a seat." It was Brendan's buck-teeth blonde and her two friends, smoking long-tipped cigarettes with bottles of Coca Cola in their free hands. "Look, girls, it's Paddy an' his friends," the blonde warned. "You've come to see the Quarrymen, hav' ye? Me brudder went to school with half of dem," the blonde advised Brendan through a cloud of cigarette smoke, sweat and the tantalising view of nylon stocking knees. "Where's the big one gone?"

"You mean Ron? He's looking around the dance floor. My name's Brendan. This is Don and that's Tim. Come and sit alongside Don, Tim," Brendan encouraged, waiting for his blonde friend to introduce herself. Just then there was movement on the low stage ahead of them "There's Paul," shouted Blondie. "Look, Nuala, there's Paul, and who's that? Doan' know him," Blondie said, as a third member of the youthful band strutted onto stage dressed in scruffy jeans and cardigan.

"We're waiting for John to come on," Blondie explained to Brendan. "He was in the same class as me brudder. Used to come to me house for tea... He's real cool. JOHN! Mary here," shrieked the blonde as the fourth member of the group sidled onto the stage with a slight bow to the room, proceeding to pick up one of the guitars resting against a kitchen chair.

Laughing, Brendan leaned over to Don. "This is Mary, Don, and her friend beside her is Nuala."

"Shush! Paddy, they're goin' to start. John's goin' to speak. Me other friend is Ruth. Now shurrup and listen."

With a nonchalant air, John Lennon raised his hand for attention, and in the expectant reduction in the noise he introduced himself and the Quarrymen with Paul McCartney on guitar, Colin Hanton on drums, the latest recruits—George Harrison on guitar and John Lowe on piano. The youngster called Paul shouted out something like, "Git on wid it, John, we haven't got all night."

Lennon turned around with a scornful look on his face, made a gentle fingers sign to McCartney, turned back to the expectant audience and announced "That'll be the day. Let it go, boys," and the members of the band all started to make music with a catchy rhythm.

"Come on, Mary," called Brendan. "Let's dance."

"OK, big boy," agreed Mary. "Yer jokin', dancin'? But let's hav' a go."

Stepping onto the crowded stone floor amidst the claustrophobic surroundings, with his head in the cloud of cigarette smoke due to the low ceiling, Brendan was aware of the smell of disinfectant, the gyrating bodies, the beat of the drums, the noise of chattering dancers and the smell of unwashed bodies as he started to shuffle around with Mary, noticing Don had encouraged Nuala to join him on the floor. Tim was standing with a shroud of cigarette smoke haloed around him from the bright light on the stage, looking quite lost. He could see Ron, deeply engrossed in a conversation at one of the small tables with a disinterested older girl, looking around the room as if for a saviour.

Mary, Brendan was pleased to discover, was slightly taller than he had expected, and it was nice to press himself up against her and smell the lacquer in her hair. The off-the-shoulder dress she was wearing gave a tantalising glimpse of her breasts, sheltering under her bra.

God, what am I thinking, thought Brendan to himself. *Bras and breasts. There's Don grinning at me with the thumbs up sign…* "What's that you said, Mary?" Brendan asked, bending down as Mary turned her head, catching Brendan's nose with her protruding teeth.

"Oh! Sorry, Paddy, I was jus' going to say, before your nose got inna way, that I've noticed how pleased ye are, down there, to see me. Are ye goin' t' do anything about it?" she questioned as she pressed up against him.

Quite startled by Mary's reaction and comment, Brendan drew back and blushed mightily. *Thank God it's so dark she can't see me. What do I say? Is she offering? Surely not, is she having me on?*

Mary, noticing his confusion and indecision, leaned back, grinning. "Got ya der, Paddy," she laughed. "Now put it in your pocket and keep dancin'. Der's Paul playing' de gee-tar. I bet he's goin' places. Isn't he good? Whose de little kid on the other gee-tar? Of course, yer a Paddy, ye wouldn't kno'," stated Mary. "Nuala!" she shouted, over the heads of the other dancers. "Nuala! Who's the young lad on the gee-tar?"

Before Nuala could answer, a dancer alongside, rocking furiously, answered in gasps, "Dat's me next—" *gasp* "—door—" *gasp* "—neighbour's son—" *gasp* "—George. Wee Georgie Harrison. Wait until ye hear him—" *gasp* "—sing."

"Thanks der. God, Paddy, he only looks 'bout fourteen. Will ye' get me a drink, Paddy? I think I've earned it."

Brendan, very pleased with the outcome of his approaches, looked to catch Don's eye and glanced towards the coffee bar, giving the thumbs-up. Nodding in the affirmative, Don was seen to speak to Nuala, who glanced over to get a nod from Mary. Brendan, concerned about Tim, noticed he was surprisingly engrossed in a conversation with a very feminine looking male, and Ron had disappeared.

With glasses of orange juice and introductions all round, Brendan noticed Mary nodding to Nuala and looking at her watch.

"Look, Paddy, Don," interjected Mary, "Nuala and I want you to kno' we're going to have to leave at ten turty to catch the bus to Bootle."

Startled by this warning, Brendan put his arm around Mary's small waist, smiled and surprised himself, announcing, "Mary! Don and I would love to have yours and Nuala's company until then, and would be delighted to take you to the bus stop. Come on, let's dance…please."

"I'm game for it, Nuala, what about you?" laughed Mary. "They don't appear dangerous. OK, Paddy, let's dance!"

Leaving the other pair looking at each other in surprise, Mary and Brendan forced their way onto the dance floor and joined in the shuffling dancers.

The remaining hours flew by. Both knew this was only a passing moment in each of their lives, both physically attracted to each other and alive to the boundaries not to be crossed, so it was with very mixed feelings Brendan waved goodbye to Mary as she boarded the bus for Bootle.

"Wonder if we'll ever meet them again, Don?" mused Brendan.

"Yeah, Bren, I wonder. I also wonder how we're going to get back to the ship. It's gone eleven, an' I'm pretty skint. Do you know your way back to The Cavern? Maybe Ron has surfaced, and Tim said he'd wait for us. He was pretty pally with that fancy looking guy."

Heading off in the approximate direction, the two friends eventually made their way back to The Cavern to find Tim waiting outside, shivering in the cold air.

"No sign of Ron, Tim?" enquired Don.

"I've not seen him," replied Tim. "Last time he was chatting up that older woman in the coffee bar. I looked for him before I left the dance, but—"

"We've gotta get back to the ship," interrupted Don. "Have we enough for a taxi, guys? I have a couple of bob, what about you, Bren?"

"I'm skint. Orange juices cost a lot of money, ye know, Don," scoffed Brendan. With a triumphant flourish, Tim interrupted, producing a whole pound note.

"Where did you get that, you wonder, Tim? A whole quid. Well done, but where's Ron? Hope he's all right. Do we go back into the club?"

"Wait!" exclaimed Don. "Could that be him? Look, there's a big guy comin' up the street. He's staggering a bit, I'll go down a' have a look."

God! He's not drunk, is he? wondered Brendan, as Don beckoned them to him as he started to support the staggering body.

"Thanks for waiting, fellas," cried Ron, wincing as he tried to straighten up. "I was beaten up by a couple of bastards. They took my wallet and watch. What's the time?"

"It's OK, Ron. Do you wanna see a doctor? What about getting the police?"

"No, it's all right, Bren, just a couple of bruised ribs and a headache. What's the time? We got to get back to the ship? Has anyone got any money for a taxi? We don't have time to go to the police an' I can easily get another watch."

"Tim has a quid, Ron. That should be more than enough. Now to find a taxi."

Arriving back to the ship, they reported to the third mate. Ron went straight to his cabin; he didn't want the third to know.

Deck and Engineering Apprentices

22

Twelfth Day in Hospital

"Hello there, my name is Jono Harris. I've come to visit my brother on Ward Six. I've been away for some time and have to leave the country shortly," Jono declared in his most pleading voice, turning on his charming smile. He hadn't seen the nurse on the desk before, so he thought he would try a bit of the Jono charm.

"Sorry, sir, the ward is closed due to a suspected infection, and no visitors are allowed," declared the nurse behind the desk, returning Jono's smile with one of her own.

"Thank you, Nurse, that's awful news. What infection is it?"

"It's…" started the nurse as she looked at a paper on her desk. "Suspected measles, sir."

"Well! I had measles when I was a youngster, so I should be all right to visit. Ward Six, you said?" said Jono, as he made to head down the corridor towards the ward.

"Sir, sir!" the nurse called after him, rising to her feet from behind the desk. "You can't go in there!" Receiving no response from Jono, who was rapidly disappearing down the corridor, she called out to a uniformed porter at the entrance.

"Paddy, there's a guy heading for Six, will ye' go stop him, quick?"

"I see him, Nurse," replied the porter, beginning to run after Jono while shouting, "You can't go in there, mister, yer not allowed. Jeasus, he's gone into the operating theatre!"

In his haste to get into Ward Six, when Jono heard the call—and with all the ward doors looking the same—he had turned into Five: the operating theatre.

"Let's be havin' ye', mister," announced the porter, grabbing hold of Jono's jacket sleeve.

"Let go!" Jono declared through clenched teeth whilst gripping the porter's wrist and squeezing it in his hold. "Let go or you'll be sorry," Jono warned again, in measured tones.

With his wrist beginning to go numb, and with Jono being taller and fitter than himself, the porter capitulated and dropped his hold, rubbing his numb wrist. "De public are not allowed in here, sir. I would be after askin' ye' te leave."

"After you then, Paddy. I was looking for Ward Six, by the way," Jono laughed, knowing there was no chance of getting in to see Brendan now. "Where will I find Mr. Larrigan?"

"Ye' can't be after goin' in there, sir, there's the measles. An' if you want to speak to Mr. Larrigan, have a word wid de nurse on de desk."

Being ushered back toward the desk by the now triumphant porter, Jono was relieved to recognise one of the nurses from Ward Six coming towards him.

Jono caught her attention with a smile and called, "Nurse, it's Nurse Fitzgerald, isn't it, from Ward Six?"

"That's right, Mr. Harris, I remember you."

"How's Brendan?" pleaded Jono. "We can get no contact with him. It's been a couple of days now without any news."

Kathleen Fitzgerald, surprised and somewhat pleased that this tall, good-looking guy should remember her name, replied in her usual direct manner, "Oh, you mean Rudi. He's still shocking us with his language, but we are glad to say he's startin' to notice things. Sorry, but I gotta go, Mr. Harris. There's Sister, callin' me." In a raised voice she acknowledged the sister's call and, in a quick aside to Jono, said, "Mr. Larrigan is in tomorra', first thing, try him den."

"I think it's daft, wearin' these face masks, as if we were goin' to catch de measles, Kath. I had them when I was a kid in Limerick. What about yerself?" Mary Sheelin asked Nurse Fitzgerald as she tucked in the corners of the hospital bed.

"I kno', I had the measles in Dublin, and had the adenoids out another time. God! That was fun, we were all sleepin' on the floor, an' the young fellas wer tryin' to get under the blankets with ye' all the time. They hadn't an idea what they were up to. Didn't kno' much about it meself den, but God der was the odd near ting. Remember one night when there was a lot of fun, the nuns came in an' began beltin' the young fellas wid a stick."

"God! Dat must of been scary. Some of the nuns I kno' were terrible," replied Nurse Mary as they finished making up the empty bed.

"Ye' kno' who I was speakin' wid last night, before I knocked off?" quizzed Nurse Fitzgerald as they approached the curtained-off corner of the ward.

"Go on, who, Kath?"

"Rudi's brother. Ye' kno', the lovely guy wid the curly hair. He was all agitated 'bout Rudi. He's a real flirt, that one," announced Fitzgerald with a knowing smile. "I think he fancies me. I told him Rudi was gettin' better an' it was best he spoke wid the consultant about dat. Ye' kno' this quarantine business is daft."

"Right, Rudi, how are ye' dis mornin'?" called Nurse Sheelin as she pulled aside the curtains shielding Brendan's bed from the ward. On hearing the voice, Brendan reacted abruptly and tried to sit up against the wrist restraints, muttering something unintelligible under his breath.

It was now twelve days since Brendan had been admitted to the ward and he was still in a coma. The cuts and bruises on his face had all about healed, as had the scars on the side of his head where the consultant had operated. His right leg was still encased in plaster from hip to toe. It was of some concern that he was still unconscious, however there was some relief that through tests they had discovered his senses were all working. It was his brain that was the worry. To what degree was it damaged?

North Thames Gas Boat

SS Politician docked at Cobh Harbour

23

The Bombing and Enjoyable Visit to Philadelphia

At ten o'clock on a bright sunny morning the following day, the *Calvex Faith* set sail from Liverpool. The *Faith* was one of the more modern tankers, built to ship the crude oil produced by the countries in the east to the refineries in the west. With the ever-growing demand for refined oils, the shipping companies were reinforcing their fleets with ever more tankers.

The *Faith* was a twenty thousand tonner, over five hundred feet long and seventy feet on the beam. Driven by steam turbines, she could do a maximum of fourteen knots. Built in 1956, at the Cammell Laird ship yard in Birkenhead, her prime purpose was to deliver the precious oil to the refineries in the western hemisphere.

Over the next few months they made regular journeys loading a full cargo of crude in Saudi Arabia and delivering it to various refineries in Europe. It was on their way from Mena Alamadhi, in the Persian Gulf, with a full cargo of crude for Antwerp, they received a change in orders. Instead of going west, the orders were to take the cargo east, to a refinery in Balikpapan, Indonesia.

Balikpapan was a little known port in the United States of Indonesia, the mystical east, Borneo. From the literature in the ship's library, Brendan discovered that before the oil boom of the early 1900s, Balikpapan was an isolated Bugis fishing village, the Bugis being an ethnic group of peoples of the area. The toponym of Balikpapan (balik or behind, and papan meaning plank) is from a folk story in which a local king threw his newborn daughter into the sea to protect her from her enemies. The baby was tied beneath some planks that were discovered by a fisherman.

Apparently the refinery was nearly destroyed after extensive wartime damage and oil production had almost ceased, until Royal Dutch Shell had completed major repairs in 1950. So the trip to Borneo was considered with some interest, and Brendan was hopeful of a visit to the town.

After a long and tedious journey across the Arabian Sea, the Indian Ocean and the Java Sea, and then to the Makassar Straits, they arrived at the port of Balikpapan. The *Calvex Faith* anchored off the port with some trepidation as there had been rumour of unrest in the country. The president, Sukarno, was pro-communist, and the USA had apparently made suggestions for Sukarno to cease his alliance with the PKI (Communist Party of Indonesia) or they would do something about it.

It was a hot, wet, sultry day off the coast of Borneo, with the *Calvex Faith* at anchor in the bay awaiting a clear berth to discharge its cargo of much needed crude oil. The delay in berthing was due to a tanker alongside the berth discharging its cargo of crude. A further tanker, riding high in the water, had just discharged and was ready to set sail. There was an Indonesian Navy corvette anchored closer to the shore, looking very ominous.

Brendan and the other apprentices had donned their working clothes—a T-shirt, shorts and sandals—and equipped themselves with buckets of soapy water and rags to start washing down the midship's white paintwork, starting at the top deck, or Monkey Island as it was known. Why the nickname? It is believed that in the ancient days, cannon balls were stored aboard ships in a brass frame or tray called a 'monkey'. During extreme cold climatic conditions, the brass tray would contract and spill the cannon balls; hence the humorous reference was established that the climate was cold enough to freeze the balls of a brass monkey.

Whatever the explanation, Brendan and Tim were certainly not freezing on the sweltering Monkey Island. The uppermost deck on the tanker was festooned with navigation aids and was a great spot to view the surrounding scene. The port of Balikpapan could be seen quite close to the starboard side, with the coast a distance away to port. Brendan and Tim were chatting about the part Balikpapan had taken in the world war when the Japanese invaded the area in 1942, and the present problems, when Brendan brought Tim's attention to the sound of aircraft engines coming from the east.

Tim, who knew something about airplanes, shielded his eyes from the sun and exclaimed, "Looks like a B-26 Invader Bomber! Wonder what it's up to? It's flying very low… God, Bren, it's bomb bays are open! It's coming in to attack! Look, they're dropping bombs over the town! It's coming this way—it's machine-gunning the oil tanks—blimey, what do we do?"

Racing down the ladder to the bridge deck, Brendan started ringing the ship's bell furiously to warn the crew members to get their heads down. Taking a pair of high magnification binoculars, he ran to the bridge wing to join Tim.

"Look, Tim, it's painted black, without any markings. It's heading for the tanker at the jetty. It's hit it—it's on fire! See, the crew are all jumping overboard. Where's she going now?"

Following the bomber with the binoculars, he could see the figure of the pilot in the cockpit. "It's heading for the other tanker. There's another bomb... Bloody hell, Tim, it's bounced off the air vent into the water. It's heading this way! No, it's going for the corvette. It's hit it and machine-gunned it. Look, it's sinking, it's heading our way!"

By now the crew and officers were all aware of the imminent attack, and the first mate was racing to the forecastle to weigh anchor with the bosun and crew when the approaching aircraft opened fire. Fortunately the crew members had reached the shelter of the raised forecastle and the bullets just bounced off the ship's deck. Another bomb was seen to be released but passed down the starboard side without exploding. The plane then increased altitude and, with a scornful waggle of its wings, roared away.

The silence was now deafening. The cries of drowning men could be heard in the distance. The tanker at the jetty was on fire, its full lifeboats hurriedly moving away. The corvette had sunk, with survivors floundering in the water. It was later discovered that the plane had machine-gunned the oil pipes on the shore. Who was behind the attack? Were there going to be any further bombing raids?

In the sweltering heat of a tropical day, the *Calvex Faith* was advised to leave the area, as all that was to be done for the survivors was in hand. Instruction also came from Calvex head office to proceed to discharge their cargo at the oil refinery in Singapore.

Somewhat shaken but immensely relieved, the crew of the *Calvex Faith* left the bay of Balikpapan and docked at the relatively peaceful port of Singapore later in the week, where they received orders to proceed to the Persian Gulf to take on another cargo of crude oil.

Shortly after the attack, an announcement on the world news said that the Indonesian and UK governments claimed that the aircraft had been flown by Indonesian rebels. What about the Americans, who had said they were going to curb Sukarno and his communistic excesses?

The reasoned conclusion was that it must have been the Americans, but why, unless they thought it would help drive foreign trade from Indonesia and weaken the economy, with the intention of undermining Sukarno's government? Well, whatever the reason, it meant the twenty thousand tons of crude oil designated for Indonesia had been lost to them.

Rumours were rife as to the reasons behind the bombing at Balikpapan. Was it the Indonesian rebels, a group called Permesta, supported by the UK government to overthrow Sukarno? Selwyn Lloyd, the foreign secretary, agreed the UK supported the US policy of support for Permesta, but disowned all responsibility for the attack.

It was now approaching the end of 1958 and Brendan had to prepare for his six-monthly company exams. It also seemed a long time since he had been home to Ireland. He was now well into his second year as Deck Apprentice. His studies had been very sporadic. Spherical trigonometry was still difficult to conquer, as was the theory of loading dry cargoes such as corn, and the intricacies of ensuring the ship's stability in a rolling sea. Oil as a cargo had its complications—temperatures, expansion, fumes, clean oils, crude oils—but was very straightforward as opposed to loading different cargoes for a number of ports.

To Brendan, what was more important was trying to get some studying done before his half-year exams. With all the distractions, the heat and the profusion of insects which seemed to consider Irish blood a delicacy, didn't aid concentration. However, by early 1959, he sat down at a separate table in the officer's saloon, together with the other apprentices, and for the next two days dug deep into the memory bank to answer questions about storing bananas with sugar, and tractors with lorries—all very different to carrying oil. There were questions on navigation—the use of the sextant, azimuth mirrors and gyro compasses—and questions on coastal navigation, deep-sea sailing and even the ship's engines.

Being what one could class as a tramp oil carrier, the *Calvex Faith* was at the beck and call of the market. As the months passed, so too did the regular trips carrying crude from the Middle East to European refineries. The *Faith* eventually received orders to call into the oil terminal port Tripoli, in Lebanon. So instead of entering the Suez Canal to journey to the Persian Gulf for a cargo of crude oil, the *Calvex Faith* continued to the easter seaboard of the Mediterranean, to the port of Tripoli in the Lebanon, and after taking the customary pilot aboard was direct to the off-shore buoys marking the underwater pipeline.

Dropping both anchors, the *Faith* discharged its water ballast and linked up with the pipeline, which had started as far away as the oil fields in Iraq. Apparently the pipeline, starting in Kirkuk in Northern Iraq, passed through Jordan and the oil, after travelling 585 miles over ten days, arrived at Tripoli. Twenty thousand tons of it was to be shipped to Philadelphia, another five thousand seven hundred miles west.

Brendan's immediate thoughts cantered around if there was any chance of seeing the nurse Joan Turbitt he had met at the mission dance in Newcastle. He had kept in touch by mail, writing the odd letter, and had received one at the last port. She had had a complete change of career and was now a research and marketing executive for a large American newspaper.

It took twelve hours to load twenty thousand tons of the smelly, life-giving substance, and the *Faith* set out on its five-and-a-half-thousand-mile journey. It was scheduled to stop at the bunker port of Ceuta, a small town on a spit of land on the northern coast of Africa, just opposite

Gibraltar, to take on fuel oil for the trip across the Atlantic. Brendan was able to get a letter to Philadelphia through the company agent in Ceuta, giving Joan the expected date he hoped to arrive in the states and the contact number for the Calvex agents in the US port.

The trip across the Atlantic was quite uneventful and took a further eleven days. However, one event occurred which bolstered the fame of Brendan Harris. A week into the journey he was called to the ship's bridge one afternoon, during Chief Officer Brian Trudy's watch, and taken to the privacy of the chartroom, a small room at the back of the bridge deck.

Slightly apprehensive, Brendan bent his head to step into the small room and, holding onto the door post, stood to guarded attention; ever since the occurrences on the last ship and Turdy's unpleasant behaviour, he had been wary of the man.

Turdy was leaning against the chart table and looked quite relaxed in his duffel coat and woollen hat, the temperature in the low forties Fahrenheit. The ship was rolling quite severely due to the large Atlantic swell, which signified either the passing of a storm or the start of a new one. Turdy had a sheet of white paper in his hand and was making pretence of reading it as he turned to acknowledge Brendan's presence.

"Harris, you know this isn't a telephone exchange," was the surprising statement from Turdy. Brendan, adjusting his body to the rolling of the ship, was somewhat nonplussed, and thought it best to agree with Turdy.

"Yes, sir," he replied. *There is something on the paper he has in his hand. Is he playing a game with me? Is it a message for me? Something wrong at home, perhaps. Come on, Turdy, out with it.*

"The Sparks has received this message from our agents in Philadelphia; you had better read it, Harris. You can read, can't you?"

"Is it in English, sir? I'm pretty good at that," muttered Brendan, half to himself, nearing the line of being cheeky to a superior.

"Well it's certainly not in Irish, now read it, Harris," retorted Turdy, waving the paper for Brendan to take. Thinking to himself what a little sod Turdy was, Brendan went to step forward, but a sudden extra roll of the ship sent him stumbling against Turdy. Grabbing at the chart table to retain his balance, Brendan fell against Turdy, knocking him off his stool. Remaining standing, Brendan leaned over to help Turdy to his feet but the ship rolled back, sending him staggering back against the doorway. The returning roll had helped Turdy regain his feet and he roared out, "Take your f---ing message, Harris, and get out of my sight."

"Sorry, sir, I lost my bal—Thank you, sir."

Grabbing the sheet of paper, Brendan stumbled his way out of the chartroom onto the bridge deck, where the helmsman looked at him questioningly. "Everything all right, Paddy?"

"Shure, Pete, all's fine," replied Brendan, making his way down the side steps to the officers' accommodation, eager to read the message.

"Well, Bren, what did he want you for?" an eager Don called as Brendan entered their cabin.

"Just a minute, Don, it's a message for me. Haven't read it yet..." Holding his hand up to silence Don, he read the message.

> To the Ship's Captain, from A. James, shipping agents. Message for Brendan Harris, Ship's Officer, from Miss J Turbitt. Letter received and understood, will meet on arrival.

Wow, thought Brendan. *No wonder Turdy was annoyed. Great news, though. Will he give me the time off? Ship's Officer Ha! Ha!*

"Well, did Turdy have anything to say? Bren! Did he say it would be alright? Isn't she the nurse you met a couple of years ago, at the dance in—"

"He said nothing, Don," interrupted Brendan. "He threw me off the bridge." Brendan recounted the events in the chartroom and confirmed it was the nurse he had met in Newcastle.

"That's Turdy back to the bastard he always was," agreed Don. "Do you want to meet her, or need I ask, Bren?" Don grinned.

"You bet," smiled Bren. "But how do we do it? If Turdy doesn't agree? Would the other two be happy to do the watches? We shouldn't take more than twenty-four hours to discharge the cargo."

"OK, Bren," Don decided, "as senior, I'll have a word with Turdy and try to arrange the day off for you. You lucky bastard. She was cute—"

"Yeh, I can remember her blonde ponytail, about up to my shoulder, two years older than me—makes her age twenty—and a lovely pair of legs. Her last letter was about nine months ago, she said she had an important job with a newspaper in Philadelphia. Thanks, Don, but with your support I'll talk to the other two and go to Turdy myself. He might think more of me. What a girl though, getting the agent to send a message. I'm sure looking forward to meeting her again," Brendan concluded, with a big grin on his face.

As expected, the other apprentices agreed if Turdy would allow it, they would share cargo watches and allow Brendan the time off.

Within hours the news had spread around the ship; every time Brendan ventured out onto deck there were knowing winks and rude hand gestures from the crew. It was difficult to ignore, but Brendan smiled it all away and sent a reply to Joan's telex, to keep in touch with the agent who would give her up-to-date ship movements.

Brendan was now in a quandary. What was he going to wear? And what were they going to do when they met? Yes. What would they do? Brendan had three quid to spend—about eight dollars—which wouldn't lead to anything lavish. The thought crossed Brendan's mind that Joan might like to show off a bit with her Merchant Navy Officer, so he decided to wear the uniform and cap with the Calvex cap badge.

The other apprentices, especially Don, were all eager to meet Brendan's 'bit of stuff', and Brendan was quite surprised to be approached by the chief officer, who professed the wish to meet this 'dolly bird'. So it was agreed that when Joan arrived to collect Brendan, she would be invited for a cup of coffee in the chief officer's office.

Hoping Joan would not mind the unexpected attention and the notoriety, Brendan awaited the meeting with great anticipation. So it was on a bright winter's day in November that the *Calvex Faith* entered the mouth of the Delaware River and picked up the river pilot to navigate the final stages before berthing.

Brendan was on bridge watch while the tanker journeyed slowly up the wide Delaware River and docked at midday at a most inhospitable jetty with oil pipelines stretching inland. The main airport for Philadelphia was only a half mile away, planes constantly arriving and leaving. Brendan's eyes were searching for any sight of Joan, and he noticed a car park a few hundred yards away at the end of the jetty. There were a few cars but no human movement.

After the ship had tied up and quarantine demands were cleared, Brendan and Ron came off duty whilst Don and Tim took watch over the next eight hours. Ron was prepared to start the next watch at eight o'clock that evening for the night, to eight the next morning. The assumption was, apparently, that Brendan would be staying away from the ship.

Well, you never know, were Brendan's thoughts. *All I can do is tell her I have twenty-four hours' leave and see what she offers. This could be very interesting.*

Shortly after they had tied up to the jetty, a group of people with ringing American accents, and one with an imposing camera, made their way into the officers' accommodation. Within ten minutes, Brendan was called by one of the stewards and informed that the captain wished to see him.

"Here we go, Ron," called Brendan, nervously adjusting the company tie and smoothing out his navy uniform jacket. "Hope this is the news I want to hear."

Led by the steward, Brendan made his way up the inside stairs to the captain's cabin. Captain Alan Hodder—a figure rarely seen by a lowly deck apprentice—was sitting behind his imposing desk with the first mate standing beside him. There were five other people in the spacious cabin, four males and a smartly dressed female with a note book in her right hand. The males were all informally dressed, two chewing away furiously. Brian Turdy stepped out from behind the desk and introduced Brendan, whereupon these two rose from their seats and welcomed him with firm handshakes and the smell of peppermint gum.

"Hiya, Bren," greeted the older of the two, dressed in a sports jacket and open-necked shirt. "I'm Carl Lansley, from the Philadelphia Inquirer, and this—" he pointed to the other male, a tall, tieless, bearded, smiling young man "—is Andrew Strauss, my assistant. His mother's a Scot, ya know." These words were bounced at Brendan through a mouthful of saliva and gum, which Lansley hurriedly mopped dry with a coloured handkerchief he swiftly whipped from his top pocket.

"Yep, Bren. I kin call ya Bren, that OK? God, you're the part. Isn't he, Andy? The uniform…smart." Rubbing his hands together, Carl turned to the desk and, resting his hands wide apart—one still clutching the handkerchief—leaned towards a startled and somewhat annoyed Captain Hodder. "He'll do, Cap'n. He's an Irishman as well, you say?" Before the scowling captain could answer, Carl continued, "Right, Marmaduke—his mother is from Japan, by the way," he announced to the room, "get some shots of everybody before we leave."

Carl then began to arrange a reluctant captain and first mate to stand alongside Brendan in different poses, all the time with continuous chatter and flying spit.

Suddenly, Carl stopped, swallowed, and turned to face a somewhat confused Brendan. "Bren! Please, old chap—they say that in England, don't they?—my apologies. I never told you what the hell's going on! Now, sit yourself down there, beside Melina, Bren. Move over, Melina, that's a good girl. Oh, of course, I haven't introduced my secretary, Miss Melina Nolan." With a flourish, Carl pointed to the notebook holder and continued his rapid announcements. "We're from the Philadelphia Tribune, an' we're doing series of programmes for the paper to celebrate the intermingling of the nations and countries. Miss Turbitt—what a gal—she hails from Blighty. She's a research and marketing executive with the paper."

Turning to face Captain Hodder, Carl continued his moist statements. "Yes Cap'n, she—that's Miss Turbitt—has been in touch with Mr. Harris here, over the years, and from the stories he had to tell, we decided it would be grand to have Bren here—" Carl turned to smile at Brendan, sitting uncomfortably on the captain's settee "—talk with some of our school kids about his adventures on the mighty oceans. Hope that's OK with you, Cap'n?"

Captain Hodder, quite taken aback by the torrent of mangled American words, sat back in his large chair and squared up the folio papers before him in his quiet, well-mannered, English way before he replied. "Yes, Mr. Lansley, I have had a request from my head office to permit you on board and to discuss the points you have raised. I shall permit you to use Mr. Harris—a valuable member of our team, I might add—in your activities. Of course, Mr. Harris will have to agree to your request. What do you say, Harris?"

"I'm keen, Sir," Brendan replied. *What a girl,* he thought, *but why isn't she here?*

"That's hunky-dory, Cap'n," Lansley interjected before anyone could comment. "Of course, we will be doing a short story on the ship, the *Calvex Trade*…Oh! Sorry, sir, the *Calvex Faith*…you know…the ocean greyhound delivering the much-needed oil from the far-east to the thirsty blossoming west. Something like that. What do you say, Cap'n?"

"Fine, Mr. Lansley, liaise with Chief Officer Turdy, here." Captain Hodder nodded toward Turdy. "You have been introduced, and do avoid interfering with the running of the ship. We are on a tight schedule…and please make sure Mr. Harris is returned before we sail." This was said with a slight smile on the captain's well-worn face. "Now, if you could take your nuisance photographs within the next ten minutes, please do so that I may get on with running the ship. Thank you."

"Thanks, Cap'n," Carl acknowledged. "Right, Marmaduke, the Cap'n's busy, now let's git cracking." Over the next ten minutes, Marmaduke lined up a resisting captain with Bren in varying poses. Melina cornered Turdy for information on the ship. Both were very conscious of the captain's disquiet and exited his cabin as soon as they could.

"Okay, Bren, you go with Melina, here. She'll take you to the offices to meet Joan Turbitt, who will brief you on what's going on. Good luck… old chap!" continued Carl, blowing a balloon from the grey gum forever wandering around his mouth. "We have booked you into The Inn Hotel for the night, so get the gear you need and Melina here will take you. Right, Marmaduke, let's git some pictures of this big oil can."

Brendan, following the Americans, looked back at Captain Hodder, who had collapsed back into his office chair. Noticing Brendan's backward look, he gave a noticeable, large wink. Brendan grinned in response, closing the cabin door behind him.

"Meester Harris, vee must get…what you say…the skates on," was the call from an anxious Melina, perched precariously in her high heels at the top of the staircase to the lower deck. Dressed in a two-piece blue office suit with a white blouse to her neck, short auburn curly hair topped a smooth brown face with a pronounced red mouth and dark eyes. Melina beckoned Brendan to follow her.

Brendan acknowledged her urgency with a smile, thinking about what he would need overnight—a change of underclothes and clean pair of pyjamas. *Staying in a hotel for the night, what a turn up! Mustn't forget my officer's cap. Must tell the lads what's happening.*

After a quick word with Ron, and after collecting his things, Brendan met with the delicious looking Melina and made his way out onto the deck, where he briefly brought Don and Tim up to date. He waved to the gawping crew members and escorted Melina down the gangplank to climb into the impressive green Chevrolet, which purred away from the busy ship.

"Wilhelm, please leave Meester Harris and myself at ze office," ordered Melina, leaning forward in the spacious backseat of the large car. "Brennan, I may call you the Brennan, pleases?" enquired Melina, with a smile on her dusky face as she settled back against the leather seat, adjusting her tight, knee-length skirt. "Missee Tur-beat will be at ze office to tell you what it is that is happening. Eeet is all very exciting, would you say, Brennan?"

Brendan, somewhat surprised by how events had turned out, opened his double-breasted jacket, put his heavy uniform cap on the seat, stretched out his long legs and grinned at the young lady sitting beside him. He took a deep breath, inhaling the leather smell and faint perfume from his companion, and replied, "Yep, Melina, do please call me Brendan. I must say I am enjoying myself, but please tell me why I am meeting Miss Turbitt at the offices? What's going on? There was something about some school kids."

"Yes! Brennan, I wait—you speak Meese Turbitt, she tell all. OK wid you?" This message was passed with an anxious smile.

"That's fine, Melina," Brendan agreed, suddenly aware of the volume of the traffic and size of the cars speeding by.

After a short drive, the car stopped at a busy pavement—or sidewalk—and the passengers alighted.

"Gosh, the size of everything!" Brendan exclaimed, standing back as the limousine sped away, leaving them on the sidewalk facing a wide expanse of revolving glass doors. It was beginning to rain slightly; there was a smell of petrol fumes and car exhaust. Brendan, beginning to feel a bit claustrophobic, felt Melina's hand taking his and encouraging him to move forward.

"Come on, Brennan. Is it that you say the 'gosh'? A joyful word. You have your hat, is good. Now, come quick." Pulling Brendan by the hand, Melina whirled them through the many revolving doors and they entered a huge carpeted reception area, with exotic plants reaching toward the ceiling, apparently looking for escape. They joined a group in a lift, which suddenly whistled upwards, the occupants disgorged and replaced at speed.

"Vee are there now, Brennan," Melina announced as the lift doors opened somewhere in the stratosphere and, laughing at Brendan's wry grin, she led him down a wide, carpeted corridor, again dotted with brooding exotic plants, to the majestic entry doors. There was an elaborate notice on the glass doorway stating 'you are now entering the offices of the Philadelphia Tribune, founded in 1845'.

"Hi, girls," Melina greeted the girls behind the reception desk. "I haf here Meester Harris, from the beeg ship in the docks. Meese Tre-bitt is there?"

"Hi, Melina, Mr. Harris. Go on through. Miss Turbitt is expecting you. I'll call."

Following Melina, Brendan gave the admiring girls the Harris confident smile and touched the peak of his cap, as John Wayne would do. Through another glass door they entered the hushed realms of the executive suite, with impressive wooden doors displaying important titles: President, Vice President, Chief Reporting Officer, Marketing Executive, and others. As they approached the last door, nearly tripping over the plush carpet, it swung open to reveal a female figure, a personification of the times. Wide shoulders, a trim waist encased in a tight two-piece tan suit with a ruffled neck, long slim legs in expensive sheer nylons, golden locks framing a near-beautiful face, standing with her arms wide open in welcome.

"Hello, Brendan. How lovely to see you again," were the very welcoming words which took Brendan quite by surprise. This wasn't the naïve, innocent nurse-to-be that he had fumbled with in the back of a car some years ago. This was an executive, a person out of his league. But what of it—her arms were welcoming, so he gave it a go.

"Joan, how lovely you look," Brendan declared, stepping forward and giving her a large hug, delighting in the smell of a perfumed body and soft hair.

Releasing herself from the bear hug, Joan readjusted her clothes and directed Brendan to a pair of two-seater settees and coffee table at the side of the well-lit room. A tall window, showing the peaks of some other city skyscrapers, loomed over a low wooden desk festooned with papers.

"Brendan, you'll have coffee, won't you?" asked Joan, already pouring some strong smelling brown liquid from a tall silver pot into a fragile porcelain cup. "Melina, what about yourself?"

"No, thank you, Meese Turbitt. If alright by you, I go wid my work," Melina replied, backing toward the door. "I am so happy meeting you, Brennan. Gosh!" exclaimed Melina with a smile as the door closed behind her.

"Now, Brendan, tell me all about your travels. I have enjoyed your letters and I must say you do look the part in your uniform," continued Joan as she sat facing Brendan, crossing her long legs with a swish of expensive nylon. Before Brendan could answer, Joan then went into the timing of the next twenty-four hours.

"It's ten thirty now, Brendan. Before we start, I'll get my secretary. He hails from County Cornwall." With that the legs unfolded, and with an alluring swish of her slim body she moved to press a button on the desk, asking Dave to present himself. On his entry to the office, Dave, small and insignificant with a notebook in his right hand, shook hands with Brendan and perched himself on the edge of the desk.

"Please, Dave, will you tell Brendan the programme for the next twenty-four hours? Time is of the essence here, as Brendan's ship will sail tomorrow, about midday. Of course, you're away for a couple of days, Dave, aren't you?"

"That's right, Miss Joan, but Melina Nolan—you've already met Melina, Mr. Harris—is standing in for me, and she is up-to-date with the programme."

In a strange mix of American and British English, Dave outlined the programme from his notes. He said there would be lunch with the principal of Philadelphia High followed by a one-hour presentation, when Brendan would speak to the pupils about his experiences as an officer in the British Merchant Navy. After the presentation, Brendan would then return to The Inn Hotel, where the Philadelphia Tribune was to hold, by coincidence, their annual staff dance. The following morning the company car would then return Brendan to his ship.

"You might like to accompany Mr. Harris to the ship that morning, Miss Joan. I have made provision for that in your diary," Dave stated with a smile.

Brendan was rather aghast at the sudden responsibilities; he had very little experience of presenting. He looked at Joan, who was awaiting his reaction. "Don't worry, Brendan. I'll spend the next hour with you, running over what we wish you to say. That's fine, Dave, thanks. I look forward to a visit to your ship, Brendan. Remember back in Newcastle?"

With Dave dismissed, Joan relaxed somewhat, and for the next few minutes gave Brendan a quick summary of her career change and rapid promotion.

"We've both done well, Bren, haven't we? It's lovely to speak with someone from the UK, Bren…even though you are an Irishman!" Her English accent was tainted with a hint of American twang, and she laughed. "The Americans love an Irishman and you should go down well with an audience of impressionable youngsters. You will be introduced by the master of ceremonies; that will be Carl. You have met Carl, I believe? I'm sure the kids would love to hear your experiences of the Suez Canal and the time your ship ran aground in Africa—at a place called Takoradi, wasn't it?"

For the next twenty minutes or so, Joan ran through the expectations of the following hours, before calling in Melina and asking her to look after Brendan whilst she got on with some other urgent business.

Over the next few hours Brendan was taken around the paper's typing pools and production lines, treated to a brief meal in the canteen, where he put together some notes on his imminent talk, and then, accompanied by Melina, he was whisked off to South Philadelphia High—or Southern High, as it was known locally—an impressive school building in the south of the city.

Feeling very conspicuous in his uniform, Brendan acknowledged the applause when he was introduced by Carl Lansley as a special addition to the day lecture and how fortunate they were to avail of his quick visit to the city. After further introductions he was treated to a rousing rendition of the school song.

O'er the field in glorious splendour
Southern colours fly
Cheers and yells like volleyed thunder
Echo in the sky
See! Our Southern team is gaining,
Gaining more and more.
So FIGHT! FIGHT! FIGHT!
We will win tonight!
Southern High forever.

The main content of the talk for the packed auditorium started with cinema shots and very professional speeches, followed by muted applause from the mix of youngsters of both sexes. There was an audible sigh of relief when Carl bounced up and, amidst his spittle, announced it was time for Mr. Harris—Mr. Brendan Harris, Ship's Officer of the British Merchant Navy—to tell them all about his experiences and why his ship was now in Philadelphia.

Brendan stood to look at the rows of boys to the left girls to the right, some ten seats deep, and saw the door at the rear open. Joan quietly sidled in to sit alongside a row of what were probably school teachers. *Right*, thought Brendan, *don't forget to speak into the microphone, smile and look around at everybody.*

"Good afternoon, everybody. Yes, my name is Brendan Harris, a ship's officer on the *Calvex Faith*, the tanker ship docked in the port. I am eighteen years of age and have been with the company for over two years, during which I have visited many ports throughout the world. There are two special instances during these years I am sure you will be interested in…"

Brendan then went into some detail of the importance of the free movement of cargoes and referred to his experiences of traversing the Suez Canal, after its closure by Nasser, and running aground off Takoradi. He brought the audience's attention to the disparity between the group of students he was now speaking to compared to the talk he gave to the missionary students in Takoradi, finishing his talk with a description of the cargo of crude oil the *Calvex Faith* had brought from the Middle East, Tripoli in Lebanon, to Philadelphia in the new world. He received a great round of applause and sat down, very pleased with his performance.

"Yes siree, you gave a great performance there, Bren. A pity yer leaving us tomorra, see ya later at the dance in The Inn. You're staying there the night, Joan, aren't you?" Carl chattered after the meeting concluded and they were on their way out to the company limo.

"Yes. That's right, Carl, but we must congratulate Brendan—well done!" exclaimed Joan as she gave Brendan a peck on the cheek, very relieved that her recommendation had resulted in such success. "We have taken a movie of the show and hope to send a copy to you when it's developed. Right, come on back to the hotel and relax for a few hours before the dancing starts." A jubilant Joan linked her arm with Brendan's and the pair of them skipped over to the waiting company limo. "Right, Wilhelm, full speed to The Inn, old chap," Joan instructed.

Feeling quite euphoric, Brendan could not stop grinning and gave Joan his *you're the girl for me* look, which made Joan shoot a warning glance at the driver. More than happy to await developments, Brendan sat back in the limo's seat, opened his jacket, loosened his company tie and listened to Joan's exploits after she had left Newcastle two years ago.

***

"Your dancing has quite improved, Brendan," Joan complimented him as they swept around the dance floor to Glenn Miller's "In the Mood", played by the Hotel Dance Orchestra. Joan had changed into a flowing green and gold dress with a low top with high heel dance shoes, and it looked quite enchanting in comparison to the strict business suit worn earlier.

"Oh, it's the music and the girl in my arms that does it," Brendan said, startled with his good fortune as he pressed his right hand against Joan's slim back and squeezed her right hand, getting a welcome response.

"I'm afraid I'm going to have to mix a bit with the staff, Brendan, love," Joan warned as the orchestra finished the number. "Look, take Melina up for the next dance and I'll probably dance with Carl, or even Andrew. Of course, they have their wives with them. Oh, I am so glad I'm single. Stop me, Bren, I'm gabbling," laughed Joan, leaning back as the couple went into a final sweeping turn on the dance floor.

On returning to the table where the management were all sitting, Brendan was approached by Andrew Strauss, the tall, bearded assistant, who introduced him to his tall, elegant wife. Joan excused herself and returned to the table.

"I must say I enjoyed your talk at the school, Brendan. It's a pity we can't avail of you anymore. Brendan sails back to England tomorrow, Ruth," explained Andrew. Before Ruth could reply, there was a rattle on the drums and the band leader stepped forward to announce the guest singers. "Ladies and gentlemen, I introduce you to Danny and the Juniors."

With a resounding rattle of drums and guitar sounds, four young men, dressed immaculately in grey suits, wearing white shirts and black ties, with the customary white handkerchiefs in their top pockets, came onto the stage. Grinning widely they lined up and started to sing their hit single, "At the Hop".

The dance floor was immediately swamped with gyrating couples. Brendan immediately linked with the catchy beat and looked anxiously toward Joan, who was speaking with a serious looking suited manager. Receiving a responsive nod, he excused himself and catching Joan's hand fell into a quick easy enthusiastic jive rhythm to the bee-bop beat. After the thunderous applause which followed "At the Hop", the foursome continued with a rock 'n' roll number to a packed floor of gyrating bodies, waving arms and sheer enjoyment. Further fast rock 'n' roll numbers were followed by their latest release, a slower rock and roll number, "I Feel So Lonely". At the end of the number, Bren and Joan fell into each other's arms with the sheer enjoyment of the mutual appreciation of the music, their bodies in accord, and the mutual attraction to each other.

"Oh God, Bren, love!" Joan exclaimed, suddenly drawing back from Brendan's eager body. "Decorum, Bren, I'm an executive. Executives do not relax in the presence of staff, particularly—" she groaned "—in the presence of upper management."

"My apologies, Miss Ter-Bitt," grinned Brendan. "Shall I take you back to your chair? I could certainly do with a rest. Boy, did I enjoy that. But yes, I understand. Decorum."

Leaving the dance floor, unconsciously holding hands, they were greeted by other happy, laughing couples. Brendan, now in shirtsleeves, his shirt damp with sweat and Joan's makeup beginning to mingle with the perspiration, they looked like what they were—a couple of youngsters enjoying themselves.

"Look, Bren, I'm away to the ladies. Get me a long cold drink and go and be an executive executive."

Brendan remained standing by the dance floor for a moment while he regained his breath and saw the familiar body of Carl approaching.

"Carl, how lovely to see you again. What an excellent night," he called out, walking to meet Carl's outstretched hand.

"Bren, I can see you are enjoying yourself, but could I suggest you act with a little less enthusiasm? You are representing the management in your role here. Hope ya understand. Miss Turbitt should have more sense. Where's your jacket?"

Quite taken aback, Brendan felt like punching the little spit-spraying weevil. "Okay, Carl, understood. I'll get my jacket. Come on, old chap, get me a drink will you, and introduce me to a few 'executives'," he replied, looking across to the table of immaculately dressed executives with their submissive wives.

Carl, quite relieved at Brendan's acceptance of the norms required, took his arm and propelled him toward the bar, picking up Brendan's jacket on the way.

Brendan caught Joan's eye as she returned from the powder room; she nodded and sat beside what looked like a staff member and started up a conversation. Brendan thought he would find out how the interviewing and filming on board had progressed, and had a lengthy spitting description from Carl of the successful day.

The evening progressed; Brendan had a dance with Melina, who implored him to go dance with Joan. "She was having such a great time with you, what has happen?" she asked.

As sufficient time had passed in Brendan's mind, he made his way over to Joan and requested the next dance. Now wearing his jacket and smiling at the executive wives, who were all nodding their heads—in agreement or condemnation was difficult to figure out—but taking Brendan's proffered hand, Joan rose and, smiling broadly, stepped out onto the dance floor as the orchestra started to play a quickstep. They eased into the rhythm of the dance and began to enjoy themselves again.

As the dance ended and they sat together, the band leader announced the next dance to be the last dance. "So take your partners for a threesome medley, 'That Old Black Magic', 'I Can Dream' and 'When You Wish Upon a Star'. Before we wish you good night, your chairman, Arthur Jacobs, would like to say a few words."

The orchestra played a quiet melody in the background, whilst the chairman, Sir Arthur, and his wife, Lady Jacobs, made their assisted way to the microphone. Brendan and Joan realised this could be goodbye, unless they could prolong the parting by some way meeting after the dance…

"Joan, I'll do anything that suits you. What do you think?"

Joan, aware of Brendan's obvious wishes, replied resignedly, "You know I want to stay with you, but if anyone found out, if we were to stay together tonight, I would be in for dismissal. The owners have a very strict moral code we have to follow."

The orchestra suddenly quietened and the chairman's querulous voice, the voice of an old, tired, man, started to ramble on about the success of the paper and thankfully finished with a recognition to all the staff for their endeavours throughout the year. He wished everyone a safe return home and finished with the Jewish *Sholes Aleikhem*—best wishes—and *Laila Tov*—goodnight.

There was a round of muted applause from the dancers and the orchestra began to play the last medley of tunes. Joan held Brendan's hand tight and they danced as one, rather scared of the final goodbye, which was fast approaching.

"Oh, yes, Bren, at the end of the night, we in management have another chore—we have to line up and say goodnight to all the staff as they leave for home. I presume you will be included in the line-up, Bren," she said, as they moved smoothly around the dance floor, smiling a goodnight to all.

"Goodnight, goodnight." All smiles, Brendan and Joan, along with the higher management, shook hands with every member of staff as they passed down the line, and then shook hands with each other. Carl appeared again, disappointingly lacking his gum, and thanked Brendan for his input. He told Brendan there would be a car waiting for him at nine o'clock the next morning, to take him back to the ship.

"Andrew and I will be with you to tie up some loose ends about the movie being made. Can you fit in the time, Joan?"

"That would be fine, Carl."

"Carl," offered Brendan, "what about a goodnight drink before we go to our rooms?" Hoping for and receiving an apology that he and the missus were retiring, as it was now one o'clock, left Brendan and Joan all aquiver in anticipation.

"What do you say, Miss Turbitt? What say I drop in for a cup of tea—sorry, I mean coffee—say goodnight and I retire to my room?"

"Yes, Mr. Harris. I am in room 905. I believe you are in 925. Perhaps you might wish to drop in for a coffee, as you say. I shall proceed with caution." Joan giggled, standing to full height and pulling her shoulders back, accentuating her bust line. Brendan could hardly contain himself and pulled her into the lift which had just arrived. With the door closed, they kissed hungrily and only stood apart as the lift arrived at the ninth floor. With nobody around, they caught hands and ran along the corridor to room 905. Hastily, they checked there was nobody there—*you never know*—and clicked the lock switch. Brendan threw his cap in the air and started to pull off his jacket, to be cautioned by Joan.

"Bren, there's still the chance they may check us, so calm down and let's have a cup of coffee. I'll go have a wash and you make the coffee." Joan backed out of the room towards the bathroom, unfastening her dance skirt and kicking her shoes off. By the time she had stepped backward into the bathroom, giving him a wave, she was down to her red knickers and bra, and closed the door behind her.

Brendan could hardly contain himself but slowly made his way to the coffee table, praying there would be no knock on the outside door. *Surely not*, he thought to himself.

Hurrah! There's no water in the kettle—will have to go to the bathroom—need to go anyway. "Joan, I'm coming in, there's no water in the kettle and I'm full of the stuff as well." Slowly the bathroom door opened and a towel clad body stepped out.

"Okay, Bren, love, get on with it. Like a bit?" she tempted, grinning mightily, opening the large towel and showing she was naked.

"Bloody hell, Joan, to hell with anyone else, I'm coming after you!"

Brendan began to step out of his trousers but fell on the floor in his haste. The laces in one of his shoes became a black knot, so he had to sit on the floor to pull the shoe off. His y-fronts got tangled up in his erection and Joan burst out laughing as he clambered up to catch her in his black socks with his white shirt still on and his erection peering out through the shirt folds.

Joan tried to contain her laughter and cried out, "Wait, Brendan, wait," as she dropped the towel and ran over to her handbag on the floor. Rummaging in it, she produced a slim package.

"Gosh! That one of those French letter things. That's great, I wondered what we were going to do about…you know what I mean, Joan. Well done! Here, let's get it on…careful now…come on, quick, I can't wait," called Brendan as he unbuttoned his shirt, with buttons pinging all over the place, and pushed the naked Joan back on the bed.

Within seconds it was all over. They lay back quite shocked at what had occurred and all so quick.

"You know, Joan, you're the first."

"You too, Bren."

"Better get dressed and find my room. You never know, the spies may be out. You do look lovely, lying there," exclaimed Brendan.

"Give me a kiss and a hug, Brendan, before you go."

Brendan gathered Joan in his arms, kissed her and reluctantly rolled off the bed. After dressing fully and donning his cap, he saluted the lovely form, receiving a wave in return, and sneaked out into the corridor.

The following morning, a bleary-eyed Brendan met the others at the breakfast table. He felt something special had occurred between him and Joan. He didn't want to leave, but it was impossible to stay. He wanted to say *Enough, I'm staying* and, looking in her eyes, he understood she wanted the same. But both knew it couldn't be, and put on a front to brave the next hours out.

Returning to the ship, Carl and the others went to speak with the captain, promising copies of the Philadelphia Tribune would be forwarded for collection at the next port of call. Brendan, with great anticipation and self-satisfaction, introduced Joan to the other apprentices and took her for a sightseeing tour of the ship. The crew made the expected semi-lewd remarks, all in good humour, and after promising to write to each other, Brendan bid Joan a tearful goodbye as the limo departed from the quay.

"Right, Harris, out of your fancy clothes and get ready for a day's work."

Back down to Earth again, away from the limelight, Brendan was still only a junior officer, a trainee still learning the job. But did Brendan now have some treasured memories.

24

Where's the Diary Gone Now?

"Doctor Larrigan, I must speak with you." Jono had waited since seven o'clock in the hospital car park for Larrigan to arrive. It was now nine, and Larrigan was in a hurry. Walking briskly toward the hospital entrance, swinging his brown briefcase, he had had only six hours' sleep the previous night and had a number of pressing complicated operations to fulfil in the next twelve hours.

"Out with it, lad, quick, what is it you want?" Giving little quarter, Larrigan was nearing escape.

"Brendan Harris, my brother, on Ward Six, will become a vegetable, sir, unless we, his family, can communicate with him."

"Go through the proper channels, young man. Now let me go on my way."

"Sir, I must implore you; all channels are shut to us," Jono said through gritted teeth as he stepped in front of Larrigan, barring his way.

"Young man, out of my way or I will call the Garda."

"Do what you will, sir, but I beg you to allow us to see my brother, Brendan Harris, Ward Six, or at least give us some of your time to discover how he is."

Larrigan, a reasonable man, stopped and looked up at Jono, towering above him, and relented. "Harris, I remember the sailor, road accident and coma. All right, young man, call my secretary and she will arrange a meeting. Now, out of my way, please."

Jono still stood his ground. "Sir! Mr. Larrigan, my brother's condition is of the greatest importance. Will your secretary be in the hospital grounds?"

"Yes! You are a persistent young man. In annex thirty-one. I will tell her you will call. Now, out of my way, or this time I will—"

"Allow me, sir," interrupted a victorious Jono, stepping aside, having reached part of his goal, and allowed Larrigan—who gave a brief smile—to enter his key number to unlock the side door and disappear behind the closed door.

Right, thought Jono. *Annex thirty-one, but first I'll have another try at getting into the ward.*

Jono made his way around to the hospital entrance and strode into the reception area. He immediately walked to the stairs to Ward Six. Finding the door ajar, he stood aside to allow a couple of nurses to enter. Neither of them were wearing gauze masks.

Maybe the quarantine has been lifted, thought Jono. *Let's go in and see what happens.* Walking purposefully into the ward, he found the same layout, nothing had changed. Brendan's bed, at the far end of the ward, was, as ever, curtained off. Jono continued his positive walk down the ward to be met by an agitated Sister Sullivan, striding toward him with the palm of her right hand held out in front of her.

"Stop, sir, stop right there, young man. Where do you think you are going?"

"Oh, hello, Sister, you may remember me, Jono Harris—Brendan Harris's brother. We had a call to say he had had a relapse. Could you tell me how he is, please?"

"Mr. Harris, please leave the ward. And make your enquiry through the proper channels. This ward is under quarantine."

"How is my brother? Sister, excuse me," Jono smiled and stepped forward as he pulled aside the bedside curtains.

He could see no change. Brendan was still lying on his back, wrists loosely tied to the side of the bed, still attached to blood and glucose drips. The bedclothes appeared not to have been changed very recently, and there was the ever pervading smell of urine. Brendan seemed to be in some discomfort, moving his lower body side to side and moaning.

Jono, quite disturbed by the sight, called out, "How are you, Bren? Jono here." The moaning stopped; Brendan turned his head toward the sound of the voice. Jono felt a quiver of expectation. *He heard me.* "Brendan, Bren, it's your brother, Jono. Can you hear me? Come on, fella, give me a smile."

There was no further recognition from Brendan as he moved his body, seemingly very uncomfortable.

"Brendan, don't worry, we're working for you. Keep fighting," cried Jono through some surprising tears as he stepped outside the curtains to find two scowling porters bearing down on him.

"It's all right, gentlemen," placated Jono. "I'm going now." Raising his hand in a submissive gesture, he walked rapidly towards the approaching threat. As the two porters went to grab his arms, Jono suddenly sped up, leaving the two of them floundering behind him.

Reaching the exit door, Jono turned to face the approaching menace and, raising his right hand to stall the advancing threat, declared in a positive voice, "Gentlemen, I am leaving, so there is no need for any physical contact."

Upon swinging around to leave, he bumped into Sister Sullivan. "Yes, Mr. Harris, a moment of your time, please. Will you be after comin' to my office, I have something to give you."

Rather surprised, Jono, in his usual polished manner when dealing with the opposite sex, put on the 'Jono smile' and followed the long-skirted, grey robed figure along the narrow corridor.

"Sister," Jono called out, moving alongside the rapidly moving figure, "what is it you have to give me? Have you any news on my brother? He does not look at all well."

"Mr. Harris, I have on my desk a very—in fact quite—dreadful compilation of stories written by your brother. I found they were in the hands of my very impressionable nurses. One moment, please." The sister rummaged in a pocket of her sweeping grey gown and produced a small brass key. Preparing to unlock the white painted wooden door, apparently to her office, she stood back in surprise. Automatically catching the glass rosary beads and cross hanging from her thin neck she exclaimed, "The door it is open. It is never unlocked. Holy Mother of God."

Jono, realising this was time for the hero in the play to step in, stepped up to the offending door with masterful insouciance. "Sister, I will check there is no danger." He pushed the door open.

The room appeared to be unoccupied. "Sister, there is nobody here," Jono advised, looking around the sparsely furnished room. He saw a large imposing desk covered in papers, a small wardrobe resting against the side wall. There was a tall unwashed, multi-pane window behind the desk, with a comfortable looking leather armchair between it and the desk.

Jono, aware the sister was referring to Brendan's notorious diary, replied, "Yes, Sister, I quite agree with you. I shall relieve you of the responsibility and thank you for looking after it for us." Whilst Jono was talking, Sister Sullivan began to get a bit agitated as she scattered papers around the desktop.

"Where is the offending article? I am certain I left it here…and the door was unlocked. Holy Mother of God, shurley no one would have stolen it? I have been so overworked these weeks," muttered Sister Sullivan, beginning to doubt herself. "Did I lock the door? Did I even put the dreadful thing on my desk?" Turning to the amused Jono, over the clacking of the rosary beads, Sister Sullivan ushered him out of the room, telling him when she found the offending diary she would destroy it, and that Jono must now leave.

Quite pleased with the results of his foray at the hospital, Jono returned to Laurel Cottage to report to his parents.

"Ma, Pop, I saw Brendan, for just a moment. He seems to be brighter—he reacted to my voice, but he's lost an awful lot of weight. I spoke to Larrigan, who said he will tell his secretary to arrange an appointment for us to talk about Bren. Best give her a ring now. Oh yes—I had a funny episode with the sister. She's got a bee in her bonnet about Brendan's diary. It seems to be getting' a life of its own," said Jono. " Firstly you had it, Ma, then Polly, then it disappeared. Then the sister claimed to have it, and now she says she has mislaid it. What's in it? The sister was quite vehement about it," laughed Jono. "She calls it 'that dreadful book'. I look forward to reading it. That's if we ever see it again."

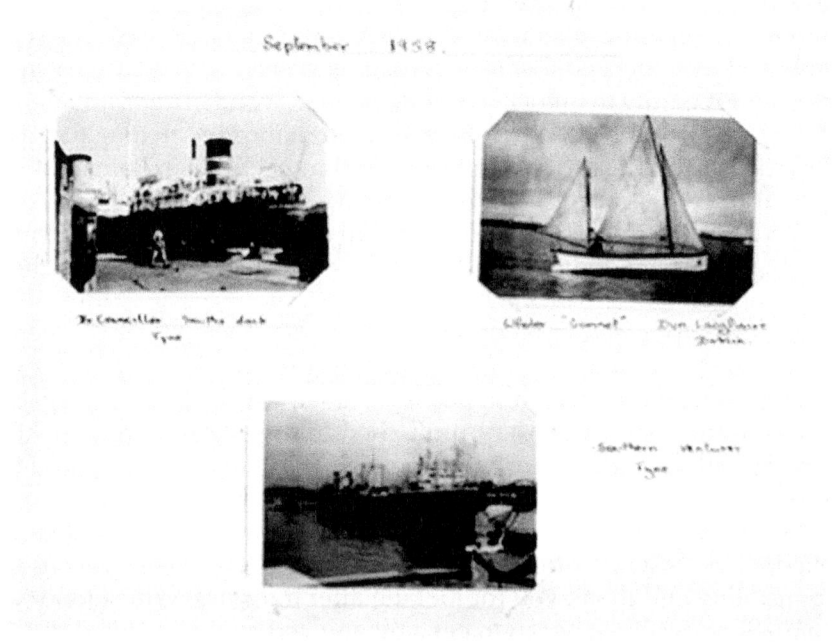

Photos from Diary

25

Back to the Beginning

So it was back to Kuwait after the excitements of Philadelphia, to load up another cargo of the foul-smelling crude oil to take back to the UK. After some months of this boring inactivity, Brendan received surprise instructions to pack his bags and transfer to the *Calvex Charity*, an eight thousand ton coastal tanker.

The *Calvex Charity*, built in 1947, now over ten years old and beginning to succumb to the ever invading rust, was due for the scrap yard, but Calvex were getting their last penny out of the old workhorse.

It was only a short walk for Brendan along the jetty at the Isle of Grain to his new home for the months ahead. Looking very small compared to the *Faith*, the *Charity* looked eager to get back out to sea. It was low in the water with a full cargo of refined oils, and flying the well-known international blue peter flag to indicate it would shortly set sail.

Brendan, feeling very mature and self-important, was now seven months away from his twenty-first birthday, with only nine months left in his apprenticeship. Now very fit and sun-tanned, a man of the world, an old sea dog successful in his studies and successful with the girls, Brendan felt quite smug as he walked up the gangplank to board when he heard a call from the deck above.

"Well! Oh well do my eyes deceive me? It's none other than the Irishman again! Hello, Brendan."

Brendan, looking to place the voice, recognised the curly head of Don Marshall peering from behind the door of the cargo office.

"Don, not you again?" exclaimed Brendan in delight, dropping his suitcases and striding forward to give his friend a spontaneous bear hug.

"Careful now, Bren," grinned Don. "Put me down! You know you're molesting a fourth officer?"

"Why, that's great, Don. You've been home and got your exams, well done. But it's great to see you again. How's your dad and…what was her name? Catherine, your step-mum? It all seems such a long time ago—"

"Don't mention her, Bren, she's gone on her way. Dad threw her out. Best to forget her. Anyway, it's great to see you again. You must be near the end of your apprenticeship, now," mused Don. "Remember you joined the *Renown* with the Welshman. Ha, ha, the bloody Welshman. That must be about four years ago. God, time flies. Enough of the reminiscing, Bren, I'll show you your cabin. We're sailing in six hours. You're the only apprentice aboard. There's another due before we sail—he's leaving it a bit short. Right, this is your cabin, pretty small, Bren, just made to fit two. I'm in the next cabin. Right, Mike, I'm coming," Don answered a call from the deck. "That'll be the second mate, Mike Read, remember him?" were the parting words as Don hurried from the cabin.

This is home for the next few months, at least, thought Brendan to himself as he looked over the small two-berth cabin. The bunks were placed one over the other against the inner wall, with a small wooden desk for each occupant and a large, well-used and drab wardrobe. Brendan, as he had a quick wash in the blue stained ceramic wash hand basin, hoped he was going to be the only occupant of the room for the duration.

Well-equipped, with warm clothes for the expected winter weather into 1961, Brendan took his long frame outside into the cold air and viewed the layout of the ship. With none of the refinements and comforts of the newer ships, the following months were going to be busy and uncomfortable.

At least there would be variety, rather than following the same dreary path to the Middle East each month, to bring a cargo of smelly crude oil back to the UK, with the everlasting chore of chipping rust in the searing heat. He would now be working cargo and navigating watches, loading many styles of refined oils for romantic places like Aarhus, Alborg, Copenhagen, Stavanger and Honningsvag.

Turning his back on the long funnel with its wisp of steam rising into the clear, cold air, and the mix of masts and rigging, ready to return to his cabin to get some sleep before the long night ahead, Brendan heard a car engine approach and turned to see a portly figure emerge from the rear of a taxi onto the dock

That figure looks familiar, thought Brendan, as the fussy body directed the taxi driver to unload the flotilla of suitcases. As the figure turned to face the ship, Brendan recognised it—yes! It was none other than Barry Jones, the Welshman. Now three years older, but still exuding the air of misled dominance and petulance.

Giving the portly body a wave of recognition, Brendan reluctantly descended the steep gangway to the shore and held out his hand.

"Well if it isn't Barry Jones," greeted Brendan, as Barry stared back in recognition.

"Brendan Harris," acknowledged the Welshman, ignoring the proffered hand. "Thought I'd seen the back of you, Paddy boyo. Grab a couple of suitcases, would you, then."

Bristling somewhat at this greeting, Brendan drew a quick breath. *Don't let him needle you.*

"Where would Sir like me take them to? Perhaps the captain's cabin?" Brendan asked with unaccustomed sarcasm, as he picked up a small suitcase, leaving the two other large leather strapped travelling trunks, with their many destination labels, for Barry to carry. Greeted by Don as he reached the top of the gangway, Brendan nodded his head to the struggling Welshman with a resigned grin. "The Welshman returned, Don, full of bonhomie as ever. Can I get a transfer?"

Don smiled back in commiseration. "I only heard within the hour that he was going to join and remembered you both started together the same time. I had a word with the mate, who has agreed for you to be Senior. It's important when there are only two of you. Must go."

Feeling sorry for the struggling Welshman on the gangway, Brendan placed the small case on the deck and descended the steep gangway. "Havin' trouble, boyo, are you den?" asked Brendan, putting on a Welsh accent. "Come on, let me take dis one. You go get the other, it's smaller den this." Reaching the cabin, Brendan confronted Barry. "Right, Barry, before we go any further…" Brendan stated as he sat on the cabin chair facing a disgruntled Welshman. "We will be working and living close together over the next months. Leave that alone and listen to me," admonished Brendan as Barry chose to ignore him and started to throw clothes onto the bottom bunk. "Barry," called Brendan, raising his voice, "will you for God's sake listen to me. I have chosen the bottom bunk, first come first choice, and to put you straight, I am Senior—"

"You, Senior? Who says so? We joined at the same time and," continued Barry, "if you think, laddo, that I'll be taking orders from you, Paddy, you've got to think again."

Looking at the small rotund body in front of him, as they stood in the cramped cabin—a body that hadn't improved in any way since their first meeting over three years ago—Brendan thought he had better put a stop to this blustering.

"Barry—I shall call you Barry—and you know full well I do not answer to Paddy. We are both approaching the end of our apprenticeship, it's probably our last trip. Barry, I want no bluster from you. The decision has been made by the first mate. I am the senior," Brendan announced, smiling and stepping closer to the short-statured Barry, towering over him with his greater height.

Barry, realising he would get nowhere, backed away with his head down. Brendan could see he was seething and thought he had better mollify the lump of Welsh blubber. He leaned forward with a conciliatory smile.

"Barry, let's call a truce, let's work together. The next few months are going to be hard. The winter is approaching and we will be docking about three times a week. What do you say?" Brendan asked, extending his right hand, offering peace.

"All right then, although I don' kno' what all the fuss is about... Brendan, but if it makes you happy, I agree," stated Barry, raising his head and accepting the proffered hand.

Gripping the limp pudgy hand, with its bitten nails, Brendan nearly dropped it, quite repelled by the feel of the soft flesh. Relieved to hear his name being called from a cabin down the short corridor, he answered it, recognising the voice as that of Mike Read. He had been third officer on the *Renown* and was now the second mate on the *Charity*.

"Right, Brendan, something like old times," smiled Read. "You've been around a bit, I hear, over the years. Here, take a seat for a moment. This will probably be your last trip before you end your time. I see you were on the *Faith*, with Brian Turdy. Heard you did English-American relations a bit of good."

"Quite a visit, Mike, quite a visit," Brendan agreed, smiling to himself, "and congratulations on your promotion."

"Yes! Thanks, Brendan, there's quite a future ahead of us in Calvex. The world is going mad for oil and they're finding the stuff all over the place." Raising his head to look directly at Brendan, he continued, "I see Barry Jones has just joined us. Everything all right there?"

"Nothing I can't deal with, Mike," Brendan replied.

"OK! That's fine, Brendan. Now, we'd better get Barry in to hear how we plan to use the two of you."

Brendan, rising to his feet, called Barry in to the second's cabin. Over the next twenty minutes it was decided that for the next month, Brendan would take four-hour watches on the bridge with Mike, on the four to eight, and Barry would stay on day work, cleaning the bridge and working with the chief officer on daytime duties.

"We're sailing in a couple of hours, that's sixteen hundred, lads," said Mike. "You can start your watch duties from then, Brendan, when we leave Grain. Barry, you go aft with Don Marshall to untie the ship. Oh, by the way, if you were not aware, our first call is to Copenhagen, and then to Malmo." Rising to his feet, Mike shook hands with both apprentices.

"Copenhagen, that's where the famous statue of the mermaid is and the Tivoli Gardens, isn't it, Barry? Wonder if we'll get any time off to see them?" Brendan asked of Barry as they returned to their cabin.

BRENDAN AFLOAT

Barry looked at Brendan with scorn on his face and, in a withering Welsh accent, stated, "Who would be bothered with such drivel? I've better things to do with my time." He turned his back on Brendan.

This is going to be fun, thought Brendan to himself, *the months ahead with this miserable Welsh creature. Whatever, I must get my uniform on and get up on the bridge to join the second mate as we'll be sailing soon.*

So it was over the next months; Brendan stood watch, four hours on eight hours off, hopping in and out of ports around Europe and Scandinavia. He and Barry fortunately saw very little of each other, as their work patterns differed. They sat their final company exams on passage from The Isle of Grain to the small port of Honningsvag, inside the Arctic Circle, and Gotenburg in Sweden. The weather was very stormy and the *Calvex Charity* rolled and pitched uncomfortably, which did not help concentration on such an important event. Brendan also updated his diary, which was now full of his experiences over the past four years, with small sketches and photos amongst the written content.

As he had spent enough time at sea to qualify for time served for his officer's exam, Calvex terminated his apprenticeship contract when the *Calvex Charity* docked in the Isle of Grain in January 1961.

Brendan's next step in his career was to register with the navigating college in Dunlaoghaire, to take a two-month course to sit his officer's exam the following April, and Calvex offered him a two-year contract to continue serving with them.

Settling down in Laurel Cottage for the winter months, Brendan met up with Polly and they went to dances, with Jono and girlfriend. One weekend, he and Jono went into the Crystal Ballroom in Dublin, in Pop's car, and met up with couple of girls, both nurses and country girls. Brendan made a date with his partner for the dance, Maureen—a good dancer, younger than him, quite tall but slightly reserved. Later in the week, after he had bought a driving licence and had a quick ten-minute lesson from Jono on how to ride his Vespa motor scooter, he borrowed same scooter and rode it into the city to meet up with Maureen outside the post office in O'Connell Street.

Arriving in good time, he waited outside the impressive stone building. Noticing the many gouge marks in the granite, he realised they must have been made by the British forces shooting at the Irish rebels back in 1918, when they occupied the Post Office. *History is all around me,* he thought. *Hey, I wonder where my date is?* He checked his watch. *Should have been here ten minutes ago.*

Looking up, he noticed a girl hurrying towards him, unsteady on high heels, wearing a light mackintosh. It was his date. Coming closer to him, he saw, under her coat, she was wearing her nurse's uniform.

"So sorry for being late, Brendan," she gasped, "but I was held up at the hospital an' I'm going to ha' to 'pologise. I've gotta get back 'mediately.

Somethin' urgent has come up. I had to run down to tell you." She took a deep breath. "Look, I'll give you a ring, so sorry."

Before Brendan could reply she had turned on her heels and disappeared into the gathering dusk.

Well, he thought to himself as he sped along the Merrion Road on the way back to Dunlaoghaire. I *won't be bothering with her again.* With the wind in his hair, a clear road and an interesting future ahead of him, Brendan Harris sped along the wide, well-lit main road. Noticing a car's headlights at the entrance to a minor road to the right, he considered… *it'll come out behind me. God! No! It's coming out fast…I'm going to hit it…*

He screamed.

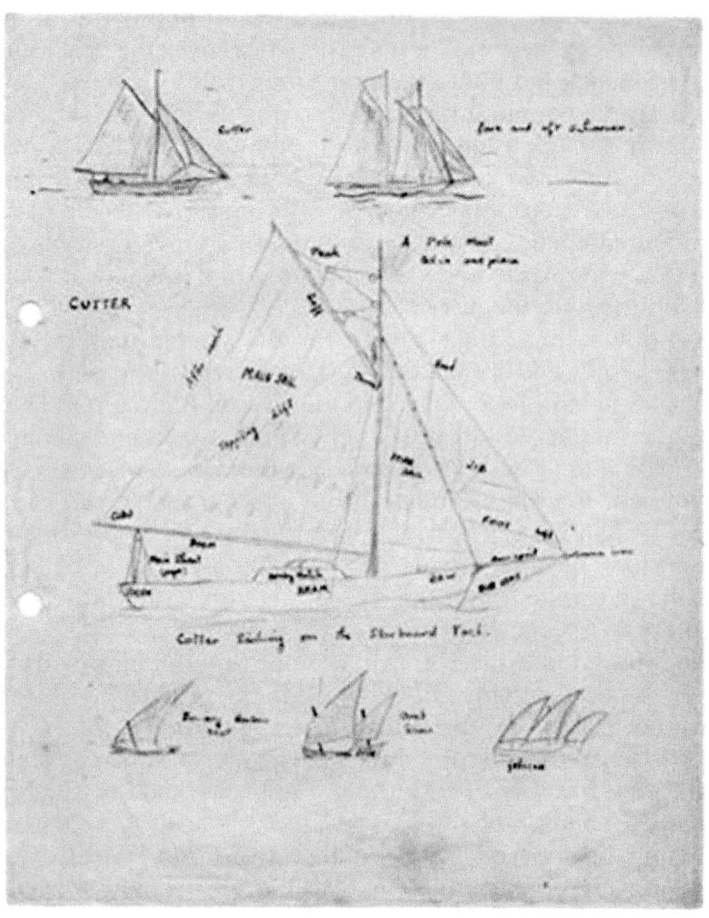

Sketches of Various Sailing Boats

26

Brendan Begins to Recover

"Tomorrow, ten a.m. at the hospital, in Mr. Larrigan's office in annex thirty-one. That's great news. Will we be able to see my son?"

"Please speak to Mr. Larrigan about that at the meeting. Thank you, Mr. Harris, goodbye."

"You heard that, everybody," Henry called out. "Mr. Larrigan will see us tomorrow at ten. Thanks, Jono, for all you've done."

"That's great, Pop, but what about the quarantine business? I got the impression it was all a bit of a false alarm," Jono replied. "Maybe a call to the hospital would tell us. Here, shall I do it, Pop?"

Upon following this suggestion, it was found the supposed quarantine was being lifted from eight o'clock the next morning, to everybody's surprise and relief.

"It's been close on three weeks since the accident, Pop. Any news from the solicitor whether Brendan can claim against the driver of the car he hit?" asked Jono. "I kno' it's more important that Bren recovers, but it would be nice to get a few quid back—the scooter was a bloody write-off."

"Go on, Alice, give Bill Faulkner a ring. He hasn't been in touch since we talked with him last week. You kno' how to deal with him," admitted Henry, reverting back to his passive mode of approach.

"Oh, alright, Hen, where's his number? I don't know why you gave him the case—he's just an ould eejit," complained Alice, with a resigned look on her face.

"Ye' kno', Alice, we've known Bill Faulkner for twenty years an' we—"

Henry was interrupted by Alice. "We don' owe him anything, Hen, remember the cock-up he made with Grannie's will…" She paused and then spoke into the phone. "Yes, hello, put me through the Mr Faulkner, please. Yes, Alice Harris."

After some fifteen minutes, Alice, getting more and more exasperated with the slow and ponderous Bill Faulkner, eventually replaced the receiver and, with a heavy sigh ending with a smile, informed the eager audience the outcome of the conversation.

"Apparently, everyone, the driver of the car was a politician and they are taking the case to court. The Garda have been informed and will interview us again. Bill Faulkner suggests they might consider Brendan was speeding and was driving without the scooter light on."

"Rubbish, Ma," interrupted Jono. "The lights were working. They can't prove that. The headlight was smashed in the collision. Wonder what politician it was?"

"OK, Jono, calm down. The case is listed to come to court in three months' time, but Faulkner suggests when they gather all facts, they will settle out of court as—"

"How does he know that, Alice?"

"Let me finish, Hen. Faulkner suggests the politician involved will try to avoid the publicity and they are just trying to scare us."

"That sounds pretty good, Ma," said Billy. "Did he say how much?"

"That's enough, Billy," continued Ma. "If we were to lose it would cost us money. Though Faulkner seems to be quite sure the other lot will cough up. Can we afford to take the chance? What's the vote, hands up to go ahead?"

Up shot Jono and Billy's hands, followed shortly by Ma's.

"Come on, Pop," Jono called to his reluctant father.

"OK, I'll vote for it."

Whilst this conversation was being held in Laurel Cottage, Nurses Fitzgerald and Sheelin were discussing Brendan's case and admitting their surprising feelings towards him.

"Nurse Dolan says Rudi spoke to her last night. His eyes were open and he smiled at her. Ye kno', Mary, I don't know If I'm beginning to get a bit fond of Rudi, an' only wish he would speak wid me," Nurse Kathleen Fitzgerald admitted with an embarrassed laugh to Mary Sheelin as they made their way off duty.

"Ye kno', I'm feelin' a bit the same about him," agreed Mary Sheelin. "It's lookin' a bit like he's comin' out of the coma an' he may be soon goin' home. The big brother has been pushin' to get things done, an' der's goin' to be a confab tomorrow morning, I hear, with the family. I'm surprised to see the Prods lookin' after each other as the Harrises are doin'. Back home, the few families there were always fightin'."

"Good morning, Mr. and Mrs. Harris, and young sirs." Larrigan welcomed Henry and Alice and nodded towards Jono and Billy, all seated in a group at the side of a small annex room. Larrigan perched on the edge of a small desk.

"I see you all have a coffee, good. So sorry this office is so small, but I thought it best we meet here, away from the ward. They are very busy at present, getting over the effects of the recent quarantine.

"Your son, Brendan. I have just returned from my rounds and was very pleased to find Brendan is now reacting to contact and speaking with the nurses, although in quite a limited way. All superficial wounds have healed, his leg is still in the plaster for support, and we intend to remove this within the next two days. We feel sure, due to the lad's healthy disposition, Brendan should realise no trouble, after physiotherapy, in recovering the use of his leg."

Smiling at the pleased expressions on the faces before him, Larrigan continued in his refined Dublin accent. "Regarding Brendan's head injury: it is still early days yet, but he is responding well. His speech does not appear to have been affected; his hearing seems fine and his sight does not appear to have been altered. A question regarding his memory is still unanswered, and I must warn you of the possibility that when he sees you, he may not immediately recognise you. If this happens, do speak with him—voices will awaken dormant memories. Please do not expect too much from him. I am sorry I cannot be more positive." Larrigan smiled as he looked around the group of worried expressions. "Yes, Mrs. Harris?" Larrigan reacted to Alice's raised eyebrows.

"How soon can we expect him to be discharged from the hospital, Mr. Larrigan?"

"Still early days yet, Mrs. Harris. A lot depends on how readily Brendan reacts to your presence at the bedside, but physically he is ready to return home within twenty-four hours. Now, if you don't mind, I shall have to leave you. Please finish your coffees in your own time and my secretary can then arrange your visit to the ward."

"This is the big day, Henry. Will Bren recognise us? Oh God, I feel like crying."

"Look, Ma," interrupted Jono. "Billy and I will hold back whilst you and Pop see him first. OK by you, Billy?" he questioned and received a nod of confirmation. "If," Jono continued, "everything's OK, maybe we could say hello to him as well."

"Yep, Jono, that's best," agreed Henry. "Billy, could you get the secretary and tell her we're ready to go to the ward?"

"OK, Pop," Billy replied, as apprehensive as the others, and returned within minutes.

"She says Sister Sullivan will be here in a minit, to take us over to the ward. She's the nasty one, isn't she?" said Billy, screwing his face up in distaste.

Shortly afterwards, Sister Sullivan arrived and, in her officious manner, led the group back to the ward, avoiding eye contact with Jono.

"Hold my hand, Hen, please?" Alice asked, reaching out to her husband. "I'm scared he won't recognise us."

"Don't you be worrien there, Alice, Brendan will be fine," consoled Henry, patting her hand.

Approaching the curtained bed they could hear laughter. Nurse Fitzgerald stepped out through the curtains, looking back at Brendan, calling out with amusement in her voice, "If sir wants them to have a cup of tea, sir will have to get it hisself."

"What's that, Nurse Fitzgerald, would you be after mindin' your manners, young lady." Startled by this admonishment, the nurse stepped aside and apologised to the sister.

Alice, overhearing this short conversation, stopped the sister with a raised hand and beckoned the nurse over to her. "Is Brendan expecting us?" she whispered, and Nurse Fitzgerald nodded her head in reply. "Oh! Thanks, Nurse, that's wonderful. Come on, Hen."

Linking arms with Henry, Alice stepped through the curtains to see Brendan sitting up in the bed, arms free of their bindings. His head was still wrapped in a bandage and his right leg encased in plaster—and strangely his right eye was shut—but he had a big welcoming smile on his face.

"Hello, Ma. Hello, Pop. What took you so long?"

Somewhat overcome by the emotion of the greeting, and the absolute relief as to its implications, both parents looked at each other and started to cry. They rushed over to hug the weeping Brendan.

After a few words, with one on each side of the bed, Jono was heard calling outside the curtains, "Everything all right, in there? Can we come in?"

Getting a nod from Brendan, Henry went to the curtain and welcomed the two of them in, and after another session of tears from everyone, and relieved laughter, Brendan's head began to droop and he fell asleep.

"C'mon, Hen, lads, let's leave him. He's in a deep sleep now. He must be exhausted. Is there a nurse around, anyone? Nurse!" called Alice.

Not receiving a reply, Henry volunteered to go and find a nurse to tell they were leaving. Patting Brendan on the shoulder, and noticing how thin he now was, Alice took Henry's hand and squeezed it with a relieved smile. "He's back again, now to get him home. Must tell Polly the news."

Brendan, whilst now conscious, was still very weak and vulnerable. His memories were all confused. In his mind he considered the bed, the smells; the sounds were his stable entity. He recognised the voices of the nurses as his subconscious had retained them over the weeks. However, the names and instances relating to his parents did not jolt any immediate memories. He knew Ma and Pop were words he associated with the two persons he had just met and knew they were people who were special to him.

BRENDAN AFLOAT

"Hiya there, Rudi," was the smiling greeting to Brendan as he wakened after a long sleep. "Nurse Fitzgerald here, time for tea. What would you like? Do you take sugar, Brendan? Better call you Brendan…" Nurse Fitzgerald realised her control of Brendan's recovery was now passing, and feeling somewhat responsible for his return to consciousness, as did Nurse Sheelin, both wished to keep an eye on his recovery and to find the real Brendan.

"A nice cup of tea, Brendan, with two sugars…ye' will need the sugar, an' here's a chocolate biscuit for ye'," smiled Nurse Fitzgerald as she placed the drink and plate, with the biscuit, on the tray over the bed and pushed it in front of Brendan. Reaching out to steady the tray, his hand brushed the nurse's arm, whereupon she took his hand and gently placed it on the bed.

"I'm knockin' off now, Bren, see you in the morning," were the passing words as Nurse Fitzgerald firstly glancing behind her, to ensure the coast was clear, then leaned over and gave Brendan a quick kiss on the cheek.

"God, I shouldn't be doin' this, Bren, don' say a word."

Brendan, seeing nothing wrong in the nurse's action, as his thought process was still accepting everything as normal, balanced the cup in his right hand and sipped the cold, over-sugared weak tea. The chocolate biscuit disappeared in two bites, as Brendan surveyed his world through his left eye. He had found, when using both eyes, he could see two of everything, and by shutting one eye he was able to focus. Brendan, in his present state of mind, did not question this.

Through the one eye, his world consisted of a bed with rails on each side, and off-white curtains shielded him from any observers. He could smell disinfectant and the background smell of urine. His right leg itched but couldn't be scratched, as it was covered in hard, white plaster. His backside felt very tender in places, and he felt he needed a shave. But more importantly, he felt hungry.

Sounds from outside his world consisted of a variety of male voices—sometimes raised, sometimes complaining—, with their regional accents from various parts of the country. Some called out in pain, others coughed, with the odd strained laugh.

Why am I here? What if I call nurse? With these thoughts chorusing through his mind, Brendan was startled to hear his name mentioned outside the curtains, and with a sudden whoosh of action they were swept aside to reveal Sister Sullivan, with two nurses alongside her, and bright windows and a line of beds with staring faces behind them. A movement to the right caught his eye; further staring faces in other beds.

Startled by this, Brendan tried to slide back under the bedclothes to hide. His right leg, encased in the plaster, caught in the blanket and pulled the covers from his body, revealing him to be naked from the waist down. Nurse Sheelin, who was standing beside Sister Sullivan, ran to cover Brendan.

"Yes, Nurse, make up that bed, it's a mess," ordered Sister Sullivan, "an' you, Nurse Fitzgerald, go let the visitors in."

"Brendan, don't mind Sister, she means well," consoled Nurse Sheelin as she tidied up the bed and asked if he was expecting any visitors.

"I don't know, nurse," admitted Brendan. "I know there are people that I know and I'm a bit concerned that I may not know them if they come in...I wish the curtains were back...God, I'm sleepy...do you think..." Brendan's eyes began to shut as the nurse adjusted the pillows behind his head, leaning very close to Brendan's face. "Boy! You smell nice," he muttered with a smile, as he dropped off asleep.

Nurse Sheelin stood back from the sleeping Brendan with confused thoughts going through her mind, and pulled the curtain down the side of the bed to shield Brendan from the ward.

"We'll look after ye', Rudi," she said softly, as she stepped back from the bed to find someone close behind her. "Oh! Sorry, Miss, didn't kno' you were there," she apologised, thinking, *this is the girlfriend, all dressed up in her bloody business suit with her blonde hair, her high heels, her perfume and her bloody posh accent.*

"Hello, Nurse," Polly greeted in her soft educated voice. "I see Mr. Harris is asleep?"

"Yes, Miss, he's just dropped off," replied Nurse Sheelin "He's had a long day an' is finding it hard."

"I can well imagine, Nurse. Will it be alright if I stay for a short while, though, he may wake up and I'd like to talk with him?"

Slightly disgruntled that this stranger should come in and take over Brendan's affections, Nurse Sheelin replied rather abruptly, looking at her watch. "There's three-quarters of an hour left visitin', Miss. I'll leave you now."

As she turned to leave, Sheelin noticed the two tall figures of Jono and Billy entering the ward and informed Polly with some delight. "I think, Miss, der's some more visitors to see Brendan."

"Hello, Polly, how's the invalid? Is he asleep...or still unconscious?"

Billy reeled off the list of questions as he drew alongside Polly, sitting beside the bed. "He looks awful," he continued, looking to Jono for agreement.

"Hello, Polly, been here long?" Jono asked, leaning over the bed where Brendan, who must have sensed the attention, opened his eyes, immediately shutting the right one. He looked around, slightly confused by all the faces. His immediate reaction was to hit out at these people invading his space, but instinct stopped him. Instead he recognised Jono and Billy, and took a moment to decide who the elegant woman sitting beside the bed was.

BRENDAN AFLOAT

"Hello, Jono. Hello, Billy." Brendan raised his hand in greeting. "And is it...Polly?" In a sudden swell of emotion, Brendan burst into tears, covering his face with his thin hands.

"Oh, Brendan. What's wrong, love?" cried Polly, rising on impulse to comfort Brendan.

"Look, Billy, we'll come back in ten minutes," called Jono, catching Billy's arm and leading him away from the bed.

"Brendan, what's wrong, love? What are you thinking? Everything's alright, the doctor says you're doing marvellously!"

Gripping Brendan's hand, Polly realised how much she had become emotionally involved with this Brendan, this invalid, this now unknown person.

Brendan, now just awakening to life again, was finding it difficult to know how he was expected to react to these different people, with their different voices and smells and their expectations. His comfortable world consisted of the hospital bed, the nurses and hospital smells. By instinct he knew his brothers and parents. He knew that he knew Polly, and there was some chemistry between them, but what was expected of him?

Why does my leg itch so badly? Why is my bottom sore? Why do I feel like crying all the time?

Polly, realising that Brendan was looking for some rapport between them, began to talk about the times they went dancing. "Remember the time we went to the Arcadia Ballroom in Bray. Victor Sylvester was the band that night. Remember, I won a spot prize." Receiving a smile from Brendan, Polly, encouraged, continued, "I remember when we went out in the yacht with Jim and Sonja...do you?" Receiving a nod in agreement from Brendan, Polly leaned forward and looking directly into Brendan's eyes said, "I never admitted it then, but I was quite scared and was very relieved when we got back to dry land."

"Oh, Polly, I thought you liked it. Oh, yes I remember it now, it was Jim's dad's whaler. I'm sorry you were scared. Where's Jim now? He went to sea, didn't he? I'm in the Merchant Navy, aren't I?"

"Bren, Bren, hold on a moment, one question at a time, please..." Polly smiled as she brushed some tears from her eyes. "There's lots to talk about, Bren. You'll be coming home soon, but may I ask..." Polly said, looking at Brendan sitting up in the wide hospital bed with his head leaning to the right and his right eye shut. "Why do you keep your eye closed?"

"I see two of everything, and when I shut an eye I see one. When I have them both open, like now," Brendan demonstrated by sitting upright with both eyes open. "I see two of you, Polly, one over the other, and when I turn my head to the right, the two of you nearly become one... So there you are," declared Brendan.

"Bren, another question...please?"

"Yes, Polly."

"Do you know why you are here?"

"Oh, look, it's Jono and Billy back. I dunno, Polly, something about an accident a long time ago? You've got some grapes, Jono, an' what's in the box, Billy?"

"Look, Bren, I'll go now, it's nearly the end of visiting time and you will want to speak with your brothers," Polly said, as she reluctantly rose to leave.

"Polly," interrupted Jono. "Don't mind us, please. We have just called in to tell Brendan how glad we are that he's recovering. Isn't that right, Billy?" Jono addressed Billy, who nodded and stepped in front of his eldest brother.

"So glad you're getting better, Bren. Come on home soon," were Billy's comments as he patted Brendan on the arm and stepped back.

"There's the end of visiting bell. Can I give you a lift home, Polly?" Jono asked as he rose from the bedside.

"That would be grand, Jono. Thanks. Goodnight, Brendan. So glad." Polly cried as she leaned over and kissed Brendan on the cheek. "Is it alright, Bren, if I go and talk to a nurse about your sight? Oh yes, another thing, where's your diary? Have either of you seen it? Jono, Billy?"

"That's a thing, Polly," replied Jono. "Last thing I knew of it, Sister Sullivan had confiscated it and threatened to destroy it."

"If she has I'll beat her to death, the bloody woman," exploded Polly. "Sorry, Bren," she apologised to Brendan, who became startled at her outburst. "You know you kept a diary whilst you were at sea."

"Did I?" replied Brendan. "That was a good idea. Must read it sometime."

""I'm going to find that sister and sort her out, and get you something for your eye, Bren."

"Thanks, Polly, that would be good," replied Brendan as he settled down behind his protective blankets and waved goodbye to these visitors who had disturbed his little world.

The following morning brought more disturbance, as Mr. Larrigan decided on his rounds that it was time Brendan got up from his bed and endeavoured to walk. Nurse Sheelin was instructed to go to the stockroom cupboard and bring back an eye patch and a pair of crutches. This she dutifully did, as Larrigan outlined Brendan's ailments to the two students alongside him.

"Right, Nurse, thank you. They're a grand pair. They should be big enough. Now, which eye would you like the patch on? I see you keep your right eye closed…cover that one?"

With a nod from Brendan, Nurse Sheelin stood on tiptoe to lean over the side of the bed and place the holding tape over Brendan's head and the black patch over his right eye.

"There ye' are now, Rudi, ye' can only see one of me, now. Isn't that grand? Yer Polly friend has been creatin' ructions about eyesight, an' she tore a strip off the sister about your diary as well," she whispered, standing back to admire her handiwork.

"Can you swing your legs over the side of the bed there now, Mr. Harris, or…you there, Miss…" Larrigan hesitated as he looked at the name tag on the tall female student. "Livingstone. Livingstone, that's a grand name you have there. Would you lean over and help Mr. Harris swing his legs over the side of the bed. That's fine, careful of the right one."

To Brendan, this was a momentous moment. He hadn't been on his feet for three weeks and was also feeling slightly embarrassed at all the attention—and he wearing only a cotton nightshirt as well. Would his legs hold him up, especially the right one with the plaster? Standing unsteadily on his two long thin legs, with Nurse Sheelin under one arm and Student Livingstone under the other, he lifted his arms to allow Mr. Larrigan to place the long wooden unwieldy crutches one under each arm and stood back.

"Put your weight on the crutches like a good man…good…now step aside, girls…and let the man see the rabbit…Ha, ha," exclaimed Larrigan as Brendan stood upright, putting his weight on the supporting crutches. "How do you feel now, Brendan?"

"A bit unsteady, Doctor."

"That's OK, put your weight on the left leg an' swing the right one… good…now quickly, weight on the right one an' then to the left. Perfect. We'll soon have you up an' running the four-minute mile. Do a few more steps an' then back to the bed. Your eye patch suits you. The only thing missing is your parrot. Ha, ha. Great. Very satisfied…we'll have you home in a few days."

Brendan, pleased that all was going so well, thanked Larrigan, gave Miss Livingstone a smile of thanks, and Nurse Sheelin a quick hug as he was assisted back to bed.

Sister Sullivan was seen walking through the ward outside her usual visits times during the day, carrying a folded blanket. She stopped for a moment, a couple of times, at Brendan's bed but continued her walk.

The following morning, after a good night's sleep, Brendan woke early with a great need to get to the toilet. Rather than disturb the nurses with the undignified use of the bed pan, he decided to make his own way to the toilet and endeavoured to swing his legs out of the bed. With his right leg still in plaster, the weight took control and it was with a heavy crash he fell out of the bed, knocking the bedside cupboard over, with glass bowls and bottles crashing to the floor. The night nurses came rushing out from the side room, all anxious but relieved to find he hadn't hurt himself—just his dignity.

Helping him to his feet and balancing him on his crutches, they aided him toward the toilet. Amongst the broken glass and bowls, Nurse Dolan noticed a sheaf of papers in the bottom of the small cupboard partially hidden in a pillow slip.

Shurley not, she thought to herself, *shurley not the famous diary.* Righting the fallen cupboard, she recovered the papers and settled on the floor to examine them. *Well o' well, the famous diary, better tidy it up. Wish I had time to read it.* "Look what I found," she called to the other night nurse, "the diary…wonder how it got here? The family will be pleased."

When Nurse Sheelin reported for day duty at eight o'clock, when time permitted she put the diary into order and gave it to Brendan to read.

Over the next couple of days, Brendan began to spend more time out of bed, sometimes assisted by his favourite nurses. He began to recover rapidly; his long term memory returned, but it was the recent months that were hard to recall. His diplopia—or double vision—remained the same; this was rectified by wearing a black eye patch. The dramatic scars on each side of his head, where Larrigan had operated on the brain, were covered by bandages, but were now also nearly covered by new hair growth. It was decided to leave the plaster on the right leg until he had returned home and physio was arranged.

The momentous day arrived where Brendan was dismissed from the hospital, three weeks to the day since he had arrived.

"Goodbye, Rudi, Brendan, Mr. Harris. Good luck," Nurses Fitzgerald and Sheelin called to Brendan as he made his self-conscious way down the ward, swinging unsteadily on his two crutches. Sister Sullivan stood at the side of the ward, having discharged Brendan from her care, giving the impression she was glad to see the back of him.

As Pop held the exit door open, Brendan turned back to view the ward where his life had been saved, where he had been reborn. He gave a last wave to the two nurses who had been such a part of his recovery. The day before leaving he had invited them to visit Laurel Cottage, and both had agreed to come.

"You OK, Bren?" Ma asked, noticing a slight hesitation in Brendan's demeanour.

"Yeh, Ma, I'm OK. A bit emotional and scared I'm leaving what I know. Hope they keep in touch." With a last wave, Brendan turned and let the door close behind him.

27

Last Sea Trip

"Back home at last, Ma, Pop. Thanks for all you have done over the past weeks. Now to start working out the future."

"Hold your horses, son," interrupted Pop, with an understanding smile. "You've got a lot of recovering to do, just take your time. You've got the summer ahead of you, so just get well."

Quite exhausted and feeling very weak, Brendan, glad to be home, would now have to adjust to the fairly spartan amenities in the cottage.

He was back to his old childhood bedroom, the room with the cracked lino, the high ceiling with the large water stain where the rain had come through some while ago, and the elaborate fireplace with fancy ceramic tiles. This room led off to a side room, where Billy now slept, and Jono had moved out to a flat close by.

The toilet, or pantry, was down to the left, off a short, dark, tiled passageway toward the kitchen. A long hallway on the right stretched to a heavy hall door, which opened into the glass porch with its wild variety of creepers and plants.

After the warm atmosphere of the hospital the cottage was very cold, and Brendan's parents had put an oil fire in the bedroom which took the chill off the air. Hoping to get back to his life prior to the accident, Brendan looked at his work books on navigation, general ship knowledge and seamanship, only to find he did not have the capacity to concentrate. He read over his diary to help recover his memory of recent years.

Life was uncomfortable; all his clothes were too large for him, having lost a lot of weight. There was very little money, and he had no savings, but at least he was getting some small recompense in sickness pay from his national insurance contributions over the previous four years.

Polly called a few times, but seemed to lose interest as Brendan had become quite depressed and was not very good company. A couple of weeks after leaving the hospital, he was alone in the cottage when there was a surprise visit from Kathleen Fitzgerald. Dressed in a jaunty brown pleated skirt, high heels, and white jersey, she brightened up Brendan's day, looking so much prettier than when dressed in her nurse's uniform. The few hours in her company flashed by and it was a much happier Brendan who walked her up to the bus stop that evening and kissed her goodbye.

The big day arrived when the plaster cast on his right leg was removed to release a long thin length of stark white bone and flesh. A programme of physiotherapy was started, to get the leg moving again. Brendan was all the while conscious of being a drain on his parents' resources. After a few months, when the leg was more mobile, he took a job working for the local petrol station as an attendant, serving petrol and washing cars.

Not feeling very well one evening, he went to bed with unpleasant stomach ache and felt he had a bit of a temperature. He expected it would clear itself overnight, but the following morning, at about six a.m., he woke with an excruciating pain in his right side. No matter which way he turned, or drew his knees up to his chest, the dreadful sharp pain remained. Pop called the doctor and within twenty minutes, Doctor Goodbody arrived with a shot of morphine, bundled the much relieved Brendan into his car, and deposited him within thirty minutes into the nearest hospital. Acute appendicitis was diagnosed and within the hour Brendan was returned to his hospital bed, relieved of his errant appendix. As a precautionary measure, in light of his recent ailments, he remained in the hospital for a further five days.

Over these few days he had some surprise visitors. Mary Sheelin, on her day off from nursing in Laurence's, made a very welcome visit. Polly, who had been absent for some time, arrived and was very apologetic and nervous. Pulling up a chair alongside the bed, she looked straight at Brendan and without any preamble asked him his intentions for the future. Did he have any intentions for marriage? Brendan, quite taken aback—as the responsibilities of marriage were the furthest things from his mind—not surprisingly, answered in the negative. Polly explained her reason as, at the age of twenty-four, she was getting pretty old and she had been offered marriage by a man she had known for a while. She had to take the opportunity, but wanted to give Brendan the chance to state his intentions.

Brendan wasn't in the state of mind to appreciate the compliment paid, laughed off the suggestion of marriage and wished her all the best. Quite selfishly, he was only considering himself and his future. Only a few months ago he had finished a successful apprenticeship in a career which had great prospects, and here he was now in a hospital bed with a gammy leg, wearing an eye patch and eager to get back into his career. The prospect of taking on any more responsibilities was furthest from his thoughts. Polly then rose from her chair, kissed him on the cheek, wished him all the best and left, probably quite glad to rid herself of the drain Brendan would be on her immediate future.

"It's Calvex on the phone, Brendan."

It was now a few weeks since Brendan returned from the hospital. He was exercising daily to get his strength back, and the mobility in his leg was improving, but he still had the double vision. He had enquired about the problem and it had been suggested there was a suitable operation which could possibly rectify the situation.

"Yes, Harris here."

"Good, Mr. Harris, Superintendent Porteous, from Calvex. We are wondering if you are in the position to return to sea? Our contract with you is still open."

"Sorry to say, I still haven't taken my officer's examination…"

"Oh, that's fine; we can offer you an uncertified third officer's position on the *Calvex Faith*, due to dock in Liverpool…"

That would be marvellous, thought Bren, but of course he had to decline the offer. He had thought about starting his studies again, to take the officer's certificate, but had been advised against it by the doctor.

One excellent piece of news, from the solicitor, was the defendants in the case Brendan had taken against the driver of the car involved in the accident had offered a sum of £3,300 to settle out of court.

This offer was gratefully accepted by Brendan, as it now gave him the ability to repay his parents, and especially Jono, for the loss of his Vespa scooter.

Brendan's main aim now was to regain his health. His good friend Doctor James Courcy, very involved with Irish Shipping and with many contacts in the coastal trade, suggested he might like a short trip on a small ship trading between the port of Cork, in the south of the country, and Liverpool.

It was now approaching the end of summer. Brendan's health was improving; he had bought himself a car for £150, a cream Ford Anglia with fawn trimmings, and had taken Kathleen Fitzgerald out dancing. Kathleen had a rented flat on the outskirts of Dublin, where Brendan sometimes stayed overnight after a late dance in Dublin, and she sometimes stayed overnight in the cottage.

One late Saturday evening, they arrived back to the ground floor flat, after a dance in the city, to find there was a great deal of laughter and noise from the flat above.

"Oh, that's Marcella, it's her birthday today an' she's having a party. I thought they would have quietened down a bit by now. Let's go up an' see what's goin' on, Bren…" Catching Brendan's hand, Kathleen pulled him up the short flight of stairs and knocked on the door on the landing.

"Hi, Marcella, party still goin' strong? Any room for two more?"

"Cum in, cum in, Kath, is this your fella? It's Brendan, isn't it?"

Brendan, standing close behind Kathleen with his arms around her narrow waist, could see a smoke-filled room over her shoulder, smelling of beer and whiskey. There was a double bed in the corner with two couples lying on it, their arms around each other, looking up in surprise; another man and girl, both with very few clothes on, were kissing furiously on the floor.

A young man with a cigarette in his right hand, bare-chested and looking quite drunk, pulled Marcella back from the door, calling out, "Cum here woman an' gie us another drink. Who's your friends, den? Jeasus, it's not the bloody Prod from downstairs, is it?" he questioned, leaning forward to see better.

"Aw, go to hell… God, it's Father John… Come on, Bren, we've better things to do dan stay here," Kathleen called out, backing away from the door as Father John burped loudly and fell against it.

"Come on, Kath, yeah, let's leave 'em to it. Seems the Church is having a night off… Come on we've better things to do," he exclaimed, catching Kath's hand and rushing down the stairs.

Over the following months, to keep himself occupied during the day, he helped the Doc—Doctor James Courcy—to put together a maritime museum in Dunlaoghaire.

Knowing Brendan's ability with the palm and needle, sail making—sewing canvas sails was an expertise he had picked up whilst at sea—the Doc introduced Brendan to a sail-making concern in Dunlaoghaire. Dunlaoghaire was renowned for its yachting fraternity and its many yacht clubs. However, this exacting job did not last very long, as Brendan took an aversion to the dust from the canvas sails and couldn't stop sneezing.

Brendan decided to take up the Doc's earlier suggestion of working on a coastal boat, threw a few clothes into a bag and set off for Cork harbour, where the *SS Politician* was loading a cargo of timber and would sail for Liverpool the next day.

After a long drive to the south of the country, over a hundred miles from Dublin traversing the wandering country roads, Brendan arrived at the harbour for the city of Cork. This was the port called Queenstown, after Queen Victoria's visit in 1850, and renamed in 1922, after independence, to Cobh. The port was renowned for the last port of call for the *Titanic* in April 1912.

Brendan locked the Ford Anglia, patted the streamlined sweeping bodywork, took a deep breath, and stopped to look at the tiny, worn out steamer alongside the quay, with its long black funnel and its deck cargo of timber.

This should be interesting. Is there anyone around? Traversing the short gangway, he jumped down onto the rusty deck, balancing himself against a stack of sawn wood and looking around.

"Anyone there?" he shouted. Without reply, he made his way to the small structure in the middle of the craft and climbed a short ladder to the bridge, a cramped structure with a large wooden wheel, small telegraph and radar set against the for'rard bulkhead.

"Anyone there?" he shouted again.

Curious to hear a shuffling sound from behind a side door, Brendan turned to see a small, bearded, balding, weather-beaten male, wearing a dark blue roll-neck sweater and smoking a pipe, standing in the doorway.

Brendan stepped forward to introduce himself, but was forestalled by the pipe smoker, who announced in a strong accent, "Yer cabin is next to de galley. We're sailin' in de mornin' at eight hundred. Mr. Courcy said ye'd be on a trip wid us… Now keep outta da way."

Taken aback by this unwelcome greeting, Brendan was not too sure who this person was. Was he the captain or one of the crew?

He asked, "Is it Captain Walsh, then?" and received a barely noticeable affirmative nod from behind a cloud of smelly black smoke.

Well, got that settled, Brendan thought, looking at his watch. "Thank you, Captain, for having me on board. My name is Brendan Harris," he said, as he stepped forward with an outstretched hand, which was ignored as Captain Walsh faded behind the door, leaving a cloud of smoke behind him.

Wondering if there was anyone in the galley, Bren, very disappointed at the lack of welcome, followed the smell of fried bacon down some steps and along a short passage, to hear activity behind a closed door, where a young male voice was singing "The Wild Colonial Boy".

Maybe the galley, he thought, pushing the door open. He viewed a small room with a deal table big enough to take six diners bolted to the floor. Two males, dressed in scruffy sweaters, were finishing off what looked like a fry up. Behind a counter, the singer stopped in mid flow, with a fish slice in one hand and a deep frying pan in the other, and called out, "Come in der, sir, is it Mr. Harris, den? Captain Walsh said ye would be needin' sometin' te eat."

"That I do, what hav' ye' got?" Brendan asked, relieved to be recognised. He nodded to the two diners who looked up when he had entered but had now returned to eating.

"Doan' mind dose two, sir, they don' know der manners. I can do you a full fry up wid some black puddin'. Will two eggs be enough, an a bit of fried bread?"

"Let's have the lot. I'm starvin', just come down from Dublin. Call me Bren, if you will."

"Okay, Sir Bren, won't be a minit," replied this very pleasant young man as he opened the tall fridge door and continued singing about the Wild Colonial Boy.

"We're sailin' at eight tomorra morning, I'm told?" asked Brendan as he sat beside one of the sweater-clad diners who had just lit up a cigarette.

"Dat's right den, Sur, fer Liverpool. Da talkative youngster up there," pointed out the speaker in a broad accent, "is called Padder. An' dis miserable eejit here," he pointed his woodbine at the other sweater clad man, "is Declan. An' I'm called Sid. So der ye are," finished Sid, drawing a long pull on the Woodbine, which almost disintegrated in his fingers as he relapsed into a hacking cough.

"Der you are now, Mr. Bren, Sir, the best of fry up dis side of Cork. Would ye want to be usin' the brown sauce, an' a mug of tea, an' there's some bread an' marge fer ye."

"Thanks a lot, Padder, I'm going to enjoy this. By the way, I'm told there's a cabin for me?"

"Next door, Bren, Sir," answered Padder. "Will ye be havin' the same fer brekki?"

"You bet, Padder."

Amidst the smoke from the Woodbines and the smell of fried grease in the hot fug of the galley, Brendan demolished his fry up and sat back, relaxed in the heavy wooden chair, and produced a twenty packet of Senior Service cigarettes.

As Dec and Sid were now keen to talk, Padder left to go see his girlfriend. Bren heard that the captain was a miserable ould sod, but the first mate was OK. He was ashore, gone home for the night. The *SS Politician* was a wreck, due for the scrap yard. The engines were just about finished, always giving trouble.

"We'll be lucky to get to Liverpool," declared Sid, as they all rose to retire for the night. It was going to be an early start next morning.

The spare cabin next door to the galley, where he was going to spend the next few days, was very claustrophobic. There was very little headroom, the bunk against the wall filled half the room and was only six feet long, just too small for Brendan's six foot two inches. The room smelt damp and reeked of stale cigarette smoke. Not feeling very comfortable with the whole business, especially with the captain's reception, he considered cancelling the whole idea and heading home, but didn't look forward to the long drive over the country roads.

Deciding to stay and see the adventure out, he had a quick wash in the small hand basin in the cabin and settled in to try to get some sleep.

What's that? Where the hell am I? were Brendan's next conscious thoughts as he heard the boat's horn and felt the ship giving a sharp lurch. There were raised voices outside and the boat's engine was running noisily. *We must be moving,* thought Brendan, *but it's only six o'clock. God, I'm cold. I'm not enjoying this at all.*

Dressing hurriedly, he walked out onto the deck to see land on either side and the funnel overhead belching thick black smoke. It was always satisfying, the feel of a boat moving through the water. *What shall I do?* he thought. *Get a cup of tea somewhere. Will Padder be up yet?* Making his way into the galley, which was empty, he filled a kettle and after some searching found the electric socket and went back outside while it boiled.

There was his new 'friend', Sid, talking with an older man, another personification of the traditional coastal seaman, small in stature, heavily built with a leathery lined face, narrow eyes and dressed in the ubiquitous blue roll necked sweater but with a well-worn and stained once brown leather jacket over it.

However, whilst Sid was wearing a cloth cap, the other sea dog had an air of authority, wearing a peaked cap with a small piece of tarnished braid attached lightly to its side. *This must be the mate, second in line to the captain.*

"Morning, gentlemen," greeted Brendan. The two men swung around in surprise.

Sid immediately raised his hand, calling out in greeting, "'Tis a grand mornin' this, Bren, Sir." Turning to the other man, he said, "Our passenger, Jack, Mr. Brendan…"

"Oh, of course. A morning to you, sir. I remember, the doctor asked if we could take you for a short trip. Settlin' in all right, are ye', den?" came the greeting in a deep melodious country drawl.

"Came on board last evening…all right to call you Jack, is it, then?"

"Yeah dat's fine, so long as you don't call me too early in the mornin'," laughed the mate. "Have you met de captain den?"

"Well, I saw him for a moment last night, but he didn't have any time to talk," replied Brendan.

"Dat's Captain Walsh fer ye den. Doesn't talk much. Hear yer on tankers. Dis must be a big change fer you, on this little ting?" Before Brendan could answer there was a shout from the bridge.

"Mr. Mate, could you cum up here an' bring Mr. Harris wid ye." It was a call from the captain, who, when they entered the bridge deck, turned on the mate and demanded to know if Brendan had been signed on as passenger.

"I don't know, Captain. As ye kno', I was ashore until five this morning an' dis is the first I have seen of the fella. He says he spoke with ye last evening."

"Well, we're well out in the channel. Can do nuttin' about it now." Turning to face Brendan, standing as high as his five foot would let him, he continued, "Don't go doing anything stupid, Mr. Harris, like fallin' overboard, or gettin' sick. Best put an entry in de log, Jack. Now git de hell off my bridge."

With that final order, which the mate took very calmly as if well used to such abruptness, he signalled to Brendan to follow him down the short steps.

"Doan mind the cap'n, he's not very nice so early in de mornin'. Now ders Padder—mornin', Padder, be in for breakfast in half an hour," he called to the youngster who was dressed in a heavy overcoat, as it was quite chilly.

"Mornin', Bren, Sir," was the greeting with a friendly wave. Bren waved back, grateful for a friendly face, and went to his cabin to put on another sweater.

Later that morning, after another substantial fry up, Brendan made his way to the front of the coaster to savour the clean sea air and had to hold on tight to the railing, as the bows were rising and falling and the boat rolling from side to side in the increasingly choppy sea. Looking back toward the bridge, which was out of sight behind the high deck cargo of timber, he had heard someone shouting to come back. He decided to make his way back alongside the restricted footing at the side of the stack of timber. With ever increasing movement, and the boat so deep in the water and the waves washing over the side, he got rather wet and was relieved to return to the safety of the bridge structure.

Whilst he would have enjoyed a visit to the bridge, he thought it better to keep his head down and went to the galley for a cup of tea and to dry out.

Padder, busy preparing the midday meal, went into great detail about how many times the ship had had to call into port to have the engines fixed and how often the captain had got drunk.

Balancing himself against the swaying and shuddering of the ship, as it rode the waves, Padder nearly lost his balance trying to place the prepared leg of lamb into the oven.

"No way, José," he called out. "I'll cook the lamb when the sea settles down. Hey, Bren, Sir, would ye' open the fridge door fer me?"

Brendan did as asked, balancing against the unsteady movement of the ship and held the door open as Padder deposited the leg into a corner of the fridge, wedging it in tight with some packs of butter.

"I'll do some sausage and a pile of chips. Easiest to do in the deep fry. Wow! That was a heavy sea!" he exclaimed as the ship suddenly lurched to the right, and both he and Brendan held onto storm handles secured to the wall, waiting for the ship to return to its equilibrium.

"Something serious?" Brendan called out. "Wonder if the timber has shifted. Any lifejackets around, Padder? We'd better get on deck quick."

"There are some around somewhere, Bren, Sir," Padder answered, making his unsteady way toward the galley door after Brendan.

Exiting out into the darkened world, with heavy clouds shielding the sun, the temperature had dropped; the wind had increased and could be heard whistling in the ship's rigging with a mournful sound. Brendan hanging onto a pillar, looked up at the bridge to see the mate waving frantically for him to come up.

"Padder, gotta go. Try an' find some life jackets," he called out to the shivering cook and made his way up the steps to the bridge to find the mate donning a life jacket and pointing out a small heap of old cork jackets.

"Look, Bren, lad, the old man is unconscious—whether from the drink or a fall I dunno, but I've gotta get down on deck to do somethin' with that timber. Can ye keep the 'Polly' head on to the sea an' the engines running fast enough to keep some headway? Right. The nearest land is ten miles to port. Right, Meehaul," he called to the helmsman, balancing behind the large wooden steering wheel at the back of the bridge, "Mr. Bren here's in charge."

Before Bren could say anything, the mate had left the bridge and could be seen stumbling his way forward in the strong wind and sheets of sea spray, to deal with the timber cargo which had shifted to the right. He could be seen directing the crew members to the starboard side—the right-hand side—with axes to hack the timber free, in the hope the ship would retain its balance.

"Mornin', Meehaul," called an exhilarated Brendan over the noise of the wind and the sound of the sea spray. "You know what yer doin'? Is there enough speed to keep headway into the wind?"

"She's yawin' a bit to starboard, Mr. Bren," was the anxious reply.

"Give her ten degrees to port, Meehaul; I'll get some more speed on the engines."

Staggering over to the engine room telegraph, Brendan moved the marker to half-speed ahead and received an acknowledgement from the engine room. With the increased speed, the bows swung into the advancing seas and settled to a steady forward movement, batting through the large waves.

Captain Bren—*or was it Sir Bren Harris?*—stood leaning into the roll of the ship as it pitched up and down and rolled sluggishly, peering through the spray-sodden wheelhouse window with his one eye.

The mate acknowledged the relaxed ship movement with a wave, and the crew renewed their axing of the ropes holding the stacks of timber to the for'rard deck.

The wind was now increasing in force and the ship was lying deeper to the starboard side on each roll of the ship.

"Meehaul, some more port wheel, the ship is dying. Next roll and she goes under." *Come on, Jack, just one more hack at that lashing,* Brendan implored the mate as he balanced precariously on the edge of being swamped by the waves crashing into the sluggish hull. To clear the rope lashings looked as if it would require just one more blow of the axe, and Jack, letting go his hold on the railing, gripped the axe with both hands and raised it above his head. He severed the last binding rope and the timber started rolling into the sea. Dropping the axe in the seething water, Jack made a frantic grab for the deck railing as the 'Polly' took a sudden lurch to port. The baulks of timber were now leaping about as they fell towards the tossing waves. Brendan winced as one piece smashed into

Jack's legs, making him lose hold of the railing. Fortunately, a fellow crew member, seeing Jack's dire position, grabbed hold of the large cork jacket and, with a fortuitous lurch to port as the stack of timber fell into the lashing seas, the ship reached an even keel and Jack and fellow saviour fell back onto the deck. Aided by a further crew member, they dragged Jack back to the accommodation structure.

"Thanks, Bren lad, I'll take over now," gasped Jack. "Sid, could ye' go git me some dry clothes? Me right leg is pretty sore. Any sign of the ould man?" Jack, sodden wet, slumped onto the floor of the bridge and took a welcome gulp of coffee from the mug proffered by Padder.

There was a sudden rush of disturbed air as the entrance door to the captain's quarters opened and a bleary-eyed captain, in crumpled trousers, sagging sweater and stocking feet, appeared on the crowded bridge.

"What de hell is goin' on here, den? Git off my bridge. Jack, what's wrong wid ye, are ye drunk?" The captain snorted scornfully, grasping hold of the door edge as the ship continued its unsettled way through the disturbed sea.

"Jeasus, where's the deck cargo gone? Can't leave you eejits fer a minit. What's that, Jack? Yer leg is broke? How'd ye do dat?"

Brendan stepped back, still on a high after the past exhilarating minutes, and sipped his lukewarm, over-sugared coffee. *What next?* he thought as he made his way down to the comfort of the galley. *I'll be glad to get off this mad ship.*

Noticing the change in the ship's movement as it turned, it was two hours later when they entered Arklow harbour and an ambulance came to take Jack. Brendan packed his bags and knocked on the captain's door to say he was leaving, and was very surprised to be welcomed by the captain wearing shoes and uniform. The captain expressed his sorrow to hear he was leaving and that he hoped he had enjoyed his stay on board the good ship 'Polly', and asked him to express his best wishes to Doctor De Courcy.

Wondering if the last frantic hours had even happened, Brendan made his way over to Arklow station and took the train for home.

The following day he took another train journey to Cork town and made his way to Cobh to collect the Ford Anglia. Upon returning home that evening, he had a serious chat with his mother. "Hey, Ma, I've been doing a bit of thinkin'. I'm gettin' nowhere at the moment. My health has improved a fair bit; the leg is pretty supple now. The only thing physically wrong with me is the double vision, though my memory is still a bit awry."

"That's right, Bren it's been over a year now, since the accident…It's up to you whether you want to go through another eye operation. What about going back to sea?"

"I'll have a go with the op, Ma, but going back to sea would mean an awful lot of study. I don't think I'm up to it at the moment. If I could get rid of the double vision an' the eye patch it would be great. I'll go see the doc to make an appointment with the eye an' ear hospital."

"Any idea what you intend to do if you don't go back to sea?" asked a concerned mother.

"Haven't a clue, Ma. Maybe go across to England an' start again. Something will turn up. I'm twenty-three now, can always start again. Now where's the number for the Royal Victoria Eye and Ear?"

Calvex Faith in the Atlantic

28

Visit to Outpatients / Next Step: the Future

"Go an' sit over there, young fella," was the order from the sullen, elderly porter as Brendan enquired where to wait for his appointment with the eye consultant. With his daily paper and book, Brendan resigned himself to a long wait as there seemed to be thousands of people waiting, all still with their winter coats on, as the room, with its off-colour, distempered walls, was quite cold. Speaking to the man next to him as he joined a row of chairs, he was told the surgery would start at nine o'clock; it was now eight thirty.

Looking around, Brendan counted some thirty persons ahead of him and worked out at ten minutes for each that meant he wouldn't be seen for another five hours, or more probably six. Three o'clock in the afternoon.

"What about that corridor down the side there?"

"Oh, that's part of the queue. As they move out from the front of the queue, we all move forward."

Resigning himself to a long wait, Brendan opened the paper.

"Look, son, there's two of them today look," was the excited call from Brendan's next-door neighbour. In the wall opposite there were four doors; two of them were open, with a white garbed attendant at each, calling out, "Next!"

As the lucky people moved toward the opened doors, a great shuffle started with everyone moving to occupy the vacant seats. It took some time before it was Brendan's turn to move.

The morning passed by with the air getting thicker from the endless cigarettes smoked. The solitary ashtray on a table at the side of the room was now overflowing, with cigarette butts falling onto the floor. *This can't be very healthy,* thought Brendan, averting his head as his neighbour went into a bout of sneezing and coughing. *At the rate this queue is reducing, I'll be lucky to be seen today,* he mused, stretching his long legs and counting those ahead of him. *Twelve o'clock, thirty in front of me, ten minutes each, three hundred minutes divided by two, say another three hours before I'm seen. That's if they the doctors don't go for lunch. Maybe some patients will die of boredom. What's this?*

The wide entrance doors behind him swung open and a large trolley with a hot water boiler appeared, followed by a smaller trolley with sandwiches and an assortment of mugs, pushed by two severe looking matronly ladies in aprons and bonnets. There was a loud rustle of bodies turning and a few people rose to make their way over to this very welcome break in the monotony. The first matronly lady raised her hand and halted the spontaneous movement. "Hod yer whist, now, ladies an' gents, I've gotta plug in de boiler first."

As they pushed the trolleys alongside the wall and plugged in the boiler, matron two, much thinner than her mountainous compatriot, announced in a weak, shrill voice, "Hav' yer monies ready. 'Twill be one an' six fer a san'wich an' a mug of tea. Der's egg…an' ham…an' egg an' ham an' tomata. We hav', as a special treet today," she announced, raising her voice, "some Jacobs Mikado biscuits…furst cum, furst served. Der two a penny. Tanks, Maureen. Now will ye' all be after makin' a queue here on de right."

With the sound of rattling coins and moving bodies, an orderly queue formed. Brendan—one of the first to get to the trolley—bought himself two pence worth of biscuits and a steaming mug of tea. Returning to his seat, he realised they had moved three seats nearer their target.

Just another ten in front of me. It's three o'clock. Maybe get in by half past.

Another half hour passed and Brendan was poised, ready to leap in to have his interview the next time one of the doors opened, when instead of calling out 'next', the white-coated junior announced the surgery was over and to call in tomorrow. A sign of disgust and annoyance spread amongst the remaining patients. After waiting so long surely…but no. The two doors were shut and bolted from the inside.

Resigned to the stupid system, Brendan returned home and came back the following morning. Arriving at seven thirty, he found he was fifth in the queue. Surgery did not start until ten am, by which time the waiting room had filled up again, but by ten thirty Brendan had had his interview and explained the reasons for his visit. Fortunately they were able to obtain his notes without too much fuss and sent him for an x-ray.

It was another ten days before he was called in to the hospital in Dublin, where he joined the queue at eight o'clock and was seen at nine thirty. After the initial interview, he was sent for a multitude of sight tests and re-joined the queue later in the morning. Resigned to hours of waiting, he was called surprisingly promptly and informed surgery could be affected to correct the double vision, but there was no guarantee it would be successful. Having come so far, Brendan agreed and was told to await a letter from the hospital when they could offer a bed.

By now, Brendan was getting very frustrated. His memory was returning, aided by re-reading his exploits whilst at sea from his diary. He was, however, somewhat daunted by the studies required to return to the officer career with Calvex tankers, and started to consider studying for another profession. Accountancy, solicitor, doctor or maybe nursing, or even to become an astronaut.

Brendan had heard on the grapevine in the close-knit community he was living in that Polly had now married her beau. Whilst on his way to the Top Hat Ballroom with Kathleen Fitzgerald, early one evening, he, bedecked in his dashing eye patch with his slim stature, happened to step off the pavement to allow a harassed looking couple, pushing a high-wheeled pram, to pass by.

Laughing at a comment passed by his companion, Brendan looked up as they passed the pram pusher, to discover it was Polly. Quite taken aback, he stopped, but Polly, with her head held down, made no sign of recognition. Her partner, a tall studious looking solicitor type, looked at Brendan, nodded his head, and they continued.

Is that what you wanted, Polly, to be stuck behind a pram for the next year or so? Oh, Polly, I am so sorry, thought Brendan. *Did I make a mistake?*

Still working as a petrol pump attendant at the local garage, and as a general odd-job man at the nearby farm, Brendan sought, through contacts and the national newspapers, opportunities for a new career without success. There were plenty of sales commission jobs available. Jono was now working in sales, and Billy had started a career in accountancy.

In July of 1963, the letter arrived from the Eye Hospital, offering a bed later in the month. It was a slightly apprehensive Brendan who settled in overnight, in a creaky uncomfortable bed, in a crowded hospital ward to prepare for his eye operation the following morning.

"Are you Brendan Harris?" asked the bespectacled attendant in the customary white coat, looking at his notepad with his biro poised.

"Yes," answered Brendan.

"Your date of birth?"

"Fifth of March, 1940."

After the customary questions to prove Brendan was himself, the next move was to bundle him onto a trolley and trundle him to theatre, where the important people, in their gowns and face masks, asked him the same questions again.

A masked female with startling blue eyes then advanced, holding a loaded syringe at arm's length. She inserted it into Brendan's arm and within seconds Brendan dropped into a deep sleep.

"Are you there, Mr. Harris? Can ye hear me…? No movement, Nurse, he's still away with the cuckoos. No wait…can you hear me, Mr. Harris?"

Brendan, coming out of the drugged sleep, could hear the voice but didn't relate it to himself. His head was aching and when he opened his eyes, all he could see was darkness, with flashing red arrows boring into his brain.

The male voice repeated its questions, receiving Brendan's answer. "Yes, I'm here."

"Good, good," was the relieved reply. "You are back from theatre now, Mr. Harris, an' yer eyes are covered. We're going to take the cover off now, Mr. Harris."

Feeling hands at the back of his head loosening the tape holding the mask over his eyes, Brendan crossed his fingers. What was he going to see? A single world…just one of everything…no more double images? With a sudden movement, the blindfold was removed. All he could see were blinding flashes of white light intermingled with red and blue. *Shut your eyes, Bren lad, and open them slowly.*

"How many pencils can you see, Mr. Harris?" was the anxious question from a disembodied voice.

"All I can see is white light…"

"God, will somebody pull the curtain?" called the voice.

In the darkened room, Brendan began to focus his eyes…*is that only one pencil I see?* he questioned himself. *Oh shit, I can see another below it. If I move my head to the right…yes they are coming closer. No difference from before. Close my right eye the top pencil is alone, close my left eye it's moved down to the right. Oh God, it's worse than it was before.*

"What do you see, Mr. Harris?" asked the disembodied voice in a resigned tone, realising there must be something wrong with the result of the operation, as Brendan's tears expressed his great disappointment.

"It's worse…it's worse than before," Brendan cried. "The gap between the pencils is greater than before. Oh! Shit! Shit! Shit!"

"Early days yet, Mr. Harris. Early days, it may improve," mollified the voice.

"At least," Brendan called in a resigned tone, "at least I only see one pencil when I shut my right eye…give me my eye patch and let me go home."

Upon returning to Laurel Cottage, Brendan reassessed his position. He was twenty-three years of age; reasonably fit, a bit underweight, suffering from diplopia and a gammy right leg. His chosen career as an officer in the Merchant Navy was over, the studying over the past four years all wasted due to his scrambled memory. What to do now was the question?

Stay in Dublin and try to start another career? His brothers were both in their chosen career paths. He wasn't an immediate drain on his parents' finances, as part of the monies from the out of court settlement had been paid to his parents as well as to finance a new scooter for Jono.

What to do? He knew how to drive a car, or at least he had a driving licence, which he had bought—it didn't guarantee he could drive. Where were the opportunities for the future in Ireland?

His good friend, Doc Courcy, was all for him going back to sea, but Brendan didn't feel he was up to the mental rigours of navigating and ship control. The Doc did offer an introduction to a couple of firms in Dublin city, but Brendan, after due deliberation, decided to return to England, and the Doc kindly gave him an address of a family in Liverpool who welcomed lodgers.

So it was with a sense of a new adventure that Brendan Harris, grateful to be alive, boarded the Dublin ferry to Liverpool again, waving goodbye to his parents, and to Ireland.

About the Author

David R. McCabe grew up in the countryside south of Dublin, Ireland and now lives in the North of England. Happily retired, David spends his time dreaming of fly fishing and working on his next book.

Website: www.anirishlad.co.uk
Facebook: www.facebook.com/pg/brendanharris11

By the Author

Brendan A Boy (An Irish Lad #1)
Brendan Afloat (An Irish Lad #2)
Brendan Ashore (An Irish Lad #3)

Printed in Great Britain
by Amazon